The Greatest Deer Hunting Book Ever

The Greatest Deer Hunting Book Ever

Jim Casada
#123/350

Edited by Jim Casada

Published by SPORTING CLASSICS

The Greatest Deer Hunting Book Ever

Published by SPORTING CLASSICS.

Editor: Jim Casada

Publisher: Chuck Wechsler

Creative Director: Ryan Coleman

Illustrations: Ron Van Gilder

Copyright 2018, *Sporting Classics*. All rights reserved. No part of this book may be reproduced, stored or introduced into a retrieval system, or transmitted in any form by any means without written permission of the publisher.

First Printing
Library of Congress Catalog Card Number 2018949128
ISBN 978-1-935342-19-9

DEDICATION

For my beloved wife, Ann, who now is in a place where she no longer knows of the early morning risings and late-evening returns which formed a part of our lives for so many years. Similarly, she is no longer able to work the culinary magic that led to many a delicious meal with venison as the featured dish. The guiding genius behind a number of co-authored cookbooks in which this wonderful meat figured prominently, her partnership has made the life of a hunter and the sometimes lonely ways of a scribe brighter and better. It's heart-wrenching to watch her decline in a nursing home, but I'm blessed by the bounty of a half-century of memories she provided. As has been the case with every book I've ever done, my debt to her is incalculable. – Jim Casada

ACKNOWLEDGEMENTS
By Jim Casada

As is the case with any book, whether an original work or a compilation such as this, input, insight and inspiration for its completion come from numerous individuals. Obviously, those whose work appears on the pages that follow deserve recognition, for theirs has been the critical role in writing—and writing wonderfully well—on a sport which in many ways is uniquely American. From pioneer days to the present, deer hunting has truly been a distinctive part of our sporting culture. Thanks to the enduring and endearing literary efforts of these sporting scribes, we can celebrate this important part of our heritage.

Chuck Wechsler has, as is the case with pretty much any project coming out of Suite 500 at 117 Alpine Circle in Columbia (headquarters of *Sporting Classics*) in recent decades, been a driving force behind the scenes. From evaluating my selections for inclusion in the anthology to proofreading material, from providing gentle goading whenever my efforts lagged to dealing with issues such as copyright permission, he has been a stellar influence in the shaping of this book.

Chuck's enthusiastic young sidekick at the magazine, Ryan Coleman, has been a willing and worthy helpmate at every step of the process, especially the layout and design.

I'm personally indebted to some of the authors represented here, notably Rob Wegner, M. R. James and Duncan Dobie, for publishing my writings, giving me an opportunity to review theirs, or simply sharing their abiding love for the whitetail quest. Likewise, a quartet of those whose work is included—Theodore Roosevelt, Archibald Rutledge, Jack O'Connor and Robert Ruark— have figured prominently in my career as literary inspirations and individuals whose writings have led me to compilations of full-length books containing their timeless tales.

Finally, in a somewhat offbeat but nonetheless heartfelt thank you, I want to express appreciation to those who have been my fellow members of the Southeastern Outdoor Press Association (SEOPA) over the years. I joined the organization in 1986 and some indication of how much it has meant to me comes from the fact that from the time I attended my first SEOPA conference to the present, I have never missed that annual gathering of kindred spirits. Today, it is the institutional home of my heart, a group of folks I consider an extended family and a constant source of professional encouragement and education.

PREFACE
By Chuck Wechsler

I was only 14 in the fall of 1956, but I was already a passionate pheasant hunter. Once the hunting season opened, while the other guys were at football practice or shooting pool and playing the pinball machines at Mel's Grill, you could usually find me walking the countryside with my trusty Model 12 shotgun in hand.

Our family lived on the outskirts of Brookings, a college town in the heart of eastern South Dakota's farm country. I knew every landowner within a three-mile radius of town and had their permission to hunt whenever I wanted. I also knew intimately the location of every woodlot and shelterbelt, slough, roadside ditch and other patches of cover that held birds.

On weekdays after school and on the weekends, hunting on foot, always alone and without a dog, I would hit as many coverts as I could, shoot a bird or two or three, and then head home, sometimes arriving after dark. My parents had come to accept my passion for hunting, and while they were no doubt concerned about my going out alone and getting back late, they never expressed that to me. Times were different then.

In those years, our county had a healthy population of ringnecks, but white-tailed deer were scarce. Indeed, despite all the time I spent in the outdoors, I had never seen a whitetail in the wild, until . . .

It was a cold, blustery Saturday morning and I had just shot my second long-tailed rooster. The next closest piece of cover was a circular stand of tall willows and bluestem grasses about a half-mile away on the far side of a cut cornfield. Adjusting my approach into the gusty wind, I headed toward the spot where I figured there had to be one or more roosters hunkered down out of the cold.

After easing ever-so-quietly across the corn stubble, I arrived at the edge of the willows. There, only 20 feet from where I stood, an enormous whitetail buck suddenly arose from his bed, then turned to stare right at me. For what seemed like minutes he just looked at me, his breath coming in thin, wispy clouds, his huge body tense and poised to explode like some kind of living missile. But what really amazed me was the size and spread of his antlers—two sets of five nearly identical tines, each long, dark and heavy.

Just as suddenly, the buck gathered his sinewy muscles, then erupted from the willows and raced away across the stubble, his long white flag waving back and forth in what seemed to be a syncopated rhythm. The field was wide open for a good mile and, as I watched, the buck's ground-eating run gradually slowed to an almost princely canter across the frozen ground until he reached a distant shelterbelt where he stopped and looked back in my direction before disappearing in the trees. I would never see him again.

The encounter was so unexpected, so breathtakingly exciting, that right then and there I decided to start back for home, eager to relate my experience to mom and dad.

Although I didn't think about it at the time, a deer hunter was born that day. Since then, I've hunted whitetails in at least a dozen states and provinces, from Michigan to Texas, from Alberta to the Carolinas. But after all my wanderings, that remarkable encounter still stands as the most unforgettable memory in my sporting life.

INTRODUCTION
By Jim Casada

For the first three-plus decades of my life, my deer hunting experiences were exclusively of a vicarious nature. Whitetails were so scarce in the Great Smokies of North Carolina where I grew up that there was not even an open season for them in my home county. Somewhat similar circumstances prevailed over much of the country. Perhaps providing a bit of personal recollection connected with my obsession with the animal as a boy and young man will help the reader understand why compiling and editing a collection of enduring deer tales holds so much meaning for me.

Despite being constantly in the woods, wading trout streams or fishing area rivers, the sum total of my direct connection with deer numbered precisely ten animals at the point when I headed off to college in the autumn of 1960. The fact that I recall every sighting, every fleeting moment of glory as a majestic animal fled my presence as if it was just yesterday is likely an indicator of obsession.

Even today, well over a half-century later, I feel confident I could set out afoot and identify, with a margin of error of 50 yards or less, every location where I had spotted a deer. That, too, suggests a fixation perhaps transcending the norm. I'll leave that judgment to others, even as I revel in my memories.

Back then, merely finding tracks was a thrill and, on one occasion when a local sportsman bagged a small four-pointer in a nearby county where hunting was allowed, it seemed half the town turned out to see the "trophy" proudly draped across the front bumper of his vehicle. It was the only deer taken by a hunter I would see until the 1970s.

For some, circumstances such as those of my younger years might have translated to disinterest in deer hunting. For me, quite the opposite was true. It meant descent into a world of dreams, with visions of one day actually being able to venture afield after the whitetails coursing through my mind with vivid and aching regularity.

Meanwhile, realization gradually dawned, thanks in part to material I read in outdoor magazines but also in early excursions into what would become my career—the study and teaching of history—that deer hunting had always been an integral part of the American experience.

In the 18th century and well into the 19th century, the white-tailed deer was an important factor in the national economic experience. For decades, hundreds of thousands of hides were annually transported from the hinterland to major ports along the Eastern Seaboard, from Boston to Charleston, for shipment to Europe. For those active on the frontier, deer hunting was not only a potential source of income but a way of life. Venison meant fresh meat; sustenance for weeks or months in the form of jerky and pemmican; raw material for clothing, shelter and many other uses taught by Native Americans. It was, in short, always our game. Given that consideration, it's small wonder so many authors have focused on the whitetail over the years.

Sadly, by the end of World War I, whitetail numbers had been seriously depleted. Relentless market hunting and the absence of seasons or regulations, which resulted in countless deer simply being shot on sight, eventually took a heavy toll.

For two or three generations spanning the middle of the last century, it was commonplace for hunters to know about white-tailed deer only through stories passed down by their elders or through the writings of sporting scribes.

That normally translated into one of two outlooks. Many hunters simply turned their attention to small game such as squirrels, rabbits and birds. In the South, for example, during the 1940s, '50s and '60s, surveys repeatedly showed quail and squirrels to be the most popular game animals. Many hunters came to believe that whitetails belonged to a world we had lost. They were firmly convinced they would never hunt deer. Others, and I was among their ranks, longed for a grand wildlife comeback story. It would ultimately transpire, and along with the resurgence of the wild turkey, the whitetail's restoration ranks as one of the great wildlife success stories of all time. Meanwhile, many hunters, myself among them, found our deer "fix" only in our reading. For the time being, that was the closest approximation of the real experience.

Throughout the 1950s and 1960s, and indeed on into the early part of the 1970s, I read voraciously about the quest for whitetails. Countless others did the same, because deer hunting in print was, for all practical purposes, all we had available. My favorite author was Archibald Rutledge, which partly explains why his work figures so prominently in this anthology.

I identified with Rutledge on several fronts. Geographically speaking, he was a fellow resident of the Southern Heartland and that meant his writings offered a potential link to reality missing in those of others in my pantheon of literary heroes such as Jack O'Connor, Edmund Ware Smith and Corey Ford. Furthermore, I had comparatively easy access to Rutledge's work, thanks to the regularity with which his deer stories graced the pages of *Field & Stream* and *Outdoor Life.* The local barber shop subscribed to both publications, and if I timed my haircuts properly to make sure the establishment was swamped with customers, chances were excellent there would be an opportunity to savor Rutledge's latest offering.

Then, too, Rutledge told tales so well that his accounts conveyed a degree of reality that had you at his side as the hounds pushed a "noble stag" (that's the kind of verbiage he brought to his writing) through the swamps and woodlands of his paradise along the Santee River in South Carolina's Low Country.

Rutledge may have held center stage in my literary leanings, with his regular magazine offerings being supplemented by a handful of his books in the local public library, but anything that dealt with deer hunting tickled my fancy.

The selections in this book represent a solid cross-section of pieces that have entertained and informed countless readers over more than a half-century. Collectively, they provide a solid sampling of several generations of fine writing on the sport and represent many of the great names, along with some lesser-known writers, who have shared the mystique and magic of our most widespread and popular big game species through the printed word.

Today, I no longer languish in the no man's whitetail land that was my lot up until I reached my late 30s. After what seemed an eternity of reading rather than direct involvement, a move to where I now live (upstate South Carolina) and burgeoning deer populations changed my personal whitetail situation in dramatic fashion.

Since that first hefty doe taken with benefit of a landowner's tag in the Palmetto Low Country, there have been scores more killed employing a variety of weapons—bows, muzzleloaders and modern rifles—along with methods as diverse as still-hunting, dog drives, man drives and patiently occupying treestands and ground blinds.

Venison has long since become a key part of my diet and, in company with my wife, I've written a number of cookbooks devoted exclusively or in appreciable measure to its culinary joys.

That transition from mere reader and vicarious hunter to direct involvement has been most welcome. Some of my most peaceful hours are spent perched on a ladder stand or tucked into a "hidey-hole" on the ground with a carefully constructed blind to conceal me.

Much of my hunting occurs on a piece of property I own, and there I can revel in links to the land where inner fulfillment sends my soul soaring. It's an opportunity to meditate, shed the burdens and stress of daily life, observe deer and, occasionally, shoot one. That translates to enjoying the best of both worlds—my decades of armchair forays into the haunts of deer with grand writers as my guides now partner with opportunities aplenty to sample and savor in person what was once only a dream.

Those of you reading these words are similarly blessed. Whitetails abound over most of their original range (and in some cases, beyond), so we once more enjoy a situation at least somewhat analogous to that known to our hardy sporting forefathers. We can hunt what might be styled "everyman's" big game animal without needing deep pockets or special privilege. Not surprisingly, given these circumstances, the sport's literature is thriving. With that in mind, here's hoping you will find these selections, more than 40 in all, the key to the reading room of a sportsman's paradise.

CONTENTS

ACKNOWLEDGMENTS *By Jim Casada* .... **VII**

PREFACE *By Chuck Wechsler* .... **IX**

INTRODUCTION *By Jim Casada* .... **XI**

PART ONE
ALWAYS OUR GAME: DEER HUNTING'S RICH HISTORY

That Christmas Eve Stag *By Archibald Rutledge* 3

The Deer of the River Bottoms *By Theodore Roosevelt* 9

The Deer Hunt *By Charles Whitehead* 25

Hunting On Snow *By Theodore S. Van Dyke* 37

Hunting Deer in Different Seasons *By Philip Tome* 45

Whitetail Hunting in 1810 *By Meshach Browning* 51

Deer Hunting in Indiana and Illinois *By Parker Gillmore* ... 55

The Last Deer Hunt *By Meshach Browning* 67

Blue-chip Deer Books: The 19th Century *By Rob Wegner* ... 71

PART TWO
GREAT WRITERS ON WHITETAIL NATURAL HISTORY

The Secret Life of the Cottontail Deer *By John Madson* 89

The Whitetail Deer *By Theodore Roosevelt* 95

Our Smartest Game Animal *By Jack O'Connor* 113

XV

PART THREE
WISDOM, WHIMSY AND THE LIGHTER SIDE

The Lady in Green *By Archibald Rutledge* _____ 125

Jake's Rangers Hunt the Whitetail *By Edmund Ware Smith* __ 133

Truthful Sam *By Charley Dickey* _____ 145

Women Own the World *By Mike Gaddis* _____ 149

Uncle Perk's Deer Lure *By Corey Ford* _____ 153

You've Got to Suffer *By Gordon MacQuarrie* _____ 157

Passing the Buck *By Charley Dickey* _____ 165

Advice of the One-eyed Poacher *By Edmund Ware Smith* __ 169

Deer Camp *By Rick Bass* _____ 177

PART FOUR
TIMELESS TALES OF GRAND HUNTS

Great Morning *By Gene Hill* _____ 187

The Comeback Buck *By Ron Spomer* _____ 191

Point Five *By Michael Altizer* _____ 199

Just Look at this Country *By Gordon McQuarrie* _____ 203

My Colonel's Last Hunt *By Archibald Rutledge* _____ 211

Lost! *By Burton Spiller* _____ 217

Northwest Whitetail Trophy *By Jack O'Connor* _____ 233

A Record Trophy *By Paulina Brandreth* _____ 241

The Deerstalkers *By Frank Forester* _____ 247

The Sunrise Buck *By Paulina Brandreth* _____ 275

PART FIVE
FICTION: WHITETAIL TALES WELL TOLD

The Kings of Curlew Island *By Archibald Rutledge* _____ 287

Strange Happenings at Chickamauga Creek *By Duncan Dobie* 301

White Deer Are Bad Luck *By Arthur R. MacDougall Jr.* _____ 307

Revenge of the Big Deer *By Duncan Dobie* _____ 317

A Rifle Named Sleigh Bells *By Edmund Ware Smith* _____ 321

PART SIX
TRICKS OF THE WHITETAIL TRADE

Woodcraft and Whitetails *By Lawrence Koller* _____ 335

Opening Day Bucks *By M. R. James* _____ 355

Hunting Whitetail Deer *By Ted Trueblood* _____ 361

Still-Hunting the Whitetail *By Lawrence Koller* _____ 367

PART SEVEN
SHORT STORIES

Mister Howard was a Real Gent *By Robert Ruark* _____ 389

Race at Morning *By William Faulkner* _____ 407

Blood Red Mackinaw *By Ryan Stalvey* _____ 423

PART EIGHT

Bibliographical & Biographical Notes *By Jim Casada* _____ 429

PART ONE

ALWAYS OUR GAME: DEER HUNTING'S RICH HISTORY

Deer hunting's storied literary history is solidly grounded in the 19th century, and with a single exception (Archibald Rutledge's piece from early in the 20th century), the nine selections offered here focus on that era. They provide a mixed sampling of the experiences of individuals who might be styled commercial hunters (Meshach Browning and Philip Tome), affluent men for whom sport was almost a metaphor for life (Charles Whitehead, Theodore S. Van Dyke and Parker Gillmore), and a concluding overview from the dean of those who have studied the literature of the sport (Rob Wegner).

Even Rutledge's "That Christmas Eve Stag" belongs, in many senses, to an earlier era, for it is redolent of traditions and styles of hunting dating back many decades prior to the time when the sage of the Santee celebrated the Yuletide season at his beloved Hampton Plantation in the Lowcountry of South Carolina with one hunt after another with family and friends.

These selections range quite widely in their coverage from a geographical standpoint—from Whitehead's adventures in Florida's Everglades to those of Roosevelt in the Dakota Badlands, from the traditional whitetail strongholds of the East (Pennsylvania, New York and Maryland) with Browning, Van Dyke and Tome, to the then hinterlands of the Midwest (Indiana and Illinois with the peripatetic British hunter Parker Gillmore). Similarly, you'll encounter a diversity of techniques such as stalking, still-hunting, tracking in the snow and giving chase with packs of hounds.

Collectively, these enduring tales remind us that the quest for whitetails was an equation with many parts. Yet there was common ground no matter where or how these great hunters pursued their quarry. That commonality included the excitement of the moment, a deeply rooted admiration for deer, and the fact that the animal has always brought exceptional storytelling ability to the forefront. Collectively, here we have rich history and richer tales, brought to us by names who are icons of what was always our game.

THAT CHRISTMAS EVE STAG

By Archibald Rutledge

***This piece was included in what is perhaps Rutledge's best-known book on the outdoors,* An American Hunter *(1937), and it is also found in* Tales of Whitetails: Archibald Rutledge's Great Deer-Hunting Stories *(1992) and* Carolina Christmas: Archibald Rutledge's Enduring Holiday Stories *(2010).*

Nearly all hunting in the northern states closes before the middle of December. Having been abroad on several zero days near the end of the season, I have heartily wished that it had closed earlier. But in the South, some seasons for hunting are open until late in the winter; and on the great plantations, venison and wild turkey for Christmas and New Year's Day are standard fare. Not to have a stag hanging up on Christmas Eve is to confess a certain degree of enfeebled manhood—almost a social disgrace.

When I met my negro driver Prince on the morning of that famous Christmas Eve, I could tell from his mien and general attitude that something was heavy on his mind. A thought of any kind on a negro's mind—barring the joyous fundamentals of eating and sleeping—is likely to be depressing.

"What's the matter, Prince?" I asked. "Did you tie your horse last night with a slip-knot round his neck?"

"Not this time," the good negro assured me. "But I was just thinkin', Cap'n, that all these years we been huntin' deer together, we ain't never yet done hang up a buck on a Christmas Eve."

"Well, let's do it today."

"We can try, Cap'n. But my wife done say we ought to be gwine to church 'stead of hunt."

"I see," I said, understanding his difficulty. "You think we are on the downgrade when we hunt on Christmas Eve?"

A gleam of humor came into Prince's eyes. "Cap'n, it ain't that, but we must use this day to show my woman that Christmas is a good time to hunt. If we can't bring nothin' back to-night, she gwine say, 'Ain't I done tole you, you triflin' sinner?'"

Prince had put it over to me that we must prove our moral soundness by bringing home a buck. I had never hunted deer before for this especial reason, but as I intended hunting anyway, I didn't mind that reason tagging along with me. Yet so long and so well had Prince hunted with me that whatever affected him had its influence on me. And, as that day in the woods advanced, the taunt of Prince's wife seemed to have more and more in it.

Eleven deer we started—six of them full-antlered bucks—but my three boys and I didn't get a single shot. It was a day on which all breaks broke the other way. Perhaps the most extraordinary escape of a stag is a matter worth recording.

For several seasons we had seen a huge creature that we had christened the Blackhorn Buck. He was one of those oversize men of the woods, and his antlers were massive, craggy and swarthy. The buck seemed to have a body as big as a swell-front barrel.

Well, after posting us at Fox Bay, Prince was riding back to the tail of the drive when he rode up this old monster. Of course, the deer headed the wrong way. Mounted on a fleet and surefooted pony, Prince undertook to race the stag to turn him. Helped somewhat by a header that the old buck took over a fallen log, the negro actually got ahead of the deer. Both stopped some 20 feet apart, horse panting and buck panting, looking at each other curiously.

But it's a darn hard thing to make a deer right-about-face, especially if he has a notion that he is the object of herding tactics. The Blackhorn estimated his chances, saw a stretch of fallen timber marking the wake of a summer storm and lithely rocked away over the obstructions. The horse could not follow.

"If I done had a rope," Prince declared to me, his honest face glistening with the perspiration of his effort to give us sport, "or jest a sling-shot, we might've had him."

"Or if it hadn't been Christmas Eve," I reminded him soberly.

By the time this deer escaped us, the sun was burning low in the crests of the yellow pines, and we knew that we might as well turn homeward. Our party divided. Some took a shortcut through the woods to the house, but my two older boys, Prince and I traveled the road.

Now I'm ready to tell you about this Christmas Eve buck. We got into the highway by the Brick Church. Before us lay a straight stretch of broad road three miles long—a stretch that was used as a race-track in Revolutionary days. The last rays of the setting sun were glinting in the forest, and the wildwoods were suffused with a rosy light. But despite the beauty of it all, our hearts were dejected. We were going home on Christmas Eve without a thing to show for our long day's hunt.

We had come a half-mile down the road in our complaining little car, with Prince's walking horse almost able to keep up with us. I saw something skulk across the road ahead of us, heading for Montgomery Branch, a dense thicket of pine and bays just off the road to the right.

"Turkeys!" I said, jamming on the brakes so suddenly that the tiny car tried to stand on her nose.

Violently I waved for Prince to come up. The three of us piled out of the car and began loading our guns with turkey-shot.

Prince was with us in a moment. In another, he had the whole situation straight. "I'll ride ahead and around," he said.

"You go across the branch. Put one boy in the thicket and leave the other on this side. Christmas Eve ain't done over yet!" he added.

I left my Gunnerman, as I call my second boy, in a tiny patch of bays a hundred yards on the near side of Montgomery—just halfway between the road and the branch. My eldest boy I posted in the branch itself, while I stole quickly forward into the open country beyond.

Just as I was emerging from the fringes of the dewy thicket, I heard a sound ahead. Then I saw a tall white flag! If I hadn't had turkey-shot in my gun, I might have let drive at him. In a moment he was lost in a thicket of young pines.

Creeping forward, I took a stand for the turkeys. At any moment they might come through the broomsedge in their swift, jerky fashion. But nary a turkey did I see or hear. The sun set. The woods seemed full of shadows. I could hear Prince riding down the thicket toward us. There seemed to be no game in front of him. When it comes to giving the hunter the slip, wild turkeys must always be given a No. 1 rating.

I turned back toward the thicket, and was halfway through it when I heard my eldest son call out. All I could catch was "A buck!"

At the same moment, I heard something split the bay-bushes wide open. I dashed forward to get into the open for a shot, at the same time changing my turkey-shot for buckshot. By the time I had cleared the branch, the buck had done the same thing.

The scene that followed is imprinted on my memory as vividly as any recollection I have of the wildwoods during nearly 40 years of roaming in them.

The buck broke the thicket about 70 yards to my right, running as if he had just turned into the home stretch of a quarter-mile Olympic race. Directly ahead of me stood my little Gunner. He had heard his brother call. He saw what I saw.

I was afraid to shout to him; besides, he appeared to be taking in the situation. Yet he was in acute distress. His gun was in his left hand, unbreeched. He had the turkey-shot shells out. His right hand was jammed in the tight pocket of his corduroy trousers, from which he was trying to pull out the buckshot shells. He could get his hand out, but not his hand and the shells too.

Meanwhile, the buck, running on a curious arc, was coming for him, apparently gaining momentum at every leap. I have seen many a deer run in my time, and certainly they have showed me some breezy capers. But I do not think I ever saw a deer run like this one. I believe that deer feel unusually frisky at twilight, and they often frolic then, just for the fun of the thing. Are they not limbering themselves after a long day's rest, and do they not feel the glamour of the twilight, just as we do—or at least to some degree?

I remember roaming the pinelands after sunset one January day and coming upon a stag that had just begun to feed. He did some fancy jumping that I have never seen another deer do—cavorting over high bushes, blowing through his nose, and then making a few more spectacular leaps, just like a pony that plays with you and won't let you catch him.

But the deer that was headed for my Gunner was not putting on any flourishes. He was just plain scared, and was running as a ringneck does when he means to get away and doesn't care to take wing. Wildly this buck ran, low to the ground, skimming over the bushes and the logs like an incredibly swift hurdler doing his stuff. He seemed to glimmer between the trees. The fading light emphasized the speed at which he was going. Probably he knew that he was in the same fix as were the chargers of the Light Brigade, who, as we learned back yonder in school days, had

Cannon to right of them,
Cannon to left of them.

That Christmas Eve Stag

When he thinks he is cornered, that is the time a deer is going to show you how to get out of a corner in a hurry. Indeed, in one sense, you can't corner a deer.

I could see from the course he was taking that the buck would run about 30 yards from my boy, crossing his front. I could see that the stander now had the breech of his gun closed. He was awaiting the moment. Between him and the deer, as the fugitive got directly in front of him, there would be a tiny pine about four feet high—a young yellow pine with a bushy top. I wondered how the Gunner would manage that obstruction. I didn't have long to wonder. The twilight hurricane was upon him. The buck looked very curious. His tail was down, his head and neck far outstretched. He was in the utmost extremity of speed.

Up went the gun with steady precision. A second later came one barrel. I saw two things distinctly: the top of the little pine was shot away, and the stag flinched, changing his stride. Such a bit of behavior is said to indicate that a deer is certainly hit. But it seems to me that a deer will sometimes flinch from the sound of a gun, if it is close to him—just as he will sometimes execute a dodging maneuver after the first shot has been fired at him. Many a hunter has claimed to have shot a deer, when, as a matter of fact, the crafty stag has only dodged.

Whether struck or not, this buck gave no evidence of having any difficulty in getting away. I wondered why my Gunner did not salute him with the second barrel. Straight toward the sunset ran the stag, far through the rosy woods—a beautiful but heartbreaking sight.

I was feeling pity for my Gunner. I knew how he would mind this. *Yet that flinching of the deer. Had he really been missed?*

A full 300 yards I watched the fleeing stag. Then he vanished in a tall growth of weeds by an old abandoned sawmill.

In another moment I was with my boy. "I think you struck him," I said. "How about the second barrel?"

"My pocket was so tight," he said, "that I couldn't pull out both shells at once, and I didn't have time to pull them out one by one."

He looked peaked and miserable, as a hunter will look after missing a fair shot at a stag.

With my hand on his shoulder, he and I started to look for any signs of blood, but the light was so bad that we couldn't see a thing to encourage us. My elder boy meanwhile came up, and Prince rode up expectantly. What he saw in my face confirmed the superstition that had haunted us both all day.

"'Bout five turkey done fly up and gone back," he announced.

"Well," I said, "at least one buck flew by here and has gone ahead."

The dusk of Christmas Eve was fast settling down—on the world and in our hearts.

"Prince," I said, "this deer flinched at the crack of the gun."

He grinned good-humoredly. "If anybody would shoot at me, Cap'n, I would flinch too. He was so close," he went on, taking on the tone of the professional hunter, "he would sure have come down."

"Well, anyhow," I told him, "ride down yonder by the old camp and see if you can see any sign at all."

My boys searched about disconsolately for blood-signs while Prince rode down the glimmering ridge. He was out of my mind for a few moments until I heard the whoop of whoops. Looking toward the far-off camp, I could barely see him, his hand raised high in ecstatic triumph, while the wildwoods rang with his superb shouts of victory.

"Gunner," I said to my young huntsman, "you killed that buck. Prince has him now."

Together, the three of us ran through the darkening woods. When we came to the place, the negro was on the ground beside the fallen stag. A beauty he was—in his prime, with good antlers. He lay within the shelter of the tall dead weeds into which I had seen him vanish.

A joyous homecoming we had that Christmas Eve. On the plantation, the negroes take the killing of a fine deer as an occasion for much festive hilarity, and certainly the white hunter has in his heart rejoicings of his own. We hung up the Gunner's buck, then went to a wild turkey dinner and an hour of perfect peace, yarning before the great open fireside.

I must add that when the stag was dressed, we found that one of the three buckshot that struck him had passed straight through his heart. Yet he had run nearly a quarter of a mile at top speed without a blunder. The vitality of wild game is a thing almost incredible.

After a day that ended so happily, I had to have a little talk with Prince before saying goodnight to him.

"Well," I asked, "what does your wife have to say now about hunting on Christmas Eve? Doesn't this deer prove to her that she was wrong?"

"Cap'n," said Prince, "I ain't never can't prove nothin' to a woman what she ain't want to believe. She done say this luck was a acci-*dent*."

And the more I think of Sue's description of our good fortune, the more inclined am I to believe that she was right.

THE DEER OF THE RIVER BOTTOMS

By Theodore Roosevelt

This selection is Chapter 4 in one of TR's best-known works on the outdoors, Hunting Trips of a Ranchman (1885). *This period in the author's life, filled as it was with a strange mixture of joy (hunting and ranching in the Dakota Badlands) and sorrow (he lost his first wife and his father in a short period of time), saw him find his feet as a writer.*

Of all the large game in the United States, the white-tailed deer is the best known and the most widely distributed. Taking the Union as a whole, fully ten hunters will be found who have killed whitetails for one who has killed any other kind of large game.

And, it is the only ruminant animal which is able to live on the land that has been pretty thickly settled. There is hardly a state wherein it does not still exist, at least in some out-of-the-way corner; and long after the elk and the buffalo have passed away, and when the big-horn and pronghorn have become rare indeed, the whitetail deer will still be common in certain parts of the country.

When, less than five years ago, cattle were first driven onto the northern plains, the whitetail were the least plentiful and the least sought-after of all the large game; but they have held their own as none of the others have begun to do, and are already in certain localities more common than any other kind. Indeed, in many places they are more common than all other kinds put together.

Ranchmen along the Powder River, for instance, now have to content themselves with whitetail venison unless they make long trips back among the hills. The same is rapidly getting to be true of the Little Missouri. This is partly because the skin and meat hunters find the chase of this deer to be the most tedious and least remunerative species of hunting, and therefore only turn their attention to it when there is nothing else left to hunt, and partly because the sheep and cattle and the herdsmen who follow them are less likely to trespass on their grounds than on the grounds of other game.

The whitetail is the deer of the river bottoms and of the large creeks, whose beds contain plenty of brush and timber running down into them. It prefers the densest cover, in which it lies hidden all day, and it is especially fond of wet, swampy places, where a horse runs the risk of being engulfed. Thus, it is very rarely jumped by accident, and when the cattle stray into its haunts, which is but seldom, the cowboys are not apt to follow them. Besides, unlike most other game, it has no aversion to the presence of cattle, and in the morning and evening will come out and feed freely among them.

This last habit was the cause of our getting a fine buck a few days before last Christmas. The weather was bitterly cold, the spirit in the thermometer sometimes going down at night to 50 degrees below zero and never for over a fortnight getting above minus 10 degrees (Fahrenheit). Snow covered the ground, to the depth, however, of but a few inches, for in cattle country the snowfall is always light. When the cold is so great, it is far from pleasant to be out-of-doors.

Still, a certain amount of riding about among the cattle and ponies had to be done, and almost every day was spent by at least one of us in the saddle. We wore the heaviest kind of all-wool underclothing, with flannels, lined boots, and great fur coats, caps, and gauntlets or mittens, but yet after each ride, one or the other of us would be almost sure to come in with a touch of frost somewhere about him.

On one ride, I froze my nose and one cheek, and each of the men froze his ears, fingers or toes at least once during the fortnight. This generally happened while riding over a plain or plateau with a strong wind blowing in our faces. When the wind was on our backs, it was not bad fun to gallop along through the white weather, but when we had to face it, it cut through us like a keen knife.

The ponies did not seem to mind the cold much, but the cattle were very uncomfortable, standing humped up in the bushes, except for an hour or two at mid-day when they ventured out to feed; some of the young stock, which were wintering on the range for the first time, died from the exposure. A very weak animal we would bring into the cow-shed and feed with hay, but this was only done in cases of the direst necessity, as such an animal has then to be fed for the rest of the winter, and the quantity of hay is limited.

In the badlands proper, cattle do not wander far, the deep ravines affording them a refuge from the bitter icy blasts of the winter gales; but if by any accident caught out on the open prairie in a blizzard, a herd will drift before it for maybe more than a hundred miles, until it finds a shelter capable of holding it.

For this reason, it is best to keep more or less of a look-out over all the bunches of beasts, riding about among them every few days, and turning back any herd that begins to straggle toward the open plains; though in winter, when weak and emaciated, the cattle must be driven as little as possible, or the loss among them will be fearful.

One afternoon, while most of us were away from the ranchhouse, one of the cowboys, riding in from his day's outing over the range, brought word that he had seen two whitetail deer, a buck and a doe, feeding with some cattle on the side of a hill across the river and not much more than half-a-mile from the house.

There was about an hour of daylight left, and one of the foremen, a tall, fine-looking fellow named Ferris, the best rider on the ranch but not an unusually good shot, started out at once after the deer, for in late fall and early winter, we generally kill a good deal of game as it then keeps well and serves as a food supply throughout the cold months. After January we hunt as little as possible.

Ferris found the deer easily enough, but they started before he could get a standing shot at them, and when he fired as they ran, he only broke one of the buck's hind legs just above the ankle. He followed it in the snow for several miles, across the river, and down near the house to the end of the bottom, and then back toward the house. The buck was a cunning old beast, keeping in the densest cover, and often doubling back on his trail and sneaking off to one side as his pursuer passed by. Finally, it grew too dark to see the tracks and Ferris came home.

Early next morning, we went out to where he had left the trail, feeling very sure from his description of the place (which was less than a mile from the house) that we would get the buck, for when he had abandoned the pursuit, the deer was in a copse of bushes and young trees some hundreds of yards across, and in this it had doubtless spent the night, for it was extremely unlikely that, wounded and tired as it was, it would go far after finding that it was no longer pursued.

When we got to the thicket, we first made a circuit round it to see if the wounded animal had broken cover, but though there were fresh deer tracks leading both in and out of it, none of them were made by a cripple, so we knew he was still within.

It would seem to be a very easy task to track up and kill a broken-legged buck in light snow, but we had to go very cautiously, for though with only three legs, he could still run a good deal faster than either of us on two, and we were anxious not to alarm him and give him a good start.

There were several well-beaten cattle trails through the thicket, and in addition to that, one or two other deer had been walking to and fro within it, so it was hard work to follow the tracks.

After working some little time, we hit on the right trail, finding where the buck had turned into the thickest growth. While Ferris carefully followed the tracks, I stationed myself farther on toward the outside, knowing the buck would in all likelihood start upwind. In a minute or two Ferris came on the bed where he had passed the night, and which he had evidently just left. A shout informed me that the game was on foot, and immediately afterward the crackling and snapping of the branches were heard as the deer rushed through them.

I ran as rapidly and quietly as possible toward the place where the sounds seemed to indicate that he would break cover, stopping under a small tree. A minute afterward, he appeared some 30 yards off on the edge of the thicket, and halted for a second to look round before going into the open. Only his head and antlers were visible above the bushes, which hid from view the rest of his body.

He turned his head sharply toward me as I raised the rifle, and the bullet went fairly into his throat, just under the jaw, breaking his neck, and bringing him down in his tracks with hardly a kick.

He was a fine buck of eight points, unusually fat, considering that the rutting season was just over. We dressed it at once, and, as the house was so near, determined we would drag it there over the snow ourselves, without going back for a horse. Each took an antler, and the body slipped along very easily, but so intense was the cold that we had to keep shifting sides all the time, the hand which grasped the horn becoming numb almost immediately.

Whitetails are very canny, and know perfectly well what threatens danger and what does not. Their larger, and to my mind nobler, relation, the black-tail, is easier to approach and kill, and yet is by no means so apt to stay in the immediate neighborhood of a ranch, where there is always more or less noise and confusion.

The bottom on which my ranch house stands is a couple of miles in length, and well wooded. All through last summer it was the home of a number of whitetails, and most of them are on it to this moment. Two fawns in especial were really amusingly tame, at one time spending their days hid in an almost impenetrable tangle of bullberry bushes, whose hither edge was barely a hundred yards from the ranch house. In the evening, they could frequently be seen from the door as they came out to feed. In walking out after sunset, or in riding home when night had fallen, we would often run across them when it was too dark to make out any thing but their flaunting white tails as they cantered out of the way.

Yet for all their seeming familiarity, they took good care not to expose themselves to danger. We were reluctant to molest them, but one day, having performed our usual weekly or fortnightly feat of eating up about everything there was in the house, it was determined that the two deer (for it was late in autumn and they were then well grown) should be sacrificed.

Accordingly, one of us sallied out, but found that the sacrifice was not to be consummated so easily, for the should-be victims appeared to distinguish perfectly well between a mere passer-by, whom they regarded with absolute indifference, and anyone who harbored sinister designs. They kept such a sharp lookout, and made off so rapidly if anyone tried to approach them, that on two evenings the appointed hunter returned empty-handed, and by the third, someone else had brought in a couple of blacktail. After that, no necessity arose for molesting the two "tame deer," for whose sound common sense we had all acquired a greatly increased respect.

When not much molested, whitetails feed in the evening or late afternoon, but if often shot at and chased, they only come out at night. They are very partial to water, and in the warm summer nights will come down into the prairie ponds and stand knee-deep in them, eating the succulent marsh plants. Most of the plains rivers flow through sandy or muddy beds with no vegetable growth, and to these, of course, the deer merely come down to drink or refresh themselves by bathing, as they contain nothing to eat.

Throughout the day, whitetails keep in the densest thickets, choosing if possible those of considerable extent. For this reason, they are confined to the bottoms of the rivers and the mouths of the largest creeks, the cover elsewhere being too scanty to suit them. It is very difficult to make them leave one of their haunts during the daytime. They lie very close, permitting a man to pass right by them, and the twigs and branches surrounding them are so thick and interlaced that they can hear the approach of anyone from a long distance off, and hence are rarely surprised.

If they think there is danger that the intruder will discover them, they arise and skulk silently off through the thickest part of the brush. If followed, they keep well ahead, moving perfectly noiselessly through the thicket, often going round in a circle and not breaking cover until hard-pressed, yet all the time stepping with such sharp-eyed caution that the pursuing hunter will never get a glimpse of the quarry, though the patch of brush may not be 50 rods across.

At times, the whitetail will lie so close that it may almost be trodden on. One June morning, I was riding down along the river and came to a long bottom crowded with rose-bushes, all in bloom. It was crossed in every direction by cattle paths, and a drove of longhorned Texans were scattered over it. A cow-pony gets accustomed to traveling at speed along the cattle trails, and the one I bestrode threaded its way among the twisted narrow paths with perfect ease, loping rapidly onward through a sea of low rose-bushes covered with the sweet, pink flowers. They gave a bright color to the whole plain, while the air was filled with the rich, full songs of the yellow-breasted meadowlarks perched on the topmost sprays of the little trees.

Suddenly, a whitetail doe sprang up almost from under the horse's feet and scudded off with her white flag flaunting. There was no reason for harming her, and she made a pretty picture as she bounded lightly among the rose-red flowers, passing without heed through the ranks of the long-horned and savage-looking steers.

Doubtless, she had a little spotted fawn not far away. These wee fellows soon after birth grow very cunning and able to take care of themselves, keeping in the densest part of the brush, through which they run and dodge like a rabbit. If taken young, they grow very tame and are most dainty pets.

One which we had round the house answered well to its name. It was at first fed with milk, which it lapped eagerly from a saucer, sharing the meal with the two cats, who rather resented its presence and cuffed it heartily when they thought it was greedy and was taking more than its share. As it grew older, it would eat bread or potatoes from our hands, and was perfectly fearless. At night, it was let go or put in the cow-shed, whichever was handiest, but it was generally round in time for breakfast next morning.

A blue ribbon with a bell attached was hung round its neck, so as to prevent its being shot, but in the end it shared the fate of all pets, for one night it went off and never came back again. Perhaps it strayed away of its own accord, but more probably some raw hand at hunting saw it and slaughtered it without noticing the bell hanging from its neck.

The best way to kill whitetails is to still-hunt carefully through their haunts at dusk, when the deer leave the deep recesses where their beds lie and come out to feed in the more open parts. For this kind of hunting, no dress is so good as a buckskin suit and moccasins. The moccasins enable one to tread softly and noiselessly, while the buckskin suit is of a most inconspicuous color and makes less rustling than any other material when passing among projecting twigs.

Care must be taken to always hunt upwind and to advance without any sudden motions, walking close to the edge of thickets, while keeping a sharp lookout, as it is of the first importance to see the game before the game sees you.

The feeding grounds of the deer may vary. If they are on a bottom studded with dense copses, they move out on the open between them; if they are in a dense wood, they feed along its edges; but, by preference, they keep in the little glades and among the bushes underneath the trees.

Wherever they may be found, they are rarely far from thick cover, and are always on the alert, lifting their heads after every few bites to see if any danger threatens them. Unlike antelope, whitetails seem to rely upon escaping observation rather than discovering danger while it is still far off, and so, are usually in sheltered places where they cannot be seen at any distance. Hence, shots at them are generally obtained at very much closer range than at any other kind of game. The average distance would be nearer 50 than 100 yards. On the other hand, more of the shots obtained are running ones than is the case with the same number taken at antelope or black-tail.

If the deer is standing just out of a fair-sized wood, it can often be obtained by creeping up along the edge. If seen among the large trees, it is even more easily still-hunted, as a tree trunk can be readily kept in line with the quarry, and thus prevent its suspecting any approach.

But only a few whitetail are killed by regular and careful stalking; in much the greater number of instances, the hunter simply beats patiently and noiselessly from the leeward, moving carefully through the clumps of trees and bushes, always prepared to see his game and with his rifle at the ready. Sooner or later, as he steals round a corner, he either sees the motionless form of a deer not a great distance off, regarding him intently for a moment before taking flight, or he hears a sudden crash and catches a glimpse of the animal as it lopes through the bushes. In either case, he must shoot quickly because the shot is a close one.

If he is heard or seen a long way off, the deer is very apt, instead of running away at full speed, to skulk off quietly through the bushes. But when suddenly startled, the whitetail makes off at a great rate at a rolling gallop, the long, broad tail, pure white, held up in the air.

In the dark or in thick woods, often all that can be seen is the flash of white from the tail. The head is carried low and well forward in running; a buck, when passing swiftly through thick underbrush, usually throws his horns back almost on his shoulders with his nose held straight in front.

Whitetail venison is, in season, most delicious eating, only inferior to the mutton of the mountain sheep.

Among the places which are most certain to contain whitetails may be mentioned the tracts of swampy ground covered with willows and the like, which are to be found in a few (and but a few) localities through the plains country. There are, for example, several such along the Powder River, just below where the Little Powder empties into it. Here is a dense growth of slim-stemmed young trees, sometimes almost impenetrable, and in other places opening out into what seem like arched passage-ways, through which a man must at times go almost on all fours. The ground may be covered with rank shrubbery, or it may be bare mud with patches of tall reeds. Scattered through these swamps, are pools of water, and sluggish ditches occasionally cut their way deep below the surface of the muddy soil.

Game trails are abundant all through them, and now and then there is a large path beaten out by the cattle; while at intervals there are glades and openings. A horse must be very careful in going through such a swamp or he will certainly get mired, and even a man must be cautious about his footing.

In the morning or late afternoon, a man stands a good chance of killing deer in such a place, if he hunts carefully through it. It is comparatively easy to make but little noise in the mud and among the wet, yielding swamp plants, and by moving cautiously along the trails and through the openings, one can see some little distance ahead.

Toward evening, the pools should be visited, and the borders as far back as possible carefully examined, for any deer that come to drink, and the glades should be searched through for any that may be feeding. In the soft mud, too, a fresh track can be followed as readily as if in snow and without exposing the hunter to such probability of detection.

If a shot is obtained at all, it is at such close quarters as to more than counterbalance the dimness of the light and to render the chance of a miss very unlikely.

Such hunting is for a change very pleasant, the perfect stillness of the place, the quiet with which one has to move, and the constant expectation of seeing game keeping one's nerves always on the stretch. But after a while, it grows tedious, and it makes a man feel cramped to be always ducking and crawling through such places. It is not to be compared, in cool weather, with still-hunting on the open hills; nevertheless, in the furious heat of the summer sun, it has its advantages, for it is not often so oppressively hot in the swamp as it is on the open prairie or in the dry thickets.

The whitetail is the only kind of large game for which the shotgun can occasionally be used. At times, if a deer is seen in dense brush at a short distance, and the shots have to be taken so hurriedly that the shotgun is really the best weapon wherewith to attempt its death.

One method of hunting is to have trained dogs hunt through a valley and drive the deer to guns stationed at the opposite end. With a single slow hound given to baying, a hunter can often follow the deer on foot in the method adapted in most of the eastern states for the capture of both the gray and red fox. If the dog is slow and noisy, the deer will play round in circles and can be cut off and shot from a stand. Any dog will soon put a deer out of a thicket or drive it down a valley.

Without a dog, it is often difficult to drive deer toward the runway or place at which the guns are stationed, for the whitetail will often skulk round and round a thicket instead of putting out of it when a man enters, and even when started, it may break back past the driver instead of going toward the guns.

In all these habits, deer are the very reverse of such game as antelope. Antelope care nothing at all about being seen, and indeed, seem to court observation, while the chief anxiety of a whitetail is to go unobserved.

In passing through a country where there are antelope, it is almost impossible not to see them; while there may be an equal number of whitetails, the odds are manifold against travelers catching a glimpse of a single individual. The pronghorn is perfectly indifferent as to whether the pursuer sees him, so long as in his turn he is able to see the pursuer, and he relies entirely upon his speed and wariness for his safety. He never trusts for a moment to eluding observation.

Whitetails, on the contrary, rely almost exclusively either upon lying perfectly still and letting the danger pass by, or skulking off so slyly as to be unobserved. It is only when hard pressed or suddenly startled that they bound boldly and freely away.

In many of the dense woodlands without any opening, the brush is higher than a man's head, and one has then practically no chance at all of getting a shot on foot when crossing through such places. But I have known instances where a man had himself driven in a tall light wagon through a place like this, and got several snapshots at the deer, as he caught momentary glimpses of them stealing off through the underbrush.

Another method of pursuit in these jungles is occasionally followed by one of my foremen, who, mounted on a quiet horse that will stand fire, pushes through the bushes and now and then gets a quick shot at a deer from horseback. I have tried this method myself, but without success, for though my hunting-horse, old Manitou, stands as steady as a rock, yet I find it impossible to shoot the rifle with any degree of accuracy from the saddle.

The Deer of the River Bottoms

Where great stretches of country have to be covered, as in antelope shooting, hunting on horseback is almost the only way followed, but the haunts and habits of the whitetail render it nearly useless to try to kill them in this way, as the horse would be sure to alarm them by making a noise, and even if he did not, there would hardly be time to dismount and take a snapshot. Only once have I ever killed a whitetail buck while hunting on horseback, and at that time I had been expecting to fall in with black-tails.

This was while we had been making a wagon trip to the westward, following the old Keogh Trail, which was made by the heavy army wagons that journeyed to Fort Keogh in the old days when the soldiers were, except a few daring trappers, the only white men to be seen on the last great hunting-ground of the Indians. It was abandoned as a military route several years earlier, and is now only rarely traveled over, either by the canvas-topped ranch-wagon of some wandering cattlemen—like ourselves—or else by a small party of emigrants in two or three prairie schooners, which contain all their household goods.

Nevertheless, the trail is still as plain and distinct as ever. The two deep parallel ruts, cut into the sod by the wheels of the heavy wagons, stretch for scores of miles in a straight line across the level prairie, and take great turns and doublings to avoid the impassable portions of the badlands. The track is always perfectly plain, for in the dry climate of the western plains, the action of the weather tends to preserve rather than to obliterate it.

When traveling along it, or one like it, the hunters can separate in all directions, and no matter how long or how far they hunt, there is never the least difficulty about finding camp. For the general direction in which the road lies, is, of course, kept in mind, and it can be reached whether the sun is down or not; then a glance tells if the wagon has passed, and all that remains to be done is to gallop along the trail until camp is found.

On the trip in question, we had at first very bad weather. Leaving the ranch in the morning, two of us, who were mounted, pushed on ahead to hunt, the wagon following slowly, with a couple of spare saddle ponies leading behind it.

Early in the afternoon, while riding over the crest of a great divide that separates the drainage basins of two important creeks, we saw that a tremendous storm was brewing with that marvellous rapidity which so marks a characteristic of weather changes on the plains.

A towering mass of clouds gathered in the northwest, turning that whole quarter of the sky to an inky blackness. From there, the storm rolled down toward us at a furious speed, obscuring by degrees the light of the sun and extending its wings toward each side, as if to overlap any that tried to avoid its path. Against the dark background of the mass could be seen pillars and clouds of gray mist, whirled hither and thither by the wind, and sheets of level rain driven before it. The edges of the wings tossed to and fro, and the wind shrieked and moaned as it swept over the prairie.

It was a storm of unusual intensity; the prairie fowl rose in flocks from before it, scudding with spread wings toward the thickest cover, and the herds of antelope ran across the plain like race horses to gather in the hollows and behind the low ridges.

We spurred hard to get out of the open, riding with loose reins for the creek. The center of the storm swept by behind us, fairly across our track, and we only got a wipe from the tail of it. Yet, this itself we could not have faced in the open. The first gust caught us a few hundred yards from the creek, almost taking us from the saddle, and driving the rain and hail in stinging level sheets against us. We galloped to the edge of a deep wash-out, scrambled into it at the risk of our necks, and huddled up with our horses underneath the windward bank. Here we remained pretty well sheltered until the storm was over.

Although it was August, the air became very cold. The wagon was fairly caught, and would have been blown over if the top had been on; the driver and horses escaped without injury, pressing under the leeward side, the storm coming so level that they did not need a roof to protect them from the hail.

Where the center of the whirlwind struck, it did great damage, sheets of hailstones as large as pigeons' eggs striking the earth with the velocity of bullets. The next day, the hailstones could have been gathered up by the bushel from the heaps that lay in the bottom of the gullies and ravines. One of my cowboys was out in the storm during whose continuance he crouched under his horse's belly. Coming home, he came across some antelope so numb and stiffened that they could barely limp out of the way.

Near my ranch, the hail killed quite a number of lambs. These were the miserable remnants of a flock of 12,000 sheep driven into the badlands a year before, four-fifths of whom had died during the first winter, to the delight of all the neighboring cattlemen.

Cattlemen hate sheep, because they eat the grass so close that cattle cannot live on the same ground The sheep-herders are a morose, melancholy set of men, generally afoot, and with no companionship except that of the bleating idiots they are hired to guard. No man can associate with sheep and retain his self-respect. Intellectually, a sheep is about on the lowest level of the brute creation; why the early Christians admired it, whether young or old, is to a good cattleman always a profound mystery.

The wagon came on to the creek, along whose banks we had taken shelter, and we then went into camp. It rained all night, and there was a thick mist with continual sharp showers, all the next day and night. The wheeling was, in consequence, very heavy, and after striking the Keogh Trail, we were able to go along it but a few miles before the fagged-out look of the team and the approach of evening warned us that we should have to go into camp while still a dozen miles from any pool or spring.

Accordingly, we made what would have been a dry camp had it not been for the incessant downpour, enabling us to gather water in the canvas wagon-sheet and in our oilskin overcoats in sufficient quantity to make coffee, having with infinite difficulty started a smouldering fire just to leeward of the wagon. The horses, feeding on the soaked grass, did not need water.

An antelope, with the bold and heedless curiosity sometimes shown by its tribe, came up within 200 yards of us as we were building the fire. One of us took a shot at him, but missed.

Our chaps and oilskins had kept us perfectly dry, and as soon as our frugal supper was over, we coiled up among the boxes and bundles inside the wagon and slept soundly till daybreak.

When the sun rose next day, the third we were out, the sky was clear, and we two horsemen at once prepared to make a hunt. Some three miles off to the south of where we were camped on a plateau, the land sloped off into a great expanse of broken ground, with chains upon chains of steep hills separated by deep valleys, winding and branching in every direction, their bottoms filled with trees and brushwood.

Toward this place we rode, intending to go into it some little distance, and then to hunt through it near the edge. As soon as we got down near the brushy ravine, we rode along without talking, guiding the horses as far as possible on earthy places, where they would neither stumble nor strike their feet against stones and not letting our rifle-barrels or spurs clink against anything.

Keeping outside of the brush, a little up the side of the hill, one of us would ride along each side of the ravine, examining intently with our eyes every clump of trees or brushwood.

For some time we saw nothing, but finally, as we were riding both together round the jutting spur of a steep hill, my companion suddenly brought his horse to a halt, and pointing across the shelving bend to a patch of trees well up on the opposite side of a broad ravine, asked me if I did not see a deer in it.

I was off the horse in a second, throwing the reins over his head. We were in the shadow of the cliff's shoulder, and with the wind in our favor, so we were unlikely to be observed by the game. I looked long and eagerly toward the spot indicated, which was about 125 yards from us, but at first could see nothing.

By this time, however, the experienced plainsman with me was satisfied that he was right in his supposition, and he told me to try again and look for a patch of red. I saw the patch at once, just glimmering through the bushes, but should certainly never have dreamed it was a deer if left to myself.

Watching it attentively, I soon saw it move enough to satisfy me where the head lay. Kneeling on one knee and (as it was a little beyond point-blank range) holding at the top of the portion visible, I pulled the trigger, and the bright-colored patch disappeared from among the bushes. The aim was a good one, for on riding up to the brink of the ravine, we saw a fine whitetail buck lying below us, shot through just behind the shoulder. He was still in the red coat, with his antlers in velvet.

A deer is far from being such an easy animal to see as the novice is apt to suppose. Until the middle of September, he is in the red coat; after that, he is in the gray. But it is curious how each one harmonizes in tint with certain of the surroundings. A red doe lying down is, at a little distance, undistinguishable from the soil on which she lies, while a buck in the gray can hardly be made out in dead timber.

While feeding quietly or standing still, they rarely show the proud, free port we are accustomed to associate with the idea of a buck, and look rather ordinary, humble-seeming animals, not at all conspicuous or likely to attract the hunter's attention. But let them be frightened, and as they stand facing danger or bound away from it, their graceful movements and lordly bearing leave nothing to be desired.

The blacktail is a nobler-looking animal, while an antelope, though as light and quick on its feet as is possible for any animal not possessing wings to be, has an angular, goat-like look, and by no means conveys to the beholder the same idea of grace that a deer does.

In coming home on this wagon trip, we made a long moonlight ride, passing over between sunset and sunrise what had taken us three days' journey on the outward march. Of our riding horses, two were still in good condition and well able to stand a 24-hour jaunt, in spite of hard work and rough usage. The spare ones, as well as the team, were pretty well done up and could get along but slowly.

All day long we had been riding beside the wagon over barren sagebrush plains, following the dusty trails made by the beefherds that had been driven toward one of the Montana shipping towns.

When we halted for the evening meal, we came near learning by practical experience how easy it is to start a prairie fire. We were camped by a dry creek on a broad bottom covered with thick, short grass, as dry as so much tinder. We wished to burn a good circle clear for the campfire. Lighting it, we stood round with branches to keep it under control. While thus standing, a puff of wind struck us, and the fire darted up, roaring like a wild beast. Our hair and eyelashes were well singed before we had beaten it out.

At one time it seemed as if, though but a very few feet in extent, the fire would actually get away from us, in which case the whole bottom would have been a blazing furnace within five minutes.

After supper, looking at the worn-out condition of the team, we realized that it would take three more days traveling at the rate we had been going to bring us in, and as the country was monotonous, without much game, we concluded we would leave the wagon with the driver and taking advantage of the full moon, push through the whole distance before breakfast next morning.

Accordingly, at nine o'clock we again saddled the tough little ponies we had ridden all day and loped off out of the circle of firelight. For nine hours we rode steadily, generally at a quick lope, across the moonlit prairie. The hoofbeats of our horses rang out in steady rhythm through the silence of the night, otherwise unbroken save now and then by the wailing cry of a coyote.

The rolling plains stretched out on all sides of us, shimmering in the clear moonlight; and occasionally a band of spectral-looking antelope swept silently away from before our path.

Once, we went by a drove of Texas cattle that stared wildly at the intruders as we passed, then charged down by us, the ground rumbling beneath their tread, while their long horns knocked against each other with a sound like the clattering of a multitude of castanets.

We could see clearly enough to keep our general course over the trackless plain, steering by the stars where the prairie was perfectly level and without landmarks; and our ride was timed well, for as we galloped down into the valley of the Little Missouri, the sky above the line of level bluffs in our front was crimson with the glow of the unrisen sun.

THE DEER HUNT
By Charles Whitehead

**First published in The Spirit of the Times *magazine, this selection forms (Chapter 7) in* Wild Sports of the South *(1860). The book was reissued with a new title,* The Camp-Fires of the Everglades, *in 1891. This chapter, along with "The Still Hunt," are the only two Whitehead stories devoted to whitetails. The work ranges widely over various types of fishing and hunting in Florida, with frequent literary side trails into natural history.*

The light broke early on the planter's shackley house and the smouldering brands of our campfire, the morning after Mike's panther story. It may not have been early, though our late hours of the evening before made it seem so to me, and I silently banned the sleepless hound and "the cock's shrill clarion, and the echoing horn," which ushered in the light and drew us to our feet, yawning and drinking in the misty sights and sounds.

Away up on the top of a live oak a mockingbird was gushing over in song. Sometimes trilling a few notes, descending an octave it would laugh and cry. Then it would sound the call of the quail twice repeated, and then tinkling, laughing, gurgling, it poured out the very music of mirth. Too happy to sit still, it fluttered up in the air a dozen feet or more, trilling its merriest song, then descending again to the branch from whence it rose, it syllabled love's deepest tones.

The sheep and cattle were crowding out of the pens and spreading over the open woods. The horses were whinnying for their food. Our boys were lighting a fire while preparing meat, singing and laughing. There were calls to negroes with fancy names and shouted answers; guns were discharged and reloaded, and saddles examined. A dozen things were wanted that could not be found, or when found were not in a condition to be used. The youngsters were running to the spring for water or to the shed for corn, or around the grounds, merely for the fun of running and shouting. They were all dressed alike, in long, brown cotton shirts, so one sex could not be distinguished from the other.

Aunty Blaze, after seeing the table was spread and the meat cooked, brought out an immense corncake on a wooden turner, and with a commendable feeling of pride, threw it down on the table, right-side up, steaming hot and brown as rosewood. Turning to go, she stumbled against a little black girl coming with the sugar-bowl; a smart slap applied with the cake-turner propels the child forward a yard and elicits a yell of disapprobation, and the sugar-bowl is dropped to the floor.

The Doctor loads his double-barrelled gun, and explains its new-fashioned lock to Miss Jackson, who comes out arrayed in a tight-fitting cap and bodice, and her eyes light up with the anticipation of the chase. Mike slowly and methodically wipes out his rifle with dry flax, and every moment is seen eating some hidden remains of last night's meal, which he has stowed away on his person, and which are to form more than half his breakfast. We eat our hurried meal—it might be called a passover, as no one takes time to sit—and then ride off down the woods.

Jackson and Mike are leading the van, Lou and the Doctor still side by side, and there goes a negro on a marsh tackey, the pony of the South, and there a neighbor that has come over for the hunt, mounted on a vicious mare as thin as a crane.

The hounds, of a dozen different colors and sizes, go along in couples, led by the negroes on foot, and on ahead to a given rendezvous shuffles Poinpey Duffield, the oldest negro on the place, driving a mule laden with two baskets of provisions intended for the dinner of the party. The mist comes up from the river in golden clouds, for the sun is just rising. Down along the bank we went with call and laughter, and the bittern arose from the sedge with a guttural cry, and the alligator sank into the water with a heavy splash as our cavalcade moved onward to the lower pinelands that skirt the big swamp. The trees were all white pine; there was no underbrush, and we could see down the long arcades they formed for nearly a mile.

Now and then a flaunting flower would rear its crimson cheek to the wind, or a vine could be seen clasping a trunk and drooping from branch to branch in long festoons, but generally the ground was covered only with the yellow siftings of the pines and free from all vegetation.

The horses trod without a sound, and save now and then a fox squirrel, we met no animal life, until we came to the hummocks and drew together to give general directions for commencing the chase, the manner of which is necessary to explain.

A hummock is a thicket often covering but an acre or two of land, and sometimes presenting an extent of several miles. The one now in view covered about 30 acres, and half-a-mile farther down the woods, we could see another. It lay in a low swale of land, and in it the haw, the alder and willow grew into a tangled copse, studded with the red leaves of the pinckneya, while above them all, a hundred feet or more, the ash and gum trees reared their long arms, and the magnolia opened its blossoms to the upper air. It was an admirable spot for game, with succulent grass and flags, and a dusky shade that was but little penetrated by the sun.

"You stay here, Doctor Pollock," said Jackson, as we rode up, "and mind your eyes, sir."

The Doctor drew himself up with a doubtful air, as if uncertain whether minding his eyes referred to the uses he had just been putting those organs to in watching Miss Jackson's face, or whether it referred to watchfulness in the future; so he answered at random, "All right, sir!"

"And you, sir," he continued, turning to me, "take your place two gun-shots off on that side, keeping always within five or six rods of the swamp. And you," turning to the neighbor that had joined us, "go on next; and you, Lou, come with Mike and me."

And away they cantered with the dogs around the other side of the swamp, dropping one or two negroes to guard some particular point of the hummock. In this way, we enclosed two sides of the swamp with a cordon of hunters stationed just so far apart that if a deer came out, one or the other was certain of a shot.

On the farther side, and the only portion of the swamp that we were unable to surround, the drivers were to enter with the hounds, and the deer would not be likely to make his escape in that direction.

The deer in Florida and the other southern states are the ordinary Virginia deer, but of small size, the bucks weighing an average of a hundred pounds, while in the northern states, they grow to an average of double that weight.

The last I saw of Jackson he was winding around the swamp with Mike, having left his daughter on a little knoll that commanded a fair view of the hummock, and where her bright bay horse and little figure stood out in relief against the dark pines beyond. I could not see the Doctor, but my negro, Scipio, stood between us and only a short distance away, and perfect stillness reigned over the pine woods and hummocks.

Moment after moment slipped away, but we could hear nothing, save the impatient champing of my horse. Away down in the woods, a fox squirrel flirted his broad tail as he chased his comrade up a tree, and a painted woodpecker passed by in undulating sweeps as silently as a moth.

At length a distant call, so faint it just reached me, but I recognized it as the driver cheering the hounds as he cast them off. Now for it. Another pause. The cry was repeated, and with it the low yelp of a dog, then another, and then a ringing shot away down the woods. My horse pricked his ears, and Scipio mounted a fallen tree, the better to survey the scene. No cheering shout announced the death of the deer, though the dogs stopped yelping.

At this moment, I heard in the bushes the rapid bound of some animal; it came nearer and nearer. From the higher ground where I stood, I could see over the bushes a pair of antlers, and I supposed it to be the same deer that had been fired at down in the swamp. I dismounted to take surer aim.

How my heart beat in unison with the bounding of his feet, while every sense converged into the coming of his presence! But alas, he did not come out by me, but between me and the Doctor, and very near to him.

Bang! Bang!

I heard his rifle, and immediately the deer turned in again, just keeping to the edge of the bushes, and showing his back at every jump. As he passed me, I took aim, and when his flag showed over the grass, I fired, but the deer only moved with an accelerated speed down past the next stand. Receiving a shot there and two from Miss Jackson, he rushed back into the swamp from whence he came.

With the firing, the dogs broke out into a louder chorus. I heard Jackson's horn nearer and nearer; he was following up the dogs, keeping in the open woods, while Mike was doing the same on the other side.

All at once the hounds broke out with a louder yell, and at the same moment a buck broke cover again in front of me, accompanied by two does, one on either side. I had just loaded, and had my foot in the stirrup, when without changing position, I fired at the stag's shoulder. I missed my mark, but shot one of the does that tumbled down in the grass.

The buck and the other doe once more turned back, and coursed down the edge of the hummock toward Poke, who fired his barrel again, and this time with some correctness, for the buck dropped his tail for an instant with an uneasy motion. Raising it again, he turned back, followed by Poke on horseback directly past my stand.

I fired my second barrel without effect, and then, not able to resist the contagion of the chase, spurred my horse after the flying animals.

Away they went down the little swale that led toward Lou Jackson's stand. One hound after another, as he came out of the rushes, caught sight of the deer and joined in the chase with a double note.

Bang! came a shot from my left, missed clear, and the hunter, not stopping to load, joined the chase.

Now it was Miss Jackson! I saw her raise her gun, her father was close behind, riding hard to get to her, and away down the woods I could see Mike trying to head off the chase, his long hair streaming behind him like a woman's. A puff of smoke and a report—the buck staggered, but still ran, drawing in behind him in one yelling, shouting, crashing train, every man, horse and dog in the woods.

"You hit him, Lou. Tally-ho! Hi on! Hi! Hurrah! Faster! There's Tip, and there's Slasher! Go it, Music! Golly! Maussa, gib him fits!"

The cries formed a medley of sound until the yelling of the dogs and the trampling of the horses drowned all words. The horses, as wild in their ardor as their riders, needed no rein.

The buck led the way directly for another hummock about three miles away, and which was now within sight; his flight was straight and well sustained, though now and then a spot of blood on the leaves showed he was wounded. The dogs were tolling on behind, not two yards away, and close behind the dogs came all the hunters, the Doctor, riding the fastest horse, taking the lead.

As we approached the hummock, the pines grew closer together, and while going between two of them, the Doctor was caught by his gun, which he held crosswise before him on the saddle, and was swept off his horse to the ground.

"There's a ten strike!" called out Jackson, as we rushed by. Closer still we came to the deer, every dog stretched to his utmost length, every rider bending to his horse's mane.

Mike was just raising his rifle to his shoulder to shoot, when without a sign, the big buck fell head first to the ground, and rolled over and over with the impetus of the chase. His heart had broken in the desperate burst just within reach of his lair, in whose close covert the doe, with one long bound, was lost.

Up came the dogs and horses so fast they ran over the game, and crowded and jostled together as they pulled up as a wave that meets a rock on the sandy beach.

Then there was dismounting and whipping off the dogs, and a search for the wounds in our quarry. Two buckshot, in the thick part of the neck from behind, came from the Doctor's second barrel.

"Where is the Doctor? Here is his horse. Oh, there he comes limping along rather sore with his fall."

A laugh and a sly joke were all the consolation we had to offer him.

Two more buckshot in the right side, close together; that is Lou Jackson's shot. They were the only ones of the party using shotguns. None of the shots were heavy enough to kill the deer, though altogether, they had broken him down in the chase.

We sounded a horn to tell the drivers we left behind our whereabouts, and putting the buck on one of the negroes' horses and coupling the dogs to keep them from entering the swamp, we turned back the way we came.

"Now for the does we left behind," said Jackson. "How many were there, sir?"

"I saw two bucks and four does," said the Doctor.

"Fudge! Those were the same deer we have been chasing, only your people turned them back into the hummock two or three times without killing them."

"I killed one," said I.

"Where is it?"

"It fell in the bushes."

"Reckon you did not hit her."

"You had better believe it; I can show you the place where she fell."

"That isn't what we want. Where is the place that she is now, can you tell me that? I fired at a doe, too, but a long way off, and she probably is where yours is."

"Doctor, how's your back?"

"He-he! Golly mighty! He quit de saddle mighty smart dat time!" remarked Caesar.

As we rode up to the hummock where we had started the game, I found the place where I had shot the doe, but she was not there, though the negroes said she had fallen.

"Throw off a dog, then," said Jackson.

"Let Music try," said his daughter, and accordingly, Music was loosened and sent in the grass. Music was a young hound, spotted white and black, like a coach-dog, and with such silky ears they felt like a satin robe in your hand. She was led to the place where the deer had fallen, and taking its track with a plaintive whimper, commenced unwinding it from among the bushes and reeds.

Presently, a louder effort warned us to beware, and cantering apart a little, so as to be able to see all around the hummock, Mike's grey eye caught sight of the doe trying to steal out of the bushes. A clear ringing shot was followed by a quick leap and she fell dead.

We laid them side by side, the stately buck and his gentle consort. The dew of the morning was still glittering on their hides—their eyes were as bright and as full as in life. I wondered if Miss Jackson felt any pity for them, as she saw the dogs licking the blood that flowed from their throats.

One of the negroes dismounted from his pony, and we put the two deer in place, tying their feet beneath the belly of the struggling horse. We then sent them where we were to meet for dinner.

"Now, one more hunt before dinner. Where shall we go, boys?"

"Saw de ole white buck fur sartin, dis day, maussa!" said the planter's head negro, coming up.

"Where did you see him?"

"Down by de run, ober dere," said the negro, pointing with his finger. "His tracks fresh as dis niggah's."

"You mean you saw his tracks?"

"Yes a maussa."

"How does he know that it is a buck?" I asked.

"How fur to know he's a buck? Haint chased dat air deers' s'often fur nuttin'; 'spect I be'ent a dun gone fool!" replied Jumping Lem, with some asperity.

"Well, if that is the buck that run in this range last winter, I kinder guess ye'll all have to rub your legs with bar's grease in order to ketch him," added Mike.

"Don't you think we can shoot him? Mike asked Lou Jackson. "No, young woman, I don't. Thar are too many here to make certain of any deer. When a man wants a deer bad, he goes alone and keeps his mouth shut."

As we rode over to inspect the tracks, I learned, partly from the exclamations of the negroes, and partly from Jackson's account, that this buck passed the winters in the pine woods, retiring when the mosquitoes become thick in the spring to the cool swamps of the Ouithlacouchee.

It has been so often hunted, and was so successful in escaping, that it became well known at the Jackson plantation, where it was the object of a covert superstition to all the negroes, which mysterious fear rather aided his escape, for when the boys saw it coming, they became so frightened they could not hit 40 paces off.

On reaching the run that Lem had mentioned, we readily found the tracks, and all drew up to examine them. The presentation of some unknown bone to a company of savants, or the appearance of a new bonnet at a country sewing society, occasions not more curiosity and sage comment than does the discovery of a new track in the woods. One mentions its size, another recognizes old peculiarities or marks, another says it was the foot of a male animal, another that it was fat in flesh and another that it was going on an easy trot. What is stranger still, from the small data of four marks in the damp soil, all these facts arrived at are the results of careful observation, though seldom incorrect.

According to the congress now assembled, this buck was the old white buck, so called from an unusually white coat, and had gone at a gentle gait into the Black Jack hummock, which lay two miles farther on, and before which we presently arrived. It was about half-a-mile in length by three-quarters broad, and was filled, like the other swamp holes, with long grass, bushes and vines, from which rose several tall trees of those species that spring in swamps and savannahs. At its upper end grew a thicket of blackjack trees. In such spots the does dropped their fawns, and young and old sheltered themselves here for their noonday rest.

Once more the members of the chase separated to take commanding positions overlooking the edges of the thicket. We were cautioned against shooting at anything that might come out, until we were certain the white buck was not there. Once more Mike and Jackson disappeared, and with them the hounds, already snuffing the air from the swamp and tugging at their leashes to get away. The forest was still.

In a short time, we could hear the cheers of the negroes, and the thrashing of the bushes as they struggled forward in the tangled underbrush. At this instant, a doe followed by a fawn almost grown came to the edge of the bushes. She looked up and down, her large ears turning this way and that, and not seeing anyone, she came out on a lope, and passing close by me, ran down the woods, making for the river.

I had my gun to my shoulder, but remembering the white buck, withheld my fire, lest the bigger game should follow the course of the doe and find me with an empty gun.

Yeow-ow-ow came from the hummock; that was Music's voice—her tone was like a bugle's. Then two or three whimpering notes from other hounds.

"What's dat air a bobbin' in yer bushes?" asked Scipio, standing near me and eagerly trying to overlook the grassy valley.

"A cat—a cat!" he shouted, "sure as gun," and a handsome specimen of the wild cat or lesser lynx sprung out of the bushes, and then seeing Scipio, darted back again to cover.

"Golly mighty, wouldn't dat cat get shook up—yah—ha, yah—ha—he!"

Now the hounds broke out in chorus, with a multitudinous cry that babbled in the bushes and wailed in the air, as though the echoes caught the sound and mellowed it down to a continuous accord.

Scipio felt the contagion, and dancing up and down, relieved himself as follows: "Dar dey come! Dar dey come! Bress de Lord! Don't dey skin 'em—dat beats dis chile; hy ah ha, hy ah ha! Go it, Music! "

The dogs had come halfway down the cover when a buck and doe broke out together. He did not appear to be of unusual size, but I could not wait any longer and fired. He fell and rose again, running over the brow of a little hill with his tail down; here he drew the fire of my neighbor on the right, and fell to rise no more.

The doe halted a moment where her comrade fell, as if waiting for him to rise, then away down the woods a rifle rung its sharp crack and she fell like a clod almost on the body of her mate. I knew Mike's rifle by the effect, even if I did not know its sound.

The hounds came closer; we could see the grass and bushes moving where they were winding about, and now and then their sickle-shaped tails above the weeds. The clamor increased, the dogs were almost through, and yet no white buck to correspond with the negro's description of the big buck they had so often hunted.

At this instant, I saw a buck rise up from the very edge of the bushes. From his stately size, I at once recognized it to be the big buck. He had evidently been watching the preparations for the hunt, and selecting the time our guns were discharged, he rushed out between me and one of the negroes, and without regarding either, flew down the open pine woods at a gallop. Hardly had he cleared the valley when I heard Jackson shouting, and saw him riding hard toward my stand, but the dogs coming out and taking the deer's track with loud clamor, prevented my hearing.

I sprang into my saddle and went flying alongside the hounds, with the air soughing through my hair, and the deer a hundred yards ahead.

In a moment or two Lou Jackson and the Doctor were in sight, their horses slamming the open woods like birds. Then came the sorrel mare, and next Scipio on the pony, and then in the distance Jackson and Mike, with all the negroes that were mounted.

Faster, still faster, heart and sense fixed on that flying buck, and the trees merged together in a mass as we swept among them.

Whoop! Why cannot a man cheer louder; why cannot a horse fly faster when a deer is in view?

There is a crash and a flash of dirt and sticks; the sorrel has gone down, and her rider rolled over and over, far ahead of his steed. There is no time to see if he can get up again.

Hurrah! There is a hummock! See Tiger and Bess turn to the left! They know the buck will not run through it, and they turn aside to cut the radius of the arc he is about to make. He sees the plan and accelerates his speed. His horns are lying on his back, his nose in air. He is stretching away at his highest speed, and whenever a bush intercepts his flight, he leaps it with a bound that must give him a bird's-eye view of his pursuers.

Far ahead of the deer is a close swamp, and from the straight line the deer was making, we knew he was looking to it for refuge. Behind, I heard Jackson calling to us, but who could stop to listen with such a buck in view?

On we went, the dogs still nearer the deer, and Tiger almost within reach of his haunches. Lou Jackson held one rein in each hand, her eyes fixed on the chase and her hair flying loose behind her.

There goes the deer in the bushes; he touched a log here and a bog there, and along he went like a rope-dancer.

"Tally ho!" On went the dogs, when to my surprise, Tiger disappeared from view, and in a second of time the whole pack was floundering in the morass.

"Hold hard," I heard again from behind.

"Hold hard, Miss Jackson!" I screamed, as the truth flashed on me. "The quicksands!"

Too late, her horse was wild with the chase, and she could not hold him. He made one or two desperate leaps as he found himself floundering, and in a second of time was half engulfed in the mud. His rider still held the reins and kept her seat on the struggling horse.

The Doctor was in equal plight, while his frightened beast pawed the air in its attempts to regain a footing. My horse, more used to such ground, turned short around when he felt it quaking, throwing me in the edge of the mud like a clown in a circus. Up came Mike as fast as he could ride, and Jackson behind him.

Mike threw himself from his horse, and while the others were cutting sticks to throw to the engulfed riders, ran out by quick jumps to the log over which the deer had run, and then cutting off with his knife a grape-vine that had climbed a neighboring tree, he wound it around his arm and swung himself out toward Miss Jackson.

The first swing did not send him far enough, but putting his foot against the trunk as his rope oscillated, he swung out to where the young girl lay up to her armpits, and rapidly sinking in the sands, and putting his hand under her arm, began to draw her from her perilous position.

When she was entirely above the surface, he swung the vine sufficiently to carry his charge to the root of the tree, from whence it was easy to reach the shore.

I would have given a year of life to get such a look of thanks from a lady I know as the breathless girl gave Mike—the ugly scamp!

The Doctor's turn came next, and then the horses, until finally, after two or three hours of hard work, we were all once more in the saddle, and some of us looking more like scavengers than gallant hunters under the greenwood tree.

"S'pose you tink dat white buck's de debbil for true now, hey?" said Scipio, as he was tightening my girths.

"No, I don't. Why do you ask?"

"Kase I 'se not sartin the niggahs here'bouts knows heaps, and dey sez dey ain't agwine to hunt dat buck nohow, and I spec as how I wouldn't nudder. 'Spec as how sumthin' wuss en what we's seen 'll come out o' dat eer chase yit. I'se not scared, but dat is very 'plexing."

The day was wearing away fast, and sending one of the boys for the two deer last killed, we all turned toward the place appointed for our meeting, where after a few minutes' riding, a blue smoke column arose among the trees and the distant gleam of water announced a dinner and a rest—two pleasant things, whose worth is only known to those who have laboured well.

From our dining place, a bend of the river showed us two vistas down the ancient woods, and the broad sheet of water, half in shadow half in sunshine, was broken by the flocks of ducks that were coasting along its banks. The trees that fringed the shore were covered with immense creeping vines that clasped the trunks and suspended themselves from the branches.

Down by the water's edge, the aster reared its purple head, and the love-vine wove its orange thread like a net over many a rank grove of water-plants. The opposite shore was lower than the bank on which we were standing, and the eye took in miles of canebrake and forest, unbroken by any sign of human labour.

"Look at those turkey buzzards, Doctor," said Miss Jackson, pointing to two birds that, with matchless grace, were floating in slow circles high in the air. "I would like to see the view they are taking in at this moment."

"So would I. They are eagles in the air and crows on the ground," replied the Doctor. "They seem never to move their wings, and yet how powerfully they fly while they watch every motion that is going on in the woods below them."

"Dinnah's ready, gemens and ladies," called out Pompey Duffield, with a marked accent on the and, while Jackson's horn played the stave of a march that made the dogs howl, and we turned away from the bank to the dinner that was spread out on the grass. There was cold wild turkey and ham, hot coffee, cornbread and bacon. It wouldn't have been a Florida dinner without the cornbread and bacon.

After dinner came the pipes and a long talk, and then as the sun went down, tracking the woods with his sanguine trail, we packed out our game, one deer to each pony and, with Pompey Duffield taking the lead, filed off through the shadowy woods for the plantation.

HUNTING ON SNOW
By Theodore S. Van Dyke

This is an edited portion of Chapter 11 in Van Dyke's timeless The Still-Hunter (1882). *While it may seem somewhat tedious and wordy to modern readers, it is worth noting that Theodore Roosevelt suggested no hunting ranchman "who loves sport can afford to be without" Van Dyke's book. A review in* Spirit of the Times *styled it as "the best, the very best work on deer hunting." No representative anthology of the sport's literature would be complete without a selection from what many consider the foundational book in the field, and here the author writes about the type of whitetail hunting he likely knew best of all.*

The climax of pleasure and generally of skill is reached in tracking up your game so as to get a good shot at it. Many of the best still-hunters will not hunt at all until snow comes, and in the Eastern and Northwestern states, the season may be said to commence only "when snow flies," as they say in the woods.

Tracking upon snow and upon bare ground are generically the same, but specifically so different as to require separate treatment. And tracking on snow being the easiest, we will consider it first.

To follow a deer's track on snow is so easy that almost any one of any tact at all can do it with a trifling bit of practice in judging the freshness of the marks and the snow thrown out ahead of the footprints. As we go on, we will notice the prominent features of a fresh trail.

Two very natural mistakes are, however, apt to be made by the novice who hunts on snow:

First. That a fresh trail is to be followed as a matter of course.

Second. That he is to follow *directly upon it*.

The advantage of snow for still-hunting lies not alone in enabling one to locate a deer and come up with him. It lies quite as much in softening the ground and deadening the sound of your steps; in making a background upon which you can more easily discover your game; in enabling you to speedily ascertain the quantity and quality of the deer about you, the direction they have taken, what they were doing, and how long since they passed, etc. etc.

To follow up tracks is often folly. An old buck in "running-time" will often lead you too long a race. A doe may then do the same. If tracks consist of jumps or half-jumps, or half-trot or half-walk and half-jump, it generally shows that the deer are alarmed, especially if there are places where they have stopped and turned around to look back. It will then be quite useless to follow them, except as hereafter directed.

If the deer are much pursued by still-hunters, they will be so likely to watch their back track even when lying down that it will be quite vain to keep on the track. Where the ground is very brushy or very level, it is rarely advisable to follow a trail unless the deer are very tame or you can use a cow-bell or horse.

Where deer are plentiful and you are well acquainted with the ground, knowing all the ridges, passes, feeding places and lying-down ground, it is often better to let tracks entirely alone and hunt as you have done heretofore—to find them on foot at feeding time, or standing in or around thickets during the day or lying down. This is the course pursued by many of the best hunters quite as often as tracking. They use the tracks only as a general guide, and depend mainly upon the other advantages of the snow I've mentioned.

But whether you follow tracks or not, there are some points ever to be remembered:

First. While snow enables you to see a deer much farther as well as more quickly and distinctly than upon bare ground, it also gives the deer precisely the same advantage over you, an advantage which you cannot in heavy timber avoid by all the white clothes and hats you can invent.

Second. Though snow deadens the *sharpness* or *distinctness* of sounds, yet dull sounds, like the crushing of dead or rotten sticks beneath the foot, will be conveyed along the ground as well as ever, and perhaps even better if the snow is wet.

Third. It may make an entirely new noise by grinding or packing under your foot when deep and dry, unless you work your foot into it toe first; or when a little stiff or crusty from thaw or rain, it may make a noise worse than any it hides. And both these new noises being conveyed *along the ground,* and being *unmistakable in their character,* will frighten a wild deer farther and more effectually than any other kind of noise. And in no respect must any of the caution to be observed in hunting on bare ground be relaxed.

Not only is it a great pleasure to work up a trail, but where deer are scarce, it is often essential to success. And, as hunting on snow without tracking does not materially differ from what we have already been over, we will pass at once to tracking.

A light feathery snow of about two inches in depth which fell last evening now covers the ground. And again we tread the woods by the time it is light enough to distinguish a deer. For the earlier we get upon a track, the less the distance we shall have to follow it, and the more likely we shall be to find our game on foot instead of lying down where we may have to depend upon a running shot.

Here is a track already. But it will not be best to follow it, as it was made last night soon after the snow ceased falling. Compare it with your own track and see how the snow thrown out ahead of the hole lacks the sparkle of that thrown from your track. You see, too, that the edges of the hole made by the deer's foot do not glisten like the edges of the one you have made. All this is because the crystals of snow have lost their keenness of edge by evaporation—a process that takes place in the very driest snow and coldest air.

Stoop low and examine the deer's tracks closely, and notice a little fallen snow and a few faint particles of fine dust from the trees in them. This dust is always falling, even in the very stillest weather. But you need nothing more reliable than the mere appearance of the snow around the edge and in front of the track.

With a few days' practice, you can tell a trail five minutes old from one five hours old, even in dry snow. But we will leave this trail, for we shall surely find fresher ones.

Here we come to one that is quite fresh. But the size of the footprints, as well as their distance apart, shows the trail to be that of a large buck. As it is the height of the rut, we will let him go.

Ah! Here is what we want—a trail of a doe and two fawns. They are going, too, toward the acorn ridges—a good place to catch them.

With watchful eye, you steal cautiously along the trails. These lead to the acorn ridges, and here they begin to separate. The deer evidently have stopped traveling, and are now straggling about here and there. Your common sense now tells you that they have probably stopped to feed a bit here and may be very close, perhaps just over the next ridge. Therefore you redouble your caution about noise, and look more keenly than ever at every spot that can possibly be a bit of a deer's coat. All of which is very well.

In a moment or two you reach the top of the first ridge, and a good long look at all the ground in sight shows you no deer. But you find where deer have pawed up the snow for acorns. The trails, too, cross and recross each other here, so that you can follow nothing. And they become mixed, too, with other deer tracks until you are quite confused.

You consider yourself fully equal, however, to this emergency, and resolve to cut the knot by the very simple device of the rabbit-tracker—a circle.

This plan is correct enough in itself. But why do it *now?* If the deer are still on these ridges, you need not follow their tracks at all, but look for them just as you would do if the ridges were bare. Your chances of seeing them in that way are quite good enough. And by the amount and variety of tracks you see, there are other deer about, and some are probably feeding on the ridges this very minute.

Never mind the tracks now, but slip around to the leeward of the breeze that you see is just beginning to sift down a little fine snow from the treetops above. Do not lose the advantage of the wind for the sake of following tracks now. You can follow those tracks in two hours as well as you can now; and if the deer have gone away to lie down or lounge, they will then be little farther away than they now are. Keep to the leeward and remain on these ridges at least an hour more.

But your anxiety to follow them is too great, and you start on a circle to find their trail again. In five minutes the circle is completed. Yet your stock of information on the subject of those three deer remains unchanged. You find only confusion worse confounded, a complete network of trails. You should have made your circle four or five times as large as you did make it.

You see this mistake, and set out upon a much larger circle than before. While doing this, one of the first things you discover is a series of long jumps down a ridge to the left. Following these back to find how you lost that deer, you discover that he was feeding just over a ridge only a hundred yards from where you began your first circle, and that by the time that circle was half completed, you with your eyes fixed upon the ground—where they had no business to be—came directly into his sight.

Two hundred yards more of your second circle brings you to another object of peculiar, often painful, interest to anxious hunters—two more sets of long jumps where two yearlings have scattered the snow, leaves and dirt with their plunging hoofs.

In the excitement of your circle business, you quite overlooked the little matter of wind, and they probably smelled you. Or they may have been stampeded by the running of the other deer, for he must have passed somewhere near here. And the running of a deer will nearly always alarm every deer within hearing of the sound of his hoofs.

By the time your circle is nearly completed, you find that the doe and two fawns have left the ridges and gone across a flat creekbottom. This does not, however, prove your circle enterprise a profitable one, for you could easily have discovered this in time without throwing away the prospects you had for a shot at the other three deer.

You follow the trail of the doe and fawns across the creek, where it turns and goes up the creekbottom some 20 or 30 yards from the creek. Thus far, they have been walking along nearly together, and at an ordinary pace. But now the trails are separating and the steps get shorter and more irregular. Here, one has wandered off a few rods to one side; here, another has stopped at a bush and nibbled a few twigs; there the old one has been traveling rather aimlessly around and through a patch of black-haws.

All these signs tell you to be careful, for they may be within sight at this instant, though they may also have gone on half-a-mile or more.

On the way to lie down, deer will often stop an hour or two in such a place to browse and stand around a while. That is what these have been doing, and as it is yet early, they may yet be here.

Priding yourself upon your caution and acuteness, you move quietly along, your eyes piercing every bush far into the distance for some 300 yards. There, on the other side of a thin patch of wild-plum bushes, you find that refreshing sight with which your eyes are already so familiar: the long-jumps. There are three sets of them, and all beautifully long.

At first you are inclined to ejaculate, but your chagrin yields at once to wonder, for a glance into the brush shows you that they were all on foot in it when they started. Yet the brush is so thin that you can see plainly all through it, and you recognize the plum-patch as one at which you looked very keenly some 200 yards back and thought then that you could see distinctly through it.

And you naturally wonder how they got started. Well, when your head first arrived in sight of that brush, deer were standing in there, two of them browsing, the other looking back in the direction from which they came. You have already been told of what an advantage the animal that is at rest has over one that is moving. You have also learned that an animal in brush can see out much better than one outside can see in. And I must again remind you that a deer standing still in brush is, even with the aid of snow as a background, one of the hardest things in the world to detect with the eye.

But you cannot comprehend how they could have run without your seeing them at all. If they saw enough of your head to take alarm, how could their whole bodies escape your eyes, especially when that bit of brush was the first thing on which your eyes rested when you came in sight of it at all?

It is rather a puzzle, but its only solution is this: A deer's eyes, when watching his back track, are as keen to detect motion in the woods as are those of the wildest antelope on the plain.

Some people who had never hunted very wild deer would doubt this, but I will show you how extremely true it is. It will reduce your opinion of yourself considerably below par, but it will reward you well in future, and also give you a good idea of the general futility of following upon the track of a deer that you have started.

Let us follow, then, the trail of these three and see if we can again get sight of them. Do not try to get a shot; be content with just a sight. Go right ahead on the trail and look into the woods as far as you can. Nearly half-a-mile you follow them, the long jumps still continuing. Here, they have skipped a high fallen log, and in three places the snow is switched from it by their descending tails. Here, one has smashed through a bush, scattering snow and branches around, and there, another has struck some boggy ground and splashed mud and water around in fine style.

Suddenly the jumps slacken to a trot; in a few yards that stops, and you find where they have stopped and huddled up, one standing sideways, the other two turning all the way around. And then the long jumps begin again, still longer now than before.

And yet the ground is all quite open. They stopped behind no brush,

Hunting on Snow

no logs, no rising ground, nothing to hide them from your sight. But it is evident they stopped here and looked back, and that they started again in sudden alarm. The wind and the distance are such that they could neither have heard nor smelled you. They must therefore have seen you; yet you saw nothing of them, although they were under full headway. Do you think this impossible? Does it seem that the second run must have been only a continuance of the first run? Then by all means follow them to the next place where they stop to look back and see what they do there.

On, on, on, on, nearly half-a-mile farther go the tracks, as if the deer were in a hurdle-race over the biggest logs to be found. Then they suddenly stop and huddle up; and then as suddenly go on again in jumps as long as ever.

And so you might keep on the livelong day, seeing perhaps two or three times a faint glimpse of dark evanescence among the distant trunks, but seeing nothing long enough to raise the rifle upon, and four-fifths of the time seeing not a trace of game at all. And yet all the time it is evident that the deer have each time seen you. And five times out of six such will be your experience with very wild deer, whether they be old bucks or young fawns. The sixth time you may perhaps get a long standing shot or a closer running one in the course of half-a-day's chase, but neither will be good enough to give you much prospect of hitting.

The principal difference between these and deer that are not very wild is that you will generally get sight of the latter, but rarely until they are running away. And when you do see them standing, it will rarely be long enough, nor will they generally be close enough, for anything like a certain shot. This applies to the latter deer only when they have once been started. Deer that are not very wild seldom or never have the trick of watching back upon their track *before* being started.

You passed a fresh track of a big buck a few moments ago that led toward the slash. He has gone there to rest a bit after his morning travels. You had better try him, for "anybody can kill a buck in running-time." At least that is what they say.

You start off upon his track with much more care than you did upon the trail of the others. But this is only time wasted. The woods here are quite open for several hundred yards, and as far as you can see, there are no windfalls, brush-patches or brushy ridges. There is no probability that he has stopped anywhere along such ground as this when, if you remember the woods as you should do, the old slash is less than half-a-mile in the direction the track is leading.

Reaching the slash, you find the trail winds over a ridge and down into a little basin. You look very carefully into the basin, thoroughly inspecting all the brush it contains. Seeing nothing, you descend and follow the trail across it and up the end of a ridge that juts into it. On the point of this ridge, in a clump of low briers, you find a large, fresh, warm bed with the well-known long jumps leading away from it.

Now, stoop low in this bed and you can still see every step of the way you came for 150 or 200 yards back. While your eyes were intently fixed upon the track, he saw you and departed.

So what was the use in going into that basin at all? Could you not just as well have wound around it out of sight behind this ridge to the right? And by so doing, could you not have found out whether the buck passed out of the basin, and just where he left it, quite as surely as you could have done by having both eyes and feet half the time in his tracks? Had you done this, he would not have seen you so soon; and when he did see you, you would have had a good running shot at him.

Turn off now to one side and keep down along the edge of the slash and see if any more deer have come from the timber to lie down in here.

A few moments' walk brings you to the trail of two yearlings. These you follow for quarter-of-a-mile into the slash, using all your care, skill, eyesight and caution about noise, moving not over half-a-mile an hour, working each foot toe first through the snow so as to feel any possible stick or brush that may crack beneath it, easing off any twig that could possibly scratch against your clothes, and looking, looking, looking oh so keenly!

You reap at last a common reward of honest, patient toil—a sight of two sets of long, plunging jumps leading away from two fresh warm beds.

The sun smiles sweetly as ever down through the bracing air; the lonely pines are as dignified and solemn as usual; the luxuriant briers embrace your trowsers as fraternally as ever; and the old logs and stumps loom up around you more smiling and bigger than before. But sight or sound of venison there is none, and you are the sole being in a dreary microcosm of snow, brush, briers, stumps, logs and dead trees.

HUNTING DEER IN DIFFERENT SEASONS

By Philip Tome

This material comes from Chapter 14 of Tome's classic 19th century book, Pioneer Life; or, Thirty Years a Hunter *(1854). The work, set in the author's native Pennsylvania, has been reprinted numerous times. As a review at the time of its original appearance suggested, this autobiography was "a source book for the mores of the fringe of the first American frontier." Its subject matter ranges widely, with considerable material on elk and bear as well as whitetails.*

In the latter part of June, deer generally keep themselves in the swales, or marshes, near the small streams, where the grass starts the earliest. The usual method of hunting them at these places was to encamp in the vicinity, and watch early in the morning and late at evening when they go out to feed. If the woods are not open, the hunter ascended a tree or eminence where he could command a more extended view.

When he discovered a deer, he slipped down and endeavored to approach it by another direction than the one in which they were moving, as they always look behind them for danger.

It is necessary for the hunter to keep on the leeward side of the deer, as their keen scent will detect his presence and flee, long before he can approach within shot if the wind blows from him to the deer.

The manner of curing the meat is the same as that of the elk. It is first cut from the bone in thin slices and salted in the skin. It is easily preserved, less than a pint of salt with a little saltpeter, being sufficient for a deer. When it has lain from 12 to 24 hours, a scaffold is built, upon which the meat is spread, and a slow fire built underneath. If the weather is stormy, the skin can be spread over the meat, and the drying still continued, the fire being gradually increased until the meat is thoroughly cured. In the meantime, the hunter could continue his operations without much interruption, as the fire has no effect in frightening away the deer.

When I went on a hunt, I usually carried a good supply of salt, and arranged it so that if I did not return at the end of three days, a man followed me with a horse, bringing me supplies and conveying home the venison I had taken.

During all my hunts, I kept a constant lookout for deer licks, and if I found none in a place favorable for deer, I made one near a spring.

The manner in which I made the lick was to bore several holes in a black oak log with an augur, which I always carried with me for the purpose, and into them put about three pints of salt, with a small quantity of saltpeter, and insert a plug in each hole. The wood soon becoming saturated with the salt, the deer would gnaw it.

If I found a lick to which the deer at the proper season resorted, I proceeded at once to build a scaffold, in order that the deer might become accustomed to the sight of it before I made use of it. If a tree stood within three or four rods of the lick, I built my scaffold upon that. If there was no tree in a favorable place, I set four crotches in the earth, lay poles across, and make a screen of bushes or bark to conceal myself from the deer.

About a month after I had prepared a log, I visited it, and if the deer had found it, I built a scaffold near it.

In hunting at these licks, I mounted the scaffold by a ladder which I drew up after me and patiently awaited the approach of the deer. If none came during the day, I prepared a torch of pitch pine, sometimes adding lard or bear's grease, which I swung upon a pole reaching from the scaffold to the ground. The torch was attached to a crane of branches and bark, made to slide upon the pole, and slipped down by a cord to within three feet of the ground. As the deer came along, they would stop and stare at the light, forming an easy mark for me.

When alone in these expeditions, I was always provided with two guns: a musket and a rifle. If several deer came at once within shot, I fired the musket, which was loaded with buckshot, and the deer frequently stood fixed to the spot, not knowing which way to flee, and I could kill three or four before coming down from the scaffold.

Beside the light near the ground, I had another upon the scaffold about as high as my head, and when firing from the scaffold, I raised the gun above the range of the deer, and lowered it gradually until the end of the barrel became dark, and then fired, scarcely ever missing my aim. When I fired from the ground by torchlight, I pointed the gun below the game and raised it till the end became dark.

After killing the first ones, there is no further chance that night as the smell of the blood will frighten away the deer.

I generally had a companion and a dog, and one of us remained at a distance with the dog, while the other watched from the scaffold. In the morning, if any deer were wounded, we set the dog on the track, if we could not track it by the blood without difficulty.

About the tenth of November, the deer begin to travel from one place to another, and by that time I had generally chosen my hunting ground. I would take my station upon the summit of some hill, where I could command a view in all directions. I would sometimes mount a tree to the height of 50 feet. On one occasion, I discovered from the top of a tree seven deer and three bears. I descended and killed two of the deer, but the bears escaped.

My first lessons in hunting were received from an old hunter, named John Mills. He lived near my father's, and wishing to remove to Canada, sold his farm to my father. He then offered to sell me his dog and teach me all he knew about deer hunting for 15 dollars, which I accepted. I had already hunted several years, but his instructions were of greater value to me than all my previous experience. The substance of his instructions I have given the reader.

The following autumn, I went on a hunting expedition, taking with me the dog I had bought of Mills and another one which I had previously owned. I followed the directions I had received, and with a success which showed their value.

From the early part of October until the first week of February, I killed 28 bears and a large number of deer.

In June, deer frequent beech and maple woods, or feed in the marshes bordering on the streams. About the last of July, they take to the highlands, among the chestnut and white oak woods, feeding on pea-vines and other herbage. In the hot weather of August, they are in the thickest shades upon high hills. At this time, the manner of hunting them is to watch by a spring as near the summit of a hill as may be found. They will come at evening to drink, and fall an easy prey to the hunter as he lies concealed within a few yards.

The last of September, the deer begin to leave the thickets and move from one place to another, and for several months they are constantly in motion. The hunter has only to station himself near one of their paths and shoot them as they pass. When the first snows come, they can be tracked to the places where herds of them lie at night, and the hunter can keep near a herd and pick them off with his rifle.

In 1805, a colony consisting of about 40 families of English people made a settlement between the first and second forks of Pine Creek. They cleared about 250 acres of land and built several good houses, but being unaccustomed to the hardships and dangers of pioneer life, they abandoned the settlement after struggling along for five years. As soon as the coast was clear, deer from all the country around came to feed in the cultivated fields and sunny pastures of the deserted settlement. This afforded a capital opportunity for hunters, and the place became a favorite resort for them.

We would lodge in the upper story of some deserted house, and in the morning, looking out of a window, could see perhaps 40 deer. I have often shot a couple of deer from the window before leaving the house in the morning.

From this congregation of deer in the openings, a man in the vicinity conceived the idea of entrapping them in fields cleared and sowed with wheat or grass. The next season, he cleared two acres, partly on a hillside, built a high fence around it and sowed it with wheat.

About the last of August, when the young wheat had obtained a good start, he made openings in the fence to admit the deer. When they had fed upon the wheat for three weeks, it was gnawed so close that he closed the fence for a few weeks to give it a fresh start.

About the first of October, he again opened the fence for a week, then he kept it closed till November. The deer had now become wonted to the place, and he made places in the fence where they could easily leap into the field, but once in, they could not get out.

In a few days he had two bucks and two does in his enclosure. He killed the bucks, and let the does stay in the field to decoy other deer. This had the desired effect, and during the season he took in this manner between 60 and 70 deer.

This method is successful only where deer are numerous. The wheat crop is not materially injured if the deer are not permitted to remain on it too long.

The best kind of dog for hunting deer is a large variety, half bloodhound, a quarter cur and the other quarter greyhound. I have had two dogs of this kind, for one of which I paid ten dollars and for the other six. They were of more practical value than four smaller dogs would have been.

When they were once in chase of a deer, they would not lose one in ten. So famous did they become for their prowess, that if any of the neighbors saw them running, they would exclaim, "There are Tome's dogs; the deer cannot be far off."

The deer could never baffle them by any of their usual strategems, and the dogs often ran them down before they reached the water. Those wishing to hunt successfully should always procure, at any cost, the largest and best dogs to be found.

A fawn when very young can be easily tamed and kept near the house. They soon become attached to their home, and if removed 20 miles will find their way back in a few days, unless forcibly prevented.

I have never succeeded in making a deer suffer me to milk her, nor in breaking one to the halter. They can be coaxed to follow, but will not be led. A doe, if at perfect liberty, will remain about half the time near the house where it was brought up and the other half in the woods, but never forgets to return.

When returning home, it always takes a straight course, through fields, streams and forests, unless attacked. They are very quiet and good-natured in a domesticated state, unless they have young, and then they will stamp, kick and drive every other animal from them.

The bucks, until they are a year old, are very mild and gentle, but even then, they will not learn to do any labor. At 2 years old, they are very untractable, and cannot be subdued by whipping or any other means, but will plunge at their keeper upon every opportunity.

At 3 years old, it is dangerous to approach them at any time after the middle of September, when their antlers have attained their full size, until they shed them in February. Their viciousness increases with their years, and unless kept in a park, they are very dangerous animals.

The color of the deer changes twice during the year. They shed their hair the last of April, and in May their color is a bright red. By the last of October, they are covered with a short coat of a blue color. The color of the young fawns is a light reddish-brown, beautifully variegated with small white spots. About the middle of October, these spots disappear, and they are then bluish, like the old ones. In November, their hindquarters become white in places.

I have seen in my life two white deer. The first one I saw with a drove of other deer eating moss in the Susquehannah River, where I was fire-hunting. Three years afterward, I saw another, while hunting for elk at night, 15 miles above the place where I had seen the first. I could have killed both, but being such rare specimens, I let them go. They are not a distinct species of deer, but are merely deviations from the general color of common deer.

Every seventh year in April, deer move west in herds of from three to 15, generally going about 30 miles from their usual haunts, and remaining, if undisturbed until some time in July. If molested, they return to their old haunts. This disposition to fly in danger to their accustomed place is always shown by them, whether in a wild or domesticated state.

I knew of a tame buck that disappeared from its owner, and nothing was heard of it for some time. At length it returned one night, very weary, but with its bell still on. It had taken up its quarters at a farm 15 miles distant, where it remained contented until attacked by dogs.

From the last of June until September, deer are light and in good condition for running, and at this season, they are not easily run down. When driven to the water by dogs, they will cross it and run a long time on the opposite side.

By late October, they are very fat, taking immediately to the water when pursued, and do not cross it, but run either up or down a mile or two, so that the dogs lose their scent. Then, leaving the water, they lie down at a short distance, keeping a keen watch for their pursuers.

I always found it desirable to have a man and dog at the water to watch for the deer, and with a good dog they seldom escaped.

A deer will not mate with any animal other than one of its own species. If one is placed when young in company with a calf, lamb or other animal, it will not form an attachment to it.

The bucks are very quarrelsome, and during the running season, desperate conflicts often ensue between them, resulting sometimes in the death of both belligerents. I have often found two of them lying dead, each bearing fatal marks of the other's antlers.

I once found one lying in the last gasp, his antlers interlocked with those of another, already dead. A neighbor once found two of them fighting with their antlers locked, and a doe standing near. He first shot the doe and then both bucks.

WHITETAIL HUNTING IN 1810

By Meshach Browning

This comes from the final portion of Chapter 6 in Forty-Four Years in the Life of a Hunter *(1859) and captures the author's activities when at the height of his considerable hunting powers. He also displays a sense of humor connected with a sudden case of "deer ague" when a wager of a keg of whiskey is in the offing. This is Browning at his best as a teller of tales.*

Shortly after returning to my home, three hunters and myself agreed to go to the glades to hunt deer. We all started for what was called the piney cabin and met at the place, but it was too late to hunt that evening, and there was no snow on the ground.

A light snow having fallen during the night, I said in the morning that I would bet any man a gallon of whiskey I would kill two deer that day.

"I'll take that bet," said a man by the name of James.

It was agreed on; and I told them to pick their course, and I would take the ground that was left. So they all made choice of a locality for that day, leaving me the very ground I wished for.

Everyone set out in great spirits, but while going to the place assigned me, I heard a buck bleat, which they will do in mating-time when they smell other deer. I walked quickly to the leeward side of him in order that he should not smell me. In doing so, I crossed a number of deer tracks.

Knowing that the buck was after them, I stood close to the tracks, where I could still hear him bleating and every time the sound was nearer. In a short time, I saw him following the tracks. I let him come within eight steps, and then stopped him by bleating as he did, when I shot him in his tracks.

I skinned him very rapidly and went on, but I had proceeded only a short distance when I saw a small buck trot along the top of a steep hill, then disappear down the opposite side.

I ran to the top, and looking down, saw him going leisurely along, whereupon I snorted like a deer, which I could do very naturally. As soon as he heard the snort, thinking it came from the other deer, which he expected to see, he stopped to look round for them.

I had with me a deer's tail, which I showed him from behind a tree, and then exposed a small portion of my clothes which were about the color of a deer. Uncertain what to do, he stood there, occasionally stamping his foot on the ground, all the while holding his head as high as he could. Then I would show the tail quietly, and as if I was not scared, and at last seeing him lick his mouth, I knew he would come to ascertain what was there.

He came on little by little, still stamping his feet on the ground, until he came within range of my rifle, when I shot at his breast and broke his shoulder. I set my dog on him, and when the deer soon turned to make fight, I shot him again.

I then skinned him, and as I was in the glades without a hat, and it was blowing and snowing as fast as the snow could fall, I started to run across a glade, out of the storm.

As I ran through the ferns, about half-a-leg high, up sprang a large buck, which, after making two or three jumps, stopped in the middle of the open glade. He had scarcely stopped before my rifle sent a ball through him. He jumped forward a few yards and fell over dead.

The storm was so severe that I was obliged to seek shelter in a grove of thick pines. After it abated, I started for camp again, still looking for deer.

I was about halfway in when I saw approaching what I took to be another buck. I stood still, but the deer saw me too, though it could not make out what I was. Each stood perfectly still, looking at the other, until I became tired.

There was between us a large fallen tree, which hid the body of the deer, so that I could see nothing but the head. Finding no other chance, I raised my gun and fired at the head. After the report, seeing nothing of the deer, I hurried forward, and there lay as fine a doe as I ever killed, with her brains blown out.

I commenced skinning her as fast as possible, as it was getting late, and I was quite ready to leave for the camp when I saw on the entrails so much tallow that I stopped to save it. As I was picking off the tallow, it occurred to me that it was a wonder a buck had not been on her track, for she was in that peculiar condition when the males will follow them, wherever they find their track.

So I raised my head to look, and there stood a stout buck within ten steps, staring at myself and the dog as I was sitting at my work, with the dog licking up the blood and eating the small pieces which fell to his share.

I dared not rise to get my gun, which was standing against a tree out of my reach. Finally, I began to creep towards it, all the time being afraid to look at the deer, lest the sight of my face should scare him, for I knew it was not pretty.

When I had secured my gun, I looked around and saw him walking off, and as I did not wish to spoil his saddle, I delayed shooting until I could get his side toward me.

All of a sudden he stopped, turned round and came walking back to look for the doe, stopping at the same place where I first saw him. That moment I pulled my trigger, and the ball, striking in the middle of the breast, killed him at once. He never attempted to jump, but reared up so high that he fell flat on his back. I skinned him, put him on the same pole with the other, and then started off for the camp.

When I arrived there, all hands seemed astonished at my good luck, but James disputed the fact, saying that I had been there the week previous and had hid those skins in the woods. But a Mr. Frazee, who had hunted with me all the previous week, during which time I had killed some eight or ten deer, told James that my boys and his had come out the last of the week with horses, and carried in all the meat both of us had killed, together with the skins. James was satisfied that there was no foul play in the matter. I told James that I could kill a deer yet that night. He was anxious to take another bet, and in order to give him a chance for his whiskey, I closed with him, for when I left the camp in the morning, I had observed a spot where a great many deer had been feeding on thorn-berries, and I knew that they would be there again at dusk after the berries.

Seizing my gun, I made for the leeward side of the thorn nursery in order that the deer should not smell me. The dog scented the deer, and therefore I crept along very cautiously, though I could see no game. Presently, a very large buck made his appearance, and I said to myself: "That will make the sixth deer, beside two gallons of whiskey, and the reputation of being the best hunter in the woods."

It will be seen that my vanity began to rise. The buck gradually drew nearer, but the pine trees stood so close together that it was a hard matter to secure a good aim, and beside, I found I was becoming so much excited that my hand was growing unsteady.

So I waited till the buck came opposite the space between two trees, when I called to him to stop, which he did, but not until he had so far passed the open space that his ribs were hid from my view. I tried to take aim, but as I could not hold my rifle steady, I waited to get rid of the shakes, though to no purpose, for the longer I delayed, the worse I became. At last, observing the buck's tail beginning to spread, I knew he was about to make off.

As this was my last chance, I put my gun against a tree, thinking thus to brace myself, but my gun absolutely knocked against the tree. As I was then compelled to shoot or to let the buck run off unharmed, I fired at his hips, at a distance of not more than 20 steps, without ever touching either hide or hair of him.

At any other time, I could have sent 20 shots into a space the size of a dollar, but the idea of a great reputation gave me the ague; and through my vanity, I lost both the buck and the whiskey.

When the report of my gun was heard at the camp, Mr. Frazee exclaimed: "There, James, you have another gallon of whiskey to pay for, as Browning never misses."

But when I returned empty-handed, the whole company enjoyed a hearty laugh at my expense.

DEER HUNTING IN INDIANA AND ILLINOIS
By Parker Gillmore

Taken from Prairie and Forest *(1874), this piece also appears in* North American Big Game Hunting in the 1800s *(1982). Gillmore hunted widely for a variety of North American big game animals, and he possibly wrote more about his experiences than any of the many Brits who came to the New World in search of sport.*

Near Vincennes, Indiana, I once knew a man who was pretty nearly master of the art of deer-stalking, and he could as well discriminate a good day for this purpose from an indifferent one as he could a thoroughbred from a mustang.

"No use going out today, Cap," he would say, in answer to an inquiry. "The woodpeckers have got their heads up, and the deer are lying; best stop at home." And best it always was.

It was in the month of December or January, I cannot precisely state which, but on rising from my bed, to my surprise I found the ground covered with a few inches of snow, just sufficient and none to spare, to track a deer with a degree of certainty. Now, I was hungry for venison, and such a chance was not to be let slip. From a very bad habit, which is unaccountable among many when they go from home, I had a morning cocktail brewed, and with a glass in each hand sought the dormitory of my friend, and over this beverage we discussed the prospects and our plan of campaign.

The horses were ordered to be in readiness after breakfast; buckshot and bullets were hunted out, shooting-boots greased, and tobacco and pocket-pistols loaded to the neck and stuffed in our saddlebags. A hard day we knew to be before us, so ample justice was done to our meal; for sportsmen, rely upon what I say, nothing so materially assists you to withstand fatigue and cold as an ample breakfast.

A ride of about five miles took us to our ground, but as our horses were fresh, and we impatient to be at work, the distance was soon traversed. We dismounted in a grove of saplings, well suited to hitch our nags to and shelter them from the wintry blast.

While we were performing the necessary operation of loading, a description of our armament will not be inappropriate. Will (as I will call him) had an antiquated, uncouth rifle with the old-fashioned double trigger, the second to set the hair-spring, an invention I had seldom previously seen and never used, which, although possessed of no finish, could shoot "plumb centre." I had my trusty double-barrel ten-bore, which, from long experience and association I was aware had only to be held straight to do correct work.

A large swamp about half-a-mile off was a favorite resort for deer, and to it we directed our steps. Before we had gone half the distance we came across numerous tracks, so fresh that we kept a sharp lookout in all directions, hoping every moment to be gratified with the sight of some antlered monarch.

Failing in this, we changed our tactics, friend Will posting me on the margin of a branch of the swamp with my back against the butt of a tree, with instructions to remain still and keep a sharp lookout while he would take a *detour*, and possibly drive some stragglers across the run which my position commanded.

Slowly, after Will started, the time passed; the forest appeared perfectly deserted, not a squirrel or bird showed itself to break the monotony, except an angry, squabbling family of woodpeckers, which appeared to have some serious disagreement in reference to the possession of a hole in the trunk of a giant dead tree.

Wet feet are never conducive to comfort, and much less so when you are prevented from taking exercise; besides, it was bitterly cold. First I stood on one leg, then on the other, after the manner of geese, which birds I began to consider I much resembled till at last the inaction became so unendurable that I was very nearly taking up my gun and starting in pursuit of my supposed recreant friend.

As I was about to put my resolution in practice, I thought I heard a voice and, on looking in the direction from whence it proceeded, I was surprised to see a couple of hunters with a cur dog passing my retreat about a hundred yards off.

He who has shot much in the timber well knows that, if he remains quiet, the possibility is great that those moving about may make the game start toward his hide. And well it was I did so, for ere five minutes had passed, a grand old turkey ran past, going like a racehorse. The turkey was not a deer, so I let him go, preferring to be without turkey to braving the wrath of Will for firing at illegitimate game.

How often patience and forbearance receive their reward! And so it was in this instance, for scarcely had the gobbler gone when a fine large buck hove in sight. From his manner, he was evidently alarmed, for every now and then he stopped, snorted and continued his route. Unfortunately, he was heading so as to pass farther off than would afford a good shot, and the ground was too clear to permit me, with any prospect of success, to better my position.

I had almost made up my mind not to shoot. However, I changed my resolution when he came abreast of me, halted and looked around. The temptation I could no longer withstand, so pitching my gun with due elevation, I let drive the first barrel, with no apparent result, for the deer only threw up his head and trotted off. The second charge I quickly determined to put in, and holding well in front and high, had the satisfaction of seeing him make a tremendous bound and drop his tail, a certain indication that some of the shot had taken effect, though the distance was so great that successful results could scarcely be expected.

Nothing is so difficult as to obtain a gun that throws buckshot well. I am inclined to believe that gun-makers have not paid the same amount of attention to discovering the proper internal construction of barrels, so as to obtain the greatest range and closeness in throwing this description of projectile. Generally, at the distance of 100 yards, the side of a barn would be none too large a target to be certain of hitting; and again, occasionally a barrel will make an unusually good pattern at one discharge, while for the next it will be quite the reverse, so that hitting a deer at 100 yards I consider more the result of luck than good guiding, if charged with buckshot.

After waiting for nearly a quarter of an hour, I was joined by my friend, who at once inquired what I had shot at. When I told him the distance, he only laughed one of those peculiar, little dry laughs, which as plainly as words, said, "You're a fool if you expect to eat any of that carcass."

Nevertheless, we together inspected the track, and I had not even the gratification to find blood. Well, Will was for giving it up, but I wished to follow it out, so after using all his powers of persuasion and argument in favor of his views, he succumbed, and consented for once to be dictated to.

For over a mile we followed our game. The line was straight, and the track distinct; moreover, the gait was steady, if one could judge from the regularity of the impressions, and there was naught to indicate that we might not with as great propriety follow any animal in these bottom-lands at which a shot had never been fired.

Will was going ahead, leading, and your humble servant bringing up the rear, when he suddenly halted and turned round. From the expression of his face I knew something was up, but was scarcely prepared for the information he gave.

"Look here," said he; "you have hit that deer, Cap, tolerably badly, and I suspect we shall get him yet. His foreleg is disabled, and he can't travel far without our overhauling him."

On inquiring how he gained his information, he pointed to the tracks, and, sure enough, the off forefoot, instead of making a clean impression, cut the snow for nearly a foot whenever raised off the ground.

"You see," said he, chuckling, "he don't use both alike, for it's all he can do to get this one up."

There was no gainsaying such conclusive evidence, and with renewed ardor we sharpened the pace of pursuit, alternately changing places, one being constantly on the lookout while the other tracked. Once or twice we got sight of the deer, but too far off, or for too limited a period, to shoot, but the view was always cheering.

Forward we pressed, exultingly hoping that each minute would finish the hunt, but the deer thought otherwise, for he was of a most unaccommodating disposition.

Soon, it became apparent that the confounded brute was traveling the same circle, and that, unless we altered our plans, we might be kept going till dark. As we were not disposed to work harder than necessary, it was agreed that I should drop behind and take up my stand in the most eligible place, while Will continued the pursuit with the hope of driving our wily foe past my ambush.

Though the plan was well devised, it failed in execution; for after an hour's tedious delay, my companion rejoined me, disgusted and dispirited, heaping anathemas upon the foe, pronouncing him to be one of the foxiest brutes he had ever come across.

After all our trouble, it would never do thus to be defeated, so I proposed doing the tracking while he took a stand, at the same time changing guns at his request.

Full of hope, and animated with the desire of distinguishing myself, I pushed forward with renewed energy. At first the trail was tolerably clear, but after some time it led and twisted in every direction through innumerable hog-paths. Never was I so sorely puzzled to keep correct, but with perseverance and care, I managed to carry the track almost across to clear ground, where I suddenly lost all signs and was completely brought to a stand-still.

I was aware that all dodges were practiced, more particularly when deer feel the effects of increasing weakness and incapacity for further exertion; so, hoping that fortune would favor me, I determined, like a skillful fox-hunter, to make a cast round the disturbed ground.

After the loss of 20 minutes, I fortunately again struck the trail, which to my surprise, led in a reverse direction, clearly indicating that the deer had retraced his steps probably in the same track, and thus, by this cunning device, almost succeeded in eluding his pursuer.

The trail of the animal now became more irregular, and the telltale track of the wounded limb greatly assisted me in distinguishing his footsteps from those of his fellows, which on every opportunity he selected. Having failed to throw me off so far, the deer adopted a new ruse, which under other circumstances would have been eminently agreeable to the sportsman, but in this instance, made me so savage that I would have indulged in the amiable weakness of breaking the gun-stock over the nearest tree if it had not been that my friend might not see the joke of his rifle being thus treated.

So intent was I watching the tracks that I did not observe the exhausted deer had halted. Becoming alarmed by my near approach, and deeming it advisable to make a fresh effort to place distance between us, he again put forth renewed energy. The brush, unfortunately, was so remarkably dense, that although I got several glimpses of his tawny hide, still never for sufficient length of time to get a fair chance to shoot, and I was unwillingly compelled to keep tracking.

About 50 yards from where I stood, a small river, not over 90 feet across, named the Ambaras, wound its sluggish, peaceful way toward its parent stream, the Wabash, and direct for the nearest part of this river the deer had gone.

Still, I could not bring myself to believe that a buck at this season, with plenty of ice in the water, would hazard an aquatic performance. My doubts were soon solved, for on reaching the margin, with surprise I saw the deer upon the ledge of ice attached to the bank struggling violently to keep his footing. The disabled leg, which appeared to hang powerless, was evidently now causing serious inconvenience to his progress over the slippery surface.

Such an opportunity to finish my work was not to be neglected, so cocking the rifle, I pitched it forward and drew a bead, but still no report followed. All my power and exertion could not pull the trigger. Again and again I looked at the lock, and essayed another effort, but with the same result.

At length, in despair, I desisted, and the deer, having altered his mind, came ashore and disappeared through the tangled brake.

Of course, to examine the gun and inform myself what was wrong was my first thought. My surprise may be well imagined when, with all my endeavors, I could not get the hammer down; there it would stand, not a particle of compromise was in the confounded thing.

All my skill in mechanism was called into play, all my past experience put to use, and not until my patience was nearly exhausted did I discover the use of the second trigger. Discouraged I was, but whether most at my own stupidity or want of luck, I know not. Still hoping for another chance, I followed on in no very amiable frame of mind.

Time fled, and the long shadows of the trees told of the rapid approach of night. Still, not a sight did I further get of the buck, and to add to my troubles, the tracks a second time led through ground that hogs had lately fed over.

Never was I so sorely puzzled. Backward and forward I searched, my eyes nearly strained to bursting, till at length I was compelled to give up the chase.

On looking round to find out as nearly as possible my situation, the better and more directly to return to my horse, I espied a splendid wild turkey feeding not over 30 yards off and still unaware of my presence.

Sheltering myself behind a fallen log, I took sight along my barrel, determining inwardly to have some reward for my labor. Although this time I worked the trigger correctly, nothing but the explosion of the cap took place; in fact, the rifle had missed fire.

The turkey, frightened at the noise, lowered his head, ran off about 20 yards, then stopped and looked around, still ignorant of the cause of his alarm.

Substituting a new cap and again taking sight was but the work of a few moments, but still the gun refused to explode. I now sprung my ramrod and placed on the nipple another cap, but the result was as before. The turkey, having become conscious that he was in a dangerous neighborhood, sought safety in flight.

How often a day's shooting is one series of blunders from morning till night, and so it was in this case. First, the game had passed too far from my stand; secondly, changing guns had lost me the deer; and thirdly, the carelessness of my friend in not sheltering his gun from the damp was the reason of my not having turkey for a future day's dinner.

Tired, hungry and bad-tempered, I struck off direct for my horse, expecting to have little more than a mile to walk, but with surprise, after having traveled that distance, I found I was turned round and lost. Already it was sunset; half-an-hour more would make it dark, and the bottomland which I was now wandering through was as intricate, densely covered a swamp as ever was inhabited by wild-cat. The season of the year, moreover, was not exactly the one to select for making your couch on the surface of mother earth, and visions of a good dinner, comfortable fire and dry clothes floated before me.

Hark! what is that—a dog barking? And so it was. Forward I pushed to the sound, and in doing so, came across a road, which on inspection, I recognized as one we had traversed in the morning.

The rest of the programme for that day was plain sailing. I found my pony where he was left, my friend's horse being gone; so concluding Will had made tracks for home, I mounted my fiery little nag, and with a sufficiently tight rein to guard against accidents, rattled home almost at racing pace.

It was nearly two hours afterward that Will turned up, wet and exhausted—down upon his luck, and deer in particular—vowing that he would be up with the sun in the morning and not return till he could boast of not having been beaten by a broken-legged deer when there was enough snow to track.

My defeat had similarly operated on myself, so that we mutually agreed to devote the morrow, blow or snow, to reestablish our tarnished honor.

The morning was well-suited to our task, still and clear, with just sufficient frost in the atmosphere to give zest to traveling. The track was easily found, my backtrack being taken as the guide.

In ten minutes, we again had our game afoot, but without getting a shot, the animal having doubled round before lying down, and consequently, rising behind us. The bed where he had passed the night was soiled with blood, and other indications were such as to justify us in hoping early success.

Although perseverance is generally rewarded, it was not so on this occasion. Hour after hour slipped by, the game appeared to moderate its pace in accordance with ours—just keeping sufficiently ahead to be out of range.

The badness of the walking (for a thaw had commenced), the continued disappointment, and the difficulty of following through the bush commenced to operate upon our spirits. But then, we struck a more open range of country, where the traveling was better or doubtless we would have given up. However, being in the vicinity of our ponies, we determined to continue the pursuit on horseback, hoping to get a view while crossing some opening, where we could give the buck a run of a few minutes, with the expectation that a sharper gait might break him down; but luck continued adverse.

Time was rapidly gliding by, a few hours more would bring on night, and as far as we could see, the prospect of a termination was as distant as ever.

Want of success or fatigue made us careless, and as we slowly wended our unthankful way—first one in front, then the other, talking aloud, deploring our misfortune and paying but little attention to the surroundings, unsportsman-like on such an occasion—my pony (for I was in front) suddenly shied, turning almost completely round, and at the same time brought me excessively near getting a spill.

And what do you imagine was the cause of this want of propriety in so experienced a steed? Simply this: the deer had lain down, and we had almost ridden over him.

To wheel round and try to bring my gun to bear was the work of a few seconds, but all my exertions and rapidity of motion were thrown away. The pony would not stand still; he had evidently been frightened, or perhaps was still in ignorance of what caused the alarm. Moreover, my maneuvering so directly intervened between my friend and the game that, for fear of peppering me, he dared not fire.

To turn round and look at one another, first sulkily, but afterward to burst into a roar of laughter at the absurdity of the whole thing, was the result, each agreeing that the buck had well-earned his safety, and that two such awkward devils had no right to a feast of venison resulting from that hunt, and therefore we had better acknowledge that we were beaten handsomely, and that by a buck on three legs.

On the following occasion the results were different. One autumn, when traveling across the Grand Prairie about 150 miles north of where the last episode occurred, I was caught in the first snowstorm of the season. The vicinity was but sparsely settled, and from the thickness of the drift, our charioteer lost his way. After getting mired times without number, and enduring one of the most disagreeable nights out-of-doors it is possible to imagine, we reached the village of Kent.

Under ordinary circumstances, it would have presented no great inducements, but the large wood-fire that blazed in the bar-room of the diminutive tavern, after our protracted night of hardship, possessed such attractions that I determined to lay over for a couple of days.

The neighborhood was well-stocked with game, I learned the following evening, when I presented myself among the *habitues,* who commonly made this public house their place of rendezvous after the toils of the day.

No small portion of the conversation was in reference to a buck, who for years had constantly been seen, yet none of the heretofore successful hunters had been able to circumvent him. It was evident that this animal was of no ordinary size, as he was dubbed by all with the *sobriquet* of the "Big Buck." One regular old Leather-stocking, whose opinion was always listened to with the reverence due to an authority, ventured to assert that the bullet would never be moulded that would tumble him (the buck) in his tracks.

This extraordinary deer had almost escaped my memory. I was resting over my next morning's pipe and beginning to fear that my visit was longer than necessary, for there was absolutely nothing to do but eat and sleep, when a man from the timber land arrived with a load of wood and held the following conversation with the mixer of mint-juleps, cocktails, etc.

"Abe, have you e'er a shooting-iron that you can loan this coon?"

Abe having replied in the negative, and inquired the reason, was told that the big buck had crossed the road about a mile off and gone into the squire's corn. Quietly going to my bedroom, I unpacked my heaviest gun, a ten-bore, in which I have particular faith, and having noted the route that the teamster had come by, I followed the back track of his sled, and true enough found the prints of a very heavy buck.

The day was still young, myself in good walking trim, and with an internal determination not to be beaten, except night overtook me, and very probably with the hope to show the neighbors that a Britisher was good for some purposes, I followed the track with unusually willing steps and light heart.

To get into the cornfield the buck had jumped the snake-fence and afterward doubled back. As the wind did not suit for me to enter at the same place, I made a considerable *detour*.

In my right barrel, I had 16 buckshot, about the size that would run one hundred to the pound, and a bullet in the left. As the corn had not yet been gathered, and the undergrowth of cockle-burs and other weeds was tolerably dense, I had little doubt but that I should get sufficiently close to make use of the former.

An old stag like my quarry, I knew from experience, would be desperately sharp, so with the utmost caution I advanced upwind, eyes and ears strained to the utmost tension.

I had only got about a fourth of the field traversed when I heard some voices right to windward encouraging a dog to hold a pig. The noise of the men, dog and porker, I concluded, would start the game off in the reverse direction, so hurriedly retracing my steps, I regained the fence, got over it, and took my stand at an angle that stretched close to a slough, which was densely covered with various aquatic weeds and bushes.

About five minutes after gaining my position, I was greeted by a sight of the beauty, who hopped the fence where there was a broken rail, and gaining the opening, for a moment halted, then tossing up his head, he offered me a fair cross-shot nearly 80 yards distant. Pitching my gun well in front, I pulled the trigger, and well I knew not fruitlessly, for he gave a short protracted jump, dropped his white tail close into his hams, and with an increased pace disappeared into the swamp.

Unless the wound was mortal, or so severe as to have seriously injured him, I was certain he would not be satisfied to remain in such close proximity to danger, so after reloading, I made a *detour* to find where he had left this cover to seek one more retired. My conjecture was correct, for after traveling nearly half-a-mile, I found the familiar telltale track.

The snow was in pretty good order, both for tracking and walking, and I did not let the grass grow under my feet. As yet, I had seen no signs of blood, which the more thoroughly impressed me that my lead had made more than a skin-wound.

In about an hour's walking, I found myself on the edge of another slough, which I was hesitating whether to enter or go round, when I espied my friend, some way beyond range, going over a neighboring swell of the prairie.

Of course, I cut off the angle and cast forward to where in the distance, I could see my friend at a stand-still, anxiously staring in my direction. My cap was of a very light color, so I concluded he did not see me, and my supposition was again correct, for after a few minutes he relaxed his pace, and turning at right angles, walked into a small expanse of dense rushes, interspersed with an occasional stunted willow.

In deer-shooting, if you suppose an animal severely wounded, never hurry him; if he once lies down, and you give him time to stiffen, you will not have half the trouble in his ultimate capture that you would have by constantly keeping him on the move.

So I practiced in this instance; carefully for 10 or 15 minutes I watched that he did not leave the cover. Then, having concluded that he had lain down, I quietly lighted my pipe and dawdled away an hour more.

Deeming that I had granted sufficient law, I renewed operations and pushed forward. The track was very irregular in length of pace from where he had reduced his gait to a walk, and several times, from want of lifting his feet high enough, he had plowed the surface of the snow with his toes.

An old deer-stalker will know these symptoms; a young one may without harm remember them. Having cautiously followed the trail three parts of the way across the cover, and almost commenced to think I would have done better by waiting half-an-hour longer, the buck jumped up within 20 yards, heading straight from me, when I gave him the contents a second time of the right-hand barrel in the back of his head.

The distance was too great to remove him home that day, so cutting a branch off a willow, I affixed my handkerchief to it, and left his banner waving to denote possession, also to furnish a hint to the prairie-wolves that they had better steer clear.

That night at the tavern bar, in the most ostentatious manner in the presence of the assembled crowd, I ordered a team to be got ready in the morning to bring in the Big Buck. Old Leather-stocking, *sotto voce,* remarked that I had not been reared on the right soil to be able to come to that game.

However, next morning, when I arrived with my trophy, the crowd congratulated me, while Leather-stocking remarked that he knew not what the world was coming to, by G—d, when a Britisher, with a bird-gun, could kill the biggest buck in Illinois.

In conclusion, I would say that in skinning, we found that at the first shot one grain had gone through the lungs, while two more had lodged farther back. The gross weight of this deer was 184 pounds.

THE LAST DEER HUNT

By Meshach Browning

This material originally appeared in Browning's widely and rightly heralded memoir, Forty-Four Years of the Life of a Hunter *(1859). None of us know whether a given outing may be our last hunt, but in this instance, the experience marks a fine and fitting conclusion to a lengthy career as a mighty slayer of whitetails. Even after the passage of almost two centuries, Browning's words and experiences retain powerful appeal to those who, like him, belong in the ranks of "hard hunters." The book has been reprinted many times and this excerpt appeared in Robert Elman's (Editor),* Timber and Tide: Hunting Tales of the Northeast *(2000). This 1842 hunt came at a point of considerable stress in Browning's life and surely must have given him welcome if temporary relief from his burdens.*

After [my last wolf] hunt, I attended to my farm and mill, which kept my family in comfortable circumstances. During the summer, my fifth son, Meshach A. Browning, gave me an invitation to visit him, saying that there was in his neighborhood a deer-lick which was much used by a large buck.

I went to see him, according to promise; and when the proper time in the evening arrived, we started for the deer-lick. As we were proceeding thither, we encountered a huge rattlesnake, with which we soon settled accounts. After fulfilling the prediction made in the Scriptures that "the seed of the woman should bruise the serpent's head," we then went to the lick and took our seats on a high rock, where we remained until dark without seeing any deer. Withdrawing a short distance, we made a fire and slept until the birds began to sing their sweet notes among the trees.

Rousing up my son, we walked lightly to the high rock, took our seats and kept a close lookout for our buck. After the sun was shining and drying up the dew, I proposed that we should eat our breakfast and go home.

At the base of the rock ran a fine spring of water, on the border of which I suggested that we should take our meal.

My son, however, objected to us leaving our seats, saying that it was possible a deer would yet come, so we continued in our places and had nearly finished our breakfast when he saw two bucks coming toward us in a great hurry. They were sometimes galloping and sometimes trotting, which paces they held until they were nearly within rifle-shot.

My son rose to his feet too soon, and was preparing to shoot at too great a distance when I took him by the arm and begged him to hold his fire until the bucks came quite near as they could not smell us, for we were on the leeward side.

But I could not prevail on him to sit down until, seeing that he was trembling with the buck fever, I told him that he would miss, and we should lose a fine buck.

He said that if he missed he would pay me the price of a buck.

I replied that it was not the price I wanted, but the buck.

I then seized his gun and told him to sit down, for he was trembling so much that he would shake the acorns off a tree if he were sitting in one.

He sat down, laughing, and said that I might take my own way.

By this time the two bucks were within range and still approaching. My son insisted that I should then fire, but as I was determined to make sure work, I let them come on until they were within 30 steps, when they both stopped to examine whether any danger was near.

Bang went my gun, or rather my son's gun in my hands, and the big buck dropped on the spot. My son loaded the gun again, and ran after the smaller one, but it made its escape.

While the young man was gone after the little buck, I went to the large one and found that he was so badly wounded he could not rise to his feet. He became furious as I approached him, and although his horns were soft and covered with velvet, he seemed willing, if he could, to put them to any use by which they could do him service. But the poor fellow was deprived of all power to do anything in his own defence. Left to abide his fate, he occasioned me little pleasure, but rather aroused in me a feeling of pity for him.

Thus was the last deer killed; and in all probability, it was the last I ever shall kill, although I have since watched licks and tried many times to kill another. Yet it is not impossible that I may someday kill one, though it seems very unlikely.

On account of the scarcity of game, my hunting was becoming laborious and, as all other hunters were not governed by the kind and fair feelings which used to regulate their actions in bygone years, they began to take my traps, use them and keep the game caught in them, thus greatly interfering with my sport. So I concluded to leave hunting, and enjoy myself with my wife at home on my little property.

Although at times I felt a strong desire to be in the woods, yet finding myself unable to undergo the fatigue, I gave up the idea of being a hunter any longer, closed my business, and sold my farm, reserving 20 acres to myself and wife during our lives.

I built a comfortable house on my reservation, and lived therein peacefully and pleasantly until the 14th day of February, 1855, when my wife was attacked with a severe stroke of palsy, which left her a complete cripple. She survived the first stroke, but on the 8th day of September, 1857, she was again stricken, on the other side of her body, and died in 25 minutes.

Thus was I a second time left alone in gloom, and almost despair, to wander from place to place in search of comfort and find but little. That little, however, I hope will be the means of keeping my feet in the paths of rectitude that, when I am called to meet the common destiny of all flesh, I may be able to do so in the full hope of a glorious immortality.

My acquaintance with this lady originated about 18 years before her death; and whilst living with me, hers was a life of continuous peace and harmony. The following verse has been dedicated to her memory:

> *We lived together sixteen years*
> *In quiet, love and peace;*
> *And then misfortune dire decreed*
> *Our happiness should cease:*
> *Death came between us, to divide,*
> *And struck the fatal blow, which took from me one loved full well*
> *Since eighteen years ago.*

The last look that I gave, she lay
With hands crossed on her breast;
I kissed the lovely, placid face,
Which spoke her spirit's rest.
And now she dwells beyond the sun and I am left below,
To mourn for her I've loved so well since eighteen years ago.

BLUE-CHIP DEER BOOKS
THE NINETEENTH CENTURY

By Robert Wegner

This selection is Chapter 14 of the second volume of Wegner's trilogy, Deer & Deer Hunting *(1987). It covers several of the authors represented on these pages as well as providing a detailed overview of early writings on deer hunting. Wegner has delved into the history and literature of the sport to a degree matched by no other student of the whitetail, and here he shares valuable insights on the evolution of writing on the sport.*

When not scouting or hunting for deer, the deer hunting aficionado searches for books that reflect his interests and dedication to the sport. For the past 20 years, I have combed the antique and second-hand book stores of this country and scoured out-of-print sporting book catalogs in search of blue-chip deer books. Indeed, ever since the age of 16, I have been an avid deer book fan, constantly checking the local stores for the newest releases. Invariably, I devour these books in one or two sessions, tucking away in my memory small snippets of information on deer and deer hunting and the literature of the sport.

Like most novice book collectors, my first volumes were primarily of a how-to nature written by dilettante outdoor writers and self-proclaimed experts. But in time and after a serious drain on the exchequer, I gradually acquired top-shelf deer books written by the nation's leading biologists and serious books on deer hunting of a where-to and wherefore nature written by first-rate authors.

Today, my library contains a collection of more than 600 volumes dealing exclusively with deer and deer hunting, with the earliest volume being William Scrope's *The Art of Deer-Stalking* (1838), and the latest vintage volume being the Wildlife Management Institute's *Whitetailed Deer: Ecology and Management* (1984).

For an annotated list of these deer books and how to obtain them, since most of them and especially the great ones are out of print, see the appendix entitled "The Deer Hunter's 400," in the author's *Deer & Deer Hunting*, Book 1 (Stackpole Books, 1984).

Many of these books were written by deer hunting guides, amateur naturalists, professional journalists, scientists, famous authors, explorers, as well as self-proclaimed experts, outdoor writers of various persuasions and backwoods pioneers without any formal training. But all of these men shared a common love for hunting white-tailed deer.

Whether we read the polished prose of T. S. Van Dyke's *The Still Hunter* (1882) or the brilliant, briar-patch philosophizing of William Long's *Following the Deer* (1901), these vintage volumes from the past provide us with an entertaining and engaging record of the American deer hunting experience.

While I was writing *Deer & Deer Hunting*, Book 1, my study of the literature of the American deer hunting experience became particularly extensive. During the preparation of that book, it became impossible to avoid comparing the different eras in which these books appeared. I reached the conclusion that the second half of the 19th century produced this country's greatest literature on deer hunting as well as the first scientific treatise on deer: John Caton's *The Antelope and Deer of America* (1877). In this chapter, I briefly examine the great deer books of the last half of the 19th century.

The first great, vintage volume appeared in 1841. In this novel, entitled *The Deerslayer*, James Fenimore Cooper (1789-1851) depicted the early American deer hunter in intimate harmony with nature. His moral character and worth, Cooper argued, depended upon his degree of reverence and respect for deer, his direct relationship to nature, and the manner in which the hunter perceived his natural environment.

Natty Bumppo, the hero of this romantic tale, killed deer only out of necessity, and then lovingly, and not for plunder.

"They call me Deerslayer. I'll own, and perhaps I deserve the name, in the way of understanding the creature's habits, as well as for the certainty in the aim; but they can't accuse me of killing an animal when there is no occasion for the meat or the skin. I may be a slayer, it's true, but I'm no slaughterer . . . I never yet pulled a trigger on buck or doe, unless when food or clothes was wanting."

The Deerslayer's chief virtue resided in the fact that he did *not* view the presence of a live deer as an insult to his powers. He hunted deer both for food and for the spiritual satisfaction of participating in the ennobling rite of the kill.

The Deerslayer's deep connection with the teachings of nature and his mastery of the intricate details of the deer forest create a rich and intensely exciting story—filled with romance and theatricality. A story to be cherished by all deer hunters, in it Cooper invested the deer kill with an ennobling purpose. But by the time of his death in 1851, Cooper's conception of the deer hunter's life as an untrammeled existence of necessary hunting was quickly evaporating—giving way to the arrival of a new social and industrial order.

Before that new social and industrial order took command, another romantic tale appeared: Frank Forester's *The Deer Stalkers* (1843). In this sketch of deer hunting in New York, Henry William Herbert (1807-1858), writing under the pen name of "Frank Forester," constructed a brilliant portrait of the chase based on the ethical proposition, as he so aptly proclaimed, "that there is not only much practical, but much moral utility in the Gentle Science of Woodcraft."

In all of his writings, Forester preached the need for adapting English sporting ethics to the American scene, taking a bitter and unrelenting stand against all poachers and pot-hunters. In the sporting journals of his time, he politicked for game laws and a sporting ethic.

Herbert's annual deer-hunting trips to the woodlands of Orange County and the lakes of the Adirondacks, especially an area known as "Old John Brown's Tract," provide the background for this classic tale unequaled in the annals of deer hunting literature. The following poem sets the stage for Forester's portrait of the early American deer hunt:

> *Mark! How they file adown the rocky pass,—*
> *Bright creatures, fleet, and beautiful, and free,—*
> *With winged bounds that spurn the unshaken grass,*

*And Swan-like necks sublime,—their eloquent eyes
Instinct with liberty,—their antlered crests,
In clear relief against the glowing sky,
Haught and majestic!*

Like most deer-hunting stories, Forester's tale begins with the first flush of autumn as Frank's boys cross the woodland hills in a horse-drawn carriage en route to the Dutchman's Tavern. Through the fast-fading twilight they rattle along—singing, laughing and jesting all the way, making the forest ring with sonorous music. Just as the young moon climbs into the sky, they arrive at the old stone Tavern nestled so closely into the wooded terrain that its existence remains largely unsuspected.

Dutch Jake, the owner, opens the door as Frank's boys enter the bar, a large room dimly lit by homemade tallow candles and blazing and snapping hickory logs in the large, open fireplace.

Forester describes the shelves of this holy sanctum for us: "They were garnished with sundry kegs of liquor, painted bright green, and labelled with the names of the contents in black characters on gilded scrolls. These, with two or three dull-looking decanters of snakeroot whiskey and other kinds of 'bitters'; a dozen heavy-bottomed tumblers, resembling in shape the half of an hour-glass, set up on the small end; and a considerable array of tobacco-pipes, constituted all the furniture of Jake's bar, and promised but little for the drinkableness of the Dutchman's drinkables."

Despite the questionable nature of Jake's snakeroot whiskey for the more refined tastes of Frank's sporting companions, they nonetheless made their way to the bar with the vociferous Fat Tom, a fictional character based on the mammoth and eccentric Tom Ward of the village tavern, a well-known man to the sportsmen of New York in those days, hollering, "Jake, you darned old cuss, look alive, can't you? and make a gallon of hot Dutch rum!"

With a burst of laughter, the deerstalkers begin to steep their souls in old Dutch Jake's strange compound of Santa Cruz rum, screeching hot water, allspice, brown sugar and peppercorns.

After several doses of this antique concoction, one of the boys howls: "I knowed it, jest as I 'spected, adzactly. Them's prime sperrits!"

Following a brace of larded grouse and brazed ham, brought forth with odoriferous steam and numerous quart pewter mugs of champagne imported to the Dutchman's Tavern from New York for the occasion, Frank's boys indulge in yarn-spinning until late into the evening. Shortly after midnight, they remove their tomahawks from their sashes, hang up their stout buckskin leggins and retire for the evening to dream of shining, antlered bucks silhouetted against the eastern sky.

When the kitchen clock strikes four, the deerstalkers are afoot. After a hearty breakfast of ham and eggs, "not least, two mighty tankards smoking with a judicious mixture of Guinness's double stout, brown sugar, spice and toast—for to no womanish delicacies of tea and coffee did the stout huntsmen seriously incline," Frank's boys shoulder their rifles and strike forth while the stars still shine in the sky.

The first flash of dawn in the eastern horizon finds several of Frank's boys—Harry Archer and Dolph Pierson in the company of Smoker, their noble, Scottish, wirehaired deer-greyhound—hunting deer from a canoe while floating down the numerous streams of the Adirondack country. After miles of floating in an unbroken silence, they suddenly encountered two bucks. Forester recalls the scene for us:

"Under the shade of a birch stood two beautiful and graceful deer, one sipping the clear water, and the other gazing down the brook in the direction opposite to that from which the hunters were coming upon them. No breath of air was stirring in those deep, sylvan haunts, so that no taint, telling of man's appalling presence, was borne to the timid nostrils of the wild animals, which were already cut off from the nearer shore before they perceived the approach of their mortal foes.

"The quick eye of Archer caught them upon the instant, and almost simultaneously the hunter had checked the way of the canoe and laid aside his paddle.

"Pierson was already stretching out his hand to grasp the ready rifle, when Archer's piece rose to his shoulder with a steady slow motion; the trigger was drawn, and ere the close report had time to reach its ears, the nearer of the two bucks had fallen, with its heart cleft asunder by the unerring bullet, into the glassy ripple out of which it had been drinking, tinging the calm pool far and wide with its life-blood.

"Quick as light, as the red flash gleamed over the umbrageous spot, long before it had caught the rifle's crack, the second, with a mighty bound, had cleared the intervening channel and lighted upon the gray granite rock. Not one second's space did it pause there, however, but gathering its agile limbs again, sprang shoreward.

"A second more it had been safe in the coppice. But in that very second, the nimble finger of the sportsman had cocked the second barrel; and while the gallant beast was suspended in mid-air, the second ball was sped on its errand.

"A dull, dead splash, heard by the hunters before the crack, announced that the ball had taken sure effect, and arrested in its leap, the noble quarry fell.

"For one moment's space it struggled in the narrow rapid, then, by a mighty effort rising again, it dashed forward, feebly fleet, keeping to the middle of the channel.

"Meanwhile the boat, unguided by the paddle and swept in by the driving current, had touched upon the gravel shoal and was motionless.

"Feeling this as it were instinctively, Harry unsheathed his long knife, and with a wild shrill cheer to Smoker, sprang first ashore, and then plunged recklessly into the knee-deep current; but ere he had made three strides, the fleet dog passed him, with his white tushes glancing from his black lips, and his eyes glaring like coals of fire as he sped mute and rapid as the wind after the wounded game.

"The vista of the wood through which the brook ran straight was not at the most above fifty paces in length, and of these the wounded buck had gained at least ten clear start.

"Ere it had gone twenty more, however, the fleet dog had it by the throat. There was a stern, short strife, and both went down together into the flashing waters. Then, ere the buck could relieve itself, or harm the noble dog, the keen knife of Archer was in its throat—one stab, and all was over."

No, you will not, unfortunately, find a copy of Frank Forester's *The Deer Stalkers* in Waldenbooks. No outdoor publisher has reissued it; you will have to locate it in a used bookstore or in an out-of-print sporting book catalog.

Since its publication, the book went through various editions, the last published by Derrydale Press in 1930. The 1985 issue of Angler's & Shooter's Bookshelf catalog lists a faded copy of the book for $50; I purchased my fine copy for $60 several years ago from Larry Barnes of Gunnerman Books. Good luck in your hunt for this jewel! It is worth every dollar spent for this short sketch of early American deer hunting.

Although this stirring sketch—written in eloquent prose with a spirited and graphic tone—provides us with a colorful portrait of the chase, in reading his great essay entitled "Deer Hunting" published in 1849, we learn that Frank Forester took a dim view of the general quality of the deer hunt during this time.

"Deer hunting proper and scientific, I may say there is none."

Too many hunters, in his opinion, were waging promiscuous havoc on the deer herd—not respecting the seasons, age or sex of the animals.

Of the two most popular modes of deer hunting during the 1840s, driving and still-hunting, Forester favored the latter.

"It is by far," he writes, "the most legitimate and exciting, as it demands both skill in woodcraft, and endurance on the part of the hunter; whereas driving requires only the patience of Job, added to enough skill with the gun to knock over a great beast as big as a Jackass and as timid as a sheep, with a heavy charge of buckshot."

Forester delivered a tremendous charge of buckshot against the idea of fire-hunting as a mode of deer hunting. His critique of this form of deer poaching resounded throughout the forest like the sudden crack of a rifle on a quiet, crisp November day:

"There is nothing of fair play about it. It is a dirty advantage taken of the stupidity of the animals; and apart from its manifest danger, ought to be discountenanced. It is utterly unsportsmanlike and butcherly. The great drawback to this species of sport, apart from the not slight odor of pot-hunting which attaches to it, is that other animals than deer often approach the treacherous blaze; and instances are not uncommon of hunters shooting their own horses and cattle—nay, every now and then, their own companions, sisters and sweethearts."

Forester's conception of a deer-hunting group never exceeded four hunters, for Frank took a mighty dim view of large parties often numbering 20 or 30 guns, presenting a situation in which as he exclaims, "the odds are, perhaps, a hundred to one against so much as even hearing the distant bay of a hound."

Whether or not we agree with these odds, I am sure that many of us can relate to his final assessment of the sport of deer hunting:

"Here there is no work for the feather-bred city hunter, the curled darling of soft dames. Here the true foot, the stout arm, the keen eye, and the instinctive prescience of the forester and mountaineer, are needed; here it will be seen who is, and who is not, the woodsman by the surest test of all—the only sure test—of true sportsmanship and lore in venerie, who can best set a-foot the wild deer of the hills, who bring him to bay or to soil most speedily, who ring aloud his death halloo, and bear the spoils in triumph to his shanty to feast on the rich loin, while weakly and unskillful rivals slink supperless to bed."

While Frank Forester and his boys tramped the picturesque passes of the Adirondack highlands in pursuit of deer, Philip Tome (1782-1855), probably the greatest Pennsylvania deer hunter of his time, wrote his memoirs of early 19th century hunting in the hills and river valleys of the Keystone state. His book of hair-raising adventures contains everything from fire-hunting deer to capturing grown elk alive on the swirling waters of the Susquehanna River. All lovers of the hunt will enjoy reading about his exciting episodes in the hills of Warren County, Pennsylvania.

Tome's thrilling adventures can only be matched by those of one of his contemporaries, Meshach Browning (1781-1859), a very successful deerslayer who hunted the Allegheny Mountain section of western Maryland. Reportedly, Meschach Browning killed somewhere between 1,800 and 2,000 deer during the first four decades of the 19th century.

One January evening, while staring at my bookshelves as the dying embers of my woodburning Morso shot their shadowy ghosts upon the antique book bindings, my eyes gradually focused on Browning's soiled, tattered, gold-colored volume entitled *Forty-Four Years of the Life of a Hunter* (1859). I had retrieved this quaint and curious volume from Paul's Used Bookstore on State Street in Madison, Wisconsin, during the Christmas holidays; shelved and forgotten about until that wintery night in January, its rare and entertaining deer hunting lore had escaped my attention.

Born in Frederick County in March of 1781, this pioneer Marylander carved a living for himself and his family of 12 out of the wilderness much like Philip Tome had done in the hills of Pennsylvania. Whitetails provided him not only with meat and hides but with a source of income as well. At that time, venison sold for 12½ cents a pound. What he could not use for his family, he sold. The money raised eventually enabled him to buy a small farm. Like Philip Tome, deer hunting represented not only Browning's favorite pastime, but his basic of livelihood as well.

He understood the whitetail's habitat; he knew their mating seasons, gestation periods and browse preferences. He used candles in bark reflectors to spotlight them at night while floating down streams in his canoe.

On the subject of deer hunting, he wrote: "If a man undertakes a dangerous enterprise with a determination to succeed or lose his life, he will do many things with ease and unharmed which a smaller degree of energy would never accomplish."

Even though his livelihood depended upon venison, Browning claimed to live by a certain ethical code toward wildlife, suggesting, in much the same way as did Cooper and Forester before him, that the chase was more important than the kill. Ultimately, he insisted that self-reliance was vital to anyone who would hunt deer. Since the rifles of his day were so inaccurate and the powder so poor that even at 30 yards they lacked killing power, Browning frequently confronted his quarry with knife in hand. While reading his autobiography, I encountered with great delight one hair-raising incident of deer hunting lore that I shall never forget: Browning's fight with a wounded buck in the Yough River.

After he badly wounded a ten-pointer with a heavy charge of buckshot, his half-breed greyhound took to the heels of the animal and drove him into the river where the dog and the buck engaged themselves in a desperate battle. Due to the river's deepness, neither hound nor deer could get a foothold. In his chilling memoirs, Browning tells us what happened:

"I concluded to leave my gun on shore, wade in, and kill him with my knife. I set my gun against a tree and waded in—the water in some places being up to my belt, and in other places about half-thigh deep. On I went until I came within reach of the buck, which I seized by one of his horns; but as soon as I took hold, the dog let go, and struck out for the shore, when the buck made a main lunge at me. I then caught him by the other horn, though he very nearly threw me backwards into the river, but I held on to him, as I was afraid of our both being carried into the deep hole by the swift current. I dared not let him go, for if I did, I knew he would dart at me with his horns. I must kill him, or he would in all probability kill me, but whenever I let go with one hand, for the purpose of using my knife, he was ready to pitch at me. I called and called the dog, but he sat on the shore looking on, without attempting to move.

"After awhile, it occurred to me to throw him under the water and drown him; whereupon I braced my right leg against his left side, and with my arms jerked him suddenly, when down he came with his feet toward me. Then it was that my whole front paid for it as his feet flew like drum-sticks, scraping my body and barking my shins, till ambition had to give way to necessity, and I was not only compelled to let him up, but even glad to help him to his feet again, though I still held on to his rough horns. From the long scuffle, my hands beginning to smart, and my arms to become weak, I took another plan.

"I threw him again, and as he fell, I twisted him around by his horns, so as to place his back toward me and his feet from me. Then came a desperate trial, for as this was the only hope I had of overcoming him, I laid all my strength and weight on him, to keep him from getting upon his feet again. This I found I could do, for the water was so deep that he had no chance of helping himself, for want of a foothold. There we had it round and round, and in the struggle my left foot was accidently placed on his lowermost horn, which was deep down in the water.

"As soon as I felt my foot touch his horn, I threw my whole weight on it, and put his head under the water, deeper than I could reach with my arm. I thought that was the very thing I wanted, but then came the hardest part of the fight, for the buck exerted all his strength and activity against me, while I was in a situation from which I dare not attempt to retreat.

"I was determined to keep his head under, although sometimes even my head and face were beneath the water. If I had not been supported by his horns, which kept me from sinking down and enabled me to stand firmer than if I had no support, that stream might have been called, with great truth, 'the troubled water'; for I know that if it was not troubled, I was, for often I wished myself out of it. I know that the buck would have had no objection to my being out, though he probably thought that, as I had come in to help that savage dog, he would give me a punch or two with his sharp points to remember him by. Indeed, that was what I most dreaded; and it was my full purpose to keep clear of them, if possible.

"In about two minutes, after I got my foot on his horn, and sank his head under water, things began to look a little more favorable, for I felt his strength failing, which gave me hopes of getting through the worst fight I had ever been engaged in during all my hunting expeditions.

"When his strength was but little, I held fast to his upper horn with my left hand, and keeping my foot firmly on his lower horn, I pressed it to the bottom of three feet of water and, taking out my knife, when his kicking was nearly over, I let his head come up high enough to be within reach, when at a single cut I laid open the one side of his neck, severing both blood vessels. This relieved me from one of the most difficult positions in which, during all my life, I had been placed for the same length of time."

I cannot imagine a better volume to read on a wintry night, especially if one is a connoisseur of great deer hunting tales and continually scouting for deer hunting anecdotes and lore. Browning's backwoods style and strange, peculiar phraseology hold great appeal. Unfortunately, Browning's book has been out of print for the past 40 years; it remains scarce, even though it went through ten editions between 1859 and 1942.

When found, a first edition of this book (1859) in fine condition will probably cost $65. For the addict of deer books, it serves as a rich compendium of American deer hunting lore of the first half of the 19th century. If you are interested in the heroic, picturesque adventures of fighting with wounded bucks and catching deer barehanded in the snow, you will want to read this exciting volume.

While Meshach Browning prowled the forests of Maryland, Judge John Dean Caton (1812-1895), that ardent deer hunter and prominent judge from Illinois, studied the natural history of whitetails under penned conditions in Ottawa, Illinois, with pen in hand. In 1877, he published America's first great treatise on deer: *The Antelope and Deer of America*. Although an amateur naturalist, his book is still regarded by scientists as a standard reference volume on the subject. Published by Hurd and Houghton, *The Antelope and Deer of America* quickly went out of print after going through a second edition.

This thorough and extraordinarily fine volume includes a very impressive chapter on the chase, in which the author discusses the true virtues of deer hunting and reminds us that "to the cultivated mind capable of understanding and appreciating the works of the Divine hand, the pleasures of the pursuit are immeasurably enhanced by a capacity to understand the object taken."

You will indeed understand "the object taken" if you read this remarkable volume of personal observations on all facets of deer anatomy and behavior.

Following in the tradition of James Fenimore Cooper, Caton placed deer hunting in the context of natural history, formulated a classic hunting ethic, and even argued that biologists have much to learn from deer hunters.

"The pleasure of the sportsman in the chase," Caton insisted, "is measured by the intelligence of the game and its capacity to elude pursuit, and in the labor and even the danger involved in the capture. No matter how abundant the game, none but a brute would ever kill it for the mere pleasure of killing. The feeling of utility must be associated with its capture. If it cannot be utilized, a pang of regret must take the place of gratification."

The glorious chapter entitled "The Chase" is worth the price of the book itself, regardless of whether you buy the first edition (1877), the second edition (1882) or the inexpensive 1974 reprint.

In that chapter we find this eloquent description of the deer kill:

"The trusty rifle is quickly brought to the cheek, and the next instant, with a lofty bound, the magnificent but graceful form of the stately stag bursts forth from the border of the covert, his face in a horizontal line, his antlers thrown back upon his shoulders, so that every branch and vine must easily glance from the backward-pointing tines, his scut erect, and his bright eyes glistening in the excitement of the moment, when instantly and while he is yet in mid-air, a sharp report is heard, when, to use a hunter's expression, 'he lets go all holds,' his hind feet, propelled by the great momentum, are thrown high in the air as if his very hoofs would be snapped off, and he falls *all in a heap* or turns a complete somersault, and then rolls upon the ground pierced through the heart, or with both fore shoulders smashed; or if the deer was descending in his leap, perhaps the shot was higher than was intended, and a stitch is dropped in the spinal column. In either case, the monarch of the forest is laid low, never to rise again. It is a glorious moment, and unsurpassed by human experience."

While the honorable Judge Caton studied, observed and stalked whitetails on the wild prairies of Illinois, T. S. Van Dyke (1842-1923), that prince of the sporting writers, still-hunted them in the primeval forests of northwestern Wisconsin. If Caton's book is the first great scientific treatise on deer, Van Dyke's *The Still-Hunter* (1882) is without doubt the first and greatest treatise on the *art* of still-hunting—the likes of which we have never seen since.

If you have not read *The Still-Hunter,* you have thus far missed the greatest, most intense happiness that could conceivably be crammed into a couple of hours in front of your fireplace. The hunter who reads this book will vividly relive his own days afield. The book's spirited and lifelike descriptions will make every hunter who has ever found enjoyment in still-hunting whitetails tingle with the delight of pleasant recollections. An unsurpassed classic! Fine copies of the later editions sell for approximately $35 to $50.

In 1899, the 19th century ended for the American deer hunter with a dramatic blast, when friends of Oliver Hazard Perry (1817-1864) posthumously published his extraordinary deer-hunting journals in *Hunting Expeditions of Oliver Hazard Perry* (1899). Unfortunately for us, they only published 100 copies, making the book extremely rare and expensive. Nonetheless, this greatly-sought-after book provides the reader with the finest account we have of the daily adventures of a mid-19th century deerslayer in the forests of northern Michigan.

Perry's journal is replete with vivid descriptions of chasing the "Old Hemlock Rangers" through Michigan's boundless and trackless forests. After reading this account, I can still hear Perry's primitive rifle belching out its thunderous notes as he tramped through cedar swamp after cedar swamp—eventually arriving at the Buck Horn Tavern, a solitary log cabin, to dine on venison, potatoes and snakeroot whiskey.

His tales of how the deer "unfurled their white flags to the breeze" have to be read to be believed. His backwoods jargon carries the reader along with great intensity. He didn't shoot deer; he "put their lights out!" After a stiff drink of "Old Bald Eye" at the Buck Horn, he spent the evening playing Euchre with the boys. First-rate whiskey, pie and cheese capped the night. Before the night ended, Perry's boys talked about "flocks of deer."

In 1899, Ernest Thompson Seton (1860-1946), that brilliant naturalist who waxed so eloquently on deer hunting, put the final touches to the blue-chip deer books of the 19th century by adding *The Trail of the Sandhill Stag* (1899), one of the most thought-provoking, sensitive, moving tales ever written on the long, endless pursuit of a black-tailed stag. In this story, Seton challenges and examines the basic philosophy of the chase.

Unlike most tales of early American deer hunting, when Yan, the main protagonist of his tale, finally encounters the Sandhill Stag in his rifle sights after several years of intensive study and elusive chase, he refrains from shooting. As he stands in front of the magnificent monarch of the woods with his nerves and senses at their tightest tone, he says to himself, "shoot, shoot, shoot now! This is what you have toiled for!" But shoot he does not. Instead, he says to himself while staring into the soul of the stag:

"We have long stood as foes, hunter and hunted, but now that is changed and we stand face to face, fellow creatures looking into each other's eyes, not knowing each other's speech—but knowing motives and feelings. Now I understand you as I never did before; surely you at least in part understand me. For your life is at last in my power, yet you have no fear. I knew a deer once, that, run down by the hounds, sought safety with the hunter, and he saved it—and you also I have run down and you boldly seek safety with me. Yes! you are as wise as you are beautiful, for I will never harm a hair of you. We are brothers, oh, bounding Blacktail! only I am the elder and stronger, and if only my strength could always be at hand to save you, you would never come to harm. Go now, without fear, to range the piney hills; never more shall I follow your trail with the wild wolf rampant in my heart. Less and less as I grow do I see in your race mere flying marks, or butcher-meat."

Although the original edition of this book is out of print—only 250 copies were published—it went through numerous editions, and copies of these later editions can be found in used bookstores and at a reasonable price. This little volume of less than 100 pages will arouse the spirit of any deer hunter. It is a fascinating record of long searches that usually end in an unsuccessful manner; it captures the spell of the woods and the joy of the hunter. A story to read and reread!

In the fall of 1899, the *New York Times* instantly recognized it as a classic. "It is in every way thoroughly pleasing, both through the beauty of the story—one which once read, we think, can never be forgotten—and in its illustrations and general makeup, all the details of which are worthy of the charm of Mr. Seton's style."

Several weeks of hunting experiences out of 52 do not thoroughly or reasonably satisfy the deer enthusiast. Consequently, we turn to good books to stretch out the season. If you're like me, you probably enjoy reading blue-chip deer books in front of the fireplace.

The books discussed in this chapter represent some of the all-time greats. In reading them, you will quickly discover that we have not learned a great deal about hunting the white-tailed deer that our forefathers did not already know. These books not only enhance the image of the American deer hunter, but the experiences found within their pages frequently parallel our own in many ways; although their deer-hunting exploits often make our modern hunting trips look like genteel tea parties. These classics not only add a universal flavor to the deer hunting tradition, but they warm our memory and provide pleasant evenings next to the fireplace.

PART TWO

GREAT WRITERS ON WHITETAIL NATURAL HISTORY

Despite the laudable efforts of groups such as the Quality Deer Management Association and Whitetails Unlimited, the undeniable fact remains that deer hunters, as a whole, devote too little attention to the nature of their quarry. They are primarily interested in the tactics and techniques designed to find them gripping the antlers of a true old "mossy horns," but to a lesser degree the factors that produce trophy bucks and sound herd balance. Similarly, for most sportsmen, tales of grand hunts, elusive bucks, the simple joys of deer camp, the camaraderie of an evening campfire and the thrill of the chase have much more reading appeal than studies of the habits and habitat of whitetails.

Yet the astute hunter, one who aspires to being well-rounded and deeply versed in the sport, readily recognizes the importance of understanding the natural history of his quarry.

Here, three giants of outdoor literature share their insights on this part of the deer-hunting equation.

A much-respected wildlife specialist, John Madson was a true rarity—a scientist who could communicate the natural world with verve and vivacity.

Theodore Roosevelt was a man for all seasons who brought his immense intellectual capacity to bear in a fashion that merits his being recognized as one of the most talented amateur natural historians of all time, and his literary grace was such he readily communicated his knowledge and enthusiasm to others.

Jack O'Connor, for his part, was a shrewd observer who understood, perhaps to a greater degree than any outdoor writer of his era, how to take a reader along with him in the field. Part of the delightful lessons he imparted in print included appreciation of the game animal in its natural setting.

These three selections may not convey quite the same excitement as a hunt involving a "deer of a lifetime" or some moment endowed with an aura of magic, but they are informative and wonderfully well expressed. They also serve as a needed reminder to us all that the hunting is but one part of a much larger picture, for with understanding of the animal in its world comes a deeper, more meaningful definition of fancying one's self a true nimrod.

THE SECRET LIFE OF THE COTTONTAIL DEER

By John Madson

First published in the October, 1977 issue of Outdoor Life, *this piece subsequently was included in* Out Home, *a collection of Madson stories and essays published in 1979. The final paragraph of the piece offers about as fine a summation of what the whitetail means to the thoughtful sportsman as has ever appeared in print.*

If there's anything dull about a whitetail deer, I don't know it. I like everything about him. His biology is fascinating. So is his management, his history, and the old legends and grandpa yarns. I like to talk about whitetails with hunters, and with such seasoned deer men as Jack Calhoun of Illinois and Bill Severinghaus of New York. I admire a deer rifle that shoots true and handles easy. I've got a hunch that good tracking snow and prime roast venison may just help a man live forever. And as the years go by, I become more and more absorbed with the essence of the whitetail—the cunning thing inside that makes him what he is.

The whitetail is the only big-game animal that has succeeded in our woodlots and field edges, and he's made it because he's sharp. His senses of smell and hearing are acute beyond belief, and his vision is probably as keen as ours, even though it's in black and white.

His success, however, doesn't just depend on the sensory information that he soaks up but on the ways that he plugs it in. Those keen senses detect the slightest changes in the deer's home range. And how he knows that home range! He knows every little break in terrain, the open ground and its edges, each windfall, thicket, rootwad, spring seep, berry tangle, cutbank and mire. No human hunter can possibly know the deer range as well.

Knowing that range, and sensing an alien presence there, the whitetail reacts in many ways. He may lie doggo, watchful and waiting, or sneak catlike around an intruder. He may explode into action, white banner astern, making spectacular leaps over obstacles and racing headlong through heavy timber—only to stop somewhere just beyond and fade into a thicket off to one side to resume lurking and spying. He has a particular genius for melting into cover that couldn't possibly conceal a deer.

A few years back, my old friend Keith Kirkpatrick was on a whitetail hunt with several friends. They were driving some farm timber known to have deer, but they hadn't seen any. One of the group, a young man who had never hunted deer, asked the farmer where the deer were. The farmer didn't know, but he figured that somebody ought to hunt a brushy draw that ran from the timber out into the fields.

The hunter worked through this cover, coming out into an open field where there was a little pond. It didn't look like much. But as he stood there wondering what to do, he heard quail chirping in the fringe of foxtail and sloughgrass. He shucked the deer slugs from his shotgun, slipped in some bird loads and stepped into the grass. The covey roared up. And at the same instant, a big buck broke cover a few yards away, tore across the fields and vanished, leaving our hero with a gun full of bird loads and egg on his face.

It was a standard whitetail trick. We should be used to it by now, especially out in the Midwest where good deer populations thrive in woodlots, thin fringes of creek brush, and all manner of little cover scraps. Still, it's always a surprise to find deer there. Even more surprising are the people who share their land with these superb animals and never know it.

There was a certain place in central Iowa where I usually could count on a pheasant or two late in the season—a little dimple in the rolling farmland that couldn't be seen by road hunters. It was in the exact center of the mile-square land section, half-a-mile from any road, the remnant of an old farm dump that was set about with sumac and undergrown with giant foxtail.

I hunted up to it one day in late December, working into the wind on an inch of snow. By the time I was within gun range of the little covert, I could sense that empty, birdless quality that a long-time pheasant hunter learns. But I played out the hand anyway. I stood in the fence corner for a couple of minutes, looking things over, knowing that this might do as much to flush a hiding rooster as any cover-kicking. Nothing. I jacked open the Model 12 and swung up on the fence.

He came to his feet in one fluid, powerful movement and was instantly on his way with that buoyant grace that even very large whitetails have. He had been lying beside a roll of rusty fencewire, his antlers melting into the sumac around him. He couldn't have been 50 feet from me. If he'd been a pheasant's head, I might have seen him. I was hunting pheasants. I hadn't expected anything like him.

I knew him for what he was. I was a professional wildlifer by that time. In fact, I had just finished working at the Lansing check station for five days, and we had weighed and aged many deer, including a dozen bucks that would take any hunter's breath away. But nothing like this one.

His broad back looked as if it might hold water in a heavy rain, the gray neck seeming as thick as a Holstein bull's. He wore a typical rack, though I haven't the slightest idea of how many points there were. It was the sheer weight of antler that stays in my mind. Between burr and brow tine, each main beam was as thick as my wrist, arching out and forward in great curves, with broad webbing where the tines arose. Ten days before we had weighed a buck that would have gone 250 pounds, and this one was bigger.

He rose weightless out of his bed and ran off down the fenceline, making no sound that I can remember. It was easily the largest whitetail I had ever seen. He left me there on the fence, heart pounding, breath coming short and legs trembling.

I asked two farmers living on that square mile if they'd seen any deer around, especially anything big. Yeah, they'd seen a few deer earlier but the hunters must have killed them all. I told the local game warden, a good friend. He was keenly interested, but hadn't seen such a buck nor heard of anyone who had. Same with several good local hunters.

That deer was probably never taken by a hunter. There'd have been no keeping it out of the record books. Nor was he killed on a road during the antlerless season. We'd have known that, too, for no car could have survived it.

The point is this: an incredible stag was living in an intensely farmed and hunted region and had not been detected. For all I knew, I was the only person who ever saw him up close.

The secret of the whitetail's success is simply his success at keeping secret. Given an option, he'll always play it sly.

I once started a buck near the head of a timbered valley. Flag up, he ran out of sight around a bend of the creek. I tracked him in the new snow. As soon as he was out of sight, he began walking slowly uphill, stopping now and then to look down his backtrail. At the top of the hill was a three-wire fence that the deer had crawled under. The bottom wire was just 17 inches from the ground. I measured it. To appreciate this, try crawling under a low fence with a small rocking chair strapped to your head. That buck did. He could have jumped that fence from a standing start. It would have been far easier, but it just wasn't the sly way to handle a fence with me coming up behind.

In manner of escape and evasion, the whitetail deer can be remarkably like the cottontail rabbit. (It's not unusual for deer to hide in big brushpiles in heavily hunted farm country.)

The cottontail starts with a burst of speed that quickly outdistances men and dogs. Then he slows or even stops and ambles around in a circle to his starting point, even though a couple of beagles may be singing down his trail. It's much the same with the cottontail deer—the flashy start and the sly circling back to home base.

Hunters long experienced in chasing deer with hounds report that such deer may not even run. At least not flat-out. Archibald Rutledge once said that in all his years of hunting, he had seen only two or three deer in full flight before dogs, and in each case the deer was wounded and about to be caught.

In front of hounds, Rutledge said, deer usually loaf along, dodge, make a few showy feints and spectacular jumps, but generally play it cool. He once watched a big buck at the head of a drive suddenly "appear like an apparition and then, with extraordinary skill, efface himself from the landscape." It was later found that the deer had turned and sneaked to safety between the hounds and the hunters.

I once played tag for four hours with a buck on a Mississippi River island. It was only about eight acres, but heavily covered. I was alone, hunting steadily and carefully, and I had one quick glimpse of the deer at the beginning and another just before I quit. So I knew that he hadn't left the island during the hunt.

We were perfectly synchronized; if we hadn't been, I might have killed him. But when I stopped, the deer stopped; when I sneaked, he sneaked. We must have cut each others' tracks a dozen times.

By the end of the day, I was kicking willows and saying things not for the young to hear. I came back the next day with Joe Martelle, my old river friend. You guessed it. The buck had left.

The whitetail's ability to adjust to man's doings is uncanny. A deer can even adjust to gunfire—if it's not being directed at him.

My son, Chris, and I were bowhunting one late October morning in the Glades, a wild tangle of Illinois River backwaters and bottomland not far from the Mississippi. We were on treestands in big silver maples looking out over a cornfield that had been sharecropped.

There were mallards and woodies back in the swamp, and duck blinds a short distance behind us. We hadn't counted on that. In the frosty dawn, the big shotguns were thunderous. And yet, stealing down a cornrow came a fat whitetail buck. At each salvo of the 12-bores back in the glades, the buck lowered his head a notch and kept walking toward the guns. He was alert but not particularly nervous. He must have had a good reason. Probably trailing a doe. Anyway, it was clear that he knew the shooting wasn't at him, and when we last saw him, he was still heading back into the swamp in the direction of the gunfire.

The whitetail is one-of-a-kind, a big-game species that thrives in small-game habitats. No other large mammal could have done it; none has that unique set of qualities and responds so well to management. In most states today, this deer is the biggest and most prized of wildlife. It has special meaning to the ordinary hunter, not just as big game, but as available big game. It is the common man's chance for high personal adventure—and often his only chance.

There's all that and something more.

Whitetails aren't often hunted in real wilderness. They are often hunted in the tamest of farmlands. But even in a horse-weed patch at the edge of a cornfield, a deer lends special wildness to the land so that wherever the deer is found, it is a truly wild place. Deer carry wilderness entangled in their antlers; their hoofprints put the stamp of wildness on tame country.

When I was growing up in the mid-1950s, our part of central Iowa held a lot for an outdoor boy. But deer weren't part of it. About the only deer we had was a little fenced herd in Ledges State Park on the Des Moines River. They were interesting, but they didn't offer much to small boys who loved to prowl the woods. They were park deer, kept deer. They were not real deer, if you see my meaning.

I was about 14 the time dad and I were fishing the Des Moines

River, and I took a shortcut across the inside of a big sandbar. There was a dead buck lying there at the edge of the willows. There was no sign of injury. The buck was just dead, maybe four or five days dead, fly-blown and swollen. It was the first wild deer I had ever seen, dead or alive, and it instantly changed my world.

He was imposing. His rack, still with some tatters of dried velvet on them, seemed huge. I had never been so close to a deer. There was no fence around this one. He had been ranging free, leaving his great, heart-shaped prints at muddy creek edges, and finally leaving his corporeal being here for a boy to find. Buzzards and possums would soon remove that, but something of the deer's presence would stay to renew the spirit that had faded from the valley 60 years before.

An almost tangible change had come over the sandbar—the thing that comes when a boy is touched by genuine wildness for the first time. It's something like falling in love. Windows had opened in my horizons, revealing wonders out back of beyond. Up until then, I had played at imagining this valley to be a wild place, though I knew it wasn't. But to find a wild deer there!

That has been 40 years ago, and I still vividly remember the quality of light on the sand and the striped willow-shade that lay across the dead deer's flanks. There suddenly seemed to be a dusty quality to the light, and a hush and suspension of all moving things. It was the old spell of wildness that other boys have felt in all other times, and it must always be the same.

I dropped my fishing rod and tore off to fetch dad. He was as impressed as I. We must have hung around there for an hour or more, marveling and speculating and not knowing what to do about it. Dad told me all he knew about deer, which wasn't much, but it was impressive at the time. So was the sudden revelation that inside my stern, graying father, there was a boy my own age. I suspected then, and know now, that men and boys are about the same when confronted with genuine wildness. It makes boys older somehow, and men younger, and they may come together at a common point on common ground.

I prize the whitetail as huntable game. There is none better. I prize his fine meat and soft leather, and I waste neither. But even more, I cherish the whitetail deer for breathing wildness into our bland, tame countrysides—reminding us of old times and old doings and the meaning of being young and free.

THE WHITETAIL DEER
By Theodore Roosevelt

This was originally published as Chapter 3 in The Deer Family *(1902). Roosevelt, who was at this stage of his career early in the first of his two terms as president, wrote the section of the book devoted to "The Deer and Antelope of North America." Although the book had three other contributors (one of whom was noted whitetail authority, T. S. Van Dyke), TR's contribution was the longest and, understandably, he garnered top billing on the book's cover and in promotions for the work.*

The whitetail deer is now, as it always has been, the most plentiful and most widely distributed of American big game. It holds its own in the land better than any other species, because it is by choice a dweller in the thick forests and swamps, the places around which the tide of civilization flows, leaving them as islets of refuge for the wild creatures which formerly haunted all the country.

The range of the whitetail is from the Atlantic to the Pacific, and from the Canadian to the Mexican borders, and somewhat to the north and far to the south of these limits. The animal shows a wide variability, both individually and locally, within these confines.

There is also a very considerable variation in habits. As compared with the mule deer, the whitetail is not a lover of the mountains. As compared with the prongbuck, it is not a lover of the treeless plains. Yet in the Alleghenies and Adirondacks, at certain seasons especially, and in some places at all seasons, it dwells high among the densely wooded mountains, wandering over their crests and sheer sides and through the deep ravines. In the old days, there were parts of Texas and the Indian Territory where deer were found in great herds far out on the prairie. Moreover, the peculiar nature of its chosen habitat, while generally enabling it to resist the onslaught of man longer than any of its fellows, sometimes exposes it to speedy extermination.

To the westward of the rich bottomlands and low prairies of the Mississippi Valley proper, when the dry plains country is reached, the natural conditions are much less favorable for whitetails than for other big game.

All over the great plains, into the foothills of the Rockies, the whitetail is found, but only in the thick timber of the riverbottoms. Throughout the regions of the Upper Missouri and Upper Platte, the Big Horn, Powder, Yellowstone and Cheyenne, over all of which I have hunted, the whitetail lives among the cottonwood groves and dense brush that fringes the rivers, and here and there extends some distance up the mouths of the large creeks. In these places, the whitetail and the mule deer may exist in close proximity, but normally neither invades the haunts of the other.

Along the ordinary plains rivers, such as the Little Missouri where I ranched for many years, there are three entirely different types of country through which a man passes as he travels away from the bed of the river. There is first the alluvial riverbottom covered with cottonwood and box-elder, together with thick brush. These bottoms may be a mile or two across, or they may shrink to but a few score yards. After the extermination of the wapiti, which roamed everywhere, the only big game animal found in them was the whitetail deer.

Beyond this level alluvial bottom, the ground changes abruptly to bare, rugged hills or fantastically carved and shaped badlands rising on either side of the river, the ravines, coulies, creeks and canyons twisting through them in every direction.

Here, are patches of ash, cedar, pines, and occasionally other trees, but the country is very rugged and the cover very scanty. This is the home of the mule deer and, in the roughest and wildest parts, of the bighorn.

The absolutely clear and sharply defined line of demarcation between this rough, hilly country flanking the river, and the alluvial riverbottom, serves as an equally clearly marked line of demarcation between the ranges of the whitetail and mule deer.

This belt of broken country may be only a few hundred yards in width; or, it may extend for a score of miles before it changes into the open prairies, the high plains proper. As soon as these are reached, the prongbuck's domain begins.

As the plains country is passed, and the vast stretches of mountainous region entered, the riverbottoms become narrower, and the plains on which the prongbuck is found become of very limited extent, shrinking to high valleys and plateaus, while the mass of rugged foothills and mountains add immensely to the area of the mule deer's habitat.

Given equal areas of the three different types alluded to, that in which the mule deer is found offers the greatest chance of success to the rifle-bearing hunter, because there is enough cover to shield him and not enough to allow his quarry to escape by stealth and hiding. On the other hand, the thick riverbottoms offer him the greatest difficulty.

In consequence, where the areas of distribution of the different game animals are about equal, the mule deer disappears first before the hunter, the prong-buck next, while the whitetail holds out the best of all.

I saw this frequently on the Yellowstone, the Powder and the Little Missouri. When the ranchman first came into this country, the mule deer swarmed and yielded a far more certain harvest to the hunter than did either the prongbuck or the whitetail. They were the first to be thinned out, the prongbuck lasting much better. The cowboys and small ranchmen, most of whom did not at the time have hounds, then followed the prongbuck, and this, in its turn, was killed out before the whitetail. But in other places, a slight change in the conditions completely reversed the order of destruction.

In parts of Wyoming and Montana, the mountainous region where the mule deer dwelt was of such vast extent, and the few riverbottoms on which whitetails were found were so easily hunted, that the whitetail was completely exterminated throughout large districts where the mule deer continued to abound. Moreover, in these regions the tablelands and plains upon which the prongbuck was found were limited in extent, and although the prongbuck outlasted the whitetail, it vanished long before the herds of the mule deer had been destroyed from among the neighboring mountains.

The whitetail was originally far less common in the forests of northern New England than was the moose, for in the deep snows the moose had a much better chance to escape from its brute foes and to withstand cold and starvation. But when man appeared upon the scene, he followed the moose so much more eagerly than he followed the deer that the conditions were reversed and the moose was killed out.

The moose thus vanished entirely from the Adirondacks, and almost entirely from Maine, but the excellent game laws of the latter state, and the honesty and efficiency with which they have been executed during the last 20 years, has resulted in an increase of moose during that time. During the same period, the whitetail deer has increased to an even greater extent.

The whitetail is now more plentiful in New York and New England than it was a quarter of a century ago. Stragglers are found in Connecticut and, what is still more extraordinary, even occasionally come into wild parts of densely populated little Rhode Island.

Of all our wild game, the whitetail responds most quickly to the efforts for its protection and except the wapiti, it thrives best in semi-domestication; in consequence, it has proved easy to preserve it, even in such places as Cape Cod in Massachusetts and Long Island in New York, while it has increased greatly in Vermont, New Hampshire and Maine, and has more than held its own in the Adirondacks.

James R. Sheffield of New York City, in the summer of 1899, spent several weeks on a fishing trip through northern Maine. He kept count of the moose and deer he saw, and came across no less than 35 of the former and over 560 of the latter; in the most lonely parts of the forest, deer were found by the score, feeding in broad daylight on the edges of the ponds. Deer are still plentiful in many parts of the Allegheny Mountains from Pennsylvania southward, and also in the swamps and canebrakes of the South Atlantic and Gulf states.

Where the differences in habitat and climate are so great, there are many changes of habits, and some of them of a noteworthy kind. John A. McIllhenny of Avery's Island, Louisiana, formerly a lieutenant in my regiment, lives in what is still a fine game country. His plantation is in the delta of the Mississippi, among the vast marshes, north of which lie the wooded swamps. Both the marshes and the swamps were formerly literally thronged with whitetail deer, and the animals are still plentiful in them.

McIllhenny has done much deer-hunting, always using hounds. He informs me that the breeding times are unexpectedly different from those of the northern deer. In the North, in different localities the rut takes place in October or November, and the fawns are dropped in May or June. In the Louisiana marshes around Avery's Island, the rut begins early in July and the fawns are dropped in February.

In the swamps immediately north of these marshes, the dates are fully a month later. The marshes are covered with tall reeds and grass and broken by bayous, while there are scattered over them what are called "islands" of firmer ground overgrown with timber.

In this locality, the deer live in the same neighborhood all the year round, just as, for instance, they do on Long Island. So on the Little Missouri, in the neighborhood of my ranch, they lived in exactly the same localities throughout the entire year. Occasionally, they would shift from one riverbottom to another or go a few miles up or downstream in search of food. But there was no general shifting.

On the Little Missouri, in one place where they were not molested, I knew a particular doe and fawn whose habits I became quite intimately acquainted. When the moon was full, they fed chiefly by night, and spent most of the day lying in the thick brush. When there was little or no moon, they would begin to feed early in the morning, then take a siesta, and then—what struck me as most curious of all—would go to a little willow-bordered pool about noon to drink, feeding for some time both before and after drinking. After another siesta, they would come out late in the afternoon and feed until dark.

In the Adirondacks, the deer often alter their habits completely at different seasons. Soon after the fawns are born, they come down to the water's edge, preferring the neighborhood of the lakes, but also haunting the streambanks.

The next three months, during the hot weather, they keep very close to the water and get a large proportion of their food by wading in after lilies and other aquatic plants. Where they are much hunted, they only come to the water's edge after dark, but in regions where they are little disturbed, they are quite as often diurnal in their habits.

I have seen dozens feeding in the neighborhood of a lake, some of them 200 or 300 yards out in shallow places, up to their bellies, and this after sunrise or two or three hours before sunset.

Before September, the deer cease coming to the water, and go back among the dense forests and on the mountains.

There is no genuine migration, as in the case of the mule deer, from one big tract to another, and no entire desertion of any locality. But the food supply which drew the animals to the water's edge during the summer months will show signs of exhaustion toward fall; the delicate water-plants have vanished, the marsh grass is dying and the lilies are less succulent.

An occasional deer still wanders along the shores or out into the lake, but most of them begin to roam the woods, eating the berries and the leaves and twig ends of the deciduous trees and even of some of the conifers, although a whitetail is fond of grazing, especially upon the tips of grass. I have seen moose feeding on the tough old lily stems and wading after them when the ice had skimmed the edges of the pool. But the whitetail has usually gone back into the woods long before freezing time.

From Long Island south there is not enough snow to make the deer alter their habits in the winter. As soon as the rut is over, which in different localities may be from October to December, whitetails are apt to band together—more apt than at any other season, although even then they are often found singly or in small parties.

While nursing, the does are thin, and at the end of the rut the bucks are gaunt, their necks swollen and distended. From that time on, bucks and does alike put on flesh very rapidly in preparation for the winter.

Where there is no snow, or not enough to interfere with their traveling, they continue to roam anywhere through the woods and across the natural pastures and meadows, eating twigs, buds, nuts and the natural hay which is cured on the stalk.

In the northern woods, they form yards during the winter. These yards are generally found in a hardwood growth, which offers a supply of winter food, and consist simply of a tangle of winding trails beaten out through the snow by the incessant passing and repassing of the animals. The yard merely enables the deer to move along the various paths in order to obtain food.

If there are many deer together, the yards may connect by interlacing paths, so that a deer can run a considerable distance through them. Often, however, each deer will yard by itself, as food is the prime consideration, and a given locality may only have enough to support a single animal.

When the snows grow deep, the deer is wholly unable to move once the yard is left, and hence it is at the mercy of a man on snowshoes, or a cougar or a wolf, if found at such times. The man on snowshoes can move very comfortably, and the cougar and the wolf, although hampered by the snow, are not rendered helpless like the deer.

I have myself scared a deer out of a yard, and seen it flounder helplessly in a great drift before it had gone 30 rods. When I came up close, it ploughed its way a very short distance through the drifts, making tremendous leaps. The snow was over six feet deep, so the deer sank below the level of the surface at each jump, and yet could not get its feet on the solid ground. It became so exhausted that it fell over on its side and bleated in terror as I came up. After looking at it, I passed on.

Hide hunters and frontier settlers sometimes go out after the deer on snowshoes when there is a crust, and hence this method of killing is called crusting. It is simple butchery, for the deer cannot, as the moose does, escape its pursuer. No self-respecting man would follow this method of hunting, save from the necessity of having meat.

In very wild localities, deer sometimes yard on the ice along the edges of lakes, eating all the twigs and branches, whether of hardwood trees or conifers, which they can reach.

At the beginning of the rut, the does flee from the bucks, which follow them by scent at full speed. The whitetail buck rarely tries to form a herd of does, though he will sometimes gather two or three. The mere fact that his tactics necessitate a long and arduous chase after each individual doe prevents his organizing herds as the wapiti bull does. Sometimes two or three bucks will be found strung out one behind the other, following the same doe.

The bucks wage desperate battle among themselves during this season, coming together with a clash, and then pushing and straining for an hour or two at a time with their mouths open, until the weakest gives way. As soon as one abandons the fight, he flees with all possible speed and usually escapes unscathed.

While head to head, there is no opportunity for a deadly thrust, but if, in the effort to retreat, the beaten buck gets caught, he might be killed.

Owing to the character of the antlers, whitetail bucks are peculiarly apt to get them interlocked in such a fight, and if the efforts of the two beasts fail to disentangle them, both ultimately perish by starvation. I have several times come across a pair of skulls with interlocked antlers. The same thing occurs, though far less frequently, to the mule deer and even the wapiti.

The whitetail is the most beautiful and graceful of all our game animals when in motion. I have never been able to agree with Judge Caton that the mule deer is clumsy and awkward in his gait.

To me, there is something very attractive in the poise and power with which one of the great bucks bounds off, all four legs striking the earth together, and shooting the body upward and forward as if they were steel springs. But there can be no question as to the infinitely superior grace and beauty of the whitetail when he either trots or runs.

If surprised close up, and much terrified, the whitetail simply runs away as hard as it can, at a gait not materially different from that of any other game animal under like circumstances, while its head is thrust forward and held down, and the tail is raised perpendicularly.

In trotting, the head and tail are both held erect, and the animal throws out its legs with a singularly proud and free motion, bringing the feet well up, while at every step there is an indescribable spring.

In the canter or gallop, the head and tail are also held erect, the flashing white tail being very conspicuous. Three or four low, long, marvelously springy bounds are taken, and then a great leap is made high in the air, which is succeeded by three or four low bounds, and then by another high leap. A whitetail going through the brush in this manner is a singularly beautiful sight.

It has been my experience that they are not usually very much frightened by an ordinary slow track-hound, and I have seen a buck play along in front of one, alternately trotting and cantering, head and flag up, and evidently feeling very little fear.

To my mind, the chase of the whitetail, as it must usually be carried on, offers less attraction than the chase of any other kind of large game. But this is a mere matter of taste, and such men as Judge Caton and George Bird Grinnell have placed it above all others as a game animal.

Personally, I feel that the chase of any animal has in it two chief elements of attraction. The first is the chance given to be in the wilderness; to see the sights and hear the sounds of wild nature. The second is the demand made by the particular kind of chase upon the qualities of manliness and hardihood.

As regards the first, some kinds of game, of course, lead the hunter into particularly remote and wild localities, and the farther one gets into the wilderness, the greater is the attraction of its lonely freedom. Yet to camp out at all implies some measure of this delight. The keen, fresh air, the breath of the pine forests, the glassy stillness of the lake at sunset, the glory of sunrise among the mountains, the shimmer of the endless prairies, the ceaseless rustle of the cottonwood leaves where the wagon is drawn up on the low bluff of the shrunken river—all these appeal intensely to any man, no matter what may be the game he happens to be following. But there is a wide variation, and indeed contrast, in the qualities called for in the chase itself.

The qualities that make a good soldier are, in large part, the qualities that make a good hunter. Most important of all is the ability to shift for one's self, the mixture of hardihood and resourcefulness, which enables a man to tramp all day in the right direction and, when night comes, to make the best of whatever opportunities for shelter and warmth may be at hand.

Skill in the use of the rifle is another trait; quickness in seeing game, another; ability to take advantage of cover, yet another; while patience, endurance, keenness of observation, resolution, good nerves and instant readiness in an emergency—are all indispensable to a really good hunter.

The chase of mountain game, especially the bighorn, demands more hardihood, power of endurance, and moral and physical soundness than any other kind of sport, and so must come first. The wapiti and mule deer rank next, for they too must be killed by stalking as a result of long tramps over very rough ground. To kill a moose by still-hunting is a feat requiring a high degree of skill and entailing severe fatigue. When game is followed on horseback, it means that the successful hunter must ride well and boldly.

The whitetail is occasionally found where it yields a very high quality of sport. But normally, it lives in regions where it is comparatively easy to kill under circumstances, which make no demand for any particular prowess on the part of the hunter.

It is far more difficult to still-hunt successfully in the dense, brushy timber frequented by the whitetail than in the open glades, the mountains and the rocky hills where the wapiti and mule deer wander.

The difficulty arises, however, because the chief requirement is stealth, noiselessness. The man who goes out into the hills for a mule deer must walk hard and far, must be able to bear fatigue, and possibly thirst and hunger, must have keen eyes and be a good shot. He does not need to display the extraordinary power of stealthy advance, which is necessary to the man who would creep up to and kill a whitetail in thick timber.

When the woods are bare and there is some snow on the ground, still-hunting the whitetail becomes not only possible, but a singularly manly and attractive kind of sport.

Where the whitetail can be followed with horse and hound, the sport is of course of a very high order. To be able to ride through woods and over rough country at full speed, rifle or shotgun in hand, and then to leap off and shoot at a running object, is to show that one has the qualities which made the cavalry of Forrest so formidable in the Civil War. There could be no better training for the mounted rifleman, the most efficient type of modern soldier.

By far the easiest way to kill the whitetail is in one or other of certain methods which entail very little work or skill on the part of the hunter. The most noxious of these, crusting in the deep snows, has already been spoken of. No sportsman worthy of the name would ever follow so butcherly a method.

Fire-hunting must also normally be ruled out. It is always mere murder if carried on by a man who sits up at a lick, and is not much better where the hunter walks through the fields—not to mention the fact that on such a walk he is quite as apt to kill stock as to kill a deer. But fire-hunting from a boat, or jacking, as it is called, though it entails absolutely no skill in the hunter, and though it is and ought to be forbidden, as it can best be carried on in the season when nursing does are particularly apt to be the victims, nevertheless has a certain charm of its own.

The first deer I ever killed, when a boy, was obtained in this way, and I have always been glad to have had the experience, though I have never been willing to repeat it. I was at the time camped out in the Adirondacks.

Two or three of us, all boys of 15 or 16, had been enjoying what was practically our first experience in camping out, having gone with two guides, Hank Martin and Mose Sawyer, from Paul Smith's on Lake St. Regis. My brother and cousin were fond of fishing and I was not, so I was deputed to try to bring in a deer. I had a double-barreled 12-bore gun, French pin-fire, with which I had industriously collected "specimens" on a trip to Egypt and around Oyster Bay, Long Island. Except for three or four enthralling, but not overly successful days after woodcock and quail, around the latter place, I had done no game shooting.

The Whitetail Deer

As to every healthy boy with a taste for outdoor life, the northern forests were to me a veritable land of enchantment. We were encamped by a stream among the tall pines, and I had enjoyed everything: poling and paddling the boat, tramping through the woods, the cries of chickadee and chipmunk, of jay, woodpecker, nuthatch and crossbill which broke the forest stillness; and, above all, the great reaches of the sombre woodland themselves.

The heart-shaped footprints where the deer had come down to drink and feed on the marshy edges of the water made my veins thrill, and the nights around the flickering campfire seemed filled with romance.

My first experiment in jacking was a failure. The jack, a bark lantern, was placed upon a stick in the bow of the boat, and I sat in a cramped huddle behind it while Mose Sawyer plied the paddle with noiseless strength and skill in the stern. I proved unable to respond even to the very small demand made upon me, for when we actually did come upon a deer, I failed to see it until it ran. When I missed it, I capped my misfortune on the way back by shooting at a large owl perched on a log projecting into the water, looking at the lantern with two glaring eyes.

All next day, I was miserably conscious of the smothered disfavor of my associates, but when night fell, I was told I would have a chance to redeem myself. This time we started across a carry, the guide carrying the light boat, and launched it in a quiet little pond about a mile off.

Dusk was just turning into darkness when we reached the edge of the little lake perhaps a mile long by three-quarters of a mile across, with indented shores. We did not push off for half an hour or so, until it was entirely dark; and then for a couple of hours we saw no deer. Nevertheless, I thoroughly enjoyed the ghostly, mysterious, absolutely silent night ride over the water.

Not the faintest splash betrayed the work of the paddler. The boat glided stealthily alongshore, the glare of the lantern bringing out for one moment every detail of the forest growth on the banks, which the next second vanished into absolute blackness. Several times we saw muskrats swimming across the lane of light cut by the lantern through the darkness, and two or three times their sudden plunging and splashing caused my heart to leap.

Once, when we crossed the lake, we came upon a loon floating buoyantly out in the middle of it. It stayed until we were within ten yards, so that I could see the minute outlines of the feathers and every movement of the eye. Then it swam off, but made no cry.

At last, while crossing the mouth of a bay, we heard a splashing sound among the lilies inshore, which even my untrained ears recognized as different from any of the other noises we had yet heard. A jarring motion of the paddle showed that the paddler wished me to be on the alert.

Without any warning, the course of the boat was suddenly changed, and I was aware that we were moving stern foremost. Then we swung around, and I could soon make out that we were going down the little bay. The forest-covered banks narrowed; then the marsh at the end was lighted up, and on its hither edge, knee-deep among the water-lilies, appeared the figure of a yearling buck still in the red. It stood motionless, gazing at the light with a curiosity wholly unmixed with alarm, and at the shot wheeled and fell at the water's edge.

We made up our mind to return to camp that night, as it was before midnight. I carried the buck and the torch, and the guide the boat, and the mile walk over the dim trail, occasionally pitching forward across a stump or root, was a thing to be remembered.

It was my first deer, and I was very glad to get it, but although only a boy, I had sense enough to realize that it was not an experience worth repeating. The paddler in such a case deserves considerable credit, but the shooter not a particle, even aside from the fact to which I have already alluded, that in too many cases such shooting results in the killing of nursing does.

No matter how young a sportsman is, if he has a healthy mind, he will not long take pleasure in any method of hunting in which somebody else shows the skill and does the work so that his share is only nominal. The minute that sport is carried on in these terms, it becomes a sham, and a sham is always detrimental to all who take part in it.

Whitetails are comparatively easily killed with hounds, and there are very many places where this is almost the only way they can be killed at all. Formerly in the Adirondacks, this method of hunting was carried on under circumstances which rendered those who took part in it objects of deserved contempt.

The sportsman stood in a boat while his guides put out one or two hounds in the chosen forest side. After a longer or shorter run, the deer took to the water, for whitetails are excellent swimmers, and when pursued by hounds, try to shake them off by wading up or downstream, or by swimming across a pond. If tired, they will come to bay in some pool or rapid.

Once the unfortunate deer was in the water, the guide rowed the boat after it. If it was yet early in the season, and the deer was still in the red summer coat, he would sink when shot, and therefore the guide would usually take hold of its tail before the would-be Nimrod butchered it. If the deer was in the blue, the carcass would float, so it was not necessary to do anything quite so palpably absurd.

Such sport, so far as the man who did the shooting was concerned, had not one redeeming feature. The use of hounds has now been prohibited by law.

In regions where there are no lakes and where the woods are thick, the shooters are stationed at runways where the deer may pass when the hounds are after them. Under such circumstances, the man has to show the skill requisite to hit the running quarry, and if he uses the rifle, this means that he must possess a certain amount of address in handling the weapon. But no other quality is called for, and so even this method, though often the only possible one (and it may be necessary to return to it in the Adirondacks) can never rank high in the eyes of men who properly appreciate what big game hunting should be.

It is the usual method of killing deer on Long Island, during the three or four days of each year when they can be legally hunted. The deer are found along the south and center of the eastern half of the island; they were nearly exterminated a dozen years ago, but under good laws, they have recently increased greatly. The extensive grounds of the various sportsmen's clubs, and the forests of scrub oak in the scantily settled inland region, give them good harbors and sanctuaries.

On the days when it is legal to shoot deer, hundreds of hunters turn out from the neighborhood, and indeed from all the island and from New York. On such a day, it is almost impossible to get any work done, for the sport is most democratic and is shared by everybody.

The hunters choose their position before dawn, lying in lines wherever deer are likely to pass, while the hounds are turned into every patch of thick cover. A most lively day follows: the fusillade being terrific, some men are invariably shot, and a goodly number of deer are killed, mostly by wily old hunters who kill ducks and quail for a living in the fall.

When the horse is used together with the hounds, the conditions are changed. To ride a horse over rough country after game always implies hardihood and good horsemanship, and therefore makes the sport a worthy one. In very open country—for instance, in Texas and the Indian Territory—the horseman could ride at the tail of the pack until the deer was fairly run down. But nowadays, I know of no place where this is possible, for the whitetail's haunts are such as to make it impracticable for any rider to keep directly behind the hounds. What he must do is to try to cut the game off by riding from point to point. He then leaps off the horse and watches his chance for a shot.

Around my ranch, I very rarely tried to still-hunt whitetail, because it was always easier to get mule deer or prongbuck if I had time to go off for an all-day's hunt. Occasionally, however, we would have hounds, usually of the black-and-tan southern type. Then, if we needed meat, and there was not time for a hunt back in the hills, we would turn out to one or two of the riverbottoms with the hounds.

If I rode off to the prairies or the hills, I went alone, but if the quarry was a whitetail, our chance of success depended upon our having a sufficient number of guns to watch the different passes and runways.

Accordingly, my own share of the chase was usually limited to the fun of listening to the hounds, and of galloping at headlong speed from one point where I thought the deer would not pass to some other, which, as a matter of fact, it did not pass either. The redeeming feature of the situation was that if I did get a shot, I almost always got my deer.

Under ordinary circumstances, to merely wound a deer is worse than not hitting it, but when there are hounds along, they are certain to bring the wounded animal to bay, and so on these hunts we usually got venison.

Of course, I did get a few whitetails while hunting alone, whether with or without the hounds. There were whitetails on the very bottom on which the ranch house stood as well as on the bottom opposite.

Occasionally, I have taken the hounds out alone, and then as they chevied the deer around the bottom, have endeavored by rapid running on foot or on horseback to get to some place from which I could obtain a shot. The deer knew perfectly well that the hounds could not overtake them, and they would usually do a great deal of sneaking round and round through the underbrush and cottonwoods before they finally made up their minds to leave the bottom.

On one occasion a buck came sneaking down a game trail through the brush where I stood, going so low that I could just see the tips of his antlers. Though I made desperate efforts, I was not able to get into a position from which I could obtain a shot.

On another occasion, while I was looking intently into a wood through which I was certain a deer would pass, it deliberately took to the open ground behind me, and I did not see it until it was just vanishing. Normally, the end of my efforts was that the deer went off and the hounds disappeared after it, not to return for six or eight hours.

Once or twice things favored me; I happened to take the right turn or go in the right direction, and the deer happened to blunder past me, and then I returned with venison for supper.

Two or three times, I shot deer about nightfall or at dawn in the immediate neighborhood of the ranch, obtaining them by sneaking as noiselessly as possible along the cattle trails through the brush and timber, or by slipping along the edge of the riverbank.

Several times, I saw deer while I was sitting on the piazza or on the doorstep of the ranch, and on one occasion, I stepped back into the house, got the rifle and dropped the animal from where I stood.

On yet other occasions, I obtained whitetails that lived among the big patches of brush and timber in the larger creeks. When they were found in such country, I hunted them very much as I hunted the mule deer, and usually shot one when I was expecting as much to see a mule deer as a whitetail.

When game was plentiful, I would often stay on my horse until the moment of obtaining the shot, especially if it was in the early morning or late evening. My method then was to ride slowly and quietly down the winding valleys and across the spurs, hugging the bank, so that if deer were feeding in the open, I could get close before either of us saw the other.

Sometimes the deer would halt for a moment when it saw me, and sometimes it would bound instantly away. In either case, my chance lay in the speed with which I could jump off the horse and take my shot. Even in favorable localities this method was of less avail with whitetails than mule deer, because the former were so much more apt to skulk.

As soon as game became less plentiful, my hunting had to be done on foot. My object was to be on the hunting ground by dawn, or else to stay out there until it grew too dark to see the sights of my rifle.

Often, all I did was to keep moving as quietly as possible through likely ground, ever on the alert for the least trace of game. Sometimes, I would select a lookout and carefully scan a likely country to see if I could not detect something moving.

On one occasion, I obtained an old whitetail buck by the simple exercise of patience. I had twice found him in a broad basin composed of several coulies, all running down to form the head of a big creek, and all of them well timbered. He dodged me on both occasions, and I made up my mind that I would spend a whole day in watching for him from a little natural ambush of sagebrush and cedar on a high point which overlooked the entire basin.

I crept up to my ambush with the utmost caution early in the morning, and there I spent the entire day with my lunch and a water bottle, continually scanning the whole region most carefully with the glasses.

The day passed less monotonously than it sounds, for every now and then I would catch a glimpse of wildlife; once a fox, a coyote, and a badger. The little chipmunks had a fine time playing all around me.

At last, about mid-afternoon, I suddenly saw the buck come quietly out of the dense thicket in which he had made his midday bed, and walk up a hillside and lie down in a thin clump of ash where the sun could get at him, for it was in September just before the rut began. There was no chance of stalking him in the place he had chosen. All I could do was wait.

It was nearly sunset before he moved again, except that I occasionally saw him shift his head. Then, he got up and after carefully scrutinizing all the neighborhood, moved down into a patch of fairly thick brush, where I could see him standing and occasionally feeding, all the time moving slowly up the valley.

I now slipped most cautiously back and trotted nearly a mile until I could come up behind one of the ridges bounding the valley where he was. The wind had dropped, and it was almost absolutely still when I crawled flat on my face to the crest, my hat in my left hand, my rifle in my right. There was a big sagebush conveniently near, and under this I peered. There was a good deal of brush in the valley below, and if I had not known that the buck was there, I would never have discovered him.

As it was, I watched for a quarter of an hour, and had about made up my mind that he must have gone somewhere else when a slight movement nearly below me attracted my attention. I caught a glimpse of him nearly 300 yards off, moving quietly along a little dry watercourse right in the middle of the brush.

I waited until he was well past, and then again slipped back with the utmost care and ran on until I was nearly opposite the head of the coulie, when I again approached the ridgeline. There was no sagebrush, only tufts of tall grass stirring in the little breeze which had just sprung up—fortunately in the right direction.

Taking advantage of a slight inequality in the soil, I managed to get behind one of these tufts and almost immediately saw the buck.

Toward the head of the coulie, the brush had become scanty and low, and he was now walking straight forward, evidently keeping a sharp lookout. The sun had just set. His course took him past me at a distance of 80 yards.

When directly opposite, I raised myself on my elbows, drawing up the rifle, which I had shoved ahead of me. The movement caught his eye at once; he halted for one second to look around and see what it was, and during that second I pulled the trigger. Away he went, his white flag switching desperately, and though he galloped over the hill, I felt he was mine.

However, when I got to the top of the rise over which he had gone, I could not see him, and as there was a deep though narrow coulie filled with brush on the other side, I had a very ugly feeling that I might have lost him, in spite of the quantity of blood he had left along his trail. It was getting dark, and I plunged quickly into the coulie.

Usually, a wounded deer should not be followed until it has had time to grow stiff, but this was just one of the cases where the rule would have worked badly. In the first place, because darkness was coming on, and in the next place, because the animal was certain to die shortly, and all that I wanted was to see where he was.

I followed his trail into the coulie and expected to find that he had turned down it, but a hurried examination in the fading light showed me that he had taken the opposite course. I scrambled hastily out on the other side, and trotted along, staring into the brush, and now and then shouting or throwing a clod of earth.

When nearly at the head, there was a crackling in the brush, and out burst the wounded buck. He disappeared behind a clump of elms, but he had a hard hill to go up, and the effort was too much for him. When I next saw him he had halted, and before I could fire again down he came.

On another occasion, I spied a whole herd of whitetails feeding in a meadow right out in the open in mid-afternoon. I was able to get so close that when I finally shot a yearling buck, the remaining deer, all does and fawns, scattered in every direction, some galloping right past me in their panic.

Once or twice I was able to perform a feat of which I had read, but in which I scarcely believed. This was to creep up to a deer feeding in the open, watching when it shook its tail and then remaining motionless. I cannot say whether the habit is a universal one, but on two occasions at least, I was able to creep up to the feeding deer, because before lifting its head, it invariably shook its tail, thereby warning me to stay without moving until it had lifted its head, scrutinized the landscape and again lowered its head to graze.

The whitetail, although it scrutinized me narrowly while I lay motionless with my head toward it, seemed to think that I must be harmless, and after a while it would go on feeding. In one instance, the animal fed over a ridge and walked off before I could get a shot; in the other instance, I killed it.

OUR SMARTEST GAME ANIMAL

By Jack O'Connor

First published in the October, 1958 issue of Outdoor Life, *this piece appears in* Classic O'Connor *(2010). The author was fascinated by the diminutive Coues deer, a resident of the arid Arizona backcountry and northern Mexico that he knew so well. So much did he write about it that the wary little whitetail was often referred to as "Jack O'Connor's deer."*

The most intelligent game animal I have ever run into on this side of the world is the pint-size Coues deer, also known as the Arizona whitetail. He's a little guy, about half as large as the mule deer he often ranges with. He is, on the other hand, about five times as smart as the mule deer. The little rascal makes up his mind quickly and gambles coolly with his life. When he knows he can no longer stay concealed, he comes out like a quail, depending on his sudden and noisy appearance to befuddle the hunter.

The only North American animals I've hunted that I'd put in the same strategy class with the little Arizona whitetail is an old desert bighorn, one that has learned the facts of life by dodging the bullets tossed at him by prospectors, fishermen and vaqueros. Yet the wild sheep gets smart the hard way. The Coues deer imbibes craft and cunning with his mother's milk.

He's a great fellow to size up a situation, work out an escape plan and stick to it. On one hunt, I watched two deer go into a patch of chaparral under a rimrock 30 feet from a spring. Soon after that, a cowboy rode his horse up to the spring, where he made a fire, boiled a can of coffee and ate his lunch. Then he snoozed for about 15 minutes before he mounted and moved on. The Coues deer stayed put.

I hadn't been able to see antlers even with my 8X glasses, but the color of the deer and the way they carried their heads made me think they were both bucks. I approached the chaparral where the bucks lay upwind and inconspicuously, but both deer sneaked out ahead of me. I just caught a glimpse of one, moving like a gray shadow with his head down and his tail clamped between his legs. Before I could shoot he was out of sight. Those deer knew the cowboy's heart was pure as driven snow, but mine was full of guile. How, I'll never know, but they did. That's why so many Coues bucks live to a ripe old age.

One afternoon years ago, another hombre and I were hunting in southern Arizona. We had separated, and in late afternoon I saw him pussyfooting down a point about 400 yards from me. Presently, I saw a deer jump ahead of my friend, and from his obvious excitement, I knew it was a buck.

The deer continued off the point as if to run along under the rimrock toward the main mountain. My friend hurried out to the brink of the ridge and stood there with his rifle ready. He was watching the spot where the oaks ended, where the buck was sure to break out of cover on his way to the mountain beyond.

But instead of doing the obvious, the buck put on his brakes as soon as he was out of sight in the scrubby little evergreen oaks under the rim. Then he turned back around the point, sneaking along under the rim with head down, tail plastered between his legs. He came out in the open about 200 yards to the left of where my pal was expecting him. Then, with the last concealing bush behind him, he flitted up his big white tail and ran.

My friend threw a hasty shot at him and missed. It was difficult to make him believe that this deer he shot at was the same one he'd jumped a few minutes earlier.

I know of no animal that's better at finding a strategic bedding ground than this smart little whitetail. This was firmly impressed on me one fall day when I was hunting a long ridge on horseback. I saw four bucks, but every single one of them was bedded so that he needed but one jump to be out of sight.

I have never seen an animal make better use of cover than the Coues deer. I recall a time years ago when I was hunting with two friends in the Canelo Hills not far from Patagonia in southern Arizona. We were climbing up a trail toward the top of a low ridge. When we got to the top, we'd figure out how to team up and work out the heads of some canyons. Then one of my friends saw a buck flip up its white tail and jump over the ridge toward a big canyon.

Yelling for us to follow, he took after it. We knew the country and thought it highly probable that we'd get another look at the deer. The big canyon into which he'd gone was quite open, with golden slopes of frost-cured grama grass and an occasional ocotillo and oaks in little groves in the side draws. There was so little cover that it would be almost impossible for a deer to move without one of us seeing it.

But nothing did we see. That deer hadn't possibly had time to run out of sight, yet he did. A couple of us searched the valley with binoculars. Not a thing could we find except a couple of crows slithering along with a lofty wind, cawing and snarling at each other against the flat blue of the sky. We decided the deer might have stopped directly below us, where the contours of the ground and a few scattered patches of mountain mahogany and cliff rose would afford cover. We rolled big stones that went crashing through that growth. Nothing moved.

Right beside us was a little patch of brush about large enough to conceal a cock pheasant. We hadn't given it a thought. Presently, one of my pals decided to roll a cigarette, so he walked over and leaned his rifle against a bush. Instantly, a fine whitetail exploded out of the little patch, head up, antlers back, snowy tail looking as large as he was. His first jump kicked leaves and twigs all over us. He passed so close to me that if I'd been less astonished, I might have grabbed him by an antler. (Don't ask me what I'd have done after I got such a hold.)

Meanwhile, the man who'd leaned his rifle on the bush, made a lunge for it and fell flat. The other hunter and I were so busy bumping into one another that the buck buzzed over the ridge without a shot being fired at him. We agreed that this buck was too hard on our nerves and set out to find a more docile one.

The career of a mossy-horned old buck that lived near Patagonia, Arizona, illustrates the amazing ability of these little deer to survive heavy hunting without much cover.

The buck's home range was a canyon-cut ridge that ran about three miles from north to south. Thin brush grew along the talus slopes below the rimrocks. Oak, mountain mahogany and cliff rose were fairly thick in a few places in the draws. The rest of this long ridge was open slopes of grama grass, limestone outcrops, an oak here and there. The ridge was within half-a-mile of a ranch house containing three hunters, within three miles of the village and a mile from a good road.

The buck lived out his long, long life almost as publicly as a goldfish in a bowl. He probably was born on the ridge and he lived about five years after his antlers had grown so large and many-pointed as to cause comment. Deer hunters came down from Tucson to try for him. High school kids matched wits with him after school and on weekends. Cowhands sniped at him.

It wasn't difficult to see the buck. Almost anyone could see him. But armed men only saw him just as he was disappearing into the brush, crossing a ridge at 400 yards, fading around a point. Yet I'm sure 200 shots were fired at that buck, maybe more.

I had a hand in this buck's undoing. Arizona rancher Frank Siebold and I knew the buck had a habit on chill fall mornings of taking the sun on a flat between a big canyon and the south slope of the mountain. If hunters came up the canyon, the deer faded over the south slope and hugged a belt of oaks as he eased away. If hunters came up that south slope, he dropped over into the canyon.

Frank and I framed him. We sent his sister, Doris, and my wife, Eleanor, up the canyon while we skirted the bottom of the south slope. When the buck came sneaking along through the belt of oaks, I took a crack at him. The bullet struck a bit low in his left shoulder. He went down, but got up as we were scrambling toward him and climbed over the rimrock. There he ran into Doris, who nailed him.

The old buck had a beautiful head with nine points to a side, but the meat was so tough, it was only edible in a stew. His teeth were about gone and he showed every sign of extreme age and decrepitude. He was somewhere between 12 and 14 years old and probably would have died of old age within a year.

Arizona whitetail is a misleading name for these little deer. That's a handle they got when they were first classified from specimens taken near Fort Crittenden, Arizona, in the days when that old army post was on guard against Apaches. Coues (pronounced cows) is a more accurate name for these little deer, and the scientific name is *Odocoileus couesi*. Other common names are fantail, Sonora whitetail and Arizona whitetail. Mexicans call it the *venado*, which simply means deer. They keep things straight by calling the mule deer, *buro*.

Coues deer are found in southern Arizona in all the hills and mountains high enough to support live oaks, from the little border town of Sasabe east to the New Mexico line. Their range is by no means continuous, but there are scattered herds as far north as central Arizona along the Mogollon Rim. In New Mexico, they are found in mountain ranges west of the Rio Grande as far north as the Datils and are quite plentiful in the Mogollons and San Franciscos. Some are found in the Davis Mountains in the Big Bend of Texas, and in the Glass and Chisos mountains in the same area. They are most plentiful in the Mexican states of Chihuahua and Sonora, and there are many in western Choahuila.

In the United States, Coues deer are generally found at altitudes above 4,000 feet, but in Sonora they range from 10,000 feet in the Sierra Madre clear down to little hills that are in sight of the Gulf of California. Distribution maps do not show them down near the saltwater, but I have seen them there by the hundreds and shot many.

Outside of the Southwest, these wonderful little deer are almost unknown. They have also undergone the ordeal of being written about by people who knew little about them. I mentioned that distribution maps do not list them as occupying the western desert portion of their range in Mexico. Writers often promote another error by making Coues deer seem smaller than they actually are. One piece I read says to imagine a jackrabbit with horns. That's silly. Vernon Bailey, Fish & Wildlife Service biologist, wrote that bucks reached a maximum weight of 100 pounds (presumably live weight) and does about 75.

I have weighed dozens of them. The average grown buck will weigh from 80 to 90 pounds after he's field dressed, and 100-pound bucks are common in any area I have hunted. It's true that a buck weighing more than 100 pounds is certainly not a maximum weight. I wrote a story some years ago about a 117½-pound Coues buck. I killed it in the Tortolita Mountains near Tucson. I thought I'd win a rifle in a heavy-buck contest, but the next day my shooting pal Carroll Lemon brought in one that weighed 128½.

Coues deer look like Eastern whitetails in miniature, except their skulls are smaller and shorter in proportion. Does and young bucks are a dove gray, but old bucks are grizzled and darker. Their antlers, ears and tails are larger in proportion to their bodies than those of their Eastern relatives. Tails range from a grizzled brown on top to a bright orange, and when they toss them up the tail appears brilliant white.

Although the little fantail is only about half the size of his northern and eastern cousins, his antlers are larger in proportion to his body. As is the case with all whitetail deer, all the points on the antlers of the fantail come off one main beam and the eye-guard points are long and conspicuous as compared with the short ones of the mule deer. However, whereas the mature Eastern whitetail generally has four points to the side in addition to the eye-guard, the Arizona deer has three. On the other hand, I have shot Coues bucks with as many as five points to a side and have seen one with nine on one side and 11 on the other.

The antlers do not freak as much as those of mule deer, and are generally very regular and symmetrical. A buck with a 17-inch beam is extraordinary, and an 18-incher is getting far up in the records if the antlers are massive. The heads may not knock your eye out, but they are one of the rarest trophies in North America. Because they are an entirely different animal from the orthodox whitetail, they are given a separate classification in Records of North American Big Game.

No matter where he's found, the little Coues deer is a hill animal. On the Sonora desert, the mule deer like to range out on the flats, but the whitetails cling to the hills like ducks to a pond. The long, rather narrow tracks of the desert mule deer are found all over the flats, but usually the hunter doesn't run into the smaller, heart-shaped tracks of the whitetail unless he's close to a hill.

The most heavily populated whitetail area I ever ran into was in the Sonora desert—a chain of low hills southwest of the little placer-mining town of La Cienega. I hunted there during the winter of 1937-38, and the deer were so thick, they obliterated the horse tracks on a trail between dusk and dawn. Apparently, they soon got too plentiful and died off. I was in there a few years later and didn't see one where I had formerly seen ten.

In spite of their wide distribution in respect to altitude, I always think of the little whitetails as creatures of what scientists call the upper Sonoran climatic zone, which means a zone with the climate and vegetation common to the higher elevations in Sonora. This is one of the most pleasant regions on earth, a zone where it seldom gets very hot or very cold, a land of eternal fall and eternal spring. In the warmest months, the nights are always cool, and in the coldest months, the sun is out bright and warm at noon. This is true of high and hilly

Sonora and also of the Arizona hills running along the Mexican border clear to the Big Bend of Texas.

All of this area has hills and mountains rising from grassy, rolling plains. It's a region where the ocotillo and the prickly pear of the desert meet the oaks of the mountains, a land of pinon and juniper, cliff rose and mountain mahogany. In this belt of country, the animals of the Rockies meet those of the semi-tropics. From the far north have come the bighorn sheep, the mule deer, the elk and the black bear. Up from the south have come our little whitetails, the peculiar coati-mundi, the mountain lion and the wild turkey. Once the grizzly ranged this country in good numbers, but it has been hunted out in the American Southwest and survives only in a few parts of Chihuahua.

Of all these animals, to me the most typical of the region is the little fantail. I always think of him as running along a grassy hillside, waving his snowy flag and disappearing into the head of an oak-filled draw.

Because the little whitetails occupy many types of country, there are many different ways of hunting them. Down on the Sonora desert, I have hunted them by walking around the bottom of the hills where they bed down and letting my rising scent flush them out. When they're found in brushy canyons, a good way to get venison is for two hunters to work together, one hiking up one side of a canyon and his companion taking the other. The hunter seldom sees deer that he himself moves. Instead, he can nail bucks on the other side of the canyon that have been put up by his pal.

As I write this, I can still see in memory one of the finest whitetails I ever shot. A friend and I were hunting together, he on one side of a draw and I on the other. I saw a buck get up about 50 feet in front of my companion and sneak off, head down, tail between his legs. He was almost as inconspicuous as a cock pheasant sneaking through the stubble ahead of a dog. My pal wasn't aware that he was within pebble-tossing distance of a fine buck, but I could see both of them on that steep hillside opposite me. I sat and carefully put a bullet right behind that buck's shoulder.

But the sportiest and most pleasant whitetail hunting is done with horses—riding cattle and game trails along the sides of the draws and canyons. Then every time a deer flashes a white tail and takes off, the hunter has to see if it's a buck or a doe and take action accordingly.

I always carry my rifle in a scabbard on the left side of my saddle, with the rifle butt to the rear and pointing up at about a 45-degree angle. It takes only seconds to get off the horse on the left side, grab the stock with my right hand and yank the rifle out of the scabbard. Then you sit down and open up.

The fantails' small, tender body doesn't offer much resistance to bullets. I use relatively light, easily expanded bullets traveling at high velocity. More often than not the bucks are shot running, and fast bullets make it easier to figure the right lead.

I have used the 87-grain bullet in the .250/3000 Savage and have found it excellent on these diminutive deer. The 7mm Mauser, with the old Western 139-grain open-point bullet, was powerful whitetail medicine, and so is the .257 with good 100-grain bullets. The new .243 Winchester and .244 Remington with bullets weighing from 90 to 100 grains should be made to order—fast, flat-shooting and quick-opening. The 150-grain bullets in the .30-06 and the 130-grain bullets in the .270 are poison on fantails. Generally, 180-grain bullets for the .30-06 open up too slowly. Some of the 150-grain bullets are excellent.

I did a lot of whitetail hunting in Mexico, from one to four trips a year for many years. I have no exact record of how many whitetails I shot there and in Arizona, but I took a good many. One thing I learned for sure is that they call for a fast-opening bullet. Back when the .257 was newly hatched, the bullets for the most part had thick, heavy jackets, and when I used them, I spent half my time chasing wounded whitetails that were well hit but still going.

The main enemy of the Coues deer is the mountain lion, and until hunters get more skillful and are allowed to shoot does as well as bucks, predation by lions is necessary for healthy whitetail herds. In areas where lions are killed down, the deer become too plentiful, destroy their own browse and die off from disease. The best Mexican deer ranges have a lot of lions—and a lot of deer. Coyotes take many fawns, and I have found where they have killed grown deer. Bobcats are likewise fawn-killers.

But nature has seen to it that the little whitetails can survive. The twin fawns, born in the offbeat months of July and August, mean a great rate of increase. The stealth and cunning of the deer make them difficult for predators to find and kill. Because of their size, an area can support about twice as many whitetails as mule deer.

The hunting pressure Coues deer can stand is amazing. There's excellent whitetail hunting, for example, in the Catalina Mountains overlooking the city of Tucson, the second largest city in Arizona.

If a country is brushy, the little fantails like it. If it's open, they can make a little cover go a long way. Many times when hunters are working out the brush in the draws and along the rimrocks, fantails bed right out in the grass where no one would expect to find them. I once jumped a dandy buck out of tall grass under a lone oak on a big grassy slope. I shedded my surprise in time to nail him, but I had no more expected a shot at a whitetail than at a tiger.

Another time, I was sitting on a ridge glassing some country below when it dawned on me that some dark points sticking out of the grass about 50 yards in front of me looked more like antler tips than dead sticks. I turned my 9X binoculars on them. They were antlers. The buck had been lying there in the grass taking the sun when I came over the ridge, and he apparently decided the smart move was not to move at all. He didn't jump until I was almost on top of him.

A Coues buck in Sonora jumped out of the grass so close that he frightened my poor horse almost out of his wits. By the time the resulting rodeo was over, the buck was long gone.

I've seen grown fantail bucks sneak along in tall grass with their knees so bent they appeared to be crawling. Once, I missed getting a shot at a fine buck I'd watched for five minutes as he crept through tall grass and thin brush. I couldn't believe it was a deer; it was so close to the ground I thought it must be a coyote.

I can think of no hunting more pleasant than a November or December shoot for fantails in Mexico. It's a hunt for a rare trophy worn by a shrewd and intelligent animal.

The deer don't rut until February and March, so the late-fall venison is always good, one of the choicest pieces of big-game meat in North America. The weather is perfect then—crisp nights and balmy days full of sun. Generally, the dude will hunt from horseback and cut the deer down on the run, which takes some doing. Then there are always the nights around a campfire of fragrant mesquite, the coals cooking steaks from the little *venados* and a pot of frijoles. Ah, me!

PART THREE

WISDOM, WHIMSY AND THE LIGHTER SIDE

The deer-hunting experience has always included a lighter side. In part, the uncertainty of the quest explains this, because a disappointed hunter beset by the sudden onset of buck ague welcomes a bit of humor. Never mind that the circumstances may in truth come close to the tragic and the comic, the average sportsman who has missed a shot, found himself the victim of a major example of ground shrinkage or come down with bad case of buck fever considers shrugging off misfortune with a grin rather than a grimace as the manly thing to do.

Similarly, a gathering of deer hunters, especially in a camp situation, provides a tailor-made setting for mischief or even outright mayhem. The nature and extent of practical jokes in such settings knows no bounds other than the collective imaginations of those involved.

For example, one of my favorite hunt camp stories from my native Smokies of North Carolina involved two erstwhile nimrods who both had dentures. After imbibing a fair amount of tanglefoot to be sure they slept soundly, the pair climbed into their respective bunks in the communal sleeping area. Their last action before entering the Land of Nod was removal of their dentures. As you can likely guess, some n'er-do-well companions switched the two sets of false teeth, and the following morning the old-time hunters awakened, put in the other man's dentures and actually consumed breakfast with the ill-fitting chompers.

That sort of mischief, best known in the form of divestiture of the shirttail of any hapless soul who misses a deer, is standard deer-hunting fare. It's mostly innocent fun, a special type of male bonding, and part and parcel of the overall experience.

Here we have eight selections, ranging from flights of literary fancy to the stuff of which belly laughs are made, sure to bring a grin to one's face or a knowing nod of approbation. There's delicious irony and whimsy in Rutledge's masterful "The Lady in Green," Corey Ford at his inimitable best as he shares a whitetail-related tale of the members of The Lower Forty, a pair of pieces from both Edmund Ware Smith and Charley Dickey, one of the few offerings Gordon MacQuarrie produced on deer hunting and the skillful storytelling of Mike Gaddis.

Loosen your belt or suspenders, settle down in comfort and prepare to be entertained. You'll leave this section of the book fully aware of the fact that some of the finest aspects of the deer hunter's world involve missteps and misadventures, misses and even downright misery, but all surrounded by an aura of good will and a wealth of whimsy.

THE LADY IN GREEN
By Archibald Rutledge

First published in Field & Stream *(October, 1941), this story subsequently appeared in* Hunter's Choice *(1946),* Fireworks in the Peafield Corner *(edited by Irvine Rutledge, 1986) and* Tales of Whitetails: Archibald Rutledge's Great Deer-Hunting Stories *(1992). The immensely popular piece has also appeared in a number of anthologies of great hunting stories.*

For a very long time we have had on the plantation a negro named Steve. For a generation he worked for us, and he is with me to this day. While we usually had certain negroes who could be counted on to accomplish even difficult material tasks, in what might be termed the realm of the psychic, Steve reigned supreme. For some reason, he was at his best when something esoteric and peculiar had to be accomplished. My Colonel early recognized Steve's strange talent, and occasionally called on him to exercise it.

Thus, when the lady in green came to us for a visit, and came with the hope of killing a regal buck, I felt called upon to enlist the darksome strategy of Steve.

"Steve," I asked, "have you ever seen a woman wear pants?"

"I ain't done seen it, Cap'n," he responded, a fervent fire of recollection kindling in his eyes, "but I has done seen some wimmins what act like dey wears dem."

"Has your Amnesia ever worn them?"

"When I is around home," he assured me, "she don't ever wear anything else but."

"Have you two been falling out again, Steve?"

"Cap'n," he said, "for yeahs and yeahs we ain't never done fell in."

"I guess she doesn't like your playing around with all these young girls and leaving her at home."

"I tole her dat woman and cat is to stay home; man and dog is to go abroad. She didn't like dat atall, atall."

"Well," I said, "this is Friday. Monday will be Christmas Day. I know just one way I can get you out of the dog-house where Amnesia has put you. Wouldn't you like to get out for Christmas?"

Steve licked his lips, a sure sign that he is about to take the bait. Besides, as I had beforehand been of assistance to him in the vital manner of domestic reconciliations, he regards me as a kind of magician.

"Tomorrow," I told him, "will be Saturday, the day before Christmas Eve. I will help you, but I expect you to help me." I was testing his loyalty in a large way.

Haunted by a sense of his own helplessness and by the mastery of his huge Amnesia, he appeared pathetically eager to do anything. In fact, such was his yielding mood that I had to be careful what I asked him to do, for he would do it. Steve can resist anything but temptation.

"I'm giving a big deer drive tomorrow," I said. "There will be twenty men and one woman—but I hear she wears pants."

"Great Gawd," was Steve's comment.

"Green ones," I went on.

"Jeedus!"

"Now, Steve, you know that old flathorn buck in the Wambaw Corner, the one that has been dodging us for about five years?"

"You mean him what hab dem yaller horns, flat same like a paddle?"

"He's the one."

"Cap'n, dat's a buck what I knows like I knows the way to another man's watermelon patch," Steve assured me grinning. "What you want me to do? And how Amnesia suddenly gwine take me back because of what you is planning for me to do?"

"Well," I told him, "you've got a job, all right. I don't want to be unfair to these men, but ordinary bucks will do very well for them. Your business is to get the *buck with the palmated horns* to run to the lady in green. If you will do this, I will give you a whole haunch of venison, a ham out of my smokehouse, a dollar in cash and a dress for Amnesia. How about it?"

Steve was stunned. When he came to, he said, "Boss, when I gits to heaben, I ain't gwine ask, 'How 'bout it?'"

"Of course," I told him, "I will put her on the Crippled Oak Stand.

You know that is the favorite buck run. Just how you are going to get him to run there I don't know, but you probably can figure it out.

"Oh," I added, "I will not hold you responsible for her killing the buck. Being a woman, she'll probably miss it anyway. But I want you to give her a chance to shoot."

I could see that Steve was already deep in his problem. Knowing the woods like an Indian, so familiar with game that he can almost talk with it, familiar also with the likelihood of big game's acting in ways unpredictable, Steve was pretty well-equipped for his task. I could almost see how he would enjoy this particular job.

"One more thing," I told him. "This lady doesn't shoot a shotgun. She always uses a rifle."

"Cap'n," he sensibly asked, "does you think she knows a deer? If she don't, I mustn't get too close to dat rifle."

"I have never seen her," I told him, "and I don't know whether she is a real huntress. All I know about her is what I have been told. But she's the daughter of one of my best friends, a gentleman from Philadelphia. I want her to have a good time. Think of what it would mean if she could kill the crowned king of Wambaw Corner!"

"I sure loves to please wimmins," Steve mused, "but so far I ain't done had too much of luck."

As we parted, I kept pounding home his job to him: "Drive the buck with the flat horns to the Crippled Oak Stand. Drive him there if you have to head him off. And remember the haunch and the ham that will be yours if you manage it right."

Not long after daylight the following morning, the crowd of Christmas hunters assembled in my plantation yard. As the season was nearing its close, every man I had invited came. And there was the lady in green.

When I saw her, I was ashamed of the way in which I had bandied words with Steve about the nature of her attire. She was slender, graceful and very lovely. She looked like Maid Marian. Clad in Lincoln green, with a jaunty feather in her Robin Hood's cap, she was the attraction of all eyes.

I could see that all the men were in love with her, and I didn't feel any too emotionally normal myself. There was nothing about her of the type of huntress I had described to Steve. She appeared a strange combination of an elf, a child and a woman, and though I do not profess to know much about such matters, that particular combination seems especially alluring, perhaps dangerously so.

While my negro drivers were getting their horses ready, and while stately deerhounds, woolly dogs and curs of low degree gathered from far and near on account of the general air of festivity and the promise of some break in the general hunger situation, I got everybody together and told them that we planned to drive the Wambaw Corner; that we had standers enough to take care of the whole place; we had drivers and dogs; we had deer. The great, and really the only, question was: *Can anybody hit anything?* That is often a pertinent question in hunting.

W ambaw Corner is peculiarly situated. A tract of nearly a thousand acres, it is bounded on two sides by the wide and deep Wambaw Creek. On one side is the famous Lucas Reserve, an immense backwater formerly used for waterpower, but now chiefly for bass and bream.

In shape, this place is a long and comparatively narrow peninsula, with water on three sides. On the south runs a wide road, along which I usually post my standers, but when I have enough (or too many), I post them along the creek. The chance there is excellent, for if a buck is suspicious, there's nothing he'll do quicker than dodge back and swim the creek.

With the woods still sparkling with dew, and fragrant with the aromas from myrtles and pines, I posted all my standers. I had sent my drivers far down on the tip of the peninsula to drive it out to the road. I had also had a last word with Steve.

"Only one mistake you might be makin', Cap'n," he told me. "I dunno how 'bout wid a gun, but with a rollin' pin or a skillet or a hatchet, a woman don't eber seem to miss. Anyhow," he particularized, "dey don't neber miss me!"

"Have you got our plan made?" I asked him. "You've got five other boys to drive. That just about sets you free to do what you want to."

"I got my plan," he said. "And," he added darkly, "if so happen it be dat I don't come out with de other drivers, you will onnerstand."

I n a place like Wambaw Corner, there are at times a great many deer. They love its remote quiet, its pine hills, its abundant food, its watery edges. I have seen as many as six fine bucks run out of there on a single drive, a flock of wild turkeys and heaven knows how many does. I have likewise seen wild boars emerge from that wilderness—huge, hulking brutes, built like oversized hyenas, and they are ugly customers to handle.

I knew that there was sure to be a good deal of shooting on this drive, certain to be some missing and possibly to be some killing. Everybody seemed keyed just right for the sport. I had men with me who had hunted all over the world, grizzled backwoodsmen who had never hunted more than 20 miles from their homes, pure amateurs, some insatiable hunters but rotten shots—and I had the lady in green.

After I had posted the men, there being no stand for me, or perhaps for a more romantic reason, I decided to stand with my Maid Marian. She seemed like such a child to shoot down a big buck, yet she was jaunty and serene.

When I had explained to certain of the standers as I posted them just how an old stag would come up to them, I could see, from the way they began to sweat and blink, that they were in the incipient stages of nervous breakdowns. But not so my Sherwood Forest girl.

Her stand by the famous Crippled Oak was on a high bank in the pinelands. Before her and behind her was dense cypress swamp, in the dark fastness of which it was almost impossible to get a shot at a deer. If the buck came, she would have to shoot him when he broke across the bank and likely on the full run—climbing it, soaring across it or launching himself down the farther bank. All this I carefully explained to her. She listened intently and intelligently.

She appeared concerned over my concern. "You need not worry," she assured, for my comfort. "If he comes, I will kill him."

"Have you killed deer before?" I asked.

"No," she admitted lightly but undaunted. "I never even saw one."

My heart failed me. "This one," I told her, hoping that Steve's maneuvering would be effective, "is likely to have big yellow horns. He's an old wildwood hero. I hope you get him."

About that time, I heard the drivers put in, and I mean they did. A Christmas hunt on a Carolina plantation brings out everything a negro has in the way of vocal eminence. Far back near the river they whooped and shouted, yelled and sang. Then I heard the hounds begin to tune up.

Maid Marian was listening, with her little head pertly tipped to one side. "What is all that noise?" she asked with devastating imbecility.

Tediously, I explained that the deer were lying down, that the negroes and the dogs roused them, and that by good fortune an old rough-shod stag might come our way.

"I understand," she nodded brightly. But I was sure she didn't.

Another thing disconcerted me: I could hear the voice of Prince, of Sam'l, of Will and of Precinct; Evergreen's voice was loud on the still air. But not once did I hear the hound-dog whoop of Steve. However, his silence did indicate that he was about some mysterious business.

In minutes, a perfect bedlam in one of the deep corners showed that a stag had been roused. The wild clamor headed northward toward the creek, and soon I heard a gun blare twice. But the pack did not stop. There was a swift veering southward. Before long, I heard shots from that direction, but whoever tried must have failed.

The pack headed northeast, toward the road on which we were standing, but far from us. I somehow felt, from his wily maneuvers, that this was the buck with the palmated horns. Ordinary bucks would do no such dodging, and the fact that he had been twice missed would indicate that the standers had seen something very disconcerting.

Watching the lady in green for any telltale sign of a break in nerves, I could discover none. She just seemed to be taking a childish delight in all the excitement. She was enjoying it without getting excited herself.

About that time, I heard the stander at the far eastern end of the road shoot; a minute later he shot again. He was a good man, a deliberate shot. Perhaps he had done what I wanted Maid Marian to do. But no. The pack now turned toward us.

Judging from the speed of the hounds, there was nothing the matter with the deer; judging by their direction, they were running parallel to the road at a little over a hundred yards from it. It was a favorite buck run, and at any moment he might flare across the road to one of the standers at the critical crossings.

Ours was the last stand on the extreme west. It seemed very unlikely that he would pass all those crossings and come to us. Now the hounds were running closer to the road, and it sounded as if the buck was about to cross.

It is now just 50 years since I shot my first buck, and I have hunted deer every year since that initial adventure. But never in all my experience as a deer hunter have I heard what I then heard on the road, on which I had 12 standers. Judging from the shots, the buck must have come within easy sight, if not within range, of every stander. The bombardment was continuous. Together with the shots, as the circus came nearer, I could hear wild and angry shouts. I thought I heard some heavy profanity, and I hoped the lady in green missed this.

She was leaning against the Crippled Oak, cool as a frosted apple. I was behind the tree, pretty nervous for her sake.

"Look out, now," I whispered. "He may cross here at any minute."

My eyes kept searching for the buck to break cover. Suddenly, directly in front of the stander next to us, I saw what I took to be the flash of a white tail. The stander fired both barrels. Then I saw him dash his hat to the ground and jump on it in a kind of frenzy that hardly indicated joy and triumph.

The next thing I knew, the little rifle of the lady in green was up. I did not even see the deer. The rifle spoke. The clamoring pack, now almost upon us, began a wild milling. Then they hushed.

"All right," said Maid Marian serenely, "I killed him."

Gentlemen, she spoke the truth, and the stag she killed was the buck with the palmated horns. At 60 yards, in a full run, he had been drilled through the heart.

On several occasions, I had seen his horns, but I had not dreamed they were so fine—perfect, ten-point, golden in color, with the palmation a full two inches. A massive and beautiful trophy it was, a kind that many a good sportsman spends a lifetime seeking and often spends it in vain.

However, mingled with my pride and satisfaction, there was a certain sense of guilt; yet I was trying to justify myself with the noble sentiment, "Women and children first."

I had told Steve to drive this buck to my lady in green. He had done it—heaven knows how. He would tell me later. But his plan had worked. But now came the critical phase of the whole proceeding. Standers and drivers began to gather, and afar off, I could hear many deep oaths. These, I felt sure, would subside in the presence of Maid Marian. They did, but not the anger and the protests.

There seemed to be one general question, asked in such a way that it would be well for the person referred to to keep his distance.

"Where's that driver?" I heard on all sides. "I mean the big, black, slue-footed driver. I believe you call him Steve. I had a good mind to shoot him."

"I'd have killed that buck if he hadn't got in the way." "What was that flag he was waving? Looked to me like he was trying to turn the buck from us."

"He was coming right on me when that driver jumped out of a bush and started waving that flag."

"Well, after all, gentlemen," I said, "here's the buck, and I must say the lady made a grand shot. Wouldn't you rather have her kill him than do so yourselves?"

Everybody had now gathered but Steve. When questioned, the other drivers disclaimed all knowledge of his whereabouts or his peculiar behavior. But they knew perfectly of both. One artfully sidetracked the whole painful discussion by saying, "Steve ain't neber been no good deer driver nohow."

Tyler Somerset, a prince of backwoodsmen, drew me aside.

"Say," he said, "I know what went on back there. You can't fool me. That's the smartest darky I ever did see. More than once he outran that buck. And he sure can dodge buckshot. I wonder where he got that red and white flag he used to turn that old buck?"

We made several other drives that day. Five more stags were slain. But the buck and the shot of the lady in green remained the records. On those later drives, Steve put in no appearance.

When my friends were safely gone, Steve shambled out of hiding to claim his just reward. I loaded him down with Christmas.

"By the way," I said, "some of the standers told me that you headed that buck with a red and white flag. Where did you get that?"

Steve grinned with massive shyness, as he does only when anything feminine comes to mind. "Dat's de biggest chance I took—wusser dan dodging buckshot. Dat was Amnesia's Sunday petticoat."

"Huh," I muttered with gloomy foreboding. "If she ever finds that one out, I'll have to take you to the hospital."

"Cap'n, I done arrange it," he told me—the old schemer! "I did tore seven holes in it with all that wavin', but I tole Amnesia I was ashamed to have my gal wear a raggety petticoat, and you was gwine give me a dollar, and I was gwine give it to her to buy a new one for Christmas."

JAKE'S RANGERS HUNT THE WHITETAIL

By Edmund Ware Smith

In the 1950s, Field & Stream *was pure gold in terms of its contributors, with columns by Robert Ruark and Corey Ford at the top of the list. The magazine also offered a series of Smith articles on "Jake's Rangers," a group of buddies somewhat reminiscent of the cast of characters in Gordon MacQuarrie's "The Old Duck Hunter's Association" or Ford's "The Lower Forty." This piece first appeared in* Field & Stream *and subsequently in various anthologies.*

Whether you call them "The Trail Blazers," or "Whitetails Limited," or simply "The Old Bunch," it means the same thing when the leaves begin to fall in the little towns in the deer-hunting states of our nation. Whatever the name, and there usually is one, you are talking about a group of men, young and old, who gather each fall to hunt the whitetail deer.

The personnel of these groups is often so varied in age and walk of life that individual members rarely meet during the rest of the year. But with the first frost, and the foliage bright on the ridges, there comes a flurry of eager telephone calls. Meetings are held, the trip is planned; and, when you reach your hunting camp, you are reunited like brothers. Your rifle stands in the gunrack where it stood last year. Your sleeping bag is on your old bunk or bed. You are fraternal in the glow of lamplight, sharing the familiar warmth of the wood stove with the old bunch and talking of just one subject—tomorrow. For tomorrow is opening day on deer.

Each fall, the phenomenon of the deer-hunting groups grows deeper into the country's grass roots. In Pennsylvania, New York, the Virginias, the Carolinas, Michigan, Maine and perhaps other states, there are groups that were first organized well over 50 years ago. Rich in tradition, and sometimes in ritual, this annual gathering of the deer-hunting clan has become an American institution.

I suspect that my own bunch is typical of at least a hundred others. We call ourselves "Jake's Rangers," and, in this description of the Rangers' 14th annual hunt, I believe you will find striking similarities to your own hunt, and perhaps a kinship between your group and ours. In fact, in what follows, you may even read words that you have actually spoken or heard spoken at night around the stove in your own hunting camp. For example:

"I was standing in a spruce knoll, when I heard this deer coming."

That opening line, with minor variations, has been uttered at least once for every whitetail deer sighted, heard, hit or missed, since deer hunting began. It can't be copyrighted, for it is always an inspired original to the hunter who is telling his story. Certain of Jake's Rangers will be speaking the magic line presently, but first I must explain who we are and where we hunt.

Officially, there are seven Rangers. Guests bring the total to ten or more. All of us reside in, or near, the small seacoast town of Damariscotta, Maine. Typically heterogeneous, our membership includes Damariscotta's postmaster, its veterinary surgeon, its Railway Express agent, a leading physician, an insurance man, a cabinet-maker, a grocer and an artist. We have named ourselves for our leader, Maurice "Jake" Day, known to his Rangers as "the Colonel." To the rest of the world, he is Maurice Day—artist, naturalist and authority on the woods and waters of the Pine Tree State. His nationally known watercolors of wilderness Maine are considered important regional documents, and in many of them, his favorite wild animal appears. Appropriately, it's the whitetail deer.

Every group of hunters, by tradition, has to have an old-timer, a colorful character or highly developed curmudgeon who is an unfailing source of camp anecdote and humor. Our candidate in this field—the man who sets Jake's Rangers apart from all other groups—is Uncle George Whitehouse, age 74.

Uncle George, who used to be a boat-builder and almost everything else, weighs in at around a 106 pounds. In build, he is virtually one-dimensional—like a canoe pole. Despite the spareness of his frame, his feats of strength and conquests of all types, as reported by himself, are without equal. He has rigged more topmasts on more four-masted schooners, felled more trees, shot more and bigger deer at greater distances, and run wilder rapids in smaller canoes—or just on logs—than any man alive. He doubts nothing that he says. His chief characteristic is his halo of invincibility.

Jake's Rangers regard Uncle George as an endowment. He is in residence year-round in the deer-hunting camp at Sprague's Falls on the Narraguagus River, near Cherryfield in Washington County. This is fortunate, because when the camp—an old farmhouse—showed signs of sagging at the sills, it was nothing for Uncle George, alone, to hold the building off the ground with one hand while he shored it up with the other.

Annually, before departing for camp and Uncle George, the Rangers go through a stage of high-octane anticipation. It has become a kind of ritual: listing and packing supplies, sighting in rifles at the local range, airing sleeping bags, applying the whetstone to hunting knives, switching from white handkerchiefs to red ones.

Bentley Glidden, Damariscotta's postmaster, invariably squeezes rare juices of drama from these preliminaries. He telephones his fellow Rangers at odd hours. You pick up the receiver. A sepulchral voice comes over the wire:

"Is your waterproof match safe full?" Or, "Have you remembered your compass?" Or, "Only *you* can prevent forest fires."

Bentley is a rotund, merry and uninhibited organizer. If you step into his Post Office in mid-October, with the opening of deer season still two weeks hence, your name is sure to be called loudly and jubilantly. Bent will snatch you into his back room and read you the camp menu for the entire ten days:

"Friday, first night in camp: hamburgers, onions, mashed potato. Saturday, opening-day night: deer liver (?) and bacon or baked beans."

Sometimes, without a word, Bent will hand you a slip of paper, turn his back on you and disappear into the darker confines of the Post Office. This year I got the paper treatment twice. The first listed the personnel of the trip as follows:

Jake (our leader), Mac (McClure Day, our veterinary surgeon, who is Jake's son), Eddie Pierce (who owns Yellow Front Grocery), Dr. Sam Belknap (The Rangers' physician), Jack (Bentley's brother, our insurance man), Bud Hauglund (Railway Express agent, a newcomer), Louis Doe (mayor of the nearby village of Sheepscott), Ed Smith (yours truly) and Bentley Glidden.

The explanatory parentheses are mine. The final words addressed to me, are Bentley's. They follow: "Please remember that you were inducted into Jake's Rangers during Be Kind to Animals Week."

The second paper that Bentley slipped me was a command that I obeyed with pleasure. It read:

"Have your station wagon in the alley back of Eddie Pierce's store at three-thirty, Thursday, October 30."

[Signed] Sgt. B. Glidden, Jake's Rangers.

The loading of grub and supplies in Eddie Pierce's back alley is always a ceremony. It's the last act in Bentley's anticipation byplay and is attended by all Rangers able to sneak a few minutes off from work. Bentley had read the camp menu to all of us, and now—passing carton by carton over the tailgate of my wagon—was the reality: a colossal turkey, an Olympian ham, a classic corned-beef brisket, enough hamburger to equip a diner, bacon, flour, canned fruits, juices, vegetables.

As the last parcel was loaded, a bystander nearby remarked with heavy sarcasm: "You poor guys are going to starve up there in the woods."

"Oh, no," Bent replied airily, "we'll eke this out with some venison and partridge."

I locked the tailgate carefully over all this bounty, drove home and locked the wagon in my barn. I was to pick up Bentley at daylight, and we were to drive to camp ahead of the others in order to make things ready and establish peace with Uncle George.

We had had five straight days of rain, but Friday morning was as clear as a bell, with mist veils hanging low in the valleys and the color of the last, lingering foliage painting the ridges in the sunrise.

Camden, Belfast, Bucksport, Ellsworth. The towns flashed by, and everywhere you could see signs announcing: "Hunters' Breakfast— 4 a.m. to 8 a.m."

We saw other hunters heading toward their camps. Tomorrow, November first, was opening day, and the deer-hunting clans were on their way to rendezvous.

Beyond Ellsworth, the road traversed the shore of Tunk Lake, with Tunk Mountain to the north. Then the magic turnoff toward Sprague's Falls, the end of blacktop, then narrow, rutted gravel. Jake's Rangers' headquarters is the last farmhouse at the dead end of Sprague Falls Road. There, Uncle George, in his tattered checked shirt, greeted us from 30 feet in the air. He was prancing along the ridgepole of the house, where he had been examining a chimney for smoke leaks.

I held my breath while Uncle George, all the time waving at us, danced down an intricate system of ladders to the ground.

"I was scared you'd fall, Uncle George," I said.

"Five, ten years ago," he said, "I'd of jumped. Once, in a shipyard in East Boothbay, I jumped sixty feet from the topmast of a—"

"Never mind, Uncle George," Bentley said. "How's the supply of firewood?"

Uncle George gave Bent an outraged look.

"Firewood? When that chimney might leak flame? Burn us all to a cinder? Would *you* of cut any?"

Uncle George was in splendid form. So was the chimney. And I had a newly filed bucksaw and an axe in the wagon.

While we unloaded the supplies, Uncle George told of new enemies he had made during the past months and of his plans for disposing of them. He had done in quite a few of them, when Bentley interrupted with The Great Hardy Perennial Hunters' Question:

"Are there many deer around, Uncle George?"

"Not a one. No deer at all."

Bent and I looked at each other in a flood of relief. Uncle George's reply was a surefire omen that the whitetails were plentiful. So eager were we to relay the glad tidings that we could hardly wait for the arrival of the rest of the Rangers. But the time went fast, and with the thunder of Sprague's Falls familiar in our ears, we went to work cutting wood, policing camp and stacking supplies on the shelves.

The smell of your hunting camp, as you step across the threshold for the first time in a year, is as familiar as the palm of your hand. There's the smoke of old fires, oilcloth, coffee, kerosene, soap, gun oil, cedar kindling and, on rainy days, the steam of damp wool and leather and rubber.

That first noon, while we were eating the lunch our wives had prepared for us, Bent and I noticed a strange new odor in camp.

Uncle George had loftily disdained to share our lunch and, instead, opened the door to his iceless, wooden icebox. The box contained nothing save a fragment of dried pollock, and the new scent emanated from the pollock. I don't know how long Uncle George had been nourishing himself from this item, but it had a perfume definitely redolent of an old Model pollock.

The old-timer shaved off a portion with his jackknife, chewed it with relish, and closed the icebox door, lest the remainder escape under its own power. The scent of mink bait vanished with the closing of the box, and we were at peace again—until Uncle George fired us up with the one burning rumor that can galvanize any hunting camp.

"I hear," he said, "that there's a white buck around."

Even if the rumor was one of Uncle George's invention, the Rangers' hunt was made. All of us would be buoyant with the individual dream of at least a running shot at the white buck.

Jake Day and Mac drove into the dooryard at midafternoon. Before they had their rifles in the rack, Bent had told them of the rumored prize. They asked Uncle George if he had seen the great white creature.

At the outset, Uncle George had just heard. Now, it developed, he had seen.

"How many points?" asked Jake.

"Where was he?" asked Mac.

Uncle George waved a hand toward the wilderness stretching northward. His gesture was wide enough to include Tunk, Bog, McCabe and Spring River Mountains, together with a 50-degree segment of the Great Barrens—in all, roughly 70 square miles.

"Right there," said Uncle George, "is where I saw him."

By the time Jack Glidden, Eddie Pierce, Dr. Sam and Bud Haugland arrived, it was dark. The night was still, except for the hollow rumble of Sprague's Falls—a sound that is built into the rafters of the old house. In a matter of a few hours, the white buck had ceased being a rumor. He was real. He was somewhere. He was everyone's goal, the substance of everyone's wakeful dreams that first night in camp.

Which rifle in the gunrack would have the honor? Would any of them?

I lay in my sleeping bag, wondering and visualizing the gleaming barrels. Most of the guns had names: "Cosmic Ray," a couple of "Betsys," and "Old Meat in the Pot"—and then there was Mac Day's .243, which came to be known as "Little Evil."

Bent and I cooked opening-day breakfast by lamplight, while, by custom, Dr. Sam made the toast and prepared the noonday sandwiches with his camp buddy, Eddie Pierce.

"Where you going to hunt today?"

That's the breakfast question. You hear it a dozen times every morning for the hunt's duration. A good question. If you know where your people are working, you avoid accidents. If a man gets lost, you know where to start looking.

Bent and Jack Glidden headed for the "Bowl," Bud for the "River Trail," Dr. Sam and Eddie for "Split Rock." These are landmark names first coined by Jake's Rangers. They are not on any map but our own. Other hunters range the same places, knowing them by different names.

Jake, Mac and I took our rifles from the rack, crossed the decaying wooden bridge at the Falls, and started out toward the Barrens. This vast, boulder-strewn area is grown to scrub oak, small beech and other hardwoods, with occasional "islands" of spruce and fir. Its high plateau fans off for miles. In the past, millions of feet of pine logs have been harvested from this reach and, latterly, millions of bushels of blueberries. An ancient tote road makes the gradual ascent to the plateau.

Mac left us and struck out alone into the woods to the westward. We watched him go. You could see his red shirt and cap, and the yellow glow of his *Fire-Glo* vest. You saw a good woodsman in action—hand instinctively fending off the sharp twig and eyes focused yards ahead, channeling the way the foot would travel, estimating the slant of ledge or boulder, testing by sight and memory the traction of the trail, and the rifle—Little Evil—cradled in his elbow, a part of the man. It has a peculiar grace and is a nice thing to see.

When Jake and I reached the Barrens, the wind had picked up to a half-gale. We heard voices, and a group of four hunters emerged from a thicket—three boys and an older man who bore the stamp of experience. His name was Grant, and he told us they hadn't seen even a track since daylight. The younger boys looked discouraged. They were pulling out for new territory.

When they had gone, Jake and I sat behind a huge boulder, out of the chill wind. Jake told of his experience of the previous year—how he was walking along the Barren's trail and a buck crossed ten yards in front of him, how he put his rifle to his shoulder, and then how a partridge boomed right up into his face between him and the deer.

"That buck should have credited the partridge with an assist," Jake said—and then we heard a shot.

Shots always fill you full of excited speculations. They have tremendous mystery—even the far ones that sound like someone whispering *pow* in your ear. Each one can mean drama or climax or both. The shot we'd just heard sounded sharp, and there wasn't a second shot. Just that single, powerful, *cr-rack!*

"That could be Mac and Little Evil," I said.

Jake was on his feet, and we hurried down the trail over which we'd just come. Two minutes later, we froze in our tracks. Three or four rifles were blazing away. You couldn't count the shots. You could tell the *Bat-bat-bat*—of an automatic. The slower cadence of a lever-action. Then came silence, except for the wind hollering in our ears.

We went on cautiously around a couple of bends in the trail. Ahead of us, standing in a group, we saw six hunters. Two of them were Mac Day and Dr. Sam Belknap; the other four were the Grant party—the discouraged ones. But they weren't discouraged now. They were dressing out a handsome doe. Mac had sighted the doe, and his shot had driven the animal up to the Grant boys.

When Jake and I joined the group, the tall Grant brother—the experienced one—was giving his boys a stern lecture on too much shooting. You couldn't blame the kids for their excitement. But it was a sound lecture, just the same.

"We had the doe after the first shot," said the older Grant. "All the other shots did was ruin good meat. You kids think of that next time. You want to have some respect for your deer."

That was a good speech, and as we started back toward camp, I thought how those boys would remember it, and someday tell their own boys the same thing.

None of the other Rangers were at camp when Jake and I got back. But Uncle George was there, and he was in a cold, trembling fury, his eyes flaming like a blow-torch. The object of his wrath was a group of Connecticut hunters who had just parked their car in our dooryard and were standing around it with their rifles. Our dooryard is the customary parking place for hunters in this vicinity, simply because there is no other place.

Uncle George now stated that they ought to pay a parking fee, and that the Connecticut hunters owed him for two years, besides this one.

He would take it out of their hides.

We watched while Uncle George, picking up a stout cudgel, went out to assault the army from Connecticut. This is what we saw.

Uncle George crossing the yard to the car under the apple tree, eagerly and companionably shaking hands with all four hunters; smiles of welcome and goodwill on all faces; a tall, red-coated Connecticut man handing Uncle George a bill; Uncle George waving the billed hand away in austere refusal.

And then we heard Uncle George say:

"You boys park here any time you want, day or night. Always glad to see you coming back."

I don't know whether it's more fun to hunt the daylight hours to the full or to spend an afternoon in camp looking up the trail, watching the Rangers come in one by one or two by two, and listening to their individual stories as they arrive at the door, unload their rifles, place them in the gun rack, take off their wet boots, and stretch their weary feet toward the fireplace fire. But this first afternoon after Jake and Mac left for The Big Pine, I decided to stay in and nurse a toe blister.

Bud Haugland came in about three o'clock.

"Any excitement, Bud?"

Bud grinned.

"An open, running shot—not twenty yards away. It was just now, a couple of hundred yards from camp."

"I didn't hear the shot—and I've been listening hard."

"There wasn't any shot," Bud said. "The safety was on."

The shadows got long. Bud cleaned lamp chimneys and filled lamps. Together, we worked up a woodpile and stacked it on the back porch.

Mac and Jake came in. No story. Dr. Sam and Eddie Pierce came in. No story.

"You boys don't seem to be very good hunters," remarked Uncle George. "I always had my buck—a big one—hung up before seven o'clock in the morning on opening day. Sixty years running."

Bud got up and lighted the big lamp over the dining table. It was twilight outside, with full dark beginning to hover down. There was that moment of anxiety so well known to any hunting camp, that strange dread of a hunter lost, of darkness. Two men were missing.

"Where did Bentley and Jack go?" Jake asked.

"The Bowl," said Dr. Sam, who has a way of keeping track of

such things.

"Maybe they got on the white buck's track," Eddie said. "That could keep them out late."

Jake began to pace up and down in front of the fireplace. Mac looked at his compass and at the framed map on the long table.

Then came the familiar voices just outside the front door. There also came a heavy thud, a groan—as in relief at dropping a heavy burden after a long, rugged haul. We grabbed flashlights and rushed outside.

Bentley and Jack, their backs steaming in the chill air, stood beside the eight-pointer they had shot on the edge of the Bowl and lugged in over that rough terrain on a pole. First buck! First blood! Opening day.

"I was sitting there on a stump," said Bentley, "and Jack sitting right near me, when I saw this deer come sneaking along—"

Both boys had fired. Both had connected. The buck had dropped instantly. Supper that night was deer liver and bacon.

The things you remember about the days and nights in camp—the things that keep coming back! The sounds of going to bed, the bunk springs twanging, the boots thudding on the floor; the penny-ante poker game with Uncle George standing by, telling of the times he had risked a thousand dollars on a single turn of a card; the chain-reaction coffee that Jack Glidden made; the day Bentley saw the black bear; the reshuffling of the contents of duffel bags, choosing the proper clothes against the probabilities of weather; the Sundays in camp—no hunting, but visiting with other hunters. And had anyone caught a glimpse of the white buck?

One afternoon it rained hard. That morning, Uncle George had told me of two mongrel dogs belonging to a neighbor, and how he planned to do away with them. They stole his food, he said, which was why he kept his dried pollock in the iceless icebox. He had decided to pinch off the animals' heads with his own hands, but only after inflicting tortures of a surgical nature.

When the rain started that afternoon, and I came back from hunting the river, I stepped into the clearing and saw Uncle George and the dogs on the back steps. He was feeding the creatures choice scraps and speaking to them in words of endearment, all the while fondling their ears. To save Uncle George the shame and guilt of being caught red-handed in an act of tenderness, I remained hidden till the scene broke up.

That was the afternoon Jake tagged an eight-pointer in the rain. He and Mac lugged it in and hung it alongside the Glidden boys' deer in the cellar under the farmhouse. It was a perfect mate for Jack's and Bentley's.

"I had just stepped over a little knoll," said Jake, "and I heard this noise, and I stopped still and—"

A clean shot high on the backbone. No spoilage.

Through the years, Jake's Rangers have had a high of nine deer, which was one apiece for that year. The low was three. This trip was about average, with a total of four. Dr. Sam tagged a fat and highly edible spikehorn near Wasse's Beaver dam on about the fifth or sixth day.

I remember it was the day I left camp late in the morning, because I saw the Rural Delivery mailman stop at Uncle George's mailbox—the last mailbox on Sprague Falls Road. Uncle George sprang hopefully from the front door and opened the box. Whatever was in it was for the Smith Camp across the river. The old-timer shook his head dejectedly.

"Nothing for me again," he said.

"Were you expecting a letter?" I asked.

"It's a long time," he sighed, "since I've heard from Theda Bara."

Jake's Rangers are a bunch of hardworking, resourceful hunters, and most of them are on the go from daylight till dark. I am content with a few hours. Maybe it's middle age or a slight lameness in my back. Or maybe it's just that I can get as big a heart bump out of someone else shooting a deer as if I did it myself.

That's probably a false statement, but on this particular day it wasn't.

Mac Day and Jake came in from their hunting on "The Mountain," a wild, rocky nubble on the west side of the river. Excitement was all over them like flame, and it caught me in its contagion. Mac drew his hunting knife and showed me the blade. It had a yellow-white coating.

"What's that, Mac?"

"It's not candle wax!"

"You got the white buck!"

"Yes—me and Little Evil. We need help hauling him in."

Then Mac told it. He had been catfooting near the top of the mountain, Jake right behind him with his camera. He had stepped up on a rock, and there in a little draw, not 60 feet away, stood the white buck. The deer dropped with Mac's first shot, lifted its head once, then slowly sank back, still.

It turned out that the famous buck wasn't pure white, but calico.

But it was an experience Mac and Jake will never forget, nor will I as I heard them tell the story.

As I write this, soon after the Rangers' return home, the four deer are hanging in the big, walk-in freezer in Eddie Pierce's grocery store. Hometown people go in for a look now and then, and anytime you happen to meet Jake, or Jack, or Bentley, or Dr. Sam, or Mac on Main Street, you can ask for the story, and it will begin with minor variations on deer hunting's immortal, and forever original opening line:

"I was standing on a spruce knoll, when I heard this deer coming."

As for Uncle George Whitehouse, I feel it just and proper that he should have the last word. There is a moment of something like sadness when you stand at the camp door and say good-bye for a year. It was particularly so when I said good-bye to Uncle George.

As I looked around over the land and forest, I thought of the snow that would come inevitably, the road closed in drifts that would cover the mailbox, the smoke from the chimney lonely and torn in the winter wind, and the old man huddled by the fire.

"Are you going to winter here?" I asked, as we shook hands.

"No," said Uncle George, nibbling the last of his dried pollock, "I've been thinking some of the French Riviera."

TRUTHFUL SAM
By Charley Dickey

First published as one of Dickey's popular "Backtrack" columns for Petersen's Hunting *magazine, this piece subsequently was included in an Amwell Press book with the title* Backtrack *(1977), which brought together a collection of those columns. It also appeared in Lamar Underwood's (Editor),* The Deer Book *(1980). A son of the Tennessee soil who became an exemplar of what it meant to be an "all rounder" in the world of freelance writing on the outdoors, Dickey was the leading light in a group of Volunteer State writers from the latter half of the last century, along with his brother, David, H. Lea Lawrence, Evan Means and Doc Jernigan who were sometimes referred to as the "Tennessee Mafia." Here we see Dickey at his outstanding best.*

Dear Sam,
    It is that time of year again! My husband is planning to spend a week at deer camp, the same as every fall. I have heard many wild stories about what goes on at these camps. Some are disturbing, so much so that I am not keen about my husband going. Could you please tell me the truth about life at a deer camp? Signed, *Anxious*

    Dear Ann,
    I realize that certain wild rumors have been circulating about deer hunting camps. It is really a mystery to me how they get started and exaggerated.
    I hear from many deer widows each fall. For 40 years, I have hunted at camps all over America. The following is a truthful description of a typical deer lodge.

Various chores are divided among the hunters. For instance, one hunter, usually with a scientific background, is named nutritionist. His main duty is to insure a balanced diet so that general health is maintained. He makes sure there are leafy foods to provide bulk and an even balance of green and yellow vegetables along with a high-protein serving. Vitamin supplements, in moderate dosage, are available at each meal.

Although pack-in conditions may preclude fresh fruit juices and whole milk, adequate substitutes of concentrated juices and powdered milk are provided. Beverages containing high caffeine content, such as coffee and tea, are discouraged. Small amounts of alcohol are permitted, but only for medicinal purposes. For instance, a hunter may arrive back at camp with aching calf muscles. The alcohol is massaged into the legs much like a liniment to increase circulation and relieve tense muscles.

A few camps may allow moderate amounts of wine, but this is strictly for cooking. For instance, two or three tablespoons of red wine may be added to venison a couple of minutes before serving. As you know, cooking removes the alcoholic content. In essence, wine is used only as a flavoring.

Of course, there is no need for cocktails such as martinis or Manhattans. The daily exercise in the stimulating fresh air, the rejuvenation of the spirit by communing with nature, and the relief from normal urban tensions—all dispel the desire for relaxants. The thought of a cocktail simply never occurs to a deer hunter.

Although the routines at different camps may vary, here is a typical schedule. At 4 a.m., the nutritionist quietly arises and begins to prepare a wholesome breakfast. At 4:30 a.m., the physical culture instructor gently awakens everyone. He then leads the group through 30 minutes of stretching and bending exercises to condition the muscles and joints for the morning hiking.

Following the yoga-like exercises, the chaplain of the day reads a spiritual paragraph or two appropriate for all religions. This is followed by 10 minutes of silent meditation; each hunter is free to let his spirit roam and dwell on metaphysical thoughts.

Breakfast is leisurely partaken, with no need to rush. The early awakening insures a calm atmosphere. It is still an hour before sunrise and each hunter has time to shave and thoroughly brush his teeth.

Naturally, the terrain, cover and general hunting conditions determine whether the hunters stay out all day or return to camp about noon. There is often a joyful contest to see who will get back first, the winner having the privilege of tidying up the camp.

Following grace, a light luncheon is served to the hunters. Perhaps 15 to 30 minutes are spent in a group discussion of the various wildflowers or unusual songbirds that were seen during the morning hunt. The hunters then take a quiet siesta, refreshing their minds and bodies before the afternoon hunt.

As the men return to camp near dusk, they compete in a spirit of good humor to see who will have the honor of doing the most difficult chores, such as cutting firewood. When all work is completed in preparation for the next day, there is a devotional period. The hunters sit in a circle and each relates his most gratifying spiritual experience of the day.

After a strenuous day in the great outdoors, the men are ravenous. If there is one small criticism of deer camps, it is that sometimes grace is overly long. Dinner is a relaxed time of good-natured banter, the men relating humorous incidents of the day or those of other years.

Cleanliness is next to godliness at deer camps. It is an inflexible tradition. After the dishes are sanitized, the men retire to a nearby creek where they plunge in, no matter how cold the water, to bathe. In extremely inclement weather, it may be necessary to heat water in a tub for a sponge bath, but the hunters always cheerfully make do with what they have.

To me, the most pleasant part of the day seems to spring up spontaneously. Someone will begin to hum an old spiritual and in a moment he will be joined by another. A clear tenor picks up with the words and is quickly joined by a baritone. A deep bass comes in with the *bum, bums* and suddenly the camp bursts into song as everyone joins in.

What joyous times these are as the merry men sing *Tenting Tonight* and *It's a Long Way to Tipperary!* They gloriously go through their repertoires of Gay Nineties songs and the popular favorites of the Big Band days. You wish that it would go on all night, but everyone realizes there is a long morrow ahead. The tenor leads into *God Bless America* and the rafters fairly come out of their sockets.

The farewell chorus of the evening is always *Swing Low, Sweet*

Chariot. The chaplain reads a bit of inspirational poetry and the hunters bid each other sweet dreams and climb into their bunks. In a few moments, all is quiet except for gentle snoring as the men sleep to restore their weary bodies.

Ann, you need have no worries about your husband at a deer camp. This is a typical day at any camp. Signed, *Truthful Sam*.

WOMEN OWN THE WORLD
By Mike Gaddis

Women may indeed own the world, but they'll never buy into what is truly important to a deer-hunting husband. It is this truism that Mike Gaddis explores in his First Light column for the November/December 2001 issue of Sporting Classics.

Sometimes, loving a woman means you have to live with one.
 We were freshly retired, early-a-purpose, for I was huntin' in the morning. I was drifting off, the deer I had been after for a month was semi-sneaking in under the stand, and I had started slowly . . . slowly . . . to draw the bow.

"What time are you getting up," Loretta asked abruptly, rolling over and poking me with the same query I've suffered for 37 years.

I awoke so suddenly the arrow fell off the rest.

"Uhhmm . . . uhh . . . what?"

"I said, what time are you getting up in the morning?"

"I don't wanna think about it," I muttered. "It makes it worse.

"*Early,*" I submitted.

"That's what you always say," she argued.

"Good, then next time you won't need to ask . . . go to sleep." I was careful to be polite.

Not careful enough.

Pretending past the alarm a few hours later, she was waiting at the back door as I arrived in my jockey shorts and boots, freshly showered in no-scent soap. I was on my way to the barn for my huntin' clothes. Scent contamination, you know. This way, they smelled like horses.

She was laughing. She always laughs.

"They didn't tell me this when I married you," she declared.

"You're a sight, you know, standing there in your baggy shorts and floppy brogans."

Baggy? I hadn't noticed baggy. "They're not brogans," I countered. It wasn't much of a retort. It *was* early.

"You going to get your clothes?" she asked. An obvious question, I thought. *Yes.*

"Are those the ones you have me wash in that non-scented, ultra-violent soap?"

"Ultra-violet," I corrected.

"What about violets?"

Oh, Boy.

"Is it really necessary to walk to the barn with no clothes on?" she continued.

"The horses don't laugh," I said, pleased with myself. She didn't smile.

"I don't want to put on anything inside after I've washed, okay?" Again, I was polite.

"Be right back," I promised.

Returning, I stopped on the deck, applying fox offal to my boots.

Loretta stepped out in her powder blue robe, sipping a cup of tea. She watched contemptuously, screwing up her nose.

"What is that stuff," she snorted, retreating a step or two. "It stinks awfully."

I didn't want to, but I had to admire the "awfully."

"Cover-up scent. Fox pee," I answered, avoiding the harsher word. I was capable of a little refinement myself.

"I don't understand," she crooned innocently. "You just bathed in scent-killing soap, you air-washed to the barn, and you've got on scent-free, ultra-violent clothes.

What's to cover up?"

This was world class, a new record in refractory logic.

"By the way," she followed, smiling brightly, "we're out of turkey. You didn't want a sandwich, did you?"

I surrendered. I pecked her on the cheek and just walked away into the night. Smugly, however.

When I got to the stand, I fished out the tube of super-stuff estrus gel, smiled to myself, and felt in my rear pocket for the tampon I'd snuck from her vanity closet. Startled, I felt again. It wasn't there. I wondered a moment, then silently mumbled it away.

Now I was gladly up a tree, celibate for a while.

At 7:20, two does frittered in. I sat at ease, enjoying the grace of their measured motion and the ever-vigilant cadence of their feeding.

At 8:40, three more arrived, joining the others within 30 yards of my stand. Munching acorns.

A half-hour later, they remained, loafing and grooming. Nice, but I needed to invite 'em elsewhere. I'd been on the stand now, captively immobile, for an hour-and-a-half. I was stiff and cramped. More than that, nature was calling and my bottle was in the pack under the seat. I couldn't move; I'd blow the stand. No deer hunter worth a snort blows his stand!

Mental control . . . it was time for mental control. Time to dampen the neurology that was flogging my brain with the insistence my bladder was tagging out. I'd done it before. It had limitations.

Fifteen minutes . . . outside.

I was well into constrictive meditation when one of the does squatted. An ugly thing, what envy can do to a grown man.

Fifteen minutes later, my lady friends were yet at hand. I was hanging on. I had too. It was a male thing. The call of Nature was now a shout.

Phase two . . . direct pressure. At the pinch of engagement, a wave of heat scorched my entire body. I crossed my legs and applied adduction. It took five minutes under watchful feminine eyes to complete the maneuver.

Thank God for the Nautilus circuit. My bow tottered precautiously on one knee. Privilege had worn into persecution. I had an urge to just jump up and holler "Uncle!" at the top of my lungs. What were a bunch of does anyway? I wanted antlers. The answer came simultaneously. Does draw bucks . . . bucks have antlers. Great. I was lapsing simple-minded.

I could just let go . . .

How sweet the relief would be. If I monitored the discharge, the result would be a slow wick down my pants and into my boots. The deer would be none the wiser. I'd be warm for a minute and then . . . It was tempting . . . for a moment.

Okay, alternate strategy. I'd go for broke and stand up. Maybe the pressure would ease. I'd gain a few minutes. I down-shifted to mental constriction, then started the eternal ascent to plantigrade, edging up the tree trunk like an inch-worm. The does fed on, endlessly.

It didn't help. I was too far gone. Any one of the next several moments the escape valve would blow and it'd all be academic.

I heard once about a man who went around peeing in deer scrapes. Odd, I had thought.

"Different with urine," he had asserted. I wondered, desperately.

Slowly, I fumbled open the bay. It took forever, while I did a stifled tango on a two-foot stage 30 feet high. I'd try for an intermittent, controlled release. Maybe they would think it was rain. *Loretta would love this*, I thought, me breaking my cool and trickling onto my ultra-violent pants. The first drops hit the dogwood leaves and dribbled to the ground.

What if they noticed the sky was clear!

The nearest pair raised their heads, looking. One walked over and sniffed the ground. Nothing. Encouraged, I disengaged anew. Another few rounds and it was mercifully over, deer unperturbed. Proud of myself, I sank weakly against the tree, basking in the after-glow.

Suddenly, all five jerked their heads up, toward the hillside behind me. I turned carefully, following their line of vision. A tremendous eight-point sauntered out, stopping about 45 yards behind two does. *Come on. Come on.* He didn't, just stood there stock-still for ten minutes, staring. They couldn't see me. I was camo, head to toe. Venturing, I grunted softly.

The big boy flared, swelled up on his toes, staring still. Meanwhile, one of the does tippy-toed a few steps forward, staring the more. My mind was reeling. What? Finally, she blew, whirled and flounced contemptuously off, her nose in the air. The horns left with her.

Collapsing against the tree, my eyes fell despondently for my feet.

Halfway, they froze, the revelation as ludicrous as the supposition. Sheepishly, I grinned, looked around, then reached down and slowly tugged my zipper back to the top.

Backing down the tree, I headed for home.

When I got there, the tampon was lying on the welcome mat. Above it was a terse, handwritten message: "The buck stopped here!"

Women own the world. I shoulda' stayed in bed.

UNCLE PERK'S DEER LURE
By Corey Ford

Originally published as one of his "The Lower Forty" columns in Field & Stream, *this story is Chapter 29 of* The Best of Corey Ford *(1975). It is vintage Ford in not only the cast of characters but with wry humor and a disparaging poke at all the folderol associated with sport (in this case, deer attractants or lures).*

Cousin Sid halted before his camp and blinked in surprise at the group of Lower Forty cars parked in the driveway. A murmur of voices came from inside, and a strange odor assailed his nostrils as he opened the door. His fellow members were gathered round the camp stove, stirring a dark brown mixture that exuded an overpowering aroma.

Cousin Sid gagged and held his breath. "What are you doing, boiling a skunk?" he asked.

"Come on in, Sid," Judge Parker said over his shoulder. "You won't even notice the smell once you get used to it."

Owl Eyes Osborn, the local warden, was checking off the items on his list. "Let's see, now. Ground meat bones, dried blood, asafetida . . . How about tincture of nicotine?"

"I've got some scrapings from Uncle Perk's corncob," Doc Hall said, adding them to the mixture. "That ought to do the job."

"Pair-r-rhops ye'd like some spoiled cabbage or a few rotten eggs," Mister MacNab suggested. "I can get them from the farmer at a vurra low pr-r-rice."

Cousin Sid rose on tiptoes to peer over their heads at the concoction on the stove. "What's it supposed to be?"

"Deer repellent," Owl Eyes replied. "It's the state biologists' formula. We make it up for folks to spread on their orchards and gardens. Never fails to drive the deer away."

"I—I don't understand." Cousin Sid was growing more confused. "Why do you want to drive the deer away with hunting season opening tomorrow?" he asked, bewildered.

Judge Parker took an empty medicine bottle from a carton, and held it upright while Doc Hall poured some of the concoction down its narrow neck.

"Guess you haven't heard," the Judge explained, "about that New York banker, Joel Timkins, who bought a summer place here. Well, it seems he's just leased the whole of Cedar Mountain, the best damn deer country in Hardscrabble—" he made a sweeping gesture with his hand "—and he's posted it so he and his city-slicker friends can have it all to themselves." He broke off and glared at Doc. "Careful how you pour that," he growled. "You've spilled half of it on my sleeve."

"Hold the bottle steady, then," Doc retorted. "The way you're waving your hand around, you're spattering it all over everybody."

Cousin Sid's confusion mounted. "What's Mr. Timkins got to do with this stuff you're making?" he persisted.

"It's Uncle Perk's idea." Judge Parker capped the full bottle and picked up another. "The trick is to spread this repellent around Timkins' posted land," he told Cousin Sid, "so the deer will hightail it out of there tomorrow and run past our stands where we'll be waiting."

"Who's going to spread it?" Sid faltered.

"Joel Timkins himself," Judge Parker smiled.

Cousin Sid shook his head in total bewilderment. "But how are you going to persuade anybody to spread deer repellent around his own—"

"That," said the Judge with a crafty wink, "is where the trick comes in." He screwed the cap on the last bottle and turned to Colonel Cobb. "You got those labels you ran off at your print shop?"

"Here," the Colonel nodded, handing him a sheaf of gummed papers.

Judge Parker peered at a label and chuckled with satisfaction. "Solve your hunting problem with deer lure," he read. "Guaranteed to bring that big buck right up to your gun."

He then proceeded to paste the labels on the bottles one by one, put them back in the carton, and hand the box to Owl Eyes.

"Will you drop this off at Uncle Perk's on your way back to town?" he asked. "Timkins phoned that he'd be coming to the store later this evening to buy some provisions." He grinned at the others as Owl Eyes departed. "The rest is up to Uncle Perk."

Cousin Sid gazed bleakly at his camp, which was smeared with the evil-smelling mixture. "How about cleaning up this mess?"

"Too late," the Judge yawned, stretching out on the sofa. "Time we all grabbed a little shuteye. We want to be out on our stands before dawn tomorrow, so we'll be ready when those deer come stampeding down off Cedar Mountain."

Uncle Perk leaned back in his swivel chair, puffing his corncob vigorously to offset the noxious odor of the bottles stacked on a shelf. The string of sleigh bells inside the front door jangled, and a stout figure with pince-nez glasses entered.

"I'm Joel Timkins," he announced. "I came to pick up those provisions I ordered—" his nose wrinkled. "Something dead in here?"

"Mos' likely it's the store mouse," Uncle Perk sighed. "Last coupla times I seen him, he didn't look none too healthy."

Joel Timkins held a handkerchief to his nose as Uncle Perk set his order on the counter. His eye encountered the row of bottles on the shelf before him. "Deer lure," he read. "Wotinell's that?"

"No hunter in these parts'd be without it," Uncle Perk shrugged. "Sold out my whole shipment today, except these last few bottles."

"How does it work?"

"Wal, you spread it around on the foliage and rub some on your hunting clothes, and them deer'll be attracted from miles away."

Mr. Timkins unscrewed the cap of a bottle, took a sniff and recapped it with a shudder. "Worst thing I ever smelt."

"That's 'cause you ain't a deer," Uncle Perk said calmly. "They think it's Paris parfum'ry. Can't resist it. One whiff, an' they'll run right to your stand. All you gotta do is shoot."

"So that's how you Yankee hunters get so many," Mr. Timkins nodded. "I'll take all the bottles you got left."

Uncle Perk watched his customer hurry out of the store, carrying the carton of Deer Lure gingerly at arm's length. He beamed contentedly, opened the front door wide, and threw up all the windows to air his store out.

"I calc'late the Lower Forty'll have a good openin' day tomorrow," he murmured.

Uncle Perk looked up from a copy of the *Hardscrabble Gazette* as his fellow members sidled into the store the following noon, heads hanging in dejection.

"No luck," Colonel Cobb reported glumly.

"Didn't get to fire a shot," added Doc Hall.

"Never saw a single deer all morning," Judge Parker muttered. "I can't explain it."

"Wal, I can," Uncle Perk grunted, backing away a few steps and averting his head. "Mebbe you fellers can't smell yourselves, but the way you slopped that repellent all over your clothes, I 'spect you drove every deer right back to Cedar Mountain."

He lit his corncob hastily and exhaled a protective cloud of smoke.

"My advice to you is burn them clothes 'an take a good bath before you go home," he added. "That stuff's prob'ly a wife repellent, too."

The Lower Forty turned in silence and filed sheepishly out of the store. Grumbling to himself, Uncle Perk hung a closed for inventory sign on the front door and took down his ancient rifle from a peg.

"Looks like I'll have to git the venison for the whole club as usual," he sighed resignedly.

YOU'VE GOT TO SUFFER
By Gordon MacQuarrie

First published in the March, 1945 issue of Outdoor Life, *this is one of the relatively few Old Duck Hunters Association pieces that departs from waterfowling and upland game. It later appeared in* Stories of the Old Duck Hunters & Other Drivel *(1967).*

The President of the Old Duck Hunters' Association, Inc. was waiting for me, so I had to get in there, even if the snow was a foot deep on the level and heavily drifted. I lay on my back in city clothes to jack up the rear wheels for tire chains, wishing that the guy who had designed those petticoat fenders was properly punished for his sins against a humanity, which at some time or other, simply must use auto chains.

The chains, momentum and good luck took me into a solid three-foot drift. Well, I got halfway through it. A half-hour of shoveling ensued, and then I turned off the back road on the narrow, twisting by-road.

It was a shambles of drooping pine trees. Jackpines 30 feet tall and up to five inches thick arched over the road, weighted down under tons of damp snow. A few clips with the pocket-ax, which I always carried in the car, snapped them; then, it was necessary to shake the clinging snow from them and drag them off the road.

There would be no deer hunting the next day—I was sure of that. Getting about in that snow would be impossible. But I had said I would get in there. The Old Man was waiting. It is amazing what a man will do to keep a date with the President of the Old Duck Hunters.

I was six hours behind schedule when I stopped the car beside Mister President's snow-shrouded car. I was sweating and unsteady afoot. There had been almost a whole day of nerve-racking driving in the storm before the final climactic effort to get over that last half-mile. I grabbed packsack and rifle and wallowed to the door of the place.

The Old Man was asleep, with his feet stretched toward the fireplace. I moved quietly. I put new wood on his fire, broke out my duffle and had the teakettle going in the kitchen before he awoke. He called from the big room, "That you, Tom?"

"Yep," I answered, sounding as much like Tom as I could.

"When did you get here?"

"Minute ago."

Tom is a neighbor who is likely to appear at the abode of the Old Duck Hunters almost any time.

The Old Man continued, still unsuspecting: "Where do you suppose that whelp of a boy is? Said he'd be here for supper, and it's midnight."

I heard him yawn and heard him wind his watch. Then he said, "Dammit, Tom, I'm worried. He might try to make it here in this storm, and he doesn't know the first thing about driving a car in snow."

"And never will. Don't worry about him. He'll hole up in some luxurious hotel down the line and wait for the snowplows."

That speech was too long. The Old Man's feet hit the floor, and he stamped to the kitchen, all sympathy vanished.

"You pup of a boy!" he snorted. "You lame-brained rooster!" He carried on over a snack of tea and toast. "Cars stuck all over the country. This is the worst storm ever hit this country before a deer season opening."

I looked around. He had brought in enough wood to last for several days. I said, "We'll just hole up, as long as we can't hunt."

"Not hunt!"

He had it all figured out. He'd looked over the nearby thoroughfare country in the storm and had found deer working down into it, out of the more open jackpine on higher ground.

"We'll hunt, all right!"

That was the last thing I heard before dropping off to sleep. I think I did not change my position once, and slept until noon, right around the clock.

"I'm saving you," he explained. "Had to get you in shape. You're going to make one little drive to me."

"I'm not mooching in this snow."

The Old Man pointed to the wall at the end of the room. "See those snowshoes? All you've done to them the last two years is varnish 'em. Today you're going to wear off some varnish."

It was bitter cold, near zero, after the snow had ceased and the clouds passed. All right, if the Old Man was going to sit on a stump in that weather, he was going to put on some clothing. I persuaded him, over his objections, to pile on plenty of underwear, a wool sweatshirt and a heavy outer shirt. He bulged rather ridiculously, I had to admit, with all that clothing, but for good measure, I made him carry along my huge, ungainly but wonderfully warm sheep-lined aviation boots.

He hated the clothes that bore him down. I knew what he wanted to wear—just his regular duck- or deer-season gear, which is not too much, topped off with the old brown mackinaw. He vowed that the only way a man could wait out a deer was to do a little personal freezing.

I had to laugh when he started out. He was so swaddled in clothes that he could hardly turn his neck above the shawl collar of the ancient mackinaw. But I did not laugh, for I was afraid he'd go back into the house and shed some of the garments, and in that searching cold, I could not see him suffering while I took what is really the easier course, moving and so keeping warm.

South of us lay Norway pine hill facing the thoroughfare, or river, between two lakes. Mister President had it all figured out. He would take an old stand at the top of Norway hill. I would circle to the south and west of him, then drive up through the thick cover lying at the edge of the thoroughfare. If anything with horns came through, he would have shooting as it hit the open Norway grove.

Northwest Wisconsin, in 20 years, never saw a storm like that one at that season. Nor did it, in that time, see cold like that so early, combined with deep snow. The freak storm kept hundreds out of the bush. It was the first day of the four-day buck season. We had the country practically to ourselves. Most of the army of hunters was waiting for the snow to settle or thaw. And a four-day doe season was coming up in seven days.

Mister President's self-imposed assignment was to mush through the snow for about a mile, hard going without snowshoes, which he does not like. I left him plodding through the stuff toward his stand and began the great circle which would bring me below him.

At any rate, that snow was good for snowshoeing. It had the solid permanence of snow that has lain and settled and proposes to stay until spring, which it most certainly did.

It felt good to be on snowshoes again, carrying a rifle. I went through a long pulpwood slashing. All the tracks in that slashing confirmed what Mister President had said—that deer were moving into the denser cover, away from the open pinelands. Down there along the thoroughfare's edge they could find protection and browse, even some white cedar, champion of all winter deer browse.

The slashing was lovely. A bluejay yammered at me. Chickadees hung upside down on branches. Will someone tell me how these minute wisps of down maintain their high spirits in the face of any weather? A red squirrel in a jackpine cussed me roundly: "Bad enough for this storm to come so early without you moving in on my property!"

Snow-bent jacks lopped to the southwest, for the snow had come from the northeast off Lake Superior. That storm gave the North a wonderful pruning. Old Lady Nature every so often throws one like that over her wild garden to nip off old branches, weed out the weak ones and compel the strong ones to prove it.

There was plenty of snow down my neck. Charlie Garvey, the forest ranger at Gordon, had warned me the evening before: "Stuff is down so much the rabbits can't get through." He knew, too, that the storm had pushed vast supplies of browse within reach of hungry deer.

Incidentally, before winter was finished in the North, the sly dame did the same thing on two more occasions, so deer got plenty to eat and the forests had a splendid pruning.

When I got to the thoroughfare where I was to turn back and drive north, I sat down a minute. At this place, the thoroughfare drops three feet. There were wings overhead, belated bluebills and early goldeneyes hunting water in the frozen lake country.

The sun was varnishing the jackpine tops as I began the drive. In the shadows, the snow was turning lavender. Downy and hairy woodpeckers hid behind tree trunks as I went along. The snowshoes creaked. I followed the thoroughfare edge. There was ice out from shore 40 yards at my right. At my left and ahead of me was thick cover.

There were many tracks, all old ones. Deer had certainly come down here out of the pinelands in the night. But where were they now? Then I saw a fresh track. You know how it is—that virgin white scar of a hoof in snow, so unlike the settled, stiffened track of 12 hours before.

The deer was moving ahead of me. Buck or doe? I do not know. Even in fresh mud I do not know, and I think that no one else can tell for certain. That track was big and brand-new. It was a mark left by a critter moving exactly the way the Old Duck Hunters wanted it to move—straight north toward the Old Man.

This deer was not plunging. It seemed to know my pace and kept just ahead of me. Likely it had heard me when I was a hundred yards away from it, had got up quietly and just sneaked away from me. You wonder at such times where the rascals get the wisdom to know that a man in snow cannot move rapidly. Deer can be very contemptuous of a man.

The wind was not a factor. There was a little drift from the northwest. Up in the open slashings it could be felt. Down along the thoroughfare bottoms, however, pipe smoke went straight up.

Sometimes this deer stayed on the beaten trails, which had been worked in the night before. Sometimes it cut across lots through fresh snow. Contemptuous of me? Indeed, and then some.

I saw where, during the night of the storm, deer had come into the thoroughfare bottoms and nibbled on cedar. Even the little fellows could live off a storm like that. Everything was caved in—trees formed solid white wigwams, branches drooped—as inviting a deer cafeteria as you might wish to see.

Why hadn't this big one moved out of the bottoms with the others? Was it an old grandfather or a grandmother that chose the easy living of this place to getting out of there and seeing country? Once I thought I saw it a hundred yards ahead, but that turned out to be mere flipping of white snow from a branch released from pressure—not a flag.

My deer had passed the place where the snow slid off the tree, a full 20 yards to the west. A calculating beggar, that animal. Just so far ahead of me—no farther.

Well, if a buck, it was venison on the pole. It went dead on toward a rendezvous with a .30-30 carbine held by a very steady old gentleman in an old brown mackinaw.

That critter had me figured out so well that sometimes it even stopped to browse. It would pay for that—if it was what Mister President called "a rooster deer." Contempt of court, that's what it was! Just wait until that old goat moved out from the thick stuff and started ambling through those open Norways! The Old Man has killed a half-dozen bucks from that stand. Most of them have dropped within an area not larger than a baseball diamond.

Good, I thought. *Whatever it was, it was right on the beam going in.*

The darkness drew down. Purple worked up to the zenith from the eastern sky. I moved that deer along the way a farm collie brings home the cows. Finally I saw him.

He was across an opening, perhaps a hundred yards off. He was big and dim. No question now what he was. He was "he." His rack went up and back like branches on an old oak. I might have had one quick fling at him, but why chance it? The Old Man was waiting, and it was better to move that deer into the open Norway grove. Then, if the first one didn't clip him, there would be other chances.

I went along. I know that terrain as well as the buck knew it—almost as well as the Old Man knows it. Pretty soon, up ahead, there would be a shot. Just one shot, it ought to be. That would be the Old Man's 150 grains of lead and copper going to its destination. Then silence—the sort of quiet after one shot that means so much to a deer hunter.

It was working out perfectly. In my mind's eye, I pictured the Old Man, alert on his hillside. I saw him scan the cover, saw the buck walk out and turn to listen along its back trail. I saw Mister President draw down on the buck, wait until the buck stood with cupped ears, raise the little rifle and squeeze it off. Yes, I even pictured him setting down the rifle and reaching for the big, bone-handled clasp-knife in his right hip pocket.

It was as easy as falling off a log. Mister President's formula had been right. If the ground had been bare, that buck might have busted through the Norway grove with his foot to the floorboard.

I wondered if we should drag him the mile home. Or if we should borrow Hank's toboggan, or just commandeer his truck, which has high wheels and is at home in deep snow. I decided that with the weather cold as it was we could dress him, hang him, cool him and have decent steaks by supper-time tomorrow.

Minutes passed. The Old Man would let him have it now. Or now. *Now, then!* The buck must be in the Norways at the foot of the hillside. Heavens above, he must be halfway up the hillside! I could see the big Norways ahead of me. The only sound was the creak of the snowshoes and the *kra-a-a-ak* of a raven.

I broke through the bottomland cover and faced the hillside. Over the hilltop in back of the old man, I saw the buck the second time, slowly and contemptuously effacing himself from me.

I took one quick shot. It was just a shot at a skulking shadow, and I knew as I pulled the trigger in the instant I had for shooting that I was over him a good two or three feet.

At the shot, Mister President waved to me from his stand. I trudged up the hill to him. He looked guilty.

"You git 'im?"

"Mister President, do not speak to me ever again."

He made a clean breast of it, then and there. "All right, I fell asleep. Your shot woke me."

It was plain as sin what had happened. Mister President had brushed the snow off a fallen Norway and sat there a while. He had lit a fire. He had banked browse against that two-foot-thick log so he could stretch out. Then—oh, my brethren!—he had fallen asleep.

"Dammit, I had too many clothes on," he said.

And then I just had to laugh. He wasn't the Mister President of other deer drives, chilled and lean and ready, with a drop on the end of his nose. He was swathed and cluttered with sleep-producing items, including those huge aviator's boots.

We went home, boiled the kettle, and ate pork chops and boiled potatoes. We drank quarts of tea. At bedtime, the Old Man announced: "If anyone tries to tell me what to wear tomorrow, I will resign the presidency of the Old Duck Hunters. I must have dozed there for two hours."

The next day, we did it again. The weather had moderated. He went to the same stand. I made the long swing south and west on the snowshoes and drove up through the thoroughfare bottoms. Making the drive, I knew that now the Old Man was standing there by his downed log in his thin swampers. I knew that sometimes he shivered, and sometimes he whapped his arms across his breast to get circulation going. I knew that he'd move up and down on his feet and wriggle his toes, and that he was standing there with his earlaps up, so that he could hear better.

The drive was easy. There were more deer in the bottoms along the thoroughfare. Plodding up through and watching the tracks ahead of me, I felt that I was pushing a whole herd into that Norway grove. One of them might be Old Horny—might be the same old fellow who beat the Old Duck Hunters yesterday, hands down.

Pow! He had shot just once. I came into the grove at the foot of the hillside, and Mister President called down to me: "He's lying over to your left. Four hens came out, and the rooster after them."

I do not know whether it was the same buck. I think it was another. The one on the day before seemed a larger animal. There he was, a good ten-pointer.

I called up the hill: "Bring your knife down here, and I'll dress him out."

He came sliding down the hill in the snow. "I'll dress him out myself. Maybe I can get warmed up that way."

Mister President was certainly a sight. His nose was red and his lips were blue. He was hunched and shivering beneath the old brown mackinaw. The wait in the cold had been a long one, but worth it. He went to work, and I went off to fetch Hank with his truck.

When we got back, the Old Man had finished the job—had even dragged the buck up his hillside and out to the road to meet the truck.

"Well, you sure got warmed up," I said.

"I did," he agreed. "But you got to suffer first."

PASSING THE BUCK
By *Charley Dickey*

First published in the November, 1974 issue of Florida Sportsman, *this piece is included in Dickey's* Backtrack (1977). *As he so often does, the author takes a mundane matter and has you smiling in short order.*

The biggest problem in going hunting is that you might kill something. This means you have to figure out some way of disposing of the meat without getting a guilty conscience. Of course, with the cost of red meat at the butcher's only a fraction under the ounce rate for raw gold, housewives are taking a closer look at rutty old bucks partly cooked on car radiators as triumphant hunters drive home.

The trouble is that the sports hunter has a rigid code of honor. Other than varmint shooting, his code demands that anything he shoots must be eaten. Further, the code requires that hunters loudly claim that any game is a great delicacy.

Some hunters insist that varmints are delectable table fare. Although they themselves have never eaten crow meat, they always have a handy story about some distant friend who eats it regularly and prefers it to roast grouse. For 20 years they have planned to eat crow, but for some obscure reason have not gotten around to it. In my experience, crow meat is not anything that will ever be written up in a gourmet magazine. However, it's considerably better than boiled owl.

If you are invited to a friend's home for venison dinner, the code expects you to declare the sinewy old buck roast you're cudding is more delicious than any U.S. prime filet mignon. The ethics of hunting demand this of you, even while you're choking and gasping on a chunk of unyielding gristle.

It is patently ridiculous to claim a scrawny deer existing on bark and leaves is infinitely more tasty than a sirloin steak from a steer fattened on feedlot grain. But any hunter will swear it, and become infuriated if you barely hint that the venison you're bending your knife on is a mite tough.

There is a certain hunter in Ocala who is invariably stricken with pangs of religion following a successful deer hunt. He takes his share of the venison, wraps it neatly in polyethylene bags and deposits them on the doorsteps of a minister. As though leaving a foundling in the night, he rings the doorbell and runs.

It's one way out of a desperate situation. He clears his conscience because he has not violated the hunter's code, taking it for granted that the minister will eat the meat or give it to the poor. Further, the hunter casually mentions his charitable work in the community. Without elaborating on specific details, he tells his friends that in his own way he is active at the church.

You may think this is an exaggeration about hunters, but have you ever known a preacher who owned a skinny cat?

The hunting season is one time the sportsman is glad he has a lot of relatives nearby. He magnanimously visits them for the first time in a year, proving his devotion by leaving behind a bag of deer shanks.

No one, in fact, becomes as benevolent as a hunter with a deer carcass. He types a variety of venison recipes and visits neighbors he hasn't nodded to for months. If a neighbor is so thoughtless as to suggest deer meat is not his favorite food, the hunter quickly shows him the recipes for stewing, roasting and how to prepare his own salami.

While pressing venison on reluctant friends, the hunter drags up old memories. He recalls his early boyhood when he went on his first big game hunt and his father roasted ribs over an open fire. Although he has since traveled the world over, he has never yet had such a delicate and tender morsel, not even in New Orleans or San Francisco.

His eyes become moist as he remembers that faraway time in his lost youth. All he is asking is that the neighbor have a chance to enjoy the ultimate culinary experience. The neighbor sees he cannot refuse and opens the freezer and deposits the package, right alongside freezer-burnt packages from the last three hunting seasons.

A compromise way of utilizing the deer is to have it ground up and padded out with beef. But this borders on violating the hunter's code. Further, it keeps the hunter from honestly bragging at the office about the tender and juicy steaks his family dined on the night before.

Every hunter who abides by the code develops his own method of disposing of his share of a deer. The favorite way to amortize a dead deer, almost a universal American tradition, is to invite one's friends for a venison dinner. This is one of those times in life when you find out who your true friends are.

They view your annual dinner the same way they look forward to visits from their mothers-in-law or a review of their income-tax returns by the IRS. There is a ritual which goes with it. All conversations about the dinner and during the dental contest are conducted in code.

When the hunter phones a friend to invite him, the friend says, "How wonderful. We were hoping you'd ask us this year."

Decoded, this means there's no way out of accepting.

On arriving at the hunter's home the night of the ordeal, the friend says, "I can't wait to get at that venison!" He tries hard to say it with sincerity and enthusiasm.

What he's really saying is, "I hope the meat was marinated in bicarbonate."

When the ancient buck is served, a guest tastes a small bite and says, "You know, it's hard to believe but this is even better than the venison we had last year."

Deciphered, it means, "If I cut the pieces small enough, I can wash them down without choking."

When a guest has a second helping urged on him, he hedges, "It's just great, but I ate too many hors d'oeuvres."

Translated this means, "Look, bud, how far do you want to push this friendship?"

Leaving the hunter's home, a guest says, "What a wonderful meal!"

Decoded this reads, "I *can't* believe I ate the whole thing."

Fortunately, there are several ways to overcome the wizened sinews of venison and make it chewable. If you have in your wine cabinet the remains of several bottles, pour the residues into a large crock and add your meat. Don't worry that you're mixing red wines and white, that you're crossing sweet wines with dry. That is not your problem. You cannot be timid. When you're loading a wildcat cartridge, you don't hold back on the powder.

Rather than marinating for a mere 24 hours, however, double the muzzle velocity with 48 hours of soaking. Don't hesitate to put in a dash of white vinegar, which adds extra cutting power.

Keep in mind that most people don't know how to cook with wines, much less what the food should taste like. There is a certain elegance and sophistication about using wines. Tell your guests that you used an old French recipe liberated by a World War II soldier during the occupation of Rheims. It was a secret formula from the Middle Ages a grateful monk donated to American culture. Not one of your guests will dare to make caustic comments about your venison. It adds to the atmosphere if you learn a few French words and toss them around.

As many hunter-chefs know, there is nothing unethical about using diversionary tactics. You prepare a big spread of gourmet novelties for appetizers such as snails, rattlesnake meat, chocolate-coated grasshoppers and fried locusts. These are expensive, but they help you abide by the code. They divert your guests in one of two ways: they are so repelled that venison suddenly sounds delicious, or, they show their courage by sampling the tidbits and after that, anything tastes good.

Barbecue sauce is great for camouflage. If you coat it thickly enough, the venison can't be tasted. Of course, this is contingent on all of your guests liking barbecue sauce. If they do, they are fully capable of eating anything on a shingle, if you shellac liberally with sauce.

As any old-time deer hunter will verify, the surest way to make certain your guests consume the venison is to cook it outside on a barbecue grill one hour after they arrive. To work this strategy, you should have a washtub filled with martinis. Keep it handy.

Hunters do not expect to drink from dainty goblets. Serve the martinis in water glasses. Remember that alcohol is a depressant, not a stimulant. When alcohol is ingested, it goes to the brain and the first part which is saturated is the center that controls judgment. That can't do anything but help your cause.

The first libation increases the appetite and releases inhibitions, both vital to your success. Additional potions numb the motor reflexes and even the taste buds. It's time to put the venison on the grill. If some of your friends wish to help with the cooking and basting, let them. Everyone needs allies.

If there are any doubts, refill the washtub. Serve the venison while it is piping hot. Your conscience should be clear as you have fulfilled the hunter's code by making sure the game you shot is eaten. But good!

ADVICE OF THE ONE-EYED POACHER

By Edmund Ware Smith

From The Further Adventures of the One-Eyed Poacher *(1947), this piece is a prime example of the inveigling tales Smith wove around the likeable renegade named Jeff Coongate. This selection reflects Smith's knowledge of setting and prevailing practices (jacklighting) in excellent fashion, and the delightful tidbits of irony so characteristic of his writings.*

I had known Jeff Coongate all of my life. So when I came last fall in November with my rifle, my canoe, my tent and a non-resident deer license, Uncle Jeff was the first person I looked for.

If you don't see Uncle Jeff brooding majestically on the public landing at the foot of the lake, there are simple rules for finding him. You can ask Zack Bourne, his lifelong partner in enterprises against the fish and game laws. You can ask Tom Corn, the game warden. Or you can drop around to the Mopang County jail, where the old poacher has whiled away many a hitch.

This time, I found Uncle Jeff standing by the canoe shed at the landing. At 70, he was as straight and supple as a canoe pole. In the crook of his left elbow, as if it had grown there, lay his battered old .45-70 Winchester. He was wearing moccasins without socks, a blue flannel shirt, dungarees and one suspender of clothesline. His one eye, a level, baleful blue, watered in the November chill, and his white mustache, notoriously icicle-bearing in winter, blew free and dry in the rising wind.

"Hello, Uncle Jeff," I said.

We were alone on the landing, and I guess the old woodsman had been half-dreaming. He had a remarkable store of dreams to draw from, too—some real, some not. It would make your scalp prickle to look at that rifle of his, if you knew half the things it had done. And his one eye had the look of horizons. The old-timer was an outlaw by any standard at all, yet he was an honest and respectable outlaw, and the game wardens were the first to admit it—specially Tom Corn.

Everyone loved and admired him, and I cherished his friendship. Ed Post, the turnkey at the Mopang jail, always grew melancholy when Uncle Jeff was released.

"Goin' to be a lonesome winter here," Ed told me once. "Old Jeff's time was up yesterday, and I got no one to spice up my life but a common horse thief."

Now, as he recognized me, Uncle Jeff's eye twinkled and he thrust out his immense hand.

"Howdy, son. What brings you back so close to freeze-up?"

"The deer season."

"Oh. Is it open?"

"Sure. Opened the first."

"It's always open for me," he said, "except on does with lambs."

He licked his lips, and somehow it brought you a picture of venison broiling on a sharpened stick and bread dunked in gravy.

"If the wind dies out, it'll be a good night to shine eyes. I know where a big ole buck hangs out. Want to come?"

It was always hard for me to decline Uncle Jeff's invitations. There was no reconciling our points of view, and my refusals made him wretched and irritable.

"No," I said, "you know I can't do that, Uncle Jeff."

He drew himself up, and his eye looked right through me.

"Young man, do you question my morrils?"

"No, it isn't that. But if I had anything to do with jacklighting a deer, I'd question my own morals."

"So be it, son," he said and, as sometimes before, I felt as though I were talking to a major prophet.

My canoe and outfit lay alongside the dock, and he was gazing at the works with an appraising eye. He moved his hand toward the canoe. It was an imperious gesture, like a god tossing a crumb to a mortal.

"That feller's got a good rig," he said. "The canoe's an Oldtown, and the paddle's second-growth ash. I wonder who belongs to it?"

"It's mine," I said. "You picked it out for me yourself couple years ago."

"That explains it," he said. "You tentin' out?"

"Yes. I want to go up beyond Leadmine Cove on the lake and hunt around there. But I've heard hunting's poor. I thought maybe you could tell me where I might find a deer."

The expression on Uncle Jeff's face indicated I had been guilty of bad etiquette. I should have realized that asking him the location of deer was about like asking an ordinary man for the loan of his wife. Still, I had just two days, and if anyone in all the Mopang country knew where the deer were, the one-eyed poacher was the man.

I was about to apologize for my question, when the notorious scheme-light flared in his eye. I should have been suspicious, but I wasn't.

"So you want to know where there's a buck, hey? All right. You take me to Zack Bourne's cabin above Leadmine Cove, an' I'll tell you."

Now, looking back on the way things happened, it seems nothing short of stupid that I didn't have an inkling of what was coming up. He had invited me to go jacklighting, which I was morally bound to refuse. He had said he knew where there was a buck. He did not say two bucks.

Immediately after my refusal, he had promised to reveal the whereabouts of this buck—on the condition that I would transport him to the cabin of his crony in a hundred crimes, Zack Bourne. If I hadn't been so intent on getting up-lake and getting my tent pitched, I might have guessed a lot of things—but not all of them, because you can't guess all the things about deer hunting.

"Could you wait just a few minutes?" I asked Uncle Jeff. "I want to pick up some supplies at Sim Pease's store."

Uncle Jeff sat down on a keg of molasses and said, "Sure. And—uh—might you do an errand for me while you're up to Sim's place?"

"Of course."

"Git me a bottle of Hernando's Fiery Dagger rum, some salt pork, an' half-a-box of .45-70 soft-point rifle ca'tridges."

He fished elaborately in his right-hand trouser pocket, then his left. He humped up off the keg and went through both hip pockets. He tried the two breast pockets in his flannel shirt and found nothing but a broken whetstone, a pipe bowl, two buttons, a faded clipping from the *Mopang Northern Light* carrying an account of his most recent arrest for salmon spearing in a closed fishway, and a dried cut of Old Jawbreaker chewing and smoking tobacco.

Patiently returning these items to their pockets, he gave me a look like a saint discovering pain for the first time, and said, "Son, I must of been robbed. Jest tell Sim to charge it. Be sure you get the rum. I got a couple ca'tridges left."

I went up the winding dirt road smiling to myself. I figured nothing but Fate would ever get the best of Thomas Jefferson Coongate.

Tom Corn, the game warden, was coming out of Sim's store as I went up the steps. He looked business-like in his uniform, and he had a good reputation in the lake and forest country. I told him where I was headed.

"Going in alone?" he asked. "Just so someone'll know where you are, in case you don't show up on time or get frozen in."

He wasn't being nosey. He was just being decently helpful, the way most wardens are nowadays.

"I was going alone, Tom," I said, "but I've picked up a passenger, as far as Zack Bourne's place."

Tom smiled on one side of his face. "Jeff Coongate?"

I nodded, feeling a little mean somehow, but Tom laughed and waved his hand, and as he walked away called over his shoulder: "You're traveling in fast company!" It made me feel better.

Inside the store, I bought two days' supplies and packed them snug in a carton, and tied it up solid. I didn't even bother to ask Sim for credit for Uncle Jeff's items, because it would almost kill Sim to give the credit, and if he refused it, Uncle Jeff would make his life miserable.

Down at the landing, I loaded my stuff in the canoe, fixed a place for Uncle Jeff to sit with his back comfortable against the tent and blanket roll, and then handed him his things.

There are three simple sights which bring to Uncle Jeff's eye expressions of equal passion: a game warden, a deer or moose, and a bottle of Hernando's Fiery Dagger rum. While I was getting the outboard motor set to start, Uncle Jeff snicked the top off the rum bottle with his fingernail and offered me a drink.

"Not now, Uncle Jeff. Wait till we land."

He looked at me as if I were a backward child, then applied his mouth to the bottle. His Adam's apple bobbed four times, then he sighed like a man getting home and capped the bottle. Then he reached inside the canoe shed door and picked up his own outfit, a marvel of simplicity. It consisted of a knapsack of the pre-Cambrian era, with shoulder straps made from scraps of harness. Before he tossed in the rum, pork and cartridges, it contained absolutely nothing but an old Ferguson jacklight with head band and a box of matches.

The motor started on the second pull, and the shoreline began to slip along fast. All the leaves were off the hardwoods. Their limbs showed a soft russet-red, and the birch boles stood out sharp and white against the green of spruce and pine. Everywhere you could smell the damp forest and the lake-smell of sun-warmed sand and granite.

We couldn't carry on any talk over the motor sound, but along by Caribou Point and Genius Island, Uncle Jeff got out the rum bottle, took a pull, and settled back. I could hear him singing. I couldn't hear the words, but the tune drifted back dolorously.

The sun was behind dark, low clouds when we rounded Leadmine and sighted Zack Bourne's cabin. But the wind had died out, and the water parted black as oil along the bows. As we pulled into Zack's little wharf, the backwash of the canoe followed in, and the wake broke noisily on the beach and died away to nothing.

Zack came down, and he and Jeff exchanged a series of amiable insults and flat-handed blows hard enough to kill a veal calf. After a first greeting, Zack had forgotten me and so had Jeff Coongate. They were remembering old crimes and laughing about them. It might have gone on forever if Zack's wife, Sarah, hadn't come down. Zack quieted down at the sight of her, and Jeff leaned close to his old crony, and I could hear him whispering about jacklights and that certain buck deer.

I was afraid Uncle Jeff would forget he owed me some information, so I asked him straight out.

He turned toward me, thought a while and swept his arm toward Big Island a mile or more away. I was incredulous.

"You mean to say there's a deer on that island?"

"It's what I'm tellin' you, son."

"But I never heard of—"

"I just told you, didn't I?"

I shook hands and said goodby and started the crossing to the island, though still I didn't believe it. Or I wouldn't have, if anyone other than Uncle Jeff had told me.

I ran the canoe into a cove and beached her. There was a sand beach and a little bluff covered with pines. I broke open the tent roll and cut some shear poles and pegs. I pegged the tent corners down and raised the shear poles. I spread out my blankets on the ground cloth inside, and there was home. I laid my rifle inside, then went down and put two stones together for a fireplace. There was a dry cedar log on the beach, and I got the axe and split off some pieces. Then I pulled the curled bark off a birch and had a fire going. The smoke smelled good, and it went up straight. For supper, I had tea and ham and beans.

I washed up and turned in early, and I lay there listening to the woods sounds. There was a mouse in the leaves back somewhere and an owl hooted, and then a loon called—they sound blue and lonesome in November. They have to go south, and they hate to go, and always in spring they're back before anything else. I worried about my canoe, because I was on an island. But I remembered I'd tied it down and drained the motor against freezing, and went to sleep the next second.

Next morning, I was hunting a little after daylight. I dropped a cartridge when I was stuffing it into my Model 99. My hands were cold and clumsy, but just the same, it's bad luck to drop a cartridge. Everyone knows that.

The island was about a mile-and-a-half long, and I zigzagged it upwind—up what wind there was. It was silent and spooky in the thick cedar growth. On the ridge, though, there were beeches and birches, and now and then a leaf rustling down or a red squirrel scolding. I ate my lunch by the base of a lone boulder the size of a house. It must have been dumped there by the melting ice sheet 22,000 years ago.

Toward dark, working back to the tent, I got jumpy. I heard a crash off to my right and still-hunted the sound with my knees shaking. There wasn't a track or an over-turned leaf. It occurred to me then that I hadn't seen a single track all day! In spite of that and the dropped cartridge, I clung to my faith in the one-eyed poacher.

But by afternoon of the next day, my faith ran thin. I still hadn't seen any sign. It was fun camping on the island, but I was sick of being alone. Two days wasn't really enough for still-hunting, anyway. I know fellows who have gone two weeks in good deer country without getting a break. The second night I didn't hear the loon. Had he taken off for the south? Did it mean a freeze-up?

Whether it did or not, there was heavy shell ice for 50 yards around shore the morning I broke camp. I could walk on it, and decided I'd wait till the sun softened it up before breaking my canoe canvas out of the ice.

I sat on the cedar log waiting. Eight o'clock; I tested the ice, and it was tough. Nine o'clock, then ten, and I figured I'd make a try. I got up off the log, stretched and turned toward the canoe—and 40 yards beyond it, standing in plain sight on the shore was my buck deer! Where he had come from, how he had got there, I don't know—or didn't, till I found his tracks where he had swum over the day before.

I reached for my rifle, and it wasn't there. It was lying in the bow of the canoe. The deer had his legs braced. He saw me, but couldn't get my scent. It was ten steps to my rifle, and I made it in three. The deer wheeled, stopped and looked directly back at me over his rump. I flipped the lever down and back and heard the shell chamber.

The first shot must have been ten feet high. The deer was running, and I wasn't looking at the sights at all. The second shot killed him clean. It went through his neck, and he never knew what hit him. I stood there, shaking like an alder in a current. He was a magnificent animal, if not a huge one. He had eight points, and weighed a 179 pounds dressed on the express company scales in Mopang. But I'm a little ahead of things.

First off, after I had dressed out the buck and got him into the canoe, I made a beeline for Zack's cabin on the mainland to thank Uncle Jeff Coongate. But the cabin was empty and the door locked, so I headed on down to Privilege. Uncle Jeff wasn't standing on the dock, and I didn't know where to find Zack Bourne, so I went up to Sim Pease's store and found Tom Corn, the warden.

I told him about my buck, and how I'd tagged it all right, and then: "By the way, Tom—have you seen Uncle Jeff Coongate?"

"I just left him," Tom said.

"Where was he?"

Tom smiled and shrugged his shoulders, half-hopelessly, half-seriously and a little humorously.

"In jail down at Mopang," he said. "See you later."

He went away fast, as if he didn't want to tell me the rest of the story.

I went back to the landing, unloaded and stored my stuff in the canoe shed for winter. Then I got Jumbo Tethergood to drive me and my buck down to Mopang, where I was going to take the train that night.

Stumpy Coldwillow was express agent that fall, and he weighed in the deer. It was sure a handsome buck. I hated to cut it up, but I had to. Stumpy helped me, and I took seven pounds of the best loin to the jail with me. Seemed that was the least I could do, since Uncle Jeff had been so kind to me—this time, and all the other times when I was a kid and he would show me things about the woods. I felt sorry for him, a kind and intelligent old man, but always in trouble and always broke.

I felt better when I saw him. He and Zack were sitting on a bench playing cribbage. They looked peaceful and contented, and it was warm and comfortable in the jail. I told Ed Post I wanted Uncle Jeff to have the venison, when it had hung long enough to be tender, and he said it was all right. Ed was happy.

"Hell, I don't wish Zack and old Jeff no harm, but I'm glad they're back. Sarah's stayin' up-street with my wife, Etta. Zack an' Jeff both got sixty days. That'll carry 'em through till after New Year."

I went away down the corridor past the cell where the horse thief once stayed, and on to the double cell where Zack and Uncle Jeff were playing cribbage. They were fighting over the score, and happy.

"Hello, boys," I said. "What brings you here?"

"Hello, son," said the one-eyed poacher. "That young Tom Corn brung us here. Caught us plump dead to rights. I had my headlight on, and we both had rifles, and he stepped into the clearin' near Zack's cabin jest as I was shinin' the eyes of that buck. The buck ran to water. We heard him splash in. I hope he made it to the island."

"What?" I said. "What buck? You mean the one you told me about?"

Uncle Jeff coughed, averted his one eye, and frowned.

I was still in the dark, and I felt kind of half-guilty and disloyal, because I figured I might have been responsible for Tom Corn following us uplake.

So I said: "Well, I got that buck on the island, Uncle Jeff. I heard you were in jail, so I brought down a nice piece of the best loin for you."

The old poacher licked his lips and his eye rolled, and Zack rubbed his hand over his stomach.

"You really done that for me?" said Uncle Jeff.

"Sure I did. Didn't you tell me where the buck was? I shot him right on the shore of the island this morning a little after ten o'clock."

Uncle Jeff groaned and bowed his majestic head.

"Dear Lord," he said, "the way of the transgressor is hard. A man's sins ketchith up with him. The buck you shot was the one that swum across last night when Tom surprised us. I never heard tell of no buck on the island before, son. I jest told you that, so you'd be out of the way when me and Zack got our lights out for him. Course, you can see why I told you. I had to git that canoe ride up to Zack's. You got any spare tobacco?"

I gave him my box, and he filled his pipe and dumped the rest of the can in his dungaree pocket, then passed me back the can, empty.

"Set down, son," he invited. "We'll play cutthroat pitch."

"I can't, Uncle Jeff. My train goes in half-an-hour."

"Well, that's too bad. Could you run up to Pease's store an' git me a bottle of Old Sabre Tooth rum? That Hernando's Fiery Dagger didn't set good. Just tell him to charge it to me, son. An' say—thanks for that there venison—only, course it was really mine, anyways."

DEER CAMP
By Rick Bass

This chapter is from A Thousand Deer *(2013), a definitive and eloquent book about deer hunting on a hardscrabble piece of land in the Texas Hill Country. In his definitive and eloquent book, Rick Bass returns to the family's "Deer Pasture," tallying up what hunting there has taught him about our need for wildness and wilderness, about cycles in nature and in the life of a family, particularly about how important it is for children to live in the natural world.*

Some years we need the woodstove, other years the air conditioner. In the old days, the season started in mid-November, around the peak of the rut, but for a long time now, opening day has been moved back to the first Saturday in November. The lore from the old days is that of hunts amid ice storms and even flurries of snow: tales befitting those from a century ago. They used to sleep in wall tents, then a shabby old bunkhouse they threw together and shared with snakes and wrens and scorpions. Not until 1987 did we build a new and more hospitable bunkhouse.

The tin roof of it gets pounded by marbled hail, and, for those of us sleeping on the upper bunks, our faces grow chilled by each night's frost, and our hair stands on end during the electrical storms that cause the tin roof to crackle. On balmier nights, the branches of overhanging oaks scrape and scratch against the roof like the soundtrack for an old horror movie. It's comforting, ancient, familiar.

Relatives of Davy Crockett had once owned this place, and before that, the Comanches. I like to think that the place was as special to them as it is to us, and from the incredible density of arrowheads scattered here and there—shards, points, spearheads, ax blades, awls—I believe it was.

On one mesa, I found ancient, lichen-spattered sandstone rocks arranged in a perfect circle the size of a teepee ring, with a view that looked over the entire Hill Country. Lower down, at the mouth of one of the canyons, there are fantastic granite monoliths, eroded into visages eerily reminiscent of the giant heads at Easter Island, and other boulders loom in the shapes of elephants, rhinos, clenched fists.

Every strong rain exposes a new sheet of shards and chips and still, all these years later, a perfect arrowhead. Now and again you encounter an old blue-tarnished bullet casing. The dozen or so of us who have hunted here every year have fired a lot of shells. If each of us shoots but once or twice a year, the math suggests there would be close to 2,000 bullet casings breech-jacked into the brush, cartwheeling gold-glinting through the sun, to be lost for a while until encountered by another perhaps decades later sitting in the same location, or passing through.

Some of us have shot more than once or twice a year. Over time, the deer tend to be drawn to the same shapes of the land—passing through the same slots and ravines and trails, often at the same crepuscular hours. By learning so well the shape of the land and the timing of the deer as they pass across it, we have found a curious way of slowing time down, or at least bending time, like a blacksmith forging an iron wagon wheel into something less linear, something with an arc and, for all we know yet, ultimately a full circle.

The slow-motion melt of our faces in the mirror, and our yearly photograph, picking up more and more lines in our faces: it's as if Granddaddy's coming back. It's as if we're all stepping forward. We're the same, yet we're different. Time is erasing the overburden of our destinies like the thunderstorms eroding the present to summon once more the past.

How can nature not develop in us a poetic sensibility? How can the specificity of the woods not spread through the canyons of our minds, bringing light and fuller understanding to all manner of broader truths, abstractions, similes and metaphors?

As some of time's advancement reveals to each of us our previously concealed futures, our youth dissolving into the past that has preceded us, so too do we see pathways of disassembly being halted by time, held loosely together by a kind of time-in-balance. The beautiful pink granite with the fantastic cubic crystals of feldspar and mica (the larger and more developed the crystals, the slower the cooling) is going to eventually disassemble. The frozen fire cannot hold together forever, but for a little while longer it appears that the rain-moistened lichens—brilliant turquoise, russet, blood red and cornflower blue—are clutching the boulders so fiercely that they will never let them crumble.

The scientist in me understands that indeed there are processes in the lichen that, by extracting faint nutrition in the interchange between roots and stones, create a kind of acid that eventually decomposes the rock further. But the poet in me sees no acid, only the wildly intricate floral patterns of lichens growing broader each year and appearing to hold the boulders together.

In the morning after a storm, the webs of garden spiders glint like necklaces in the spaces between the cedars, holding together the white spaces through which, soon, the world will begin moving once more, piercing the day, piercing the diamonds.

The more deeply we come to know this Hill Country place, the more we come to understand that there is a reassuring sameness everywhere. The green translucence of each sunfish in the little creek casts a delicate, fish-shaped shadow when sun-struck, so much so that the shadow seems more real, more visible, than the fish themselves.

A hike through the high boulders on the east side of the lease—boots scraping on the pink wash of gravel that is the detritus of the decomposing granite—takes me past the tooth-shaped crystals of quartz that lie next to the bleached skull of a wild hog; teeth and savage tusks, loosened from his jaw, appear in their repose no different from the bed of ivory crystals in which he now rests.

Elsewhere on the same hike, far back in the brush, I encounter the skull of a bobcat with its formidable rabbit-killing canines still intact, resting amidst a mound of dried rabbit pellets. Who controls whom, predator or prey?

I suppose we should be more intent upon finding and killing deer, but we have killed so many across the decades that it's not so much like there's a truce, nor is it a fatigue, as instead a desire, I think, for everything to move more slowly—to move as slowly as possible—and, as we all know, when you kill a deer, the hunt is over. At this stage of our lives, we are all less eager for the hunt to be over.

A close observation of nature cannot help but yield a poetic sensibility, and who observes nature more closely than a hunter? Not all hunters, however, devolve or evolve into poets. Certainly, Old Granddaddy did not yield or change in this regard, but remained instead a resolute slayer of deer all the way to the end, chain-smoking cigarettes around the dry cedar all day. An eater of fried foods, particularly pork—"I never see a pig I don't tip my hat"—he probably would have lived to be about 120 had he had even remotely better habits. He's gone now, though steadfastly, we each and all follow him.

Like little else in the world, the sport of hunting demands presence and attentiveness, summons an imagination electric with possibility. Even as we age and lose the fire for killing and procuring—as if made weary by our relentless success—the habit of noticing nature continues.

We watch how things in nature strive to hold together, even in the midst of massive disassembly, and we are comforted. We are comforted by the steadfast regularity of patterns—from the four seasons to the phases of the moon to the cycles of the deer in the fall breeding period and everything in-between—even as our hunter's eye stays watchful always for the anomaly, the one interesting thing outside the cycle

This ability to be two things—pattern-viewer but anomaly-seeker—has sharpened who we are as a species and as a family and as individuals, and it occurs to me that stories serve the same purpose.

Each year we retell so many of the old ones—are reassured, reknit together, by them—even as we seek new ones as well. Assembly, reassembly, disassembly: each year, we step through and between all of these stages. We keep moving forward.

Sometimes as we grow older, we just want to sit around the fire and rest, but we keep moving forward, even knowing full well that it leads us right back to where we started.

Where once Comanches raided the settlers who sought to eradicate their way of life, we now raid each other. Again and again we retell the old stories of gone-by pranks, while remaining vigilant for opportunities for new ones. Long ago, in his snake-fearing youth, a cousin who shall remain nameless killed a big rattlesnake—old-school Texas, back before people knew better—and he decided to bring it back to camp to skin and fry, curious as to whether it really did taste like chicken.

The snake was rendered headless before being tossed into the back of the truck and onto a pile of firewood that was being gathered for the campfire that evening. It was dark by the time he got back, and this nameless cousin straightaway asked his brother, Randy, for help unloading the vast scramble of limbs and branches.

Always an enthusiastic worker, Randy seized a big armful of wood, branches splaying every which-way, and as he was walking over to the fire, his face so close to the branches that he could barely see where he was going, I inquired, "Say, is that a rattlesnake in there with all that wood?"

Randy refocused upon the immense snake that was in the midst of his double-armful grip and threw the wood into the sky with a most satisfying scream.

Another time, I found myself walking back to camp alone, well after dark, without a flashlight. There was no need for one—we know every inch of the tangled thousand acres better, I think, than we know the canyons and corridors of our own minds—and walking in the darkness still far from camp, I began to smell propane. I was walking along the creek beneath the high canopy of live oaks that formed a long eerie tunnel along the trail, and a short distance farther, I saw the spot of light that was the source of the scent: Randy with his hissing gas lantern. He's too old-school to use a flashlight; he likes the more democratic throw of the lantern for his night walking, and as I watched his lantern drifting through the all-else darkness like a firefly, a plan came to mind, one too good to pass up.

Knowing that he could hear nothing over the dull roar of the lantern, I ran down the dark corridor after him and drew right up behind him. Spanish moss hung in ghostly, looping tendrils from the canopy. I took in as much air as I could and then let loose with the loudest panther scream I could muster, inches behind him, then jumped back out of the sphere of light as he dropped the lantern. The globe glass cracked and the mantles crumpled, but the twin burners kept jetting orange firelight.

Randy sat down promptly—in that tiny sphere of light, he looked pale and sick—and he peered wild-eyed into the darkness. "Richard?" he said, and I did not have the heart to scream again.

That was 20 years ago, and those days are gone now, all our hearts are too frail and worn-out for such shenanigans.

It's not just Randy who's the target of pranks; we all are. No one escapes. One year Russell shot a nice eight-point down in the creek. I heard his single shot and knew he'd been successful. A few moments later, I saw a nice little forkhorn slipping through an opening on the other side of the creek, illuminated by the mid-morning sun on the side of Buck Hill.

It was a long shot but I had a good brace and was confident; I made the shot, and the buck dropped instantly. I climbed down out of the rocks, crossed the creek, ascended Buck Hill, cleaned the little buck and then, feeling strong, began dragging him out, back toward camp, as had been done in the old days, rather than going to get a truck.

I had dragged it for only about 15 minutes before coming through a clearing and seeing Russell's much larger buck, also gutted, hanging in a tree; Russell had already gone back to camp for a truck. His was a very nice buck, and I had no qualms about untying it from its limb, hiding it in the bushes, and replacing it with mine.

I then continued on to camp, where Russell was regaling everyone with the tale of his big deer. We were all excited to hear about it, and he was proud to show us, so after lunch we all drove out there in a caravan.

It pleases me to recall the confusion with which Russell slowly approached the deer—the disbelief in his face—and the way he turned to us slowly and said *"This is not my deer."*

"Oh Russell," my father said, "they always look bigger when they're in the woods."

Other times we're less brutal. As we age, we take midmorning naps more and more often, and our hearing is no longer keen. It's easy to sneak up on one another. We'll spy a hunter dozing against the trunk of a tree, camouflaged within the ground shrubbery of agarita or shin oak, and will slip right in and place a wildflower—a late-season aster—in the gun barrel, then pass on, unaccounted.

We used to kill deer like crazy. They were drawn to us as if by our desire alone. There were times known to each of us when we knew the day beforehand—the night beforehand—where we would see the deer. It was not with confidence that such certainty impressed itself upon us, but instead a kind of wonder. The incandescence of our yearning for the hunter's contract—the way the world had lathed us for at least the last 180,000 years—was at times a kind of brilliance within us, and we never took such dreams or foreknowledge for granted, but instead marveled at them, and the next day, moved toward those places—those appointments, those rendezvous—with the surety of faith.

And when the deer appeared, in much the time and manner as we had imagined, we were grateful, never arrogant. We understood that the success of such ventures never depended on our skill, but was always instead the decision of some larger thing, some larger force—something a little like the electricity created by the confluence of our desire, the landscape and the deer, as well as the world's desire to keep on moving.

To be hunters, we *had* to hunt—and to hunt, we had to be willing to gather our own meat. And back then, we were enthused about it.

Those kinds of dreams no longer occur. A central strand of the electrical current—our desire to find deer—has gone silent. Instead, now we sit quietly among the oaks and cedars. Sometimes the deer pass by us anyway, and sometimes—unless it is only my imagination—they almost look confused, as if wondering why their world has tipped, and where the hunters have gone.

We admire the morning sunlight in their eyes. We admire the smooth grace of their muscles. They have been here far longer than we have. They may or may not outlast us. Watching them pass by, it is very hard to imagine that any of it ever ends, but that instead, it all goes on forever; that it, that current in which we once so enthusiastically participated, will last even longer than the stone itself.

PART FOUR

TIMELESS TALES OF GRAND HUNTS

Recounting memorable outings, whether they involve magic or misery, delight or disenchantment, is as much of the whitetail hunter's world as pre-season preparation, sighting in, scouting and other activities integral to the overall experience. Excitement associated with a hunt of a lifetime, the taking of grand trophies, sightings of elusive bucks, or any of the many other aspects of the sport provide the fodder for campfire tales or gunroom gossip.

We all revel in sharing our own stories of the quest, but by the same token, we recognize that it takes a special talent to capture the thrill of the chase and the anticipation of a telling shot in irresistible fashion. That talent is one the seven men and lone woman whose works comprise this section of the book possess at a rare level.

To accompany Archibald Rutledge's father, a man who saw arduous duty from the beginning of the Civil War right through to Appomattox, on his last hunt is to know joy beyond compare. Or, who can resist the superb skills of Gene Hill or Gordon MacQuarrie? Add pieces by two of the giants of sporting letters from the last century, Jack O'Connor and Burton Spiller, with ample spicing of two selections by a woman who must rank as *the* Diana of all time when deer enter the picture, and you have the stuff of wonder. Topped off by selections from two *Sporting Classics* columnists, Ron Spomer and Mike Altizer, you have a can't fail menu for a literary feast.

GREAT MORNING
By Gene Hill

Originally published as a piece in his "Tailfeathers" column for Sports Afield, *this tale is a splendid example of the author's genius in pulling on the heartstrings of his readers. It subsequently appeared in one of the many collections of Hill's tight, bright little essays,* Mostly Tailfeathers *(1971). It also appears in* The Greatest Hunting Stories Ever Told *(2000).*

I guess I've been deer hunting for something over 30 years, and I suppose I've killed my fair share of deer. I can look back on many moments when everything seemed to come alive at the fleeting footfall of a buck—his very awareness made the forest ring with silence. These times are everlasting in the memory, but even more memorable are the times when I've been really warm.

Deer hunting and subzero weather seem to go hand in hand in my part of the East. And I doubt it has ever been colder on an opening day than the year I got my very first buck.

I woke up that morning about four and crept downstairs to start the fire in the kitchen stove. About the time the fire got going good, the men began to drift in from early morning chores. The kitchen smelled wonderful once all the men had gotten warm. The air was heavy with woodsmoke, tobacco, odors of dog and barnyard. And the not-so-secret source of most of these damp smells was the long-lost and wonderfully warm felt boots.

Felt boots were a standard item in every farmer's wardrobe. If you remember, they were made in two parts. A long, thick, felt, socklike affair that came to the knee was covered by a separate heavy rubber shoe that came just above the ankle and fastened by two or three metal buckles. They were heavy as hell, but they were warm! Naturally I had a pair. I also had on a heavy woolen union suit (over a pair of regular underwear), two pairs of heavy bib overalls, I forget how many shirts, and topping all this was a blanket-lined denim coat we called an "overall jacket."

My grandfather put me on the first stand, behind a giant, fallen chestnut log. I was told to stay put.

"What if I shoot a deer?" I asked, positive that I would.

"Stay put," was the answer.

And stay put I did. I really didn't have too much choice. Wrapped all around me was a giant horse blanket, the kind with a raft of buckles and straps on it. Nestled between my legs was a kerosene hand lantern. I sat there like a human tent with my own personal furnace going.

In those days, we didn't worry too much about a deer smelling any of us. I guess because we all smelled like so many horses and cows ourselves. If I didn't smell like a horse, it wasn't the fault of the blanket and the kerosene lamp forcing the odor out for a couple of country miles. I probably would have smelled like a horse anyway—and the outfit was plenty of insurance.

The real point of all this is the absolute fact that I was deliciously warm. I was more than warm—I was downright cozy. By the time the sun had risen completely over the horizon, I had, of course, eaten all my lunch.

Grandpa came by about ten o'clock and asked me how I was. I was just fine and told him so, adding that I was getting a little hungry. He gave me a couple of sandwiches and a handful of cookies that must have weighed a quarter of a pound apiece, and told me again to stay put. I don't think I could have gotten out of that rig if I'd wanted to, but I promised him, and off he went again.

Under the blanket, I held my most cherished possession—an old 1897 Winchester pump gun. It wasn't really mine. Pop had borrowed it for me to use. The 30-inch, full-choke barrel stuck up out of the blanket like a chimney, and I kept swiveling it around as best I could without disturbing the oven arrangement. I can tell you, I was mighty eager to use it.

Along about noon, I was about half asleep from so much food and the warmth from the old lantern when a sharp crack of a broken branch brought my eyes open. Against the snow, about a quarter-mile off through the woods, I could see the four legs of a deer cautiously working its way down toward my stand. Buck or doe, I couldn't be sure because of the hazel and birch thickets between us.

As slowly as I could, I eased the old '97 up out of the blanket and across the chestnut log and began following the legs of that deer closer toward me through the woods.

About 50 yards directly in front of me was a tiny brook with a clearing or two on the other side along the bank. With absolute certainty, the deer—whatever it was—was heading toward one of those clearings.

I eased the hammer back on the Winchester with a very shaky thumb; buck fever was coming on a little faster than the deer. But if I had seen this sight once in my dreams and my imagination, I'd seen it a thousand times.

I couldn't take my eyes off those four legs . . . three or four more steps, and he'd be in the clearing by the brook. And suddenly, there he was! A buck—a big curving Y.

Somehow, as the barrel swung back and forth over the clearing, I managed to shoot. Just one shot. I don't believe I could have pumped that gun if my life depended on it.

At the shot, the buck twitched, stepped carefully back from the brook and, just as cautiously as he had come down, began to walk away as I helplessly watched him. I really never thought of the second shell (I was only allowed to have two buckshot). With a feeling of abject shame, I saw him disappear into the woods. I had missed him. How would I ever tell Grandpa and Pop?

Well, I sat there feeling lower than a cricket's knee. If I hadn't been 11, I might have cried. Sooner or later, I knew, the hard part had to come—in the form of my father, and it wasn't 15 minutes until he showed up. He was kind of smiling, as I remember it.

"You shoot?" he asked.

I nodded.

"Where's the dead deer?"

I said there wasn't any dead deer; that he had just walked away.

"Which way did he walk?"

"Around behind that big beech tree was the last I saw," I told him, fearful that I'd be dealt with pretty harshly for wasting a shell.

"Well, you'd better come along and show me," Pop said as he uncovered me, blew out the lantern and started off toward the beech tree. He made me unload the gun, and I felt pretty small as I shucked out the empty shell that had sat in the chamber, forgotten. I put the other shell in my pocket and trudged along behind him.

I should have suspected something when he quickened his pace as we passed the spot where I had last seen the buck, but deep in misery and head down, I just tried to walk in his tracks and keep up. I almost fell over the deer.

"This is him, isn't it?" he said, standing by a fallen forkhorn, about 50 yards beyond the big beech.

"Yep," I said, trying to indicate by my tone of voice that I wasn't the most surprised person in the world.

"Well, boy, you'd better drag him down by the brook so's we can clean him out."

I guess I could have dragged a bull moose right then, and drag I did, right into the flowing water where we cleaned and washed him out.

By the time the other men had gathered, and I told how I had shot my first deer, the carcass had frozen solid.

Grandpa had come along and gathered up my blanket and lantern and asked me if I'd been warm enough. I said I had, but that I was getting mighty cold again.

"Here, boy," he said, handing me a two-foot loop of rope, "warmest thing in the world."

"How's that going to keep me warm?" I asked.

"Simple," he said. " Just wrap one end around the deer's neck and the other around your hand and start walking toward the wagon."

Well, I miss the old felt boots, and I still think the blanket—provided it smells like a dapple-gray—and the lantern are pretty comforting. But to really keep a deer hunter warm, there's nothing like a two-foot rope around a man's hand, with a sleek December buck on the other end.

THE COMEBACK BUCK
By Ron Spomer

Longtime Rifles columnist for Sporting Classics, **Ron Spomer headed to the prairie grasslands of western Kansas where he pursued a record-book buck—the biggest of his life. His story originally appeared in the July/August 1999 issue of the magazine.**

By 8:00 o'clock the night's snow was melting. Huge drops ballooned under dark oak limbs and drummed the leaf litter. I had seen gray forms ghost through this narrow wood in the dull light. One had antlers. Tracks came up from the creek bottom and angled across an open pasture toward a distant stand of timber.

I sat against an oak trunk 80 yards from the trail and lay the single-shot .25-06 across my lap. After a half-hour, a whitetail stepped out from behind a big tree on the far edge of the woods. I could almost feel heat radiating from its dark pelt as it pranced nervously, eight antler points protruding high above its ears.

"There's a nice four-point hanging around and a huge ten-pointer that will make Boone and Crockett," the landowner had told me the night before. Carl, who has lived on this small farm in northeast Kansas most of his life, had seen both deer during bow season and was holding out for the biggest. I had promised him I wouldn't shoot the big one, though I don't think he really believed me, and I wasn't too sure I believed it myself. To avoid temptation, I had decided to shoot the first good buck I saw, and this eight-point was it.

My chest heaved as I slowly lifted the rifle. The buck stuck his nose to the ground as if sniffing out acorns, then moved his head behind a tree.

I centered the animal's chest in the scope and, after one fleeting second-thought, pulled the trigger.

The deer ran off, but fell over while I fumbled another silver cartridge into the chamber. He was fat and sleek, just reaching his prime.

He bore none of the puncture wounds, ripped ears or broken tines of older bucks. His antlers, though only 14 inches wide, rose high enough to score an honest 135 B&C points green. Here was buck enough for most hunters, bragging rights in many states. But in Kansas, it was just a good meat buck. I was pleased to get him so early on my first hunt of the season. Doubly pleased because, at 9:30 a.m. on opening day, I was free to begin my trophy whitetail hunt.

Have you ever dreamed of having two tags in a trophy hunting unit so you could shoot a good buck yet still be able to look for a better one? Sounds selfish, but in this age of overabundant whitetails, it really isn't. Many states dole out multiple deer tags to hunters. Mostly, however, these are doe or buck tags in places where trophy whitetails are as common as trophy polar bears.

Kansas is different. For decades the Sunflower State's Parks & Wildlife Department has carefully regulated its deer harvest through a system of limited entry permits in order to maintain a high buck-doe ratio and broad age structure. Trophy bucks are now relatively common in Kansas. Tags to hunt them, however, haven't been.

Then, in 1997, for the first time in decades, excess buck tags were available in a few units after the initial drawing. Any Kansas resident was entitled to apply for them, even those of us who had already drawn buck tags in the initial lottery. As a former resident and holder of a Kansas lifetime hunting license, I qualified. That explains how I was able to take the tall, eight- pointer and then, on the very next morning, pursue a record-book whitetail on a ranch less than a hundred miles away.

My "trophy ranch," which I have been hunting most every year since 1986, sprawls over several square miles of prairie grasslands dissected by deep, narrow draws lined with shadowy cedars and dotted with buttes, small mesas and isolated cropfields. Native bluestem, switchgrass and Indian grass stand tall and thick even in drought years. Ponds sparkle in wet years. Weeds and erosion are almost impossible to find and the cattle are always fat.

It is the best-run cattle ranch I have ever seen, thanks to the careful attentions of manager Larry, his wife Phyllis, and long-time assistant Chris. They guard this corner of paradise respectfully, watching the timeless play of light and shadow, rain and drought, frost and heat. They know and appreciate the bobwhites and bobcats, coyotes and whitetails, wildflowers and grasses as much as the wheat and cattle. They rise to melodious meadowlarks and retire to serenading coyotes, season after season, year after year. And they allow this displaced country boy to share these wonders for a few days each fall, for which I shall be forever grateful. This is the land, the wildlife and the people I will return to in memories. My good old days.

This is also the American Serengeti, the land that lured mid-19th century hunters like Custer and Cody. It was home to the Pawnee, Kiowa and great herds of bison. The bison are gone. In their place have come pheasants, quail and whitetails. Big whitetails.

During my many hunts on the ranch, Phyllis and Larry had teased me when I shot bucks that scored 150 to 163 points. "You'll have to come back for the big one next year" was their standard retort. This was next year.

"We saw the twelve-pointer on the eighty all summer," Larry said over dinner at the ranch house that night. "He's real wide." I knew better than to ask just where the buck was hanging out now. Larry, like Chris and Phyllis, will describe the bucks that live on the ranch, but it's each hunter's job to find them.

The 80-acre cropfield Larry referred to lay near the center of the property. Deer feeding on it could hole up anywhere. Three miles west in a maze of wooded canyons. Two miles south in a wooded creek bottom. A mile east in a broad, brushy draw.

One thing I knew from experience, though. Any buck foraging in an open grainfield at night would hike one to four miles from it before bedding at dawn. I suspect this is a genetic trait selected over millennia by predation from wolves and coyotes. The farther a deer walks from the heavily scented feeding site before bedding, the greater its chances of avoiding detection. Or maybe they just like the exercise.

"If he's as big as you say, he's been around long enough to know where it's safe," I told Larry.

"He's no dummy, that's for sure," Phyllis added.

"Well, ordinarily I'd guess he's hiding in the thickets down by the creek, except you say some bowhunters have been in there, right?"

I watched Larry's face carefully. His expression never changed. He just looked at me and nodded.

"If he's been disturbed in there, he could have moved into the canyons on the west side. A buck could hide in there all season."

Again Larry looked at me and nodded.

"Of course the forest is even more isolated . . . " Larry continued nodding, but this time he stared at his stocking feet and curled his toes back.

The forest was a 10-acre creekbottom thicket in an isolated corner of the ranch. Dawn caught me halfway to it, crossing side canyons as I went. I had already bumped a doe and her fawns, and now I could see others working their way ahead of me. This was odd. Most years, the females stayed up on the fields until well after sunup.

I moved cautiously, watching for bucks slipping down through the dark ravines. Eight years earlier this technique had put me within 60 yards of a burly 10-pointer that had scored 155 B&C points. Four years later the same approach netted a buck with an even wider, taller rack, but several broken tines pushed its score down to the high 140s. The following season I walked up behind an honest 163 buck.

This time, despite finding more tracks and trails than usual in the draws, I saw no bucks. Three lesser prairie chickens passed overhead. By 9:00 a.m. I had crawled over a small, grassy hill and tucked myself into the shadows of the tall grass overlooking the forest—plum thickets, cedars, willows, ash and other hardwoods mixed with head-high Indian grass and switchgrass.

A tiny creek looped and gurgled through the cover. A rising wind hit me in the face.

For the next two hours, the whitetails paraded by. Does, fawns, two small bucks. By the time I left, the little pocket of timber was hiding some two dozen whitetails. But no 12-point bucks.

"I think I saw a big ten-point this morning," Phyllis said at lunch.

"Where?" I asked.

"Heading off the eighty. I was up there trying to get Theresa a shot at a doe. It was pretty dark yet when he ran off, but I'm sure it was him. I think he was chasing some does into the canyon to the north."

That particular canyon led three miles to a dense stand of cedars and cottonwoods. A buck bedding there would not leave early enough to reach the feeding-field before dark. But if he were consorting with a ripe doe, he would follow her come hell or high water, and she would likely hurry to the green winter wheat before sundown.

Phyllis and I went to intercept him. She knows the ranch as well as anyone and loves to roam it. To approach the field with the wind in our favor, we had to hike two miles and cross the same canyon the deer would eventually move up, so we started at 3:30, just in time to discover four other hunters driving out of the area.

"They've probably spooked everything around here," I said. "Look at the tracks."

Tire tracks crisscrossed several big draws.

"They must'a been lost," Phyllis guessed.

"Or trying to flush deer with the truck," I countered.

"They better not have been."

It was a disheartening discovery, but it was too late to move. We pushed on to the field and settled in to wait, each of us watching a different draw.

"Psssst. Psssst!" It was Phyllis. She waved me over. "It's a big buck," she said.

"Is it him?"

"Don't know, but I think so. Looked pretty tall."

"Where?"

He was standing behind an old elm in the bottom of the draw we had just crossed. We had passed within a few hundred yards of it. So had the vehicle hunters.

There was a dense pocket of plum bushes several feet behind the elm. It was a classic hiding place, but almost never used by bucks so close to a feeding-field.

Then I saw the doe. She was making a pretense of foraging some 50 yards in front of the buck. He stood like a pointer, staring at her. She was almost ready to mate, and that's what had enticed the buck to hole up in such an unusual location.

"I'm sneaking closer," I said, and I started to trot, knowing that Phyllis would stay behind to watch the buck. I kept to the shadowy side-draws, closing within a quarter-mile before sitting and pulling the tripod and spotting scope from my pack.

The buck was in the clear. Dark, thick, heavy. Four tines on the 10-point rack looked as if each would measure 12 inches or more. The main beams reached almost to his nose. His only shortcoming was width—barely past his spread ear-tips. I guessed he would score about 170. *Hmmm.*

The sun was setting. I would have to decide soon. I abandoned the pack and scope, slithered into the last side draw and slipped within about 300 yards of the big elm. Here, I parted the grass and began studying the buck through my binocular. Five points per side. Nicely balanced. Eighteen inches inside.

How much bigger was that 12-pointer? Should I pass up on this opportunity to hunt for it?

This was only the first day of the hunt, but those four vehicle-hunters were prowling, and six more were scheduled to arrive on the weekend. The 12-point might go into hiding, move off the ranch, get shot by someone else.

While I pondered, the buck started walking closer. "Keep on coming, buddy."

I centered the scope on his chest. I could make the shot.

I would make the shot. To heck with that phantom 12-point. This deer was too good to pass up. I'll take him when he stops.

He did. Directly behind a branch. No problem. Still plenty of time. The wind was in my favor. He suspected nothing. His doe was slowly browsing my way. He would eventually follow and when he stopped in the clear . . .

Five minutes slipped away. Six. Seven. *Come on, come on.* Finally, he lowered his head and started to walk.

I lined up the crosshairs, started the trigger squeeze.

No, I'll let him stop. Why risk a walking shot? He's only getting closer.

And then he got too close. The doe tossed her head, kicked her heels and gamboled back toward the plum thicket, her eager swain hot on her hoofs. And then they were gone.

I studied that dark thicket. No deer. She was hiding from him. I had seen this trick before, does using brush to keep overly eager bucks off their backs. He would simply wait her out. But I couldn't. At best, I had ten minutes of legal shooting light and 400 yards of grass between me and my quarry.

Trusting that the buck was preoccupied, I scurried to the creek, keeping the big elm between us. Then I moved toward the cut bank of the creek itself, watching the grassy slope above the plum thicket in case they broke out.

I ran out of cover 150 yards from the thicket. Two minutes of legal shooting time left. No deer visible.

Had they slipped out unseen? Their brush pocket was thick enough to hide an elephant.

I walked closer. The doe broke from the far side of the thicket and ran uphill. I kneeled, wrapped the sling around my arm and waited, thumb on the safety. The buck popped out behind the doe, his body language clearly showing he thought this more foreplay. The object of his passion, however, knew better. She stopped halfway up the grass slope, ears forward, body tense and turned to confirm what she suspected. Then she blew and bounded up the hill.

At that, the buck caught the alarm and metamorphosed from courtesan to prey. No more prancing, no bobbing the head. He turned 90 degrees from the doe's line of escape, put his ears back and flat out fled.

Oddly, I found myself calm and still undecided. The buck was angling away and slightly to my right. The crosshairs settled on a narrow slice of shoulder as I tracked him, noting again the narrow spread, wondering if I should take him or continue hunting for the 12-pointer. I might never see this buck again.

I knew the shot was good even as I was pressing the trigger. A satisfying *whock* echoed immediately after the shot. When I recovered from the recoil, I saw a tall set of antlers protruding above the grass. I put a finishing shot into his heart and was gutting him when Phyllis walked up.

The moon wouldn't rise for a couple of hours, so I hung my blaze vest on my tripod to mark the spot before we started hiking. Larry found us on a ranch trail about a half-hour later.

"Did you get one, Spomer?" Larry kidded. "Or did you miss again."

I held up my bloody hands.

"Any size to 'im? I suppose you shot another Bambi."

I feigned modest disappointment. "It's not the big twelve you were talking about."

"Hop in," Larry instructed. "We'll go get him after we pick up my ten-pointer."

"Your ten-pointer?"

Larry had shot a fair-sized buck on the back side of another field, and we were able to drive right to the carcass.

"Hey, that's a nice deer."

"Aw, it's not much. Grab ahold there." We swung the buck onto the flatbed, our breath steaming against the headlights.

"Now where's your buck?"

It took some searching before we caught the glow of my vest in the headlights. We stood 'round that buck for some time, admiring it beneath an inky sky shot with silver. Finally, Larry knelt and hefted a massive beam.

"This time, Spomer, you don't have to come back next year."

But I will anyway.

POINT FIVE
By Mike Altizer

This story first appeared as Mike Altizer's Ramblings Column in the September/October 2016 issue of Sporting Classics.

I *remember how it looked,* the distant ridges more fog than forest, while my tree alone retained any significant color or detail. The mountain beneath me plummeted in all directions through the murky woods, and the surface of the distant lake lay still and coy beneath a blanket of blue-grey mist that swirled Heavenward in great undulating columns of cold condensation, like warm and heartfelt prayers.

I remember how it smelled, subtle wisps of locust smoke wafting up the mountain toward me from distant dying embers glowing weak and rust-red back on shore. The sweet tobacco smell of new-fallen leaves rose damp and fragrant from the forest floor, and from somewhere out in the shrouded sunrise floated the faint, lingering aroma of hot coffee still steaming from the campers far below.

And I remember how it sounded, the thickened mist dripping in syncopated spatters from dew-laden leaves, along with the songs of cicadas finishing the raspy refrains they had begun during the night. The awakening birds murmured softly one to another, still reluctant to abandon their nighttime perches, while the deep muffled cadence of a hammer maul from somewhere out in the gathering dawn bore evidence of one lonely soul just now beginning his long day's labor.

And all of it incidental to the whisper of the wind and the warm steady pulse of my own beating heart.

It was one of those mornings whose spirit transcends its purpose.

The thick fog isolated my brother and me from the world and each other as we stood perched in our respective trees, suspended between patience and hope as we eagerly awaited the sunrise.

We had come in by boat during the night, guided by mist and memory and broad bands of stars that framed the black, moonless mountains that towered over us as we slowly motored east beneath the Butler Bridge, then north up the narrowing channel on our midnight run to Point Five.

As we rounded the final bend, we could see two small glows on the shoreline still a mile ahead, one blue and one a bright russet-orange—latent evidence of a lantern and a campfire.

We eased in across the cove from the campers and secured our boat to an old embedded snag. With our bows already strung and our gear arranged for a pre-dawn departure, we slipped into our sleeping bags, stuffed our boots and shooting gloves deep inside to protect them from the night, and drifted off amid dreams of daybreak.

Alan woke me at 3:40. We knew we must be on our way early, lest some overlanders try to get onto our ridge ahead of us. We shared a couple of cold biscuits, then scattered the crumbs on the water as we passed the canteen. We each took a single practice shot, holding the flashlight for one another, then retrieved and re-sharpened our arrows.

By 4:05 we were set to go.

I left a minute or so ahead of Alan, moving slowly as I ascended the first steep pitch with my bow, pack and small tree stand. I could hear him behind me as he turned straight up the ridge to his tree.

For my part, I intended to climb all the way to the head of the hollow before turning up to the crest. I topped out slightly higher than I'd intended, eased back down the ridge toward the lake and found my own tree, a perfectly leaning locust on the edge of the wooded flat.

Eighteen yards below the base of my tree ran a long-abandoned fencerow that angled back down the ridge. We knew that bucks like to work these old, overgrown fencelines, for it was here we'd been finding steady deer sign for the past month.

It had taken over an hour from the time I'd left the boat until I was in my stand. With nearly two hours to go before shooting light, I made certain everything was in its proper place, then settled down with nothing to do but listen to the sounds of the waning night.

At 6:10 I saw flashlights slicing through the mist. *Overlanders!*

There were four of them, bumbling through the darkness made darker by their errant beams, and we exchanged not-so-pleasant words as they passed. Still, I sensed they wouldn't stay long in one place come daylight, and so they might move deer for us later in the morning. The commotion finally faded, but I suspected that one or more of them had set up farther down the ridge near my brother. Meanwhile, I could hear the campers down on shore beginning to stir.

At 6:50 I heard the first squirrel scurry through the leaves 40 yards below me. I knew there would be others and that I must carefully check each one I heard—*for sometimes they turn out not to be squirrels at all.*

To my delight, I discovered I could lay my bow, arrow nocked and ready, across the flattened limb to my left. This would make standing a little more comfortable, allowing me to rest my arms occasionally.

THERE! . . . *nope, just another squirrel.*

Later in the morning I might try the camouflaged stool I'd left hanging hidden in this tree a few days earlier and see how it fit my small portable platform.

WHAT?

Yet another squirrel . . . but like the others, one that must be checked.

I wondered if Alan had seen anything yet.

Time for my first drink of the morning. Canteen in the top pouch of my pack. Lay my bow across the limb to my left. Loosen the top. Drink. Replace the top. *Careful—don't drop it!* Canteen back into the pack.

Yeah, that's better, I thought. *I was thirstier than I realized. It sure would feel good to lie down for a few minutes. But it really is pretty up here in the sky, with the wind and the woods and the wakening birds . . . 'nuther squirrel, off to the right behind me.*

I turned to look. He was dogtrotting, head down, antlers forward, his nose into the breeze.

"DEER!!!"

My bow seemed to move all on its own as I turned and swung and drew, all in one motion. I held dead-on horizontal and three body lengths out in front of his shoulder as I released the arrow, watching each lovely rotation of its bright yellow fletching as it flew swiftly through the morning woods and slipped silently through his chest.

He stumbled, regained his stride, then bolted straight out the ridge. I gave two quick lip whistles and heard another arrow released without wondering whose it was, for I knew well the whisper of my brother's bow.

Mindful of the other hunters, I turned my watch cap orange-side-out before climbing from my tree and heading down the ridge. I passed one of the overlanders barely ten feet up a tree facing down the hollow we had ascended earlier, and he asked if I had heard something.

When I got to my brother, he was still high in his tree, waiting for me.

"You hit him good!" he said softly, but emphatically. I puzzled for a moment before realizing he had probably heard the impact of my arrow at a distant angle better than I had straight on at 25 yards.

"Did you see him?" I asked anxiously.

"I *hit* him," my brother replied.

As he roped down his bow, he asked, "Where did *you* hit him?"

I pointed to my right chest and he grinned and said, "He's headed for the water." And so did I, trying to cut him off as Alan took up his trail.

When I broke out of the woods, I could see the lake below. Nothing rippled its still surface so I bore left, searching the edges of the trees. Finding neither track nor blood trail, I turned back up the ridge, wondering how this story we would share for the rest of our lives would end.

I whistled softly.

Nothing.

I eased a little farther back up the ridge and whistled again.

My brother's voice. But *where?*

"Do you have him?" I called.

"Yeah. C'mon up and see your deer!"

It was as sweet a summons as I have ever received.

I found them together, my brother sitting cross-legged in the leaves, our buck laid out before him with an arrow protruding from his chest, precisely where I had hit him.

But it wasn't *my* arrow—it was *Alan's*.

We were perplexed for a moment, until finally realizing we had both hit him in the exact same spot, the three-bladed hole made by Alan's broadhead overlapping that of my own.

My arrow had completely penetrated the buck's chest, and backtracking up the ridge, I found *it* where it had found *him*, its point buried deep in the leaves, a bloody smear on the young sweet gum tree next to it. I replaced it in my quiver, gathered my tree stand and gear from the old locust, and moved back down to join my brother.

We dragged our deer off the ridge together that morning and field-dressed him by the edge of the lake, then lifted him respectfully into the boat and shoved off.

He was a fine little eight-pointer and is, in fact, the smallest buck I ever took.

But to this day, he occupies a most honored place—both on my wall and in my heart.

JUST LOOK AT THIS COUNTRY

By Gordon MacQuarrie

Judging by the sparseness of his writing on the subject, MacQuarrie and his compatriots in the Old Duck Hunters Association probably didn't do a great deal of deer hunting, yet there can be no doubt he knew and appreciated the sport and all its intricacies. In this piece from the November, 1939 issue of Field & Stream *MacQuarrie captures some of its nuances with his customary flair while demonstrating his talent for handling physical settings as well as he did character descriptions.*

L*ook at this country. Just look at it!"* The words leaped up in me like that on the opening day of Wisconsin's 1938 deer season. I stood on the top of a high hill with a rifle in my hand and looked across miles of grand, rugged hunting country.

You've made that same exclamation yourself, perhaps at the end of a hard portage trail when a blue, spruce-girded lake opened before you. Or when you saw sweeping country below you at the end of a hard climb.

The sight of that Wisconsin wilderness made me feel like getting back in there for a prowl instead of proceeding to the immediate business of hunting deer. I had never seen this big, rough patch of Wisconsin before, although I had fished and hunted around its edges for years. It was like discovering a pearl in an oyster.

Thousands of acres of madly arranged hills. Some pyramidal, some cone-shaped. Snaky ridges with slopes ranging from steep to gentle. Little valleys and big valleys. None more than 200 feet below the highest elevations. Some just potholes, round as the inside of an old kettle. Others long, V-shaped troughs.

Country like that makes me want to go look-see. I have a keener appreciation of what Kipling meant when he wrote: *"Something lost behind the ranges, lost and waiting for you. Go!"*

Our group included only three hunters. There was Dr. Patrick Tierney, a broth of a huntsman with a flair for far-going. And there was that redoubtable, that peerless, that matchless gentleman and woodsman of the cut-over—the President of the Old Duck Hunters' Association, Inc.

Pat Tierney, a lithe-legged rascal, had been telling me about this country for years. When I looked at it—and kept on looking—there came over his face an expression of deep gratification such as his ancestors wore when they unveiled the Blarney stone. We stood and discussed it, Pat and I. His black Irish eyes snapped.

"I've hunted it for years," he said. "Sometimes I get my buck, sometimes not. I just like to get in there and travel."

The President of the Old Duck Hunters observed this meeting of Scotch and Irish minds with misgivings. He looked at the country, of course. He even tossed in a few superlatives of his own, but the tenor of his conversation was businesslike.

"It looks like mighty tough going for a couple of old fellows like you and Pat," he said while loading his "far reachin'" gun, a .38-55. "Don't laugh, oh my brethren of the flat-shootin' stuff, for what reaches far for Mister President may not reach so far for Joe Doakes."

As Pat said, eying the noble arm, "You can't tell from the looks of a frog how far he'll jump."

Then the President cleared his throat impatiently.

"Gentlemen," he began, "it's high noon of opening day. There is no snow. The sun is bright. I did not come here to listen to an oral survey of this hunk of God-forgotten sand. We'll drive, of course. There aren't enough of us to do it right, but we can get along. You two work west through those gullies, and I'll be over by that old rampike, waitin'."

We still surveyed the country, talking. The President said it was getting on, and we hadn't yet seen anything with horns on it. Finally, Pat made up his mind.

"Mister President," he said, "I am tired. I want to get more tired—a different kind of tired. I want to go out in those hills and walk my legs off, all by myself."

"You don't mean to say," snorted the President, "that you won't make even one little push through the alders?"

The drive is the thing in Wisconsin. The President—all of us, in fact—were brought up with deer hunters who drive. Still-hunting? Grand sport, indeed, but the rules are upset when 100,000 hunters go into the woods. I told the President I felt as Pat did: that I'd like nothing better than a long, hard swing through the hills. He was aghast.

"A couple of naturalists, eh?" he shot at us. "Going out to enjoy the beauties of nature. Sorry I didn't bring my wife along. She loves to gather wintergreen berries at this season!"

We protested. It wasn't that, exactly.

It was just that a couple of city-pent fellows wanted to tramp the bush. He could hardly believe it.

He waggled a finger under my nose and exploded: "I'd never have come if I'd known it! There are anyway a hundred bucks back in those hills. A little drive—nothing to it. We shouldn't settle for anything less than one today. It's opening day!"

We finally convinced him we preferred it our way, every man for himself. He moved quickly then. He pumped the cartridges out of the .38-55 and put the gun back in its case. He dived into my car and from its depths yelled: "Have you got that old pig-iron shotgun here?"

I had. It is an ancient arm, the open barrel of which will throw a shotgun slug about as accurately as your grandmother would pitch 'em over at the Polo Grounds. But the choke barrel is accurate with slugs. I explained this to him. I explained further that it was an exceedingly temperamental cannon, given to letting off both barrels if you pulled the rear trigger. He said all he wanted was one crack at whatever he saw, because he was going to be almighty close to it. He dug in the inexhaustible pocket of the old brown mackinaw and found two 12-gauge slugs, pocket-worn but lethal.

Pat offered his .250-3000, but he declined. No, sir!

"As long as it's still-hunting with the cards stacked against you and the herd running wild everywhere, I'll take the elephant gun!"

He inspected the old shotgun.

"I never shot one of these things at a deer in my life," he declared. "But you boys have put me on the spot. You've made an Indian out of me in fifteen minutes. What I want now is something that'll plow through brush. I feel like a fool toting a shotgun in deer woods, but somebody's got to get meat for this camp. I can see that right now!"

He left us, a sturdy, indignant figure in the old brown mackinaw, buttoned as always only at the throat, its brown checks bedizened with red bandanas. We wear red in the Wisconsin deer woods. Pat and I went into the brush and separated within a mile.

It was one of the grandest hunting days I remember. The kindly old hills took me in. They let me become a part of them. Up this ridge and down that one. Across that draw on the outside near yonder hump. Maybe a buck would come along. Who cares? Still-hunting? Not even that. Just poking about in the hills.

I had been tired, but now seemed refreshed. The previous day I had driven 460 miles over a large part of Wisconsin's deer country. I felt I needed to get out and replace the fatigue of driving and city life with the honest weariness of the woods. I wanted to get out and perspire and breathe hard while climbing hills.

That country has an enthralling sweep. It fascinated me as it had fascinated Pat for years. It seems more like a mountain country than anything I know of in Wisconsin. Not in the sense of possessing high ranges; indeed not. But it has contrast, and contrast is what counts. Sometimes a child's sand mounds in the back yard can look more like mountains than the real thing.

A mountain country in miniature. But quite accessible to a man on foot. A place where a man can feel a giant by his conquest of one range after another. A bewildering assortment, of crazily strewn sandhills, the product of the last glacier.

A place where a hunting man can find a thousand spots to stand with a modern arm and command a mile of country. A place where high, wooded ridges run helter-skelter. One of those rare, pock-marked terrains of the lake states where you can actually put field-glasses to good use, where hunting can be made more like bighorn stalking than deer hunting.

It's north of the town of Barnes in Bayfield County, but you've got to get off the town roads and fire lanes to see it. Furthermore, if you're interested in the travelogue angle, have a peek some day at the somewhat less rolling land south of the Eau Claire Lakes in that same county, along what they call the Hayward Road. One opening day of deer season I counted—but hold on; we're off the trail.

Fifty years ago, the lumbermen took off the white pine. "The finest white pine that ever grew," they tell. They've been pecking away since at the smaller stuff. Now they're down to jackpine pulpwood, but an amazingly benevolent nature is building back. Leave it alone and keep the fires out, and it will come back, they who know tell us.

Stand on one of those ridges and look far away. Have you ever tried to look at anything far away in a city? Or even in a town? I mean something that rests the eye. The eye seems to forget it can be made to focus at long distances. Far-off, misty blue hills, one draped behind the other; ropy, twisted hills; tree-clad ridges; old potholes that once were lakes; long, inviting draws. No part of it like any other part.

Perhaps what Pat and I saw in those hills that day is of small moment. Perhaps here, in an outdoor magazine devoted to fishing, hunting and kindred sports, is no place to confess hunting was secondary out there in the sun-drenched hills. Perhaps . . .

But I doubt it. I know too many Pats and Jims and Johns. I know how they feel some days. I grew up in deer country. As a boy, it was important that my dad get his two legal deer that the law allowed. It was meat for the winter. I grew up, like many another youngster in north Wisconsin, with venison a familiar and delicious taste. From about 7 on, I used to be as thrilled as any adult hunter when enough snow fell on the opener to "make for good trackin'."

But it is something to be alone in the bush with a .30-30 under your arm, the wind in the trees, and the feeling that if there are such things as big cities, they must have existed in some ancient past. It is a fine thing to climb a rise, sit in the tumbleweeds, smoke a pipe and look off for miles at more of the same country you just came through.

Some people ask why men go hunting. They must be the kind of people who seldom get far from highways. What do they know of the tryst a hunting man keeps with the wind and the trees and the sky? Hunting? The means are greater than the end, and every deer hunter knows it.

The yellow November daylight was fading fast when I turned back toward the parked car. The last half-mile took me over the highest hill I had found. I hadn't seen a deer. But the sun was molten and round in the west over the upper Brule country. South, like a straight brown carpet, ran a wide, new fire lane. Here and there lights on hunters' cars were already gleaming in the dusk.

At the car, I found Pat. He had just arrived. We were both leg-weary but uplifted. The President had not appeared. The sun went behind the hills, and the quick November darkness came on from the east. Pat was reminded that we had played a rather shabby trick on Mister President. He rubbed his chin and remarked, "If he gets a critter, we'll never hear the end of this."

I felt guilty myself. "But, of course," I reminded Pat, "he won't get a deer." The President is a "drive man."

An old car creaked out of the narrow trail down which we had seen the President vanish four hours ago. The driver, a sturdy son of the hills, rolled down a window and shouted: "You fellows looking for an old gent with a shotgun?"

"Not exactly," I said. "He usually looked for us. He was pretty well able to take care of himself."

"Well, he took care of himself today," our farmer explained. "He's back there 'bout half-a-mile with a 180-pound buck, and he told me to tell you boys he'd be d— if he'd move him an inch from where he dropped him."

"Man with a brown mackinaw draped with bandanas?"

"That's your man. He can't tote that buck out alone."

The messenger of the hills drove off. Pat spoke first. "Maybe we'd better just go home and go quietly to bed with the covers over our heads."

"I am beginning to get your idea, Dr. Tierney."

"He's had me under suspicion ever since the last day of the duck season." Pat went on. "I wanted to quit at noon because I was cold."

We drove the car down the trail among the scratchy oaks. The President was sitting at the roadside smoking a cigarette. The buck lay in the center of the trail, where he had dropped it. He had dressed it, sat down and waited.

"I told that fellow in the car I wouldn't move him," the President explained. "Told him why, too. Told him I had a couple naturalists with me who liked hard work. He seemed to enjoy it. Anyway, he drove his car through the brush to avoid running over the buck. And how did my—er—er—companions of the chase make out?"

At that, he didn't bear down so hard. He seemed to be waiting for something. He wouldn't touch the buck. No, sir. Not with two, strong, heavily muscled young athletes around the place. He'd take care of the winter's meat. But the menial tasks? For the women and children, he said.

We stowed that limp, five-point animal in the trunk of my car, and there was room for the guns. Then, in the last of the daylight, we looked over the place.

It was easy to see what had happened, once the President showed us. The trail was an old logging road. The President had looked it over carefully for a distance of several hundred yards. It lay just on the edge of that wide hill country. He chose the brushiest spot in the road because, going into the woods from the trail on each side, he had found a deer runway, hard-packed in places, with hooked brush where bucks had worked off steam.

Thirty yards from that crossing, almost invisible from the trail itself, the President had sat down to wait. One hour. Two hours. Two and a half. He knew which way the buck would come. From the hills where "you two boys were running up and down the ridges."

A twig snapped. A hundred yards back from the trail, on a rise, came the buck, walking, nibbling a bit here and there. He was obviously working cagily out of the hills toward a game refuge to the west. The President held his fire. He wasn't sure of that first barrel. The buck would stay on his own runway and hit the road. The wind was right. The President doesn't make that kind of mistake. The buck walked leisurely into the open center of the road.

He was 30 yards away.

"I decided right then and there to pull the rear trigger!" the President explained. "That buck never knew what hit him. Both slugs at once through the neck. Say, that shotgun's got the old flat-shooter beat at close range."

We made it to the camp, hung the buck on the pole and went inside. It was warm in there. Pat and I removed our heavy flannel mackinaws and then our flannel shirts. We sat and talked.

The President's revenge was not forthcoming. Maybe he had forgotten about it in the elation at getting his buck. He was very kind to us. He made two trips to the kitchen to pump us cold drinks from the big red pump. What with him being so nice, we could hardly refuse when he asked us to carry in an armload of wood apiece for the fireplace.

We returned. The wood clattered to the floor beside the hearth. The light was poor, I noticed. Something was draped over the shade of the big gasoline lamp. I removed it—two pieces of flannel, one green and black, the other red and black. It was, in fact, the major portions of the shirt-tails of Pat Tierney and your reporter. The President had deftly snipped them off when we had gone for the wood.

From a corner of the room, where he lay wreathed in tobacco smoke, the President of the old Duck Hunters peered at us and chortled.

"Now" he said, "you danged naturalists can get me my supper."

MY COLONEL'S LAST HUNT

By Archibald Rutledge

First published in Outdoor Life *(January, 1942), this piece later appeared in* Hunter's Choice *(1946) and in* Tales of Whitetails: Archibald Rutledge's Great Deer-Hunting Stories *(1992). Family bonds with his father and his three sons were of great importance to Rutledge, and this tale reveals the close link he enjoyed with the man he always referred to as "My Colonel" (his rank in the Confederate Army).*

Not only do I admire hunters as a class, but I have learned greatly to love certain woodsmen and to treasure the details of some of their famous hunts. Such a man was my father, and such a hunt was his last one.

Though my father had, throughout his long and active life, little occasion to consult a doctor, and though he hunted until his 82nd year, there came a day when it was necessary to call in a physician for the old gentleman, and this heartless and tactless man told my Colonel that his hunting days were over. At the time, I was living nearly a thousand miles from home, but I soon got a report of this distressing affair.

"The old idiot [my father wrote me in his usual spirited fashion] says I must hang up my hunting horn and lean my gun in a corner—for keeps. I'll hang him up, or stand him in the corner for keeps before I'll stay out of the woods. I'm only eighty-two, Benjamin. [He always called me that because I was his youngest son.] Why quit so young?"

My Colonel, judged by his skill and by his sportsmanship, was the best hunter I ever knew. Not to my knowledge did he ever break a game law; yet, hunting like a gentleman, he killed in the old plantation regions of our home more than 600 whitetail deer; and his record of 30 double shots on deer (one with each barrel) is, so far as I know, still good in South Carolina.

When the brusque doctor's verdict came to the old huntsman, I was, as I have said, far away, but I knew very well from his letters—and just from knowing him—how he took the thing. He simply wouldn't take it. Give up hunting? Not while he could draw a breath. Give up life, if the call came, but not the grand sport that he had followed since earliest boyhood!

After the physician left the house, I know my Colonel looked thoughtfully at himself in the glass, and probably admitted the meaning of that silvery hair; yet surely the blue eyes had lost none of their glinting fire. He probably took a rather fierce five-mile walk, just to prove that the doctor was an old mountebank. Again and again he took his beloved shotgun out on the big front porch and sighted it at imaginary deer at various distances. He could still put it on them. Quit the woods? Not he!

But the real test of his age came when he went down to the stable lot to interview his ancient handy man, Will Alston, a negro of exactly the Colonel's own age, who had faithfully served his master well for more than 60 years. Will was still milking the cows and feeding the stock, and up to that very time, whenever my Colonel felt like taking a turn in the woods, Will had acted as his guide and his deer driver. As he walked down to interview the old darky, my father wondered if the years were telling on his faithful old servant as much as they were on him.

As he approached the dusky figure crouched beside the cow, the Colonel wondered just how he was going to introduce this delicate subject of their relative ages and their fitness for the chase. The cow settled that question. She, a skittish young thing, had just been waiting for some excuse to kick over the bucket, and my father's coming supplied it. She gave it a resounding *wham*, at the same time jumping away from Will. The old negro gaily saluted her in the ribs with a double-barreled kick, with a jauntiness that amazed both the cow and the Colonel.

"Why, Will," he said, "you don't seem to feel old."

"No cow ain't gwine tarrigate me," he said defensively.

At this show of mildly defiant spirit, the Colonel felt younger himself. But he doubted that he could have delivered those kicks with the same spontaneous accuracy and vim that Will had used.

"You are pretty sassy with a cow," the Colonel ventured. "How about a deer? You and I have given many a one a ramble. Are you going to be game to hunt this winter, Will?"

"My wife done tole me I mustn't go in the woods no mo'," Will confessed sadly.

"That's what they are telling me too, Will. But we aren't through yet, are we?"

There was an eager pathos to the question.

"As long as a buck grow horns, and we got two feet, we gwine to follow him. Huntin' is all."

As the Colonel returned to the house he was whistling an old ballad.

A gentle rain was falling, but to this he paid no attention. Nature had never hurt him, and he never learned to coddle himself. But his wife and his three daughters met him on the porch—one with a shawl for his shoulders, one with a cup of hot tea, and two with anxious insistency that he sit in his big chair by the fire. With artful strategy he accepted all these ministrations, but his was a wildwood heart, and tea could not tame it. Slippers and a fireside had no allurements when an old stag might even then be bedded up in the Thickhead or the Rattlesnake or some other famous plantation thicket. He might be a ten-pointer; he might run straight for the Double Pine stand. What was a little rain? Damn all doctors! If Will could kick a cow gaily, he could surely drive out a deer branch. A man can't get up an appetite for dinner by drowsing by the fire.

"My dear," he said to his wife a half-hour later, "tell Will to come in here. I must see him on important business."

This affair called for ancient strategy. For a man, there is no evasion quite so difficult as that of feminine care.

When Will appeared, the two old cronies sat by the fire and talked in whispers of the great crime and affair of state about to be committed.

"It isn't raining hard, is it, Will?" asked the Colonel in so pleading a tone that but one answer was possible.

"She gwine hol' up after a while," lied Will encouragingly.

"We can't use the horses, or we'll get caught," my father advised. "Do you think the bushes out in the Thickhead are very wet?"

"No, sah, not as wet as sometimes," replied the incorrigible negro.

"You hide my gun under your overcoat and slip out by the stable lot. I'll bring the shells. I am going down by the river, make a circle and meet you at the gate."

While the feminine members of the family were busy about their domestic affairs, the Colonel tiptoed down the hallway to the back porch, whence, with an air of indifference, he sauntered through the shrubbery toward the river. Once out of sight of the house, he made a fast detour, and in 10 minutes joined the waiting Will at the edge of the big woods, then dripping and misty under the slow but incessant rain. The two old culprits grinned guiltily but delightedly when they saw each other.

Down the puddly, sandy road they went, making for the deer drive known as the Thickhead, more than a mile from the house. As they approached this famous hangout for deer, a green thicket of myrtles and bays set in the wide and lonely pinelands, the two wily old strategists laid their plans as they had a hundred times before. Only now, they had no horses and no hounds; besides, there should be four standers for the Thickhead, and now there was only one.

"Bossman," said Will calculatingly, "is you want me to compass 'um or to focus 'um?"

Translated, this meant simply: Shall I go round the thicket or shall I come straight through it?

With the deliberation that so momentous a question merited, the Colonel considered long. Finally, he said, "Focus it, Will. I am going to stand at the Double Pine. Give me fifteen minutes to get there."

Will waited in the steady rain while the old huntsman, his cherished gun under his coat, made a circuit of the drive—far through the dripping bushes—coming at last to the famous stand where he had killed more than 40 deer. A yellow pine stood at the critical place; a pine that forked two feet from the ground, sending two mighty shafts towering into the blue. For more than a generation it had marked the place where deer might emerge from the Thickhead, 200 yards straight ahead.

But what of the Pond Stand, and the White Stand, and the Opening to the West? These, too, were famous runs.

The Colonel, with mingled feelings of guilt and the old excitement of the chase, looked the situation over. There might be no deer in the Thickhead. If there were a buck lying in that dripping sea of greenery, he might run over one of the empty stands; or, since Will had been directed to come straight through, he might easily double back.

Bucks, when pushed, have almost a habit of running round the driver. The Colonel knew also that a deer will almost invariably start out of his bed in the direction toward which his head was pointed when he was couched. It was all a great gamble.

There was not a sign of life in the woods. The pines' mournful, sweet song was hushed in the shower. All the birds were hidden and still. The squirrels were asleep in their holes. My Colonel felt that only two foolish and incorrigible old men were out to get a thorough wetting. What would they say at home when he returned bedraggled and empty-handed? And Martha, Will's ebony consort, would blame my father for the whole sinful escapade.

But Will had begun to drive. The Colonel could hear the old fellow's voice quavering at the far end of the Thickhead. The lone stander broke open his gun carefully and made certain that he had in the right shells. He was all set.

The Thickhead looked so dense and so wet that it seemed incredible that Will would ever start anything from those reeking bushes. On he came, rapping the pines with a club and shouting manfully. There was an ardent and a cheerful quality in Will's shouting that showed that he had in mind sweet venison steaks.

He was now near the very middle of the green wilderness of bays. It was a likely place for a jump. But nothing happened. The Colonel's keenness and tension abated somewhat. *Poor old Will!* he thought. He must be as drenched as a sponge. But he was making a manful effort. He didn't seem old, and his voice had that old ring. Through the deep thicket the driver came. The stander could see him. Well, they had hunted anyhow, even if they hadn't killed.

But wait . . . A sudden wild change in Will's voice meant that he had spotted something. Then . . . well, what happened is best told in my father's words, in a letter he wrote me the very day of the Great Affair:

"I had about given up, Benjamin, when old Will sang out, as if he had got religion, or found a jug of liquor. I knew he had seen a deer, but I was not prepared for what followed. You remember that little point of huckleberries that makes out toward the Double Pine? There's a little rosemary pine there not ten feet high, all overrun with smilax. It was under that canopy that this stag was lying.

"Will heard his first rush, and I saw him come tearing out—a great monster of a deer—as if he had lighted firecrackers tied to his tail. When he got within thirty yards I showed myself to make him turn. As he presented his broadside, I saluted him. The gun kindled and he went down—it was all over. He was a true monarch of the glen—a ten-pointer, and so large an animal that it seemed incredible that he should be found right here in the home woods.

"After my shot, I glanced toward the Thickhead, and here came Will, clearing the bushes like a yearling! He got to the deer as soon as I did just as it gave a final, convulsive heave. Over the stag's splendid prostrate form we solemnly shook hands—we two old sinners, we two old down-and-outs whose hunting days were over!"

Such was my Colonel's last deer hunt. He died in his 83rd year.

LOST!
By Burton Spiller

This selection comes from Firelight *(1937), one of Spiller's exquisitely crafted books published by the legendary Derrydale Press. It also appears in* The Deer Book *(1980). Any hunter who says he has never been lost either is a stranger to the truth or hasn't roamed much. Even Daniel Boone, while disclaiming that he had never been lost, acknowledged that he "was once temporarily misplaced for three weeks."*

I had parted with Wilson at daybreak that morning. We had come into camp together the previous evening, riding the 11 miles in from Eustis on a springless, horse-drawn vehicle which jounced and pounded over the corduroy road until we flinched at each recurrent blow of the lightly padded rest at the small of our backs.

It was snowing hard before we had completed the two-hour journey: great, moist flakes, which persisted in finding their way down inside our upturned collars, and left our necks cold and clammy and uncomfortable. They melted less readily, though, on the cool earth, where the cedar boughs began to bend low with the accumulation of the white burden.

Sitting between us and ever pushing his body back to wedge us more distressingly against the torturing seat, the driver flapped his reins and chirruped to the plodding horse. "You fellas are gettin' in at just the right time. First snow of the season," he said. "Oughta be good trackin' tomorrow and next day."

He proved to be a good prophet, for when we rose the next morning before dawn, and went outside to verify his observation, we found a four-inch carpet upon the ground, a moist and heavy blanket which made it possible to move soundlessly through the heavy wood. The clouds were lifting and breaking up. Occasionally a star gleamed momentarily in an opening and gave promise of a clear day.

We ate breakfast by lamplight in the long, low kitchen of Downey's camp to the accompaniment of the confused babel of voices of a half-score sportsmen who ate hurriedly as they formulated plans for the day's hunt.

We listened while we munched our toast and tried to assimilate information from the scraps of conversation, for this was our first visit in that rough and rugged wilderness lying between the last frontier town in the Dead River region and Rangeley Lakes, some 30 miles to the south.

Our gleanings were of little value, though, for these men were old-timers who had spent many seasons in the locality. A group of three was going to drive the "burn." A grizzled old chap and a black-haired fellow of 40 were pinning their faith in the "gap" to produce a head worth mounting. Another pair was going to work the "ridges."

To the men who mentioned them so glibly, these names signified a definite area, a choice preserve which was theirs by the right of discovery, and which they had located only after tramping many a weary mile. But to us they meant less than nothing. The knowledge would eventually be ours, but we must acquire it as the others had done.

We built an imposing pair of sandwiches from generous slices of bread and thick and juicy venison, stuffed them in our pockets, picked up our rifles and struck out in the halflight of early dawn.

The trail of the hunters who had preceded us followed a well-defined path leading toward a bit of rising ground to the southwest, and this path we elected to follow. In the east, the sky was already crimson with the miracle of another day, while in the west, a lone star blazed and paled as it fought for supremacy over the inevitable brightness which must soon efface it.

Two hundred yards farther on, we came to a spot where three men had left the trail and swung off to the right. These would be the three who were going to drive the "burn." It must lie somewhere off there to the northward in that stretch of wood which extended to the Chaudiere River in Canada. Farther on, a couple had turned to the left. Somewhere off to the south must lie either the "ridges" or the "gap," and these men were striking confidently toward them with hope burning strong in their breasts that a mighty buck or a sleek doe awaited them there.

Oh, well. In a few days we, too, would be familiar with the country, and strike off as unhesitatingly as they toward some spot of our own choosing, which we believed to be superior.

A splash of green attracted my attention: a dark spot among the snow-laden limbs of the almost impenetrable cedar thicket which fringed our path. Something had moved beneath that limb since the snow had ceased falling. The white covering had slid earthward, leaving the bare branch to indicate the passing of some unknown forest dweller.

Stepping from the trail, I scanned the newly fallen snow beside the disturbed branch. Sure enough, there was the trail I had expected to find: the imprint of the cloven feet sharply defined. It was now light enough to distinguish the well-rounded toe prints which identified the sex of the animal.

"It's a buck, and a good one," I said to Wilson. "No need to look further. Let's follow this one."

"You take him," he answered, "and I will look up one of my own. If the sun comes out, this snow will be gone before night. We had better make the most of it while it lasts and hunt separately."

Now, I have always liked to have a companion when I follow a deer. I like to have one pair of eyes free to watch the country ahead, without the necessity of glancing down momentarily at the elusive trail. Then, too, I have found it is often good strategy to post a partner at some likely spot after a deer has been jumped and starts circling as they oftentimes will. More than one wily old fellow has experienced the surprise of his life while playing hide and seek with me, because of that little coup which he had not anticipated.

Wilson, though, was more experienced than I, and I acceded to his opinion.

"All right," I said, "but pick a good one if you expect to beat this fellow. If he weighs less than two hundred I am no judge of footprints."

He laughed and advised me to take my time on the trail.

"The foolish ones don't live to grow so big as that." With that bit of wisdom, he left me.

The tracks led toward the south. I verified that with my compass before I started off, and checked it at frequent intervals afterward. The trail meandered back and forth as the buck chose the easier footing, but the general direction was unvarying. So fresh were the tracks that I knew he was but a short distance ahead, yet I was certain he was unaware of my presence behind him. His pace was unhurried, and I could see where he had stopped occasionally to nibble a shoot of the not-too-common moosewood. The sun emerged from the retreating bank of clouds, and the trees began to drip as the already moist snow felt the warming rays.

Still, the buck traveled steadily onward. At nine o'clock, he detoured to a low knoll where the telltale tracks showed that a doe had joined him. Together and unhurriedly they went on, still traveling southward through the wilderness as accurately as though they followed a blazed trail. An hour later, they were joined by another smaller doe, but possessed with the same common purpose to learn what lay beyond the ever-receding horizon to the south.

For at least another hour I followed them. Then, all at once, the trail took on an appearance of extreme freshness. It would be hard to explain why, for the footprints were not one whit more clearly defined than before, but I had a feeling they were but a few minutes old, and knew that foolish and often laughed-at inclination to feel if they were still warm.

For the first time that morning, I began moving with extreme caution, testing each step for a concealed and betraying bit of dry wood beneath my foot before I bore my weight upon it, while scanning the forest ahead with an intentness of gaze which was eye-straining.

There was little wind, but, such as it was, it favored my approach, and I felt certain I would see them before they were aware of my presence. But their sense of hearing was keener than I had thought, or else some flaw in the wind carried my scent to them, for all at once there came a startled snort and the crash of leaping bodies in the tangle ahead of me.

I threw the rifle to my shoulder and was made aware of the commotion ahead of me, not only by the sound, but by the violent agitation of an occasional branch or a more sturdy sapling. Of those plunging brown bodies, however, I caught not the slightest glimpse.

Then, for one fleeting instant, the buck was plainly visible, outlined as though he were engraved upon the darker background of the forest as he leaped over some obstruction barring his path. I tried to swing my gun on him but failed, for he was out of sight in the space of a single heartbeat.

To my ears came the sound of a few more crashing bounds, then silence descended as I pushed ahead to read the story in the snow. It was plain enough. They had detected my presence and had bounded away: the two does going straight ahead, the buck, choosing to desert them and seek safety somewhere off to their right.

I knew that his desertion was only a temporary one, and that sooner or later he would try to rejoin the females, and I resolved to put into practice a plan whereby any such gallantry on his part might prove to be his undoing.

Calling on my already tiring legs to do double duty for a few minutes, I set off on the trail of the does and followed them for perhaps 300 yards before I had the satisfaction of again hearing them jump before me.

A hasty examination of their tracks showed they had not doubled back on their former course, so I retreated some 20 yards downward from the trail, brushed the snow from a fallen log and sat down to await developments.

My position, I felt, was a strategic one. The buck was separated from the does and was anxious to rejoin them. The obvious thing for him to do would be to wait until I was well out of the way, on whatever mysterious errand had brought me across his path, and then cautiously smell out the trail of the two entrancing young ladies who had so hurriedly departed. Yes, it seemed likely he would follow that plan, and it seemed equally likely he would not guess I was sitting there beside the trail, waiting for him to come along.

I glanced at my watch. It was 11:50. Almost noon. The thought reminded me of the sandwich in my pocket. I secured it and ate it slowly, meditatively, as I kept a keen eye on the trail.

The minutes dragged past; many of them. The sandwich was long since consumed and my perspiring body was beginning to know the chill of inactivity. I looked cautiously at my watch once more. 12:45! I had been sitting inert for nearly an hour. Evidently the plan was not going to work. The old fellow was either too cautious or else he had slipped around me and rejoined his companions.

If I was to get back to camp before dark, I would have to hurry. I slid the watch back in my pocket and was about to stand up when I distinctly heard the crackle of brush from down the trail whence the does had gone. I started to turn my head cautiously that way, but the motion was arrested by a louder and nearer sound from that quarter of the woods from which I had expected the buck to emerge.

The significance of it dawned upon me. Each party was seeking the other, and if my luck held just a few minutes longer, they were going to meet almost exactly in front of the spot I had chosen. What a nice little party we were going to have!

Their approach was cautious. At intervals I could hear the swish of a branch as a sleek body disturbed it sufficiently to relieve it of its weight of snow. Once I heard a doe emit a soft little *ba-a*, but otherwise there was silence as only a great wood can know silence.

Then, from the corner of my eye, I caught a hint of movement down the trail and, almost instantly afterward, another from the direction from which I expected the buck to appear.

Focusing my eyes on that spot, I saw him clearly as he emerged into a little opening. He carried his head low as he sniffed the path he followed, and his ears twitched alternately forward and back as he listened for a sound that would send him less cautiously forward, or one that would cause him to bound tumultuously away.

Waiting until a thicket screened him, I slid the safety, brought the rifle to my shoulder and leveled it at the next opening ahead of him. He stepped into it almost at once, scarcely 50 yards away and almost broadside. When I touched the trigger, he went down as though poleaxed. I saw him kick convulsively as I worked the action and swung about in an effort to locate the does.

A white flag became visible at once, moving in quick, erratic flashes as its owner dodged in and out through the thickly growing timber. Following that waving beacon with my rifle sight, I saw her clearly for a moment, swung well toward the front of her and touched the trigger once again. Her flag went down at the report, then showed white once more as she leaped ahead in startled frenzy, and she was gone before I could shoot again.

I glanced back again at the buck. He lay where he had fallen, his head drawn stiffly back and a forefoot pawing listlessly in an ineffectual and pathetic effort to impart motion to his stricken body. That he was done for I knew, for I had held just back of his shoulder, low down for a heart shot, and the distance had been as nothing. I turned my back on him and hurried down the trail after the doe that I was certain my bullet had reached.

There was blood on her trail. Not much, but a spatter of it here and there on the watery snow. I pushed on after her with hope strong in my heart, but it died gradually as the red flecks became less frequent.

My aim had been faulty and my bullet had no more than creased her skin or nicked one of her generous ears. Oh, well! It was too much to expect to kill a pair on the first day out.

I would go back to my buck and perform the rather messy and disagreeable task of dressing him and, by the time that was done, it would be necessary to make all possible haste to camp if I expected to reach it before dark.

Hastening along on my back track, I came, before many minutes had passed, to the spot from whence I had done my shooting. From there, I looked across the intervening space to where my prize lay. For some unknown reason, I was unable to see him. With an uneasy feeling in my heart, I hurried over to where he had fallen.

He was gone. There could be no denying that fact. There was the place in the snow where he had dropped, the imprint of his body enlarged and misshapen where he had twisted about in a vain effort to rise, but no tuft of hair or minute carmine stain to indicate that my bullet had struck any part of him. I was sure that my eyes could not have deceived me. He had gone down as though hit by a lightning bolt, and I would have taken any bet that he would never regain his feet. He had accomplished the task, nevertheless. The track showed that he had risen, stumbled once to his knees, and then leaped cleanly away.

I tried to reason the thing out. I knew my aim had been accurate. I did not claim to be an expert rifle shot, but at that distance, and shooting from a sitting position, I knew I could place a dozen shots in a group which my hand could span. The only possible error I could have made would have been in the manner of distance. It might have been farther than I had thought. I glanced back to the log where I had sat and knew that I had not erred. The distance was not an inch more than 50 yards.

Standing thus, with my gaze taking in the route my bullet had traveled, I became aware of an unusual white spot on a cedar sapling about halfway to the fallen log. I went back and examined it. The sapling was a tiny thing, no thicker than my thumb, but my bullet had centered it accurately. The copper jacket had peeled back and was still in the ragged hole.

Going over the territory carefully, I found that the bullet had shattered. A grain of it had creased a larger cedar some three feet to the right of the correct line of flight. Probing a fresh wound in a white birch some 15 feet to the left, I dug out another goodly chunk of lead. An almost severed branch showed where a third piece had zoomed upward at an unbelievable elevation.

What minute portion of it hit the buck, and what part of his anatomy, I have never been able to determine. I followed his track for more than a mile, but found no indication that he had been injured in the slightest degree. There was not so much as one fleck of blood in all that discouraging distance. His leaps were sturdy and strong, indicating that he was possessed with an irresistible yearning to occupy any other spot in the universe than the one that he was at that moment vacating.

I became so absorbed with the intriguing mystery that time and place were forgotten, until a chill breath of air and an absence of warmth in the sun's rays brought me to myself at last. I consulted my watch. The hands pointed to three o'clock. In two hours' time it would be dark. The thought was startling. I had less than two hours in which to retrace a trail I had been making for eight hours. The thing was absolutely impossible of accomplishment.

My only chance was to lay a course due north according to my compass, and follow it as accurately and as speedily as possible. My plan had only one drawback. Downey's camp lay at the end of the corduroy road, and the road ran north and south in an almost exact line with the route I proposed to travel. Should I err and miss it by passing to the right, I would, in the course of time, come either to civilization or a road leading to it; but if I chanced to pass to the left, I might well travel to the Canadian boundary without finding so much as a lumberman's camp.

The safer way would be to travel in a northeasterly direction, and then swing northward until I came to the road leading to camp, but that would occupy a longer space of time than I had at my disposal.

My ultimate decision was to try, with what little woodsmanship I possess, to come out within sight of camp.

Looking back now upon the events of that entire day, I am impressed with my utter lack of common sense. The country was of a monotonous sameness, with no distinguishing landmarks to arrest the eye of a newcomer. No scarred peak thrust its spire upward as an easily read sign-board, which even a novice could understand. No babbling brook or rushing river intervened to form a barrier, which one would know he must not cross. The whole country was uniformly flat and of an unvarying sameness until one had learned it as he learns to accurately know his own dooryard.

I was aware of these things, but I had utter confidence in my ability as a woodsman. There was no slightest doubt in my mind concerning my power to eventually reach either the camp or the adjacent road. The only disturbing thought was whether or not I would have time to do so before dark. I brushed the snow from a fallen log, leveled my compass upon it, took an accurate bearing due north and started off at the best pace possible in the loose and uneven footing.

For the first hour, the way was easy. The forest was not too thick, while the land sloped almost imperceptibly in the direction I was traveling. Then I ran into difficulty. Before me stretched a cedar swamp, a thick and almost impenetrable tangle of closely set young trees whose branches touched the ground. How far the swamp extended to the right or left I had no means of knowing, and neither had I any conception of the distance it stretched before me.

There was no time left for a trip of exploration along its fringes. My way led straight ahead—and that way I went.

I believe the swamp was less than a quarter-mile in width, but some distances may not be accurately measured by such standards. Occasionally, one encounters a bit of terrain whose span may only be estimated by the toll it exacts of spent muscles and aching limbs. Of such nature was the cedar swamp.

For untold centuries, the trees had grown and died and fallen to the ground in a jackstraw confusion through which other trees had sprung. The only means of progress was by crawling through spaces barely large enough to permit the passage of my body, under logs too high to climb, and over others too low to crawl under. Many of the latter lay in crisscross tangles, which persisted in breaking rottenly in that moment when I had almost reached their summit: a bit of stratagem on their part which invariably threw me, with football tactics, for a loss of one or two hard-won yards.

Adding to my difficulties, the ground, when I did get down to it through the rotten wood, was a quagmire into which I sank almost to my knees, while the snow, which still lay thickly on each hindering branch and twig, showered me and melted with the heat of my body until every thread of my clothing was saturated with it.

The sun was shining when I first pushed into the tangled mass, but twilight had already fallen when I finally won through to the firm ground on the other side. I have never known a more heartbreaking hour in the wilderness.

It seemed hopeless, now, to push on. Darkness was but a half-hour away and my judgment told me I was still some two or three miles from camp. If the way chanced to be open, I might make it, but another tangle like the one I had just traversed would effectually bar me from further progress for the night.

I deliberated whether or not to push on or pause here and gather wood for a tiny fire, which would keep me from freezing through the long hours that lay ahead. With my saturated garments, the latter plan held little of pleasurable anticipation. For that matter, the thought of forging ahead through the darkness was not conducive to merriment, but there was a chance I would find an easier trail ahead. Accordingly, I went on, hurrying as best I could, but ever mindful of the disaster that would inevitably follow a slip, resulting in a sprained ankle or a fractured leg.

The twilight deepened and the light died in the west. Presently a star came out, winking brightly at me from the pale sky. Others followed at intervals until the heavens were studded with them, and I welcomed their dim but friendly light.

Another hour passed and the way grew rougher. Little rolling ridges intercepted my progress. Ridges down which I had to grope with caution, and up which I climbed with an effort that took a toll from my leg muscles and lifeless knees.

Well, I thought, here is the situation which you have visualized for more than ten years. You know what to do. Don't wait any longer. If it is necessary to spend a night in the woods, spend it as comfortably as possible. Make camp—and make it now.

That this was good advice I knew full well. Many a man has perished under similar conditions, because in his panic, he forgot that the human body weakened rapidly through cold and exposure, and that even a sleepless and supperless night spent before a rousing campfire would restore more energy than would the heaviest repast if the latter were followed by a night of aimless wandering.

I was quite confident I had not erred much in the matter of direction, but the distance to camp was still a matter of conjecture. That cedar swamp had been my undoing and, in the darkness, I cursed the almost impregnable entanglement which had robbed me of the hour of daylight I had so sorely needed.

Then, too, the matter of selecting a camping spot was not an easy one, now that night had fallen. I needed a background of cliff or boulder or steeply cut bank to reflect the heat of my fire and cut off the freezing air, which was now settling rapidly from the starlit space above me. If I could find such a spot, the night would not be too uncomfortable to endure.

I slid down into another gully and began ascending the sharply rising ground before me. It seemed steeper and higher than the others I had climbed, and there was an occasional outcropping of ledge where the snow had melted. I decided to push along to its crest and try to find an upthrust boulder which would serve my purpose.

The trees thinned as I neared the top and my hopes arose. Somewhere along this ridge, which an ancient glacier had molded in its passing, I would find a friendly niche where a minimum of fuel would give me a maximum amount of heat.

Swinging to the right, I traveled a few yards while my eyes strained to pierce the darkness. Then, directly ahead, a square of light glowed through an opening in the trees. It was shining through a rear window in Downey's camp! No harbor light ever loomed fairer to a storm-tossed mariner than did that yellow glare to me.

To reach it was only a matter of minutes. I lifted the latch and entered. A dozen faces confronted me and relief was written plainly upon them. A dozen pairs of eyes glanced questioningly at me as I closed the door and strode into the room. A dozen voices lifted in simultaneous clamor for details as I searched the circle of faces for the only one I knew.

"Get lost, did you?" a grizzled old-timer asked.

"Oh, no," I boasted, secretly a little vain of my success in running a course so accurately. "Only slightly delayed. Where is Wilson? Isn't he in yet?"

"Wasn't he with you?" The chorus was a general one.

"No. We separated at daylight. I followed a buck until three o'clock and then took a straight line for camp."

"This friend of yours—what's his name? Wilson? Is he a—does he know his way around in the woods?"

It was Downey who spoke, and I could detect the uneasiness in his voice: a host troubled for the safety of his guests.

"Yes," I assured him. "Yes, he's a good man." I tried to extract some grain of comfort from the thought but knew a growing feeling of apprehension.

"Did he have a compass?"

"Yes."

"Well, I guess he'll be all right—if he knows how to use it—and keeps his head. You better get some dry clothes on and eat your supper. You look cold."

I had not noticed it until then, but now I could feel a tremor in my body as the sensitive nerves shrank away from my soaked garments. When I undressed, I found my limbs were blue and wrinkled, and never have I known a more grateful warmth than that imparted by the feel of dry woolens against my tingling skin and a pot of hot tea, which all but blistered my tongue.

Ten minutes later, I would have been physically content once more had it not been for my worry concerning Wilson's safety. Save for the natural reluctance to experience the discomfort of a night spent in the open, I had known no uneasiness concerning my own safety or my ability to speedily find camp with the coming of daylight. But now that I knew my friend was somewhere out there in the cheerless night, a score of disquieting possibilities presented themselves and added to the depressing weight, which was already bearing heavily upon my soul.

Nor was the burden lifted when, warmed and refreshed, I again entered the lounging room where a crackling fire glowed in the huge fireplace, flooding the room with both light and friendly heat.

In the face of impending disaster, man has a propensity to talk of incidents which have come under his observation where tragedy actually occurred. More than once, while riding out a howling squall in an open boat, some comforting soul has ceased his bailing long enough to observe, "This is like the blow in which Joe Doakes and his wife and three kids were drowned in Lake Suchandsuch. The motor stopped and—"

Or, while sitting with a group of friends during a severe electrical storm, how common it is to hear someone say, "This reminds me of a shower we had down in Honkatonk two years ago. It came up just like this one—so dark you could hardly see across the room. It burned four stands of buildings and killed three people in that one town alone. I was standing in the doorway when the bolt came down, which struck the town hall. It split three ways and—"

Evidently, Downey also possessed that characteristically human trait for his voice, attuned to the open spaces, flooded the little room.

". . . looked like a woodsman," he was saying, "and I supposed he knew a little something. I found out afterward that he was one of them city gunners who never hunted a patch of woods that had more than two acres in it. We found him in a birch country, but he'd used up every match he had, tryin' to light a fire of green brush. Guess he didn't know that birchbark would burn. Both feet was froze, and we thought for a while they would have to come off, but he got out of it by losin' most of his toes. It beats all how a feller will go off his nut just as soon as it begins to get dark."

"There's lots of things can happen—especially when a man is alone." The seamed and wind-tanned face of the speaker marked him as a man who had spent much of his life in the open.

"I remember the time Folsom disappeared. He had been gathering gum before the deer season opened. We all knew he was working Black Nubble, but it was weeks before we found him. I guess a dozen men had gone within twenty feet of him, but they didn't look high enough. His spurs had slipped in a bit of rotten wood.

"He was sitting bolt upright, about twenty feet from the ground, and looked as though he was perched up there for fun—kinda grinning down at us. I guess he didn't laugh much, though. He had come down on a dead branch that was pointing straight up, and it was driven the whole length of his body. Made me kinda sick when we pulled him off from it."

Then someone remembered Alcide Perrault. Old Alcide had slipped on a snow-covered rock and broken his leg. Dazed, bewildered and wracked with pain, he had crawled for miles and dragged that tortured limb behind him. A tough bird, Old Alcide. One of the kind who die hard. He had crawled for miles, but in the wrong direction. When they found him, he was frozen stiff, while the wood mice had . . .

"Queer things happen," said one I had come to know as Bates. "Sometimes you can't find a reasonable explanation for them, and then again you can. Take the case of Hoffman. For a businessman, who only got into the woods a few weeks each year, he was just about as good as they come. I suppose that was what made him successful in business— what I mean is that if he took an interest in anything, he studied it until he knew all the angles. He certainly was a good woodsman.

"He knew this section, too. He had been coming up here for years and never asked anything of any guide but to keep out of his way. He tried to get his wife interested in hunting, but I guess society appealed to her more. She was a lot younger than he, anyway. He did manage to get her up here one fall, but three days of it was all she could stand.

"The next fall, he brought in a sleek-looking young fellow he was taking into his business. He was a smooth chap and looked like one of those collar ads you see in the magazines, but I disliked him from the first minute I saw him. That's funny, too, for when I tried to find something about him that I could object to, I couldn't think of a thing, with the exception of the way he brushed back his hair and the oily look it had.

"Queer, isn't it, how we sometimes dislike a person at the first glance? Well, I didn't like him—but Hoffman did—so it was none of my business.

"They went out together the second day, and that night Stavel— the young chap—came in alone. He was scratched by branches and bruised by falls, and he said the camp certainly looked like the snake's hips to him. He had separated from Hoffman early in the morning and had become confused, he said, and had no idea where he was until he struck the tote road leading to camp.

"As darkness came on, he began to worry, and suggested getting up a searching party, but we laughed at the idea. We knew Hoffman. He had a compass and he knew how to use it. If it had become damaged, he still had the stars to guide him. If it was necessary for him to sleep out, why he knew how to build a leanto and how to keep it warm.

Hoffman was all right.

"He didn't come in that night, so we started a search for him the next morning. The next day we sent after more help and made an organized hunt, but with no success.

"Stavel was wild. He telegraphed Mrs. Hoffman and she pulled in that night, in a big car with a chauffeur and a private detective.

"Then the governor got interested in the case and put a hundred men in the woods. Every possible outlet was watched, and we had a plane scouting the territory for two days, searching for a trace of smoke, which might be his campfire.

"We couldn't pick up his track the first day, and after the army was turned loose on us, it was impossible to follow any one man's track.

"Stavel offered a reward of five thousand dollars to any person who would find Hoffman, either dead or alive, and that brought in a lot more men. The young fellow was pretty nearly frantic, but he stuck to the story he had first told, telling that and no other, and no amount of questioning could cause him to change it in the slightest degree.

"Mrs. Hoffman bore up under it remarkably well. She said she felt it would somehow come out all right. She put in quite a lot of time comforting Stavel, who was suffering the tortures of the damned, if you could judge by his looks.

"After a week the governor called in his men, and although we hunted more or less until winter closed in, it was useless. Hoffman had vanished.

"The next spring a few of us went over the ground pretty carefully. We poled up the rivers and paddled around the lakes without finding anything. We even drained Beaver Bog, and went over every foot of it on snowshoes, with the same lack of results.

"Mrs. Hoffman waited a few months longer and then took the matter to the courts. After some deliberation, they arrived at a decision. They pronounced Hoffman legally dead—at least so far as she was concerned."

He paused a moment while he selected a cigarette from its metal case. The lighter clicked, the flame flared, and he blew a cloud of smoke upward.

"I respect the court's decision," he said. "So far as she was concerned, I think Hoffman was dead long before that morning when he started out with Stavel. I may be wrong—but I never liked the way that guy brushed his hair. I guess she liked it, though. Anyway, she married him."

We sat silent for a moment, and, in that moment, the latch lifted and Wilson stamped in. There was blood on his hands, but the eyes which sought out mine from all those others focused upon him knew a contented look. It was good to see him and to note that a self-satisfied little smile lurked at the corners of his mouth.

"Well, how big was yours?" he asked. "He'll have to be good if he beats the one I hung up just before dark. Ten points—and his head is a perfect one, too!"

NORTHWEST WHITETAIL TROPHY
By Jack O'Connor

As was the case with so much of his writing, this adventure originally appeared in Outdoor Life *and subsequently in* Outdoor Life's Deer Hunting Book *(1974). Always a master at giving his readers the utmost in vicarious experience, O'Connor takes us along on a memorable hunt in his inimitable fashion.*

The northwestern variety of the whitetail deer in its various forms is the most widely distributed big-game animal in the United States. Found from Maine to Oregon, it furnishes more sport to hunters than any other big-game animal and is responsible for the sale of more rifles and ammunition for the manufacturers and more telescope sights for the scope-makers. And, because sportsmen buy licenses to hunt it, the money it brings in keeps most game departments functioning.

But until recently, the northern whitetail was to me as strange a trophy as the greater kudu, the desert bighorn and the ibex are to most hunters. I have hunted all of these fine animals and others just as exotic, but the northern whitetail had always eluded me.

Of all the varieties of northern whitetails, the least known is the one found in the Northwest. The more plentiful mule deer and the elk sell the out-of-state licenses and get the publicity. In fact, many hunters do not even realize that some of the largest whitetail deer in North America and some of the best trophies come from Idaho, Washington, Montana and Oregon, and from the Canadian province of British Columbia. These northwestern whitetails are probably just about as heavy as the famous whitetails of Maine, and their heads compare favorably with those of whitetails shot anywhere. The Number 4 listing in the 1964 edition of *Records of North American Big Game* is a whitetail shot in Flathead County, Montana, in 1963, and I have seen handsome and very large antlers nailed to barns and garages and poorly mounted on walls of backwoods bars and country stores. Most of these big whitetails were taken not by trophy hunters, but by backwoodsmen and farmers who are after meat.

These whitetails of the Northwest are classified as *Odocoileus virginianus ochrourus*.

I grew up in the Southwest country where I hunted Coues whitetails. I have hunted these fine little deer in Arizona, in Sonora, and in the Big Bend of Texas, and I have taken many handsome bucks of this diminutive species. Such small skill as I have at hitting running game I owe to the Arizona jackrabbit and the Arizona whitetail. I have also shot the small but quite different Texas whitetail found around San Antonio. But a good northern whitetail was one of the few major North American trophies I did not have.

I had never laid eyes on a northern whitetail until I moved from Arizona to Idaho more than 20 years ago, and then it took me about three years to see one. I'll never forget the first one I saw.

I was hunting pheasants with a wonderful Brittany spaniel named Mike. He had been cruising through a field of rich, golden wheat stubble when he went on point at the edge of a grassy swale. I thought he had pinned a cock pheasant, but when I got up to him, he looked at me out of the corner of his eyes and wore the sneaky expression he assumed when he was doing something he knew he should not do.

I picked up a stone to flush whatever it was, and threw it at the spot in the grass where Mike's nose was pointed. Out burst a little whitetail doe. Most dogs are convinced that they have been born to be deer and rabbit hounds, but Mike almost fell backward in surprise.

Another time, Mike hauled up on the edge of a brushy draw on solid point. I walked in and kicked the brush. A pair of cackling roosters came barreling out. I shot, dropped one of them, was about to take the other when a big whitetail buck sailed out of the brush and headed across the stubble toward a patch of woods.

For the rest of the bird season, which mostly at the time ran concurrently with the deer season, I carried a couple of rifled slugs in my pants pocket so if I jumped another whitetail, I could jerk out a shotshell and slam a shell loaded with a slug into the chamber. But the news must have got around; I never saw a buck.

A farmer I knew told me he just about had a big whitetail buck tied up for me. He said that the old boy lived in a canyon bordering one of his wheat fields. That buck fed on wheat all summer and in the fall feasted on the sweet, stunted apples that fell in an abandoned orchard in one corner of his place.

So I spent about ten days hunting him off and on during the season. His tracks were everywhere—in the orchard, in the wheat stubble, along the deer and cattle trails among the brush and trees, and on the bank of the little trout stream that ran through the canyon.

Keeping the wind in my favor, I still-hunted cautiously and quietly along the trails, taking a few steps, stopping, listening, watching. Once I heard something moving quietly off through thick brush, and I found his bed below a ledge in a warm spot where the sun had melted the frost off the grass. Another time I heard a crash below me and caught a glimpse of his white flag flying. I sat for hours with my back to a tree waiting for him to show up. He didn't.

"I can't understand why you can't see that buck," my farmer friend said. "I seen him yesterday when I was looking for a stray cow, and Bill Jones seen him from his pickup when he was coming back from getting the mail four or five days ago. Said he wasn't a danged bit wild; stood there looking at him. He could have hit him with a slingshot."

Another year, while scouting for good pheasant areas in eastern Washington, I found a pretty little valley full of trees and brush and with a clear brook wandering through it. It lay between two grassy hillsides that ran down from rolling wheat fields. The valley was full of pheasants. The hillsides supported several coveys of Huns. Quail roosted in the trees. The valley also contained a herd of whitetails. I saw a doe, a fawn, one small buck and the tracks of a big buck.

I made up my mind to be in a strategic spot in the valley as soon as it was light enough to shoot on opening day. So when the day came, I parked my station wagon along the road half-a-mile from the valley and left my Model 21 Winchester 12 gauge and my puzzled, whining Brittany spaniel locked up. Wearing a pair of binoculars around my neck and carrying a light 7x57, I walked through a wheat field toward the head of the valley.

I was almost at the spot I had in mind when I heard the crash of a rifle. A startled doe streaked by me. Running along the grassy hillside and up into the wheat stubble were the dim forms of about a dozen deer flaunting white tails. I sat down and got them in the field of the binoculars. All were does and fawns. Then something caught my attention just under the skyline about a quarter-mile away. I put the glasses on a buck sneaking along. When he topped out, I saw heavy antlers.

About 20 shots had been fired, but now the last deer was out of sight. I could hear voices coming from the valley. It was quite light now. I walked a little farther until I saw four men gathered around a small and very dead buck. One was gutting him. I talked to the men a few minutes. Before long they departed in triumph, each holding a leg of the buck. I went back to my car and stowed the rifle and binoculars. Then I let my joyful dog out and set off to see if I could have any luck on birds.

In Arizona and Sonora, Coues deer are found high up. In southern Arizona, they are seldom lower than the altitude where the evergreen oaks the Mexicans call *encinos* grow—about 4,000 to 4,500 feet. The desert variety of mule deer are out in the mesquite and cactus of the flats and the low rolling hills. Out on the flat Sonoran desert west of the railroad that runs south from Nogales, Arizona, the mule deer are on the perfectly flat, sandy, aboreal desert where they range among the mesquites, ironwoods and chollas. Low hills and little ranges rise from the desert floor, and on all of them are (or used to be) whitetails. Sometimes the whitetails are in easily navigable foothills of the tall, rocky, desert-sheep mountains.

But in the Northwest, at least in areas with which I am familiar, whitetails are found lower than the mule deer, on the brushy hillsides near wheatfields, and in the wooded riverbottoms back in the elk mountains. They are bold but furtive, and they'll live all summer in a farmer's woodlot.

Some of them grow to be very large. I once knew a man who ran a meat locker in Lewiston, Idaho, my home town. He told me that the heaviest buck ever weighed at his plant was a whitetail. As I remember, it field-dressed around 335 pounds. I have heard of Northwest whitetails in Washington as well as Idaho that were about as heavy. I have never seen a deer of any sort that I thought would dress out at anything like 300 pounds, but now and then, one undoubtedly turns out to be that heavy.

I started closing in on my first Northwestern whitetail in the fall of 1969 when my wife and I drove to the ranch of our friend Dave

Christensen on the Salmon River downstream from Riggins, Idaho. Dave operates an elk-hunting camp on Moose Creek in the Selway Wilderness Area and lives most of the year on the beautiful Salmon River ranch. When I first knew the elk-hunting camp, it was Moose Creek Lodge, a luxurious bit of civilization out in the wilderness. A hunter could go out after elk all day and return at night to a drink around the fireplace, a good meal served with silver and linen, a hot shower and a sound sleep on an inner-spring mattress. But the area was declared a wilderness. The federal government bought the lodge and burned it down.

Now in the fall, Dave's dudes fly in to a U.S. Forest Service landing strip a few miles away and hunt elk from a comfortable tent camp near the spot where the lodge used to be. I have shot five-, six- and seven-point elk out of Moose Creek. Dave and his father, Ken, took the money they got from the sale of the lodge and their land, and put it into the Salmon River ranch.

As my wife and I drove in that November day in '69, we saw a whitetail buck in a field a mile or so from the ranch house. Not long afterward we saw some whitetail does and fawns.

"You must have a lot of whitetails around here," I said when Dave came out to meet us.

"Plenty," he told me. "The whitetails are mostly low down along the creek and in the brushy draws that run into it. The mule deer are higher."

The season around Dave's place was closed then, so my wife and I had to forgo the whitetails. We hunted mule deer in another management area about 20 miles away. But we made a promise to take a run at the whitetails.

Along in August, 1971, Dave called me.
"You haven't forgotten our date to hunt whitetails?" he asked. "No? Well, the season opens October second. Drive down the afternoon of the first and we'll have at them."

My son, Bradford, who is outdoor editor of the *Seattle Times* and who is a longtime pal of Dave Christensen and his wife, Ann, flew from Seattle and joined us on the drive to the ranch.

One of Dave's successful elk hunters from Moose Creek had come down to the Salmon to try for a deer, and three other elk hunters who were on their way into Moose Creek were camped down the creek a mile or so from the ranchhouse.

The strategy was simple. Eleanor, Bradford and I, accompanied by a guide named Stan Rock, would climb about 1,000 feet above the ranch near the head of a canyon where a little stream ran into Dave's creek. After giving us time to get into position, Dave would walk up the canyon on a deer and cattle trail that ran along the bottom. There were whitetails and mule deer in those canyons, and with luck we would get some shooting.

It was dark and chilly when we started out, and the sun was not up when we arrived near the head of the canyon on a grassy ridge. The canyon dropped sharply below us, and the bottom was a tangle of trees and brush. The far side of the canyon was steep, mostly rocks with a few low bushes and sparse grass.

Eleanor had gone on to the brink of the canyon; Bradford was about 20 feet or so to her left. I was in the process of filling up the magazine of an old pet .270 I had used from northern British Columbia to Botswana and Iran. It is a pre-1964 Winchester Model 70 Featherweight stocked in plain but hard French walnut by Al Biesen of Spokane and fitted with a Leupold 4X scope on the now-obsolete Tilden mount. It has the original Winchester barrel with the original Featherweight contour. The only thing Biesen did to the metal was to put the release lever for the hinged floorplate in the forward portion of the trigger guard and checker the bolt knob.

This is a terrific rifle. I bought it from the Erb Hardware Company of Lewiston, Idaho. Year after year, it holds its point of impact. Carry it in a saddle scabbard, jounce it around in a hunting car on safari, ship it a few thousand miles by air, let it get rained on for hours in a Scottish deer forest, shoot it at sea level or at 10,000 feet, in the crackling heat of the Kalahari Desert or under the glaciers in the sub-arctic Stone sheep country of British Columbia, and it always lays them in the same place. It is also one of those rare light sporters that will group into a minute of angle—if I am using good bullets and do my part.

I had just finished slipping the last cartridge into the chamber and putting on the safety when Eleanor, who has eyes like an eagle, said, "Deer . . . two deer. The lower one's a buck."

Two deer were scooting up the far side of the canyon about 250 yards away. Both were waving big white tails. I could dimly make out antlers on the lower one.

The sight of those flaunting flags across the canyon made me shed

25 years. Once again I was back in my favorite Calelo Hills along the Mexican border of southern Arizona, where I had some small reputation among the local yeomanry of being a fair hand on running whitetails.

I sat down quickly, put the intersection of the crosswires just to the left of the buck's head for lead, and squeezed the trigger. So far as results went, it was almost as spectacular as a brain shot on an elephant. The buck fell, started rolling, and tumbled clear out of sight into the brush and timber at the bottom of the canyon.

"Some shot!" said Bradford.

The buck was a big one. It had long brow points and four points on each beam—a four-pointer Western count, an eight-pointer Eastern count. He had been hit rather far back through the lungs. Down there in that narrow canyon, it was so dark that the exposure meter said half-a-second at f/2 would be about right. Since we had no flash, good pictures under those conditions were impossible. Later someone would come out from the ranch with a packhorse and get him.

By now, the sun was up and bright, and while the others went along around the head of the canyon where I had shot the buck and to the head of the next, I stayed behind to admire the scenery. Far below, the little creek glistened through the timber along its banks and as it twisted through the meadows. The meadows were still green, the pines dark and somber, but along the creek, cottonwoods and willows were shimmering gold, and patches of crimson sumac blazed on the hillsides.

Up in the high country at the head of the creek where the elk ran along the ridges, an early storm had frosted the dark timber with snow. Far below against the green of a pasture I saw some moving black dots. The glasses showed me I was looking at a flock of wild turkeys.

Clear down in the bottom of the main canyon I heard a fusillade of shots. I made a mental note that they were probably fired by the Californians who were going to try for deer before they went into Moose Creek for elk. I hurried to catch up with the other O'Connors, who were out of sight over a ridge.

I heard two quick shots. Then I saw Eleanor and Bradford, rifles in hand, sitting on the hillside looking down.

"Get anything?" I asked.

"Buck mule deer . . . sort of a collaboration," Bradford said.

"The heck it was," Eleanor said. "I shot behind it and then Bradford dumped it. See? It's lying down there on the road."

The glasses revealed a young buck mule deer close to 300 yards away.

Back at the ranchhouse, we found that the Californians had taken three whitetail bucks out of a herd of eight. The largest had heavy antlers, with three points and a brow tine on each side. Though their measurements were the same as those of my deer, this buck appeared to be heavier. The next buck was somewhat smaller than mine and the third was a youngster.

Soon a packhorse came in with my buck. He and the largest buck shot by the Californians measured 18 inches in a straight line from the top of the shoulder to the bottom of the brisket. Both were fat and in fine condition, weighing between 185 and 195 pounds. These two whitetail bucks in weight and measurements were every bit as large as mature four-point mule deer bucks.

I was interested in comparing them to Arizona whitetails I had hunted so long. They were about twice as large, since an average mature Arizona whitetail will weigh from 90 to 100 pounds. As is true among Arizona whitetails, the top of the tails of the old bucks is a grizzled brown whereas the upper portion of the tails of the young bucks is bright orange. Oddly, the tails of these big bucks looked to be the same size as those of their Southern cousins.

The beams of my buck's antlers were a bit over 23 inches long, and the inside spread was 18 inches. I have never shot an Arizona whitetail with beams anything like that long, but I did take one that had a 20-inch spread. Though the northwestern whitetail is twice as heavy as his southwestern cousin, his antlers aren't twice as large.

The coats of the big deer were a bit more brownish and less grayish than those of Coues deer. The young Northwest whitetails have much more grizzled coats than those worn by young Arizona whitetails. These are quite bluish.

Sad to say, my underprivileged wife didn't get another shot. We drove up a precarious ranch road late that afternoon and early next morning when the deer should have been moving. We hunted the heads of several canyons and glassed the points and ridges, but all we saw were does and fawns. The bucks had gotten the message.

A RECORD TROPHY
By Paulina Brandreth

This is Chapter 20 in Trails of Enchantment *(1930—reprinted in 2003 in the "Sisters of the Hunt" series). It recounts, in Brandreth's delightful fashion, killing a 13-point Adirondacks trophy with massive, palmated antlers.*

At the summit of a low-lying hardwood ridge, Rube paused and scanned the outlook carefully. Around him stretched the vistas of the forest—white, mysterious, silent. Directly below, the ridge slope fell away toward a swampy piece of ground fringed thickly with young spruce that resembled, under their covering of snow, so many little Christmas trees. To the right, a monumental skidway piled high with glistening yellow logs testified to the presence of lumberjacks; while to the left, a big boulder, the relic of some pristine upheaval, thrust its lichen-streaked sides above the snow. Toward this boulder Rube's glance became immediately directed.

"There's a good rock ter build a fire against," he remarked after due consideration. "We kin eat our lunch, boil a cup of tea and git dried off—"

The prospect of a hot cup of tea was a pleasant one. We had been hunting since early morning, and since early morning had searched in vain for the track of a big deer. Not that there was any lack of fresh signs. Everywhere we had found them plentiful, and once had stirred out a trio of does, dark-hued, velvety creatures feeding in the green timber. But the bucks apparently were not yet moving. Either that or else we had not been lucky enough to run across the trail of anything sufficiently large to suit our fancy.

Several inches of snow lay in the woods, and all day the moist, feathery flakes had fallen from a heavy, brooding sky. It was approaching two o'clock, and still the storm hung around us in ghostly veils and windy uproar. Not a leaf remained upon the trees; not a shred of bright autumnal coloring glowed through the deepening mantle of cold, glittering white.

Although it was only the second week in November, it seemed that winter had already set her heel upon the wilderness and was challenging from the skies.

While Rube chopped some dry wood from the heart of a dead spruce, I set about foraging for birchbark. Very soon, in spite of the decidedly moist weather conditions, we had a good fire roaring and snapping against the wall of rock.

While on the subject of fires, if you are ever hunting or otherwise occupied in the woods on a cold, comfortless day and want to get warmed up, always remember to build your fire, if possible, against a rock, ledge or boulder. The heat is then never wasted, and the warmth thus reflected is much more gratifying than the scattered flames of a blaze kindled in the open.

From his pack, Rube produced a package of venison sandwiches, a tea pail and two tin cups. The pail he filled from a little stream that trickled down the ridge slope. Then he cut a long stick, drove one end of it in the ground, and hung the pail deftly on the other. It sagged to exactly the correct distance over the flames, and in five minutes our brew of tea was simmering fragrantly and ready to be poured.

"I think we'll try them ridges betwixt North Pond and the lake," Rube said presently in a voice muffled by a sandwich. "Deer ought ter be feedin' in there this afternoon, and we're likely to run on a big one."

With this plan in view we finished lunch while our wet clothes steamed and got partially dried off. Just as we were about to leave the shelter of the rock, there came an unexpected and welcome lull in the storm, and for the rest of the afternoon the weather cleared gradually, patches of blue sky opening up beyond the glittering treetops.

From a strip of virgin timber, we presently struck a section of forest threaded with log roads and bearing the marks of recent cuttings. Near and far loomed great skidways piled with spruce, balsam and hemlock that at a distance resembled a village of log cabins under their cap of snow. Very often we passed slabs of hemlock bark, valuable for tanning purposes, stacked in long rows; and in all directions lay lopped branches, defective logs and the mute stumps of a fallen wilderness.

As we were following along a log road, we came on the fresh tracks of several deer, one of which was evidently that of a good-sized buck. Trailing conditions were perfect now that the snow had stopped falling, and some 20 minutes later, we jumped two does near the base of a steep hill. Then, while rounding the end of a skidway, we came suddenly on the buck. He was so close we could have struck him with a stone, and against the wintry background, his body fairly seemed to glow with life and grace and color. He carried a pair of long, sharp horns that were polished to a tint of old ivory. The white markings on his face, ears, neck and legs were very pronounced, and as he stood broadside, gazing at us curiously, it would have been hard to have found a more beautiful specimen of his kind.

In stepping up beside Rube, I had cocked the rifle but on seeing the animal's head, I dropped the hammer and we both stood silently enjoying the picture before us. I have no idea what made this buck so tame, and even had he carried a fine set of antlers, I doubt if I should have had any desire to shoot him. After scrutinizing us for several seconds, he began feeding again, and we watched him until he had wandered leisurely out of sight.

"There ain't much use followin' up any more tracks today," Rube said as we retraced our steps to the log road. "It's gettin' late and we just got about time enough to make camp before dark."

Successively he pulled out his watch and compass. The latter he studied with deliberation. Then, he turned sharply to the left and started off through the woods at a fast walk.

The traveling underfoot was bad, there being at least six inches of moist, heavy snow which kept balling up at the soles of our shoe-packs. Both of us cut some queer capers. More than once I caught the old woodsman balancing like a Russian dancer on the back of a snow-covered log, with arms outstretched and one leg waving wildly in mid-air. But always at the critical moment, he managed to regain his equilibrium and continue placidly on his way. Not once did he fall down; I marveled at him every time I measured my own length, and decided then and there, it was futile to worry about his breaking any bones!

We were nearing a ridge which overlooked North Pond when we ran across a stretch of ground literally cut up with fresh deer signs.

"Looks as if a whole band of 'em had been in here, don't it?" remarked Rube.

A little farther along, he stopped again and beckoned to me over his shoulder.

"How's that fer a buck's track?"

Discouraged as I felt with the outcome of our long day's hunt, the sight of that track seemed to put new life in me. It was as big as a heifer's and evidently had just been made. The realization, however, that it was too late to think of following the animal reestablished immediately a sense of gloom and disappointment.

"Never cuss yer luck till yer git home," Rube advised cheerfully. And the wisdom of this remark was soon made manifest.

We kept on toward the top of the ridge and once more stumbled onto the buck's tracks. Then, as we looked over and down into the sweep of a wide valley, the old hunter stiffened.

Directly below us, under the brink of the ridge, stood a big doe. She had evidently heard us, for her ears were thrust forward while her whole attitude denoted alertness and suspicion.

"Jist stand quiet," Rube warned in a whisper.

We remained motionless, searching every foot of ground for a possible patch of gray, the glimmer of a horn, the flicker of a tail. The buck was there, *somewhere*—of that we felt certain. During this interval, the doe grew very uneasy, and at length, after having stamped nervously and raised her nose several times into the wind, she made off at a brisk trot along the slope of the hill.

No sooner did she get under way than our eyes caught a sudden motion under the top of a fallen spruce, which lay to the right of where she had been standing. Next minute, we glimpsed a mighty set of horns as the buck burst from cover and fled up the ridge. He did not bound, but seemed to slip like a shadow over the ground, his head carried low, his great dusky antlers laid back on his shoulders. Twice we obtained a fair view of him, and twice I tried to get a snap-shot, but each time, with almost uncanny precision, he managed to put a barrier of lopped treetops between us.

The thing had happened so quickly that we just stood there and looked at each other. Rube grinned. "Wasn't that an awful head?"

"It's plain rotten luck," I said. "What are you going to do now?"

"I'm goin' ter take a circle round and see if we can't run on ter him again," was the old man's reply.

We swung down into the valley and began a rapid detour, bearing to the left in order to have the wind in our favor. Time being so precious, it seemed that twilight closed about us with greater rapidity. The woodland distances suddenly grew veiled and dimmed; near objects loomed up darkly, while those farther away melted into gray uncertainties. A strip of sunset sky, which had brightened the west a moment before, was now turning silver, and high overhead, the faint pin-point of an early star glimmered vaguely.

With his keen eyes covering the woods ahead, Rube fell into a swinging gait. There was no chance for any pussy-footing or cautious still-hunting. It was getting dark too fast. Coming to a skid trail that led down the hill, he followed it a short distance, and then striking a log road, turned to the left again. Just at that moment, I caught the outline of a deer moving at a walk down the ridge in our direction. I touched Rube on the arm.

"Here comes the doe," I said, and we both dropped on our knees in the snow.

About halfway between our position and the point at which the log road broke over the hill stood a mammoth yellow birch. This tree shut off our outlook most effectually until Rube, who could stand the strain of uncertainties no longer, risked a motion, and craning his head off to one side, obtained a glimpse of the approaching animal. He turned to me with eyes snapping.

"It ain't the doe that's comin'," he articulated softly. "It's *the* buck!"

The next few seconds were crammed with excitement. Looking back on the experience, it seems always to assume more and more an element of the ridiculous. Certainly, it proves, like many other incidents, that the game of hunting is more often than anything else a game of chance.

Here were we, the hunters, being literally hunted by the deer, which a short time previous we believed had given us the slip. In other words, we had been whisked around within 15 minutes from the extreme of bad to the extreme of good luck.

We knelt in the snow, waiting for the buck to appear from behind the intervening trunk of the big birch. The suspense was harrowing. And then at last he loomed suddenly before us.

Enough of daylight still remained for us to see him in detail, and certainly he was a magnificent creature. He came at a swinging walk, his head lowered, his nose close to the ground. There was something almost formidable in his appearance, and I believe that, not having winded us the first time he was scared out, he had gotten the idea that another buck had started the doe, and was therefore returning to administer a sound thrashing to the intruder.

I have seen a number of large heads during the years I have spent in the woods, but the head of this buck overshadowed all the others. The horns were so massive they made the animal look top-heavy. As he came toward us, he swung them from side to side with a motion similar to that of a belligerent bull.

When he had passed a few feet beyond the birch, I gave a loud whistle. Instantly, he froze into rigid suspicion and threw up his head. He stood facing us, slightly quartering and offered a deadly shot. At the crack of the rifle, he plunged forward in his tracks, struggled a few paces, and just as Rube fired a second shot, rolled over stone dead.

We ran up the log road rejoicing. It was one of those rare occasions when Rube's habitual taciturnity dissolved completely in a burst of enthusiasm, and it is quite needless to describe my own feelings. This was a trophy worth many days of hard hunting, and we were not slow to appreciate the fact.

On close inspection we found that the antlers bore a striking resemblance to those of a blacktail. Several of the prongs were quite broadly palmated, and there were 13 points in all. The tips of the horns were blunt, as though the old warrior had done a lot of prodding and rooting with them.

It was now almost dark, and we hurried in the business of hanging up our prize. Rube brought out his rope, block and pulley, and slung the former over the stout limb of a beech. We were soon ready to haul, and haul we did with a vengeance.

Quite unexpectedly came the catastrophe. I had a momentary glimpse of my companion sailing backwards into a brush pile. Then the falling mass of the deer caught me a glancing blow and knocked me flat.

"That dum rope busted," the old man explained as we picked ourselves out of the snow. No great damage had been done, however, and after giving the tackle an overhauling, we went at the job again. This time everything went well, and in 20 minutes we were able to get underway.

Gathering our rifles and packs, we decamped hastily, for already the stars were shining with wintry brilliancy and night had fallen in the woods.

THE DEERSTALKERS
By Frank Forester

Frank Forester was the pseudonym of William Henry Herbert, an amazingly prolific 19th century writer. This piece, based on true experience although written in novelistic form, comes from The Deerstalkers: A Sporting Tale of the South-Western Counties *(1843). It is also included in John E. Howard (editor),* North American Big Game Hunts in the 1800's *(1982). The setting was what the author described as a "beautiful and lonely dell" in the then sparsely populated section of New York State lying between the Hudson and Delaware rivers and along the latter stream's eastern branch, the Mohawk River. Waxing lyrical after the fashion of the era, the author takes us along to dream-like settings in the rocky hills of New York at the outermost reaches of the ancient Laurentian Shield. Both his literary style and the unfolding events are evocative of the Scottish Highlands of Forester's native British Isles.*

The mountains, on either side the narrow glen, loomed up superbly dark, like perpendicular walls of the deepest purple hue, opaque, solid, earthfast, against the liquid and transparent blackness of the starry firmament. The broad, clear mill-pond at their base lay calm and breezeless, with no reflection on its silvery breast, save the faint specks of purer whiteness which mirrored the eternal planets, motionless, sad and silent, yet how beautiful. The dews were still falling heavily, and there was in the air, among the trees, on the waters, that undefinable soft rustling sound, which yet is scarce a sound that we cannot determine, even when sensible of it, whether we hear or feel; but other sound of man or beast there came none through that deep and narrow valley. Ever near morning, although before the earliest east has paled, the accurate observer will find in nature the deepest stillness.

The shrill cry of the katydid, the cicada of the west, which carols so exultingly all the night long over her goblets of night-dew, has lulled itself at last to rest. The owls that hooted from every dell and dingle, so long as the moon rode the heavens, have betaken themselves to their morning slumbers. The night-frogs have ceased to croak from the wooded hill; the very cocks, which have crowed twice, are silent; and the watch-dogs, feeling that their sagacity will be required but a few hours longer, have withdrawn to their cozy kennels.

There is in this stillness something peculiarly grand, solemn and affecting. It reminds one of the morning sleep of the young child, which perturbed and restless during the earlier watches of the night, falls ever into the soundest and most refreshing slumber, when the moment is nearest at which it shall start up, reinvigorated and renewed, to fresh hope, fresh life, fresh happiness.

And in the mind of Harry Archer, ever alive to thick-coming fancies, thoughts such as these were awakened during their swift walk up the vale on that clear, still autumnal morning, far more than the keen sportsman's eagerness or the exciting ardor of the chase.

After they had walked some 20 minutes in complete silence, the whole program of the day's sport having been abandoned to the old hunter's sagacity, Harry became curious to know what were his arrangements for the contemplated still-hunt.

Withdrawing from his mouth the cigar which he had been sedulously cultivating, he said to the hunter in a low voice—"Well, Dolph, how is it to be?"

"You goes with me, in course," said Dolph Pierson "We'll take the birch canoe at the bridge and follow the crick down, still as death, to Green's Pond. It's like we'll catch them as they come down to drink at daybreak. Then, when we reach the pond edge, we'll round the western end and creep up the brook that comes down through the cedars clear from the mountain top, and work up that to leeward 'till we strikes Old Bald-head yander."

As he spoke, he designated the huge crest of a distant hill, crowned far above its robe of many-colored foliage with a gray diadem of everlasting granite.

"There's a green feedin' ground jest under yan bare crag, with only a few stunted yellow birches and a red cedar here and there. There's a herd a'most alius, and if we happen on 'em there, they've no chance to wind us, nor to see us, unless they've got a doe set out sentinel-like up the rocks."

"Then, we'll stalk the whole west mountain down to the outlet, where we'll meet the rest of 'em, and take a bit and sup at something. Maybe we'll send the boys with the ponies to fetch up the game if we've the luck to kill any on't. Then, we'll all paddle up the crick agin at night, and so take chance to git 'em at the evenin' drink. The flies has quit botherin' 'em, since the cold has set in, and we wunt find none in the pond, I'm a thinkin'."

"But what will you do with Tom Draw and Mr. Forester? You must remember that old Tom cannot foot it now—"

"Not as he used to could," replied Dolph. "It 'ud take more nor a slouch to worry the old critter down. And that green-coated chap; I guess he ar'n't no great shines at travelin', nohow—"

"Ah, that's just where you're wrong, Dolph, and you're not very often. He can travel like a hunted wolf, I tell you, and he's a prime sportsman and a crack shot at small game, though not much used to work of this kind. But you must send them where they'll get shots, or they'll be mad at us; and it would not be fair either to throw them over."

"In course not; I counts to put them on the best easy ground. When we take the canoe, three of my boys will meet them with two ponies, so they can ride down to Cobus Vanderbeck's mill on the outlet, where it's broad and full of islands like, and channels. They'll git canoes there sure, and two o' the boys will paddle them, and the t'other, why he'll follow with the ponies. It'll be all they'll do to git to the pond by the time we strikes it, though we've got fourteen miles to walk, not countin' what we crosses over and agin'.

"Oh, that's prime feedin' grounds, them islands, and the boys, they knows every inch on 'em. They'll come on the deer quarterin' upwind, too, so they won't smell 'em. I wouldn't wonder, not one mite, if they was to git ten shots this day. But Lord, heart alive! We'll beat 'em some."

"Why, how many do you count upon our getting?"

"I'll be most mighty unsatisfied, now I tell you, if we don't git six fair ones."

"I'll kill five out of six, sartin."

"So will Tom, easy."

"Yes, if they stand still and wait for him. Don't you tell me; if we get six, and they ten shots, we'll beat them to eternal smash."

"I hardly think we shall get sixteen shots among us."

"I do, Mister Archer. Deers is as plenty this fall as they's been scarce these six years agone."

"Here we are at the bridge; but I don't see the boys or the ponies."

"Oh! they'll be here. I'll call 'em."

And, putting his forefinger into his mouth, he produced a long, shrieking whistle, which rang through the hills more like the cry of some fierce bird-of-prey than any sound of the human voice.

Such as it was, however, it found a reply in a second, and directly afterward the clatter of horses' hoofs was heard coming rapidly down the hard road. Within a minute, the boys came in sight, riding a couple of rough, hardy-looking, round-barreled ponies.

"Here we leave you, Frank. You and Tom go today with Dolph's son," said Harry Archer. "You will ride about three miles and then take the canoes. You have the best ground and the easiest walking—or I should rather say the least walking, for yours will be almost all boat-work. Dolph says that you will get ten shots to our six; so look sharp. We don't want to beat you."

"I wisht to heaven you may git ten and we six, boy," cried Tom, "and then you'd see who'd beat, I reckon. Oh, I am most almighty glad to see them ponies. You've been comin' too fast for the old man, altogether—another mile would have busted me up clean. I am glad, by Gin, to see the pony."

Weary work was before them, ere they met again at the outlet of the lake, at which they were to arrive from two diametrically opposite quarters.

Harry stepped lightly into the birch canoe, which lay moored in very shallow water, and the sagacious hound, accustomed of yore to every variety of field sport, crept into it as gingerly as if he were treading upon eggs, and coiled himself in the very center of the frail vessel, as if he knew exactly how to balance it, in a position from which nothing could have disturbed him short of the command of his master.

Last, Dolph the hunter entered and assumed his place in the stern, Harry occupying the bow, but with their faces toward the head of the canoe and their rifles ready to be grasped at the shortest notice.

"Ready!" said Dolph, in that low guarded tone which is peculiar to the forester of North America.

"Ready!" responded Archer. And at the word, each dipped his paddle in the clear water and away shot the light vessel, propelled almost without an effort on the part of the rowers. Within two or three minutes, they had lost sight of the rustic bridge and the group assembled to watch their departure. The stream was in this place very narrow, in no spot above 12 or 14 feet across, but proportionably deep and rapid, flowing over a bottom of yellow sand and gravel through a wide boggy meadow.

"Are there trout here, Dolph?"

"Lots of 'em, clear down to the pond. But no one niver catched none in the pond; nor no pickerel, which is plenty in the pond, up hereaways in the crick, and that seems to me cur'ous."

"Not at all, Dolph. Not at all curious. The pond water is too warm for the trout, and this spring brook is too cold for pickerel."

"Likely. I ar'n't no fisherman, nohow."

"How far do you call it down to the pond? I have forgotten."

"Six mile."

"And how far to the first chance for deer?"

"That's it," he answered, pointing forward to a low tract of scrubby brushwood about half-a-mile's distance, into which some 20 minutes afterward the canoe was borne by the rapid current of the brook under a deep arch of emerald verdure.

"Lay by your paddle, take up the rifle now and lay flat on your face. I'll keep her goin' as slick as can be."

No sooner had he spoken than Harry did as he was directed, and making his rifle ready for the most sudden emergency, he stretched himself out horizontally in the bottom of the boat with his keen eye alone gleaming out watchfully above the sharp bow, and lay there as quietly as if he had been a statue carved in wood.

At this instant, the birch canoe shot under the arch of dense umbrage composed principally of alders, but in places colored by the autumnal frosts in almost every hue of the rainbow, varying from the deepest crimson to the most brilliant orange and chrome yellow.

By this time the sun had risen, and a yellow luster had crept inch by inch over the pale horizon, till the stars were all out, each after each according to the various degrees of their intensity, and the whole universe was laughing in the glorious sunlight.

Mile after mile they floated on in silence—silence unbroken except by the dash of the mute hunter's paddle—now darting across lonely pools encircled by tall trees clad in gorgeous tints and carpeted with the broad, smooth green leaves of the water-lily—pools from which the gay summer-duck, or the blue-winged teal, flashed up on sudden wing before their glancing prow—now shooting down swift rapids, overarched by bushes so dense that it was difficult to force a way between their tangled masses.

Still no sight or sound met their eyes or ears, which betokened in any sense the vicinity of the wild cattle of the hills. Archer was beginning to wax impatient and uneasy. Suddenly, bursting from out of a thick, heavy arbor, the canoe shot into a little pond below which was a quick-glancing rapid divided into three channels by a small green island nearly before the boat's head and a huge block of granite, which had been swept down in some remote period from the overtopping hills.

The island was not at the utmost three yards across, yet on it there grew a tall, silver-barked birch, and under the shade of the birch stood two beautiful and graceful deer, one sipping the clear water, and the other gazing down the brook in the direction opposite to that from which the hunters were coming upon them.

Neither of the three channels of the stream was above 12 or 14 feet across. The one to the right was somewhat the deepest, and through this the hunter had intended to guide his boat, even before he saw the quarry.

No breath of air was stirring in those deep, sylvan haunts, so that no taint telling of man's appalling presence was borne to the timid nostrils of the wild animals, which were already cut off from the nearer shore, before they perceived the approach of their mortal foes.

The quick eye of Archer caught them upon the instant, and almost simultaneously the hunter had checked the way of the canoe and laid aside his paddle.

He was stretching out his hand to grasp the ready rifle, when Archer's piece rose to his shoulder with a steady slow motion, the trigger was drawn, and ere the close report had time to reach its ears, the nearer of the two bucks had fallen, its heart cleft asunder by the unerring bullet, into the glassy ripple out of which it had been drinking, tingeing the calm pool far and wide with its lifeblood.

Long before it had caught the rifle's crack, the second, with a mighty bound, had cleared the intervening channel and lighted upon the gray granite rock. Not one second's space did it pause there, however, but gathering its agile limbs again, sprang shoreward.

A second more it had been safe in the coppice. But in that very second, the nimble finger of the sportsman had cocked the second barrel, and while the gallant beast was suspended in mid-air, the second ball was sped on its errand.

A dull, dead splash heard by the hunters announced that the ball had taken sure effect, and arrested in its leap, the noble quarry fell.

For one moment's space it struggled in the narrow rapid, then by a mighty effort rising again, it dashed forward, feebly fleet, keeping to the middle of the channel.

Meanwhile the boat, unguided by the paddle and swept in by the driving current, had touched upon the gravel shoal and was motionless.

Feeling this as it were instinctively, Harry unsheathed his long knife, and with a wild, shrill cheer to Smoker, sprang first ashore and then plunged recklessly into the knee-deep current. Ere he had made three strides, the fleet dog passed him with his white tushes glancing from his black lips, his eyes glaring like coals of fire as he sped mute and rapid as the wind after the wounded game.

The vista of the wood through which the brook ran straight was not at the most above 50 paces in length, and of these the wounded buck had gained at least 10 clear start.

Ere it had gone 20 more, however, the fleet dog had it by the throat. There was a stern, short strife, and both went down together into the flashing waters. Then, ere the buck could relieve itself or harm the noble dog, the keen knife of Archer was in its throat—one sob, and all was over.

"I won," cried the hunter, "them was two smart shots anyhow—and that ere dog's hard to beat. Let's liquor."

Liquor they did accordingly, and after that proceeded to disembowel the two deer, to flesh the gallant Smoker, and then to hoist their quarry up into the forks of two lofty maples, where they should be beyond the reach of any passing quadruped or biped plunderer.

This done, they again paddled onward, and shortly after ten o'clock reached the Green Pond without obtaining any other shot. An hour more carried them around the head of that great forest lake, but without moving any worthier game than a team or two of wild ducks, and two or three large blue-winged herons.

At the lake's head, they moored their little skiff, and thence struggled up the difficult and perilous chasm of its headwaters, through breaks of tufted cedars, over smooth, slippery rocks, up white and foamy ledges to the gray summit of the mighty hill. Three hours had been consumed in this strong toil, and though every trunk against which a stag might fray his antlers had been noted; every tuft of moss; every sere leaf that might bear a footprint had been wistfully examined. No trail had been found, and their hearts begin to wax as faint as their limbs were weary.

Both were toil-worn and broken when they reached the summit, but even so, the hunter declined the proffered cup of Ferintosh. Content with bathing his brow and hands in the cold element of which he dared not drink, so weary was he and so faint he soon announced that he was ready to proceed.

A few steps brought them to the very crest of the huge mountain, and there, casting himself down on the bare rock, he wormed his way like a serpent to the brink which overhung the valley, and signed Harry to follow his example.

For nearly ten minutes they dragged themselves painfully over the rough, gray stones before they reached the abrupt ledge of the rocky platform. A moment before they reached it, however, Dolph Pierson paused, took off his cap and laid it on the rock, looked to the caps of his rifle and made a gesture of his hand, indicating the necessity of the greatest caution.

Ten seconds afterward they had reached the extreme verge, and carefully advancing their heads beyond the brink, they gazed anxiously down into the valley at their feet.

Gods! What a view! The sheer and perpendicular precipice fell down at once above 200 feet in one vast wall of primitive rock, with here and there the stem of a bleached and thunder-splintered pine thrusting its ghastly skeleton forth into the air from some crevice or fissure wherein its roots had found a casual hold to support its precarious and difficult existence.

Beneath this gigantic mountain wall, the hillside sloped away very steep and abrupt but unbroken by any knoll or crag for several miles in length to the margin of the clear lake, which lay embosomed in its pine forests like a mirror surrounded by a wreath of evergreens. A bright brook rushed into it, rapid and turbulent, and the pellucid, brimful river, which stole forth from it in the opposite direction, wound among the verdant meadows and many-colored woodlands like a long silver ribbon.

Beyond the little lake stretched miles and miles of gorgeous autumnal woodland to the southward, miles and miles of dark piney forest, with here and there a cultivated clearing laughing out among the foliage, its white-walled cottages and village steeple glinting back the long sunbeams. Farther yet aloof were still other lakes isle-dotted, other streams blue glimmering, and leagues away on the horizon a long line of blue mountains, scarcely distinguishable from the azure of the sky, veiled as they were by the thin, golden haze of an American autumn and flooded by the unrivaled splendor of its shimmering sunshine.

The hillside between the rocky wall and the lake had been swept by fire many years before, and was now covered with a rich growth of tall grass and low, bushy shrubs, with here and there the black-scathed trunk of some gigantic cedar towering up, a monument of past devastation, and here and there a group of young, graceful trees which had shot up vigorously from the ashes of their sires towards the clear skies and bright sun, which they could now behold, no longer cowed and opposed by the tyrannous verdure of their gigantic ancestry.

This was the famous feeding ground to overlook, which our hunters had toiled so painfully to the summit of that towering precipice. As Dolph had observed, rarely was it, indeed, that its rich and succulent pasture could not display one herd, at least, to the sportsman's ken.

The gentle southwest wind blew full and fresh into the faces of Harry and the hunter, so that no taint could be carried from the persons by the nimble atmosphere to the delicate organs of their intended. It was the quick eyes, therefore, of the sentinel does only that it was necessary for them now to avoid.

The first glance was enough to fill a hunter's heart with rapture, for close below the crags and within easy shot of the platform on which they lay, a noble herd was pasturing: three gallant bucks, and twice the number of slim and graceful hinds. A seventh deer stood a few hundred paces from the rest on a little knoll, its head erect, ears pricked and expanded to catch the smallest sound, widely distended nostrils snuffing the breeze to detect some taint on its fresh balmy breath, its eyes keenly roving over the whole expanse of rock, wood, pasture, lake and river.

No rash or boyish excitement at the view prevented those skillful foresters from taking an accurate survey of all that lay within the range of their vision. No burst of eager impulse led them to discharge their rifles at the nearer herd until such time as they should have accurately scanned the whole pasture range to see if there might not be some other deer within reach.

Their scrutiny was speedily and well rewarded, for in several points of the landscape they detected the noble animals of which they were in quest, tranquilly feeding on the long grass and incumbent branches of the underwood, entirely unconscious of their deadly enemies.

In one open glade about a mile to the eastward was a noble hart of the largest size, with a yearling buck, or prickhorn, and two barren hinds. Among the dense coppicewood, yet half-a-mile farther to the east, the wood-brown backs and hornless heads of several more hinds might be distinguished by a practiced eye, though it was not easy to make out their exact number.

Far away, on the margin of the woods skirting the lake, was a yet larger herd, the deer licking their glossy coats or scratching their ears with their cloven hoofs, resting in perfect security and fearlessness.

In a word, from the elevated station on which they lay overlooking the wide valley, not less than 40 or 50 head of deer were visible at once, among which the hunters had been at first glance able to detect with certainty two harts of the first head, or what in the Scottish forests would be called harts royal, and two other stags of six or eight branches besides the yearling prick-horn. The farthest herd was too distant to distinguish the age or even the sex of the animals.

Ten minutes were perhaps devoted by the hunters to survey their scene of action, during which neither of the two moved hand or foot, or indeed gave any sign of life except by the keen glances of their watchful and roving eyes. At length, when each was apparently satisfied with what he had seen, their eyes met with a look of mutual intelligence, and drawing back their heads as warily as they had thrust them forward, they wormed their way backward foot by foot over the craggy platform until they reached a little hollow in the rocks at about a hundred yards' distance from the brink. There, safely out of eyeshot and earshot of the wary herds, they paused in consultation.

"Well, Mister Archer," the old hunter began, "yan is a noble sight for a hunter's eye! You niver seed jest sich another, I'm a thinkin'. There's fawty head of deer on the range, if there's one. Do tell now, did you iver see the like?"

"Many's the time, Dolph. Many's the time, on Braemar and from the craigs of Ben-y-Ghoil. But never mind that now. How do you mean to work them? How many can we get? I make four parcels within eye-range that may be worked up to, but one of the four is all hinds and of no account."

"Four passels," replied the hunter, doubtfully. "Four passels there be, sure enough, but how the heavens and airth you'd work up to the big lot by the pond edge is more than I can calkilate."

"No, no, boy. There's three passels only 'at can be shot at by this party; and, as you says right, one of them's all does, and of no account. That nighest bunch to the eastward has got one fine biggest sort of buck in it, but if we goes to shoot it fust, I'm afeard that the wind, which takes a swirl like oncet and agin, amongst these gib gray stones, will bring down the scent of us and mayhap the crack of the rifles too, and so skear these away. I guess it's best to pick the three bucks out of this nighest passel and let the others go."

"I think not, Dolph," replied Archer, confidently. "I assure you that there are four parcels, beside that by the lake. Your eyes, good as they are, have failed you for once. You know the deep narrow gully that forks from the glen were we came up to the mountain and cuts right across the pasturage from the west, eastward—"

"Cattycornered like," interrupted the hunter. "Yes, I knows it, and knowed it afore iver you was thought on. What on't, Archer?"

"Why, about twenty yards below it, there lies a great round-headed gray rock, what I call a boulder, which must have fallen from these crags ages since. Below that a hundred yards again or thereabout stands a tall, black half-burnt cedar with a thicket of briars and wild raspberry bushes about its foot.

"Look here, Dolph," he continued, pointing to the scathed top of a pine projecting from the face of the crags, "bring that white pine top into a range with the spot where the feeder comes into the Green Pond, and you will have rock, cedar-stump and all in one range. That done, look close at the bottom of the cedar and among the briars, you will see a monstrous stag, couched all alone."

"I do think, Dolph, it is the big mouse-colored hart you wounded last fall on the northern slope; the hart, I mean, that we tracked thirty miles in the snow and lost after all."

"Do you though, Archer? By H—we must have him, if so be, it be he. He had twelve branches on his horns then, and he'll have thirteen now—don't you mind that, for sartin?"

"Surely I do, but he is too far off now for me to mark that distinctly; and as we lay, I could not get my glass out. Here it is, fit it to your focus, and creep forward and examine him. I would rather have your judgment than my own, by one-half."

"I dun' know—I dun' know," replied the old hunter, gazing at him with not a little of admiration, and perhaps a slight shade of half good-humored envy. "Them eyes o' yourn is young, and I thinks as how they grows younger like and keener ivery year, and mine's a failin' me for sartin.

"I'll go, though, I'll go, boy. But fust tell a feller how you thinks to deal with them, so I'll be able to make out and settle all slick and to rights. We woun't be creepin' anymore to the edge like, if we don't warnt to skear 'em. What's your plan, say?"

"My plan's soon told, Dolph. It is that you should lie here on the brow, keeping that royal hart under your rifle all the time. That I should creep down the ravine, or gully, to the gray stone, and if I can once get to that, I can fetch him sure.

"There's a strong run of water in the gully, and the ripple of that will drown the noise of my feet. The ravine is so deep, and its face on this side is so steep and broken that I think this light wind will sweep right over it without bringing any taint of me to the nostrils of that knowing doe.

"Then, if I can manage it rightly and shoot the big hart before he bounces, there'll be nothing but the rifle-crack, which will only sound like a squib in the open, and a puff of smoke, which if they neither see nor smell me, will scarce alarm them. But if it does, and you shoot down the old stag, as you can do certainly, the herd will either strike downhill toward the east end of the gully, where I can race for it under cover, and perhaps get another double shot at them, or they will dash directly eastward along the base of the crags, taking that other big hart, the prick-horn and the two does along with them. In that case, you must head them along the cliff-tops where they trend northerly away, where you will probably drive the whole of the two parcels down to the outlet, where Tom and Frank Forester will be ready by that time to give an account of them.

"Again, if none of them take the alarm, I'll steal up the gorge back to you, without bleeding him or breaking him up, till after we have done with all the other parcels. Then I can creep along the summit here, till I get opposite the big stag and the prick-horn, when perhaps I can get both of them, while you knock over this chap here below you. That's all. What do you think of it, Dolph?"

"I dun' know yit awhiles," replied the old forester, as he brought Harry's glass to the right focus for his eye. "I'll go off and see how't looks and be back torights, and we'll fix it one way. Seems to me the wind is kind o' breezin' stronger up, and drawin' westerly more, and that'll be agin your not skearin' 'em. But we'll see."

And off he crawled for the second time, leaving his rifle and his cap behind him, and carrying Harry's fine Dolland telescope carefully in his right hand, while with the left he wormed himself along the surface of the ground.

Archer, thus left alone, applied himself to a careful examination of his rifle. He took off the caps to see that the powder was well up in the nipples and, satisfied that all was right, wiped the cones with a piece of greased leather, renewed the caps, ran his rod down the barrels, and finding that everything was in right working order, drew out his dram-bottle, ate a sandwich, and washed it down with a moderate sup of the old Ferintosh.

This done, he shook himself, and with a well-satisfied air, raised the heavy rifle two or three times to his eye, and as he laid it aside muttered to himself: "I'll have that hart royal for a thousand!"

As he spoke, Dolph returned from his reconnaissance, and thrust the joints of the telescope together between the palms of his horny hands.

"All right," he said. "Mr. Archer, your plan is the best, I think. We'll git the two best bucks inyhow, and maybe another. But, as it is, I'd rather have that 'ere big 'un of all than three common-sized.

"The wind has hauled a pint more to the westward nor it was, and it's kind o' freshenin' up, so I kind o' thinks as your shot'll skear this passel. But I'll keep well ahead on 'em to the eastward. When I shoot and show myself like, and if you hears me shout, then strick it down like anything along the holler.

"Now, be off with you. That big fellow lies still yet awhiles. But if I shoots afore you git to the gray rock, then you may know as he's bounced and come stret back to me. I'd like to git a good shoot today, for I'm afeard it'll rain to-night or to-morrow."

"Let it rain," replied Archer, cheerily. "I'll have that mouse-colored fellow, anyway. I say, Dolph, keep your Smoker here, and after you shoot at this herd, point them to him, and wave your hand well eastward as he starts, and ten to one he'll course them right down to me. Good-bye, old boy!"

And with the word, he dropped the telescope into his pocket, snatched up his rifle, donned his cap and, after motioning Smoker to lie quiet until such time as he should return, stole away quietly for a few yards till he had cleared the plateau of rocks. Then he dashed down the mountain gully, at a pace widely different from the toilsome labor by which they had dragged themselves to the upper from the lower elevation within half-an-hour.

Now racing rapidly down the soft, peaty margin of the brook where it spread out into marshy swales; now bounding fearlessly from rock to rock, where it flowed among big round boulders; now swinging himself by the pendulous arms of hemlocks and cedars from ledge to ledge where it fell in mimic cataracts and rapids, over long rifts of slatey limestone, he effected in less than 20 minutes the descent of the gorge, to ascend which it had cost him and Dolph Pierson two hours of difficult and painful labor.

By this time, he had reached the point at which a large, fresh spring boils up from the bottom of the bed of the brook, and leaving the old stream to persist in a direct course to the lake below, shoots off at an acute angle between two shoulders of black dripping rock and forms the ravine, of which I have spoken as diagonally crossing the green pasturage, or as it is generally termed in that part of the country, "The burnt feeding-grounds."

At this spot the view does not extend more than 50 yards in any direction, for the new stream turns a second angle before it strikes the open ground, and the whole space about the forks is covered with so dense a forest of pine, hemlock and cedar, with a few tamarack about the edges of the brook, that the sight is circumscribed within very narrow limits.

Here, Archer paused for a moment to recover his breath, bathed his face and hands in the cool stream, and then turned down the gorge to his left with a wary and crouching step, very different from the free bounding pace at which he had dashed down the precipitous hillside.

Within five minutes, he reached the jaws of the ravine, where the wood broke off in sparse masses to the right and left, and the little torrent rushing through a scarped natural pass plunged down a pitch of some 40 feet into the deep, gravelly trench through which it seethed and chafed on its way to join the distant outlet.

Here again Archer paused and looked warily abroad. From his altered position, he could now see only three of the separate lots, or parcels, as they are more correctly termed, five of which he had noted from the summit. He could see the large, solitary hart, which had arisen from his lair and was now browsing lazily among the boughs, which had of late afforded him their shelter. He could also see the herd of three bucks and seven does, which had moved though without taking the alarm, some hundred yards nearer to himself.

This was all in his favor, since if his taint, or the smell of his powder, should reach them, it would find them sheltered, as it were, in the angle between the crags and the gorge, so that Dolph would have every opportunity of heading them again and driving them down to the mouth of the ravine.

A minute sufficed him wherein to observe all this, and carrying his rifle, half-cocked and ready, he stole down the center of the streamlet's bed, knee-deep in water, stooping low and with every sense on the alert, toward the well-marked point directly opposite the big gray boulder, which was his guide and landmark.

Before he struck the watercourse, however, he took his bearings accurately, knowing that he could not lift his head above the verge of the ravine to ascertain his whereabouts, without the certainty of terrifying the animal of which he was in pursuit from the place where he was likely to fall an easy victim to his rapid and unerring aim.

This was soon done, for a stunted oak grew on the left side of the watercourse exactly opposite to the rock, so that he had nothing to do but to steal silently, keeping his head low to that tree, with the certainty of success should he reach it undiscovered.

Meanwhile, old Dolph, with Smoker crouching at his heel, had again crawled to the brink, and with his rifle ready for instant service, was watching with anxious eye the movements of his young comrade.

The deer which it was his peculiar duty to keep under his aim had indeed moved a little farther to the westward, but he cared not for that, well knowing that on the sound of Harry's rifle below them, they would come, if alarmed, directly toward him.

To Harry, crawling as he was down a gorge midway between the little pack and the solitary stag, the operation in which he was engaged was as nice a one as any that can be imagined in the whole range of deerstalking. And admirably well did he perform it.

The eye of the veteran marked him as Harry appeared and disappeared, and reappeared again, among the sinuosities of the wild gorge, never raising his head sufficiently to let the keenest eye catch a glimpse of it above the grassy banks, or exposing his person to the gusts of wind, which were now beginning to sweep fitfully across the open and bleak hill-side.

Dolph rubbed his hands in ecstasy as he observed the care, the toil, the active yet deliberate patience with which his pupil made his way toward the goal at which he aimed.

"Ah! he's a great 'un," he muttered to himself inaudibly, "for all he's a Britisher. I niver seed his like nohow, for quickness at kitchin' inything. I wisht one of my boys 'un take arter him, but Lord! they ar'n't half a beginnin'. He'll git that stag yit, I swar; and not start them long-yeared does nuther, and that's what I'd not a' promised to a' done in my youngest and spryest days. He's as 'cute all for one as a Feeladelfy lawyer . . . as true as a good hounddog's nose . . . and as quick as a greased bullet out a smart-shootin' rifle."

But while he was yet speaking, Harry had reached the point where the most care and management was needed to escape discovery.

The banks had for some time been gradually becoming lower and less abrupt, and the brook flowed tranquilly for a hundred yards, scarcely a foot below the level of the surrounding slope. At the end of this hundred yards was a deep rapid which burst down to a yet lower level some 60 feet beneath.

Should the young hunter succeed in crossing the hundred level yards unseen, and conveying himself to the lower level, his success might be certain, but to do so appeared well nigh impossible, since he had to turn down the gorge to his left with a wary and crouching step, very different from the free-bounding pace at which he had dashed down the precipitous hillside.

Within five minutes, he reached the jaws of the ravine, where the wood broke off in sparse masses to the right hand and left, and the little torrent, rushing through a scarped natural pass, plunged down a pitch of some 40 feet into a deep, gravelly trench through which it seethed and chafed on its way to join the distant outlet.

Here again Archer paused, and looked warily abroad. From his altered position, he could now see only three of the separate lots he had noted from the summit. The large, solitary hart had risen from his lair and was browsing lazily among the boughs which had of late afforded him their shelter. The three bucks and seven does by the lake's edge had moved, though without taking the alarm, some hundred yards nearer to himself.

It now seemed almost certain that the wind must strike his person, and carry the telltale odor uphill to the pasturing herd at the crag's foot. But he had decided on all his measures beforehand, and they were executed in an instant. Turning his head to the source of the stream, he worked his way down the center of the current, which was some eight or ten inches deep, flat upon his belly, until he reached the verge of the fall, down which he suffered himself to slide, retarding the rapidity of his descent by clutching at the ledges with his hands.

It was a perilous attempt even for a practiced cragsman, but in his case fairly successful, for in less than five minutes from his entering the dangerous pass, he stood at the bottom of the cataract unseen and unsuspected.

Dolph clapped his hands in ecstasy, and seeing that Archer's success was now certain, prepared himself for his share of the action.

Harry, meanwhile, as he stood dripping from his ice-cold bath, shook himself like a water-dog, drew a long breath, imbibed a deep draught of Ferintosh and unslung and examined his trusty rifle. Then, having reached the spot opposite the gray boulder, he crawled up the western bank, with his thumb on the rifle-cock and the nail of his forefinger close pressed on the trigger-guard.

Now he attained the brink, crouching low, and keeping his whole form concealed among the long grass and low bushes which crowned the abrupt steep. Only his eye glanced quickly through the dry stems and sere leaves.

For a moment, he fancied that his quarry had escaped him, for it no longer occupied the station at which he had previously observed it. But just as he was beginning to despair, a quick rustle caught his ear from the right, or the direction opposite to that in which he had been gazing, and turning his head quickly, he saw the noble beast standing within 20 paces of him, tossing his "beamed frontlet to the sky" and snuffing the atmosphere eagerly, as if he suspected the presence of a foe, though ignorant as yet of his exact whereabout.

With the speed of light, the rifle rose to Harry's unerring eye, a quick flash gleamed through the brushwood, a small puff of smoke rose into the cloudless air, and a flat, quick crack followed it. Before the small puff had cleared away, so truly was that snapshot aimed, the gallant hart had fallen lifeless, literally without a struggle, on the green sward.

Lowering his butt instantly, Harry poured the measured powder into the muzzle, drove down the well-patched ball, applied the cap and was ready for another shot in less time than it has taken to describe the operation.

The next moment, another rifle exploded on the hill above him, its sharp crack was reverberating and repeating in a hundred ringing echoes from the rocks and the gnarled trunks. Instantly, a long clear whoop, in the well-known stentorian voice of Dolph, announced that the upper herd was in motion.

At this sound, Harry raised his head, and looking back, perceived the two second-rate stags with the seven does preceding them, coursing at all their speed along the base of the crags due eastward. Along the summit, he could discern the tall, gaunt form of the Dutch hunter bounding forward with what seemed almost supernatural agility, with the dog Smoker at his heels, in the hope of yet cutting them off and forcing them toward the ravine in which Harry stood, half-doubtful, half-expectant.

"Well!" Archer soliloquized, "he has shot the stag. That is two royal harts in one day's stalking; not so bad, but we shall not get a chance at the others. Since there's no hope left of them, I'll bleed this fellow."

And with the word his keen blade was out, and buried in the flesh of the superb animal, which lay out-stretched lifeless on the greensward, which it had trod but a little while before, so full of graceful life and fiery vigor.

"A splended hart, by heaven! Twenty stone, horseman's weight, I'll warrant him, after he's *gralloched*. He never stirred after the ball struck him. It must have pierced the cavity of the heart. Halloo! What the devil's that?" Harry asked as the deep bay of a hound struck his ear.

"It's Smoker's tongue, but surely, surely, he is not going to run musical and get himself shot nowadays by those cursed Dutchmen!"

The cry was not repeated, but Harry's telescope was out in a moment, and by its aid, he saw the fleet deer-hound dashing down a fissure in the rocks, heading the two stags which he had cut off from the hinds, directly down upon the ravine within which he was standing.

In his impatient joy at finding a pass by which he could descend upon his quarry, the staunch hound had given vent to his pleasure in that one wild cry, and was now running, fleet as the wind and silent as the night, upon the track of the game. The two stately harts came bounding down the slope with the hound hard upon their haunches, right toward the lower end of the ravine.

As the fleet and graceful animals came dashing down the hill, clearing the scattered bushes and blocks of rifted stone with long and easy bounds, Harry almost instinctively perceived that they had not as yet scented him, though they were well to leeward of him owing to his position in the deep channel of the stream.

About a mile's distance below him to the eastward, the gorge of the stream melted away into the level plain on the border of the lakelet, and evidently it was at this point that the deer intended to cross the water.

If, therefore, by dint of his utmost speed Harry could reach that point, ere they should cross it, he was sure of at least one shot. As he noted the direction of their course, he dashed, reckless of all impediment, at the top of his pace down the gully.

There was no level ground on either side of the brook, only the gravelly or peaty banks which fell steep and sheer from the plain above to the water's level. The channel of the stream was his course, therefore, and a right difficult course for such a headlong race.

Yet he sped fearlessly and fleetly onward. He could not see anything of the chase he was pursuing, but he needed not the aid of the eye to know that they would hold their course straight and unaltered to their point.

Here, he leaped with long active bounds from block to block of granite as they peered with their slippery white heads above the chafing current; here he splashed recklessly through the swift rippling shallows, seeing the swift brook trout dart through the eddies from before his feet; there, he floundered almost waist-deep in the dark pools, where it flowed through peat bogs and tussocks.

Onward he sped, long-breathed and unwearied, and ever and anon he learned by the long cheery huzzas of the old hunter on the hill that he was holding his own at least, if not gaining on the chase.

It must be understood that the lines on which Archer and the two harts were running lay nearly at right angles to each other. Harry had about one mile to run, and the deer about twice that distance before their courses should intersect one another.

Harry had now cleared above two-thirds of the distance, and without slackening his pace, had pitched up his rifle into the hollow of his left hand and was examining the caps as he ran, to see whether they had been damaged by the water dashed up from his feet in his headlong run.

The banks grew gradually lower, and the stream, spreading over a wider bed and running on a bright gravel bottom, afforded him a better foothold than he had hitherto encountered.

At this moment, a long piercing yell from Dolph, who from his station on the crags could see everything that was passing, gave him notice that the crisis was at hand.

An instant more, and before he had even checked his pace, the two harts dashed across the gorge scarce 20 feet apart, their proud heads aloft, their wild eyes glancing fearfully around them, and their nostrils distended to the upmost. It almost seemed that they were no sooner in sight than they disappeared, so rapid was their transit, and so completely did the bold bank conceal them after they had once cleared the channel of the stream.

But swift as was their transit, swifter yet was the motion of hand and eye, which brought the ponderous rifle truly and surely to the runner's shoulder, and discharged both barrels in such quick succession that the two reports were almost blended into a single sound.

No eye of man, however near or quick-sighted, could have noted that either of the balls had taken effect, but the deerstalker had another sense by which he was assured that neither of his messengers had failed to perform its errand. For a dull flat *thud* met his ear almost simultaneously with each discharge, which he recognized at once as the sound of the ball plunging into its living target.

Before he had lowered the weapon from his eye, Smoker had swept across the stream in one long, swinging leap and was away on the traces of the quarry, still mute, although the slaver on his lip, the glare in his fierce eye, and the wiry bristles erect on his back and shoulders proved clearly how earnest and fiery was his excitement.

Scarce was he out of sight over the ridge before his master

scrambled up out of the gorge and, scaling the right-hand bank, found one of the two harts prostrate and struggling in the death agony, which his sharp knife soon mercifully terminated. He then saw the other, now some 300 yards away, striving, with desperate but useless efforts to escape the pursuit of the deer-hound.

Casting down his unloaded rifle by the side of the slain hart, and fixing the spot in his memory by a marking glance, he now bounded onward to the aid of the gallant hound, who he perceived would ere long overtake the wounded stag, and would in all probability receive some injury, should he attack it single-handed.

Fast as he ran, however, exerting himself till every sinew in his frame appeared to crack, and till the sweat rolled in big drops down his face, despite the coldness of the weather, his speed was put forth to no purpose. For wearied by its gigantic efforts and weakened by the loss of blood which flowed freely from the large wound made by the ounce-ball of Harry's rifle, the hart turned to bay.

But it was all too late, for as he turned, the fierce dog sprang, fastened his sharp white tusks into his gullet and bore him to the ground, before he had time to strike with his cloven hoofs or aim a thrust with his formidable antlers.

Then followed a desperate and confused struggle. The hart, strong in its last extremity, rose to its knees again, tossing its antlered head frantically in fruitless endeavors to break the hold of its cruel enemy, bleating and braying piteously the while, with the big tears rolling down its hairy cheeks, and blood and foam issuing from its distended jaws.

For a second's space, it seemed that the stag had the advantage, but it was for a second only. Again, with a sharp angry growl, the dog tore him down; and ere he could struggle up again, the man was added to the strife. His foot was on its neck, his knife in its gullet—one sharp gasp, one long, heaving shudder, and the bright eye glazed, and the wide nostril collapsed.

And now, weak himself with the violence of his exertions and overcome with toil, Harry Archer waved his cap in the air above his head, and sent forth his note of triumph in a long drawn *"Who-whoop—"* to which a cheery shout replied from the lips of Pierson, who was now running toward him midway between the cliffs and the streamlet.

But ere the shout had well died from his tongue, Harry staggered and sank down beside the slaughtered game, half fainting and almost insensible.

Two minutes had not passed between Archer's sinking to the ground exhausted, and Pierson's arrival on the scene of action. For seeing his young companion fall so suddenly, as it seemed to him, he imagined that he had received some hurt from the antlers of the wounded stag in its death-struggle, and in consequence redoubled his pace down the uneven slope, throwing away his rifle in order to reach the place more speedily.

During the few seconds that Harry's insensibility lasted, Smoker had applied himself assiduously in the height of his dog-affection, licking the face and hands of his master over and over again until he had communicated to them no small quantity of the blood, which had flowed from the hart's death-wound, and which he had been lapping greedily.

So that when Pierson came up, Harry presented a singularly ghastly and almost appalling spectacle; for between fatigue, loss of breath and excitement, his face was ashy pale, and the streaks of frothy arterial blood which crossed it in many places gave it exactly the resemblance of the countenance of one violently slain.

A loud exclamation of dismay and grief burst from the lips of the rude forester as he knelt down by Harry's side, raised his head upon his knee and gazed wistfully into his face.

At this moment, however, the brief fit of exhaustion and faintness passed away and, as Archer's eyes reopened and fell full upon the hard angular features of the Dutch hunter, grotesquely distorted from the effects of sorrow and apprehension, he burst at once into a loud hearty laugh, which instantly reassured his friend and satisfied him that he was not seriously endangered.

"That's right; that's right, Mr. Archer!" cried the good fellow cheerfully though a big tear, the offspring of strangely mingled feelings, which was rolling down his dry withered cheek.

"Laugh at the old fool e'en as much as you will; right glad I am to hear you laugh inyhow. I niver thought to hear you laugh again, I didn't."

"Why, what the deuce ails you, Dolph?" cried Harry, springing to his feet, as brisk as ever. "Or what should ail *me* that I should never laugh again? The devil's in it, if, after running two miles over such ground as I have just run, and at such a pace too, a fellow may not lie down on the grass and rest himself. I was dead blown, old fellow, nothing more. A good pull at the Ferintosh will bring me about in a jiffy."

"But whar's all that 'ere blood comed from, say?"

"Blood! What blood? Man-alive, I believe you are either drunk or dreaming!"

"On your face, Mister Archer. Arn't it *your* blood? Well, I thought it was, for sartin!"

"I do not know," said Archer. "No, it's not my blood, I'm not hurt," and as he spoke, he raised his handkerchief to his face, and with the aid of a little water from the brook soon washed away the filthy wetness from his face.

Then seeing Smoker, who relieved from all anxiety about his master, had buried his sharp muzzle in the wide death-wound of the buck.

"There is the culprit," he added. "Poor devil. I suppose he fell to licking my face when he saw me lie down."

"Well, yes, he was a kind o' nuzzlin' at you when I seed him, and I'm an old fool, inyhow, not to have thought of that afore. But do you call that lyin' down? It looked a darned sight liker failin'."

"Well, well, never mind which it was, Dolph. All's right now, so don't say a word about it when those chaps come up. Fat Tom would crow for a whole month if he got hold of such a story on me."

"Niver a word, I," replied the hunter. "But come, it's past now, and we've got more than we can do to git these four bucks broken and hung up, so as we can jine old Tom and that 'ere fancy chap down at the outlet."

"Well, let's be doing," answered Harry, "but first run to the brook, Dolph, won't you, and fetch us up your big tin-cup full of water. For all the water's so cold, I want a long drink, I tell you."

"Here 'tis," replied old Dolph, as quick as light. "I've drinkt out on't, myself. But I guess you won't stand for that."

"Not I, indeed," said Harry, bolting the liquor. "Now I'm your man for anything—what's to be done first?"

"Fust! Why fust we've jest got to go and find our rifles and load up. Where's yourn?"

"By the other hart, on the brook's edge. I threw it down that I might help Smoker with this fellow who would, I thought, prove too tough a match for him. Where's yours?"

"Somewheres on yan hillside. I throwed it down when I seed you fall. I dun' know wheres, but I can find it by taking the back track."

"Look here, then, let us gralloch this hart first and hang him somewhere. We'll have to carry him a hundred yards to that tree. As we have got four to look after, we must lose no time, and take no steps twice over. I'll break him up," he added, tucking up his sleeves and drawing his long knife.

"Do you run and cut a ten-foot pole, stout enough to carry him in the coppice yonder."

No sooner said than done, and before Harry had cleared the carcass of the offal, on which Master Smoker blew himself out till he could hardly stir, Dolph returned bearing a young, straight dogwood tree of some three inches diameter at the butt by 12 feet in length, which he had hewn down and shaped crudely with his keen tomahawk.

"That's your sort, Dolph!" cried the young Englishman, who had by this time interlinked the legs of the hart through the perforated sinews, as cooks will do those of a partridge before roasting.

"Shove it through here. Put your shoulder to that end, and I'll hoist this. Oh-he-ave!"

And with the word, they raised the noble buck from the pole, back and head downward, and walked away cheerily under the heavy load to the spot where the other had fallen close to the ravine's edge.

Here, Archer's rifle was recovered and duly loaded, and the operation of breaking, or butchering, having been performed on that hart likewise, Harry mounted the deer to the fork of a young hickory which grew hard by. Then, with Pierson's assistance, they hoisted one up on either side of the stem, and left them hanging there, a noble trophy, the one with six points, the other with seven to its widespread and formidable antlers.

Thence, they had a long and tedious walk uphill to the spot where Dolph had cast down his rifle, and a weary search ere they found it. A search rewarded only by success at last, in consequence of the extreme sagacity of the Dutch hunter, and the houndlike, instinctive skill with which he tracked the light prints, invisible to any eye less practiced than his own, of his own bounding footsteps on the dry grass and among the leafless bushes.

This task at last accomplished, and the unerring piece loaded with the minute and patient exactness which is so perfectly characteristic of the true backwoodsman, the hardy pair set forth again; and after scrambling up the tangled and broken slopes of the burnt pasturage for something better than half-an-hour, reached the foot of the cliffs at about half-a-mile's distance from the mouth of the ravine through which Harry had descended.

Here, the same ceremony was performed on Dolph's stag which they had already completed on the others, and when he had been drawn up by the heels to a dwarf oak which shot out of the crag's face, nothing remained for them to do but to descend leisurely by the brook's edge to the scathed tree, at the foot of which lay the great mouse-colored hart, which had rewarded Archer's toilsome descent of the gully.

"It's him, by the Etarnal!" cried old Dolph, the moment his eye fell on the carcass of the monstrous animal. "It's him, Archer, else I'll niver pull a trigger after this day!

"Give us your hand, boy; you've done that this day, as'll be talked on hereaways after we're both cold and under the green sod. Yes, yes, it's him, sartin. There's the crook horn, and there's the white spot on his hither side whar' poor Jim Buckley's bullet went clar through him, as I've heern say by them that was alivin' them days, these fourscore years agone and better.

"And they do tell as he was *then*, what *you* calls a hart royal, with a full head I means. There's not a hunter in the range, as his father and his grand'ther hasn't run this fellow as lies here now so quiet, with hounds, on snowshoes, in light snows and on deep crusts fifty times, and niver got within rifle range, 'ceptin Jim Buckley.

"He lied in wait for him like over ten nights in May, up in the crotch of a big tree, whar' he come bellin' for his hinds, nigh whares he'd seen the frayin' of his horns like on the ragged stems, and so he shot him through and through, with an ounce-bullet from an old-fashioned yager, as was took from them Hoosian chaps at Trenton in the Jarseys.

"But Lord a' massy, Mr. Archer, he stopped no mores for that ounce-bullet than you'd stop for a musquito bite when the hounds was makin' music in a runway. He rared right stret an end and shuck himself, and looked kind a savage-like at Jim, and went off through the woods jest the same as though nothin' ailed him . . . and nothin' did ail him, likely."

Here, the old hunter paused, looked about him with a furtive and uneasy eye, and then added in a low voice, as if he were half ashamed of the thoughts to which he was about to give utterance, or fearful of uttering them.

"But su'thin ailed Jim Buckley afterward, they does say, Mr. Archer, for that same day one year after, a rifle went off of itself like in his partner's hand, and the ball struck him nigh the blade-bone of his right shoulder, quartered through him, and comed out jest in his flank under the lowest rib—jest the identical shot as he gave the stag—but Jim was a dead man in five minutes.

"The ball, it warn't nothin' but a little triflin' fawty-to-the-pound slug. I'm kinder sorry after all that you shot him; they doos tell 'at no one niver had no luck afterward that had as so much as chased him, let alone shot him."

"Ha! ha! ha!" shouted Archer merrily. "Why, Dolph, old lad, are you beside yourself this fine morning! Why, to my certain knowledge you have hunted him with me there several times yourself and shot *at* him once. I never heard yet of any bad luck that had befallen you."

"Nor of none very good, nuther, I'm athinkin'," interpolated Dolph with an incredulous shake of the head. But Harry proceeded as if he had not heard him.

"And for the rest, Dolph, you may be perfectly easy for this time, I think. For you had certainly no hand in this job from the beginning to the end. It was I who viewed him from the crags with my naked eye, when you overlooked him; it was I who recognized him for the old crookhorn, with my glass; I who stalked, I who shot, I who bled him, and I, Dolph, who will bear the brunt right merrily of anything that is like to befall me in consequence. Come, man, don't look so woe-begone after the best morning's work that has been done on the burnt pasture these ten years or better."

"These twenty year, I guess. But I ar'nt downcast none, nor I don't believe the one-half of their parleyin'. But you keeps a askin' me ivery now and then to tell you the old talk of our woods-lads hereaways, and then when I doos, you laughs at me."

"Not I! not I!" said Archer, who had been busy cleaning the carcass, while Dolph was ruminating on the old-time superstition.

"By the Lord Harry, four inches of clear fat on the brisket!" he ejaculated on a sudden. "I will dissect a dozen or so of these short ribs, Dolph, and with a bit of salt and pepper out of my pouch, we will make a broil down by the lakeshore yonder, and with the hard biscuit and cold pork and onions, and the drop of Ferintosh, we will have a feast fit for kings by the time those fellows come along. I'd bet a trifle they haven't beat us yet awhile."

"There ar'nt no *two* men on this arth as kin," replied the old hunter, looking with an admiring eye at his companion. "For I will say that afore your face, as I've said many's the time ahind your back, yourn is the quickest eye, the steadiest hand, the coolest heart and the fastest foot I iver see on hill or in valley. Mine ar'n't so quick, or sure, or cool, by many a sight, nowadays. I dun' know as they iver was; and for fastness, why when I was a boy, you'd have outrun me jest as I can a mud-turtle, then for knowin' sign and followin' trail, and specially for puttin' things together, and seein' what the hull sum of them tells—though you was green as grass and helpless as a year-old babby when I seed you fust—there's not a many as kin beat you hereaways, nor in the far west nuther.

"Now, if I'd bin and done a wrong thing inyhow, and kivered it up close so's no one should find out who dun it, and then med tracks, I'd rather have fifty Feeladelfy lawyers and half the woodsmen in the range after my heels, as jest you unaccompanied like."

"Hush! hush! Dolph. You'll put me to the blush, old boy. Whatever little I may know of the woods and woodcraft. I owe it all to you."

"There ain't nothin', Archer, in hearin' the truth or in tellin' the truth, right out, up and down, as should make no gal blush, let alone no man. And it's truth that I tell you. Hallo! what's that—?"

The distant crack of a rifle came up the light air to their ears, from the lakeshore. Both turned their eyes instantly toward the point whence the sound came, and a thin wreath of bluish smoke was seen to curl lazily above the underwood and to melt into the transparent skies.

A moment later, at about 200 paces from the spot where the smoke was disappearing, a noble buck darted from the covert at full speed and, plunging into the lake, oared himself with his fleet limbs gallantly across the limpid sheet, his graceful neck and antlered crest showing like the prow and figure-head of some stately galley, with the blue water rippling before the smooth velocity of his motion.

Another minute afterward, a man showed himself, rifle in hand, examining the bushes and the grass underfoot, in search of blood or hair, or the track of the bullet, thereby to judge whether his shot had been effective.

"Ay! ay!" said Archer, laughing, as he recognized the gay garb of his friend by aid of his telescope. "You may look there these ten years, Master Frank, and find no sign. That was a clear miss, hey, Dolph?"

"In course it was. Who iver see a man in sich fancy garments as them are do anything but miss?"

"He does not always miss, I can tell you, by a long way, Dolph," said Harry. "But come, let's be tramping. They are nigher to our meeting place than we are."

"But we'll do the distance in jest half the time."

"True. But let's do it easy."

THE SUNRISE BUCK
By Paulina Brandreth

This is Chapter 17 in Trails of Enchantment (1930), *which was reprinted in 2003 in the "Sisters of the Hunt" series with a new foreword by Robert Wegner. The story, which is in effect a "stand alone" piece, offers an important lesson when it comes to patience in dealing with and ultimately tracking wounded deer.*

There are places in the woods one never forgets. Sometimes we put a stamp of ownership on them in the shape of a hunting or fishing camp. Sometimes we see them and pass, and never go exactly the same way again. The vista of that lonely log road; that spruce-studded, park-like little beaver meadow stumbled upon unawares; that rain-fed brooklet cascading down a hitherto undiscovered ledge are seldom seen twice. The woods are big. Unless you blaze a trail to these charmed spots, the difficulty of finding them a second time is only appreciated when you undertake the task.

Many years ago, we fell in with such a place and determined not to lose it. This was before lumbermen visited the locality and more or less changed the face of things. It was as solitary and wild and beautiful as one could wish. We built a camp there and made it our hunting headquarters. Usually we breakfasted under the stars and traveled from sunup to sundown. Being young and enthusiastic, I wanted to eat up the miles, and eat them up we did in spite of Rube's arguments against such over-strenuous methods.

The camp was situated near a sheet of water known as Panther Pond—the name itself adding a flavor of wildness to an environment already replete with the charms of solitude. Rube and Everett, if I remember correctly, were the architects and builders, and its unique character has never faded from my mind.

In shape it resembled a large Indian tepee. Great rolls of spruce bark had been ingeniously wrapped around a framework of poles, and a wide opening in front faced the fireplace. In many ways, it was warmer and more comfortable than a lean-to. Inside, three people could sleep without crowding on the thick, fragrant mat of balsam boughs.

Besides the tepee, we possessed the remains of an old tent, which stretched to its limit between four trees, gave protection to our store of provisions and made a good shelter for the mess table. The latter was an extremely rickety affair and the seats we used were worse. These consisted of a slab of pine nailed to a short block of wood, the sharpened point of which was driven into the ground as you sat down. Occasionally, if the point didn't happen to go in deep enough, you were likely to capsize ludicrously backwards or sideways in the middle of a meal. If you grabbed the table in a frantic effort to regain your balance, that equally unstable piece of furniture would, as likely as not, upend and turn turtle (the boards being laid on loosely), and the catastrophe would then be complete.

Yet, in spite of these faulty luxuries, food served on those uneasy boards tasted as though it had been dropped right down from the table of the gods.

The tepee stood on a knoll sown thick with big balsams. They were not the kind that snapped off easily in a windstorm, but were trees of antiquity, and their aromatic spires towered high above the camp. On the south side of the knoll at the bottom of a shallow ravine coursed a clear, spring-fed brook, which emptied and lost itself a little farther on in the heart of a dense, black spruce swamp. Beyond this swamp a spacious beaver meadow reached to the brink of Panther Pond and extended for almost the entire length of its easterly shore.

The pond itself was long and narrow. At no point was it more than a hundred yards wide. Banked with virgin timber on all sides except that taken up by the meadow, its surface was invariably unruffled, mirroring like some fabled pool the massive figures of white pines, the yellow, frost-withered grasses, the fleecy October clouds. Food for the whitetail was abundant along its shallow margins as the network of runways and trampled mud attested.

The Sunrise Buck

Undoubtedly the work of beavers in time long past, Panther Pond in those days, unmarred by human endeavors, unsoiled by wasteful dominion, knew the quietude, the primitive beauty, the freshness of a wilderness built up by the accumulated patience of centuries, and was something to be looked upon with reverence, considering the destiny which even then overshadowed its future.

We breakfasted (as I have already said) very often under the stars. The flavor of those early morning repasts was eloquent with promise. And certainly, at no other time (provided the weather was clear) did the planets and constellations appear more resplendent, more intimate, more freighted with mystery than between the hours of four a.m. and the moment of gradual fading with the approach of day.

Nor indeed, for that matter, are there any hours so pregnant with vitality, so beautifully adorned, so altogether exquisite in their intimations.

Once you have bridged the difficulty of getting awake, the splendor of night, ready to break at the first imperceptible change in the eastern sky, seems to enfold the forest in a shining and hallowed secrecy. A frosty breath from this chamber of enchantment is sweet as a rose garden. All is still with the stillness that is a prelude not to death but to life.

In the small hours of a certain memorable morning, I was wakened by our unfailing camp alarm clock—a loud decisive cough from Rube. Luxuriously, with the blankets pulled up over my head, I waited developments. Presently, a warming glow followed by a brisk crackling animated the opening in the tepee.

"Hev some eggs fer breakfast?" the old hunter inquired as I slipped out and joined him beside the fire. In one hand he held a frying pan, in the other, a large spoon with which he kept a golden island of butter circling and sizzling on the bottom of the pan.

"Eggs?" echoed a voice behind us. "I thought they was all used up."

"No, they ain't. I put some away where you couldn't find 'em," replied Rube mildly, without turning around. "If you want somethin' ter do, you kin stir that pancake batter on the table."

"My hands are too cold," Wallace demurred with a wink in my direction. "I like ter froze stiff after you let the fire go out."

Rube maintained a cynical silence as he broke half-a-dozen eggs deftly into the pan. Wallace, balking in his attempt to evoke an enlivening argument, grumblingly went in search of the pancake batter.

"Awful still, ain't it?" the former remarked as we sat at breakfast a short time later.

It was, indeed, a breathless autumn morning. Not a leaf stirred. The stars, blotted out by a thick curtain of mist, failed to look in upon us from their appointed places. Underfoot, the painted foliage was drenched with moisture.

"You won't be able to do still-huntin' today, not after the sun gets up," Wallace said as he poured the coffee.

"No, I guess you're right," agreed Rube. "We'll set down by the pond somewheres and watch."

Imperceptibly, the mist hanging between the tree trunks around camp took on a pearly tint. By the time the last pancake had been baked, it was light enough for us to get underway. Far off in some remote corner of the woods, a bluejay chimed melodiously.

"I've got a lot of firewood ter split up, so I'm goin' to stay in camp," Wallace announced.

"Don't work too hard," Rube threw back as we started off. "You might get laid up, so we wouldn't hev no one ter tend the fire at night."

"Well, by gravy, you're doin' some real talkin' now," Wallace drawled sarcastically. "If it wasn't fer me, you two would starve ter death and freeze way out here in these lonesome woods. I suppose I got ter clean up all these dirty dishes."

The trail to Panther Pond led north from camp. For the first few hundred yards, it zigzagged through the mazes of the black spruce swamp and then entered the beaver meadow. As we stepped out into the latter, a pair of hawks volplaned over our heads, mysteriously silent. A moment later, the first shaft of sunlight struck the distant treetops.

Clumps of alders, stunted evergreens and giant dead tamaracks decked out with streamers of gray-green moss were scattered near and far. On either side of the trail, the little spruces were wreathed with silver cobwebs, and through this glittering miniature forest we advanced noiselessly, our feet sinking ankle-deep in the water-soaked sphagnum. Behind us, over the rim of a hog-backed ridge, the rising sun blazed for an instant between snowy rifts of vapor and touched the cobwebs with prismatic fires. Above the phantom sea of mist overhanging the marsh, it resembled a lurid moon. But as quickly as it had broken its cloudy nightcap, it disappeared again, drowned in a gulf of milky fog.

As we drew near the shores of the pond, the mist grew even denser than before. Runways that threaded the meadow gave evidence of many nocturnal wanderers and made us realize the number of deer that must be located in the neighborhood. In one, we found the fresh imprint of a medium-sized bear. A moment later, coming abreast of the pond, we were treated to a rare and beautiful picture of wildlife.

The surface of the water was smooth as a mirror, shrouded partially by moving clouds of mist, and reflecting translucently sections of the opposite shore. Suddenly, a black object, which at first glance we took to be a large muskrat, broke the polished surface and began swimming up the pond. Almost immediately it was joined by four others. As we stood staring, one of the five rose seal-fashion from the water and dove with a resounding splash.

Rube gave a chuckle.

"Why, them's otters," he said with a note of deep satisfaction.

For ten minutes or longer, we stood and watched the gambols of these sinuous and splendid fur-bearers. Playful as schoolboys, they chased each other back and forth across the pond, dove with the swirl of a monster trout, and often reared, glossy and shining, three-quarters of their length out of the water. Against the snowy streamers of fog they appeared black as ink.

Doubtless, these five otters belonged to one family, but as the female rarely brings forth more than two pups, there must have been three full-grown adults in the party, judging from their size.

Gradually they moved off toward the opposite shore, and evidently having become suspicious of human presence, their frolickings abruptly ceased; nor did we ever see them again during frequent visits to the pond.

Following a runway, we continued our hunt, with the idea of skirting the shore until we found a favorable place to watch. Nearing the head of the pond, we stepped out on a grassy point in order to get a better look around.

"Right behind that little spruce," Rube whispered sharply, grabbing me by the arm. "A nice buck . . . can't you see him?"

Through the mist curling off the water-like steam, I caught the outline of a deer. He was standing broadside, motionless as a statue, his head partly hidden behind a small tree, his blue coat glistening velvety through the shifting vapors. It was a picture I have never forgotten—the water with its cloudy breath and sharp reflections, the yellowish marsh grass struck by smoky sunbeams, the gold and scarlet autumn foliage, the dark figure of the deer looming and fading through the thin clouds of mist.

"Sure it's a buck?"

"Sure," replied the old man . . . "I seen his horns."

Shoving the sight on the rifle up to the second notch for long range, I knelt down on the boggy ground, got a good knee-rest, planted the bead on the center of the animal's foreshoulder and touched off. The roar of the old .40-65 broke the silence like a thunderclap. As the smoke cleared, I saw the buck standing in exactly the same position. Suddenly, he turned and started for the woods.

"You didn't touch him," cried Rube in exasperation. "Shoot agin—shoot agin!"

The palsy of buck fever laid hold of me with deadly fingers. The rifle sights seemed to wobble all over the map. Groaning in spirit at this awful exhibition, I fired three shots in rapid succession. At the last report, the buck made a quick bound sideways and vanished behind a screen of alders.

Rube gave his beard a thoughtful tug and looked around for a place to sit down.

"Think he's hit?" I ventured.

"Oh, he's hit all right—but we want ter give him a little time before we foller him up."

I wondered then just how long the old man meant by a "little time." I knew his failings when it came to time and shortcuts through the woods. Both were liable to remarkable extensions, and being in no patient frame of mind, I had small relish for remaining inactive when every moment might be precious in securing our trophy. Had I been alone, I would, without doubt, have chased after the buck and probably lost him. Rube's wisdom in the hunting field taught me many valuable lessons that served me well in later years.

As we sat by the pond, the fog gradually cleared away, and the sun came out warm and mellow. It was one of those rare October mornings when the brilliant foliage of the forest glowed softly through a bluish haze, and not a breath of wind stirred the leaves or ruffled the glassy surface of the water. Now and again, an insect shrilled in the dry marsh grass. Occasionally, a broad-winged hawk sailed out over the treetops, and rising to greater heights, spun slow, measureless circles against the filmy blue of the sky.

Quite oblivious to the fact that they were being watched by human eyes, a pair of does, sleek and graceful, wandered along the shore until they came opposite to where we were sitting. There, they grew suspicious, jerked their tails upright and disappeared into the woods with slow mincing steps.

After what seemed like a considerable length of time, Rube stood up and hitched his pack into place.

"I guess we'll move now," he said.

We followed the shore down to the inlet, crossed on a log and struck up along the opposite side. Instead of picking up the trail where the buck had last been seen, the old hunter went in diagonally and nosed around for ten or fifteen minutes amid a network of runways. Suddenly he stooped down, touched a leaf, then straightened up with a smile.

"Here's where he went. I don't believe he'll go far, neither."

It was a neat piece of work. The trail led up a steep, spruce-clad hill. Halfway to the top, it swung off at right angles. Just ahead, a big hemlock had tumbled down the slope, its great roots matted with dirt and boulders flung upright like a barrier across the trail. As we came up close to it, Rube paused, craned his neck, took a step forward, and clapping his rifle to his shoulder, fired. Behind the upturned roots lay our trophy, a swift bullet having put an end to further suffering.

"I didn't darst wait for you," he apologized. "He had quite a lot of life left, and I wasn't givin' him no chance ter skip again. Well, he's a nice deer, ain't he?"

"Let's see where he's hit," I said. "I held for his shoulder on both those first shots, and Lord knows where the last ones went!"

We turned the buck over and found a bullet hole in a place that makes even a tyro blush with shame.

"Held for his shoulder and hit him in the ham," the old man remarked with an unsympathetic grin.

"That fog was what threw me off," I explained.

"Well, it wasn't no easy shot," he returned. "And just remember one thing," he added. "It's gettin' your deer that counts, once you've hit him. Lots of people would have lost that buck by rushin' right after him, and he might have traveled miles and died a lingerin' death. No, sir, it don't pay ter go tearin' after an animal that ain't got a bullet in a place that's goin' ter kill 'em quick. I don't mind seein' deer missed, but I do hate to have one hit and then lose him—a bad job all the way 'round."

Out of the little pack he always carried, Rube produced a coil of rope and a small block and pulley. Nothing is handier in the woods than a rig of this kind, for it facilitates easy handling of the quarry. Twenty minutes later we were on our way back to camp.

The resonant blows of an ax greeted us as we approached the tepee. Wallace, with one foot on a log, paused and stared at us in surprise. "I thought you wasn't comin' back ter lunch?"

Rube threw off his pack and went for a basin and towel. "It don't take us all day ter git a good deer," he remarked from the rear of the mess tent. "Didn't you hear the shot?"

"I was too busy ter hear anythin'," replied Wallace. "Why didn't you bring him along with you?"

"He was too big. We got ter have some help."

Wallace regarded us suspiciously.

"I suppose that means you'll load me up like a horse," he said. "I wish ter gracious you'd build a shed, so we could have Fred out here ter do the totin'. (Fred being an equine possession of Rube's in which he took considerable pride.)

"What's the matter with you anyway?" the old man rejoined in scornful amusement. "Are yer losin' all yer strength? Why, when I was a young man of your age, I could pack out half-a-dozen deer on a huntin' trip and never think nothing of it."

Wallace smiled tolerantly.

"You could, eh? What was they—fawns?"

Momentarily, this shot took the wind out of Rube's sails. He switched abruptly and attacked from a fresh quarter.

"Hearin' you groan about carryin' meat out of the woods reminds me of a feller who used ter work fer me by the name of St. Clair. He had plenty of bean and weight, but he was always coddlin' hisself. He had more affection fer a rockin' chair than any man I ever seen. We was makin' maple syrup one spring and luggin' all the sap by hand. St. Clair got fed up on handlin' them pails and yoke.

" 'Say, when are you goin' ter quit this job?' he asked me one day. 'Oh, when the millers come out,' I sez, and not long afterwards he walks in with two brimmin' sap buckets, lookin' as pleased as Punch, and holds out his hand.

" 'There's one of your damn millers,' he sez—and that's just the way you'll be gettin'," Rube ended up.

Early in the afternoon, we set out to bring in the buck. Rube decided to take one of his shortcuts instead of going around by the pond, and at the announcement, Wallace's jaw dropped, but he said nothing. Rube's shortcuts were sadly familiar to us both. On this occasion we tramped steadily for two hours. Noticing our disconsolate expressions, the old woodsman finally called a halt and examined the contour of the land.

"We'll just clim' this knoll," he said reflectively, "and then—"

"Clim' another," finished Wallace. Rube, however, ignored the thrust and resumed his skirmishing.

"The route we come by is a good deal easier than wallerin' through the marsh," he remarked later when we finally arrived at the place where the buck was hung.

"I'd ruther swim the pond than go back that way," Wallace declared, mopping his face.

When the trophy was skinned and packed, the argument broke out afresh, but this time Wallace was the winner. We pulled into camp in about half the time it had taken us to go out.

All this happened, as I have said, many years ago. The tepee has long since crumbled away; the big balsams have been ground into pulp, have passed into the printed sheet from which you have been informed of the happenings of the day—murder, theft, politics, war, scandal, international grievances, etc., and yet the beauty of that once virgin and isolated territory lingers despite mutilation.

Panther Pond is still the favored haunt of the whitetail, and the stars cannot be commercialized.

PART FIVE

FICTION:
WHITETAIL TALES WELL TOLD

The entirety of the whitetail experience lends itself to fiction. After all, what hunter worth his salt hasn't sat in a stand or eased through the autumn woods with visions of a majestic buck taking center stage? We indulge in realms of fiction almost as a second nature with deer hunting. Or, as my Grandpa Joe liked to put it, we devote quiet times and long hours of patient waiting to "dreamin' and schemin'."

Grandpa performed all his indulgence in flights of fancy orally, with a rocking chair forming a poor man's throne, and his hands constantly in motion as he used them to punctuate, emphasize and generally embellish his tales. That grand old man who filled my boyhood with magic was at best marginally literate, but that educational limitation in no way imposed on his excursions into telling of tall tales. There was an element of fact underlying his stories, but Grandpa could embellish with the best of them. He fully understood the old Southern chestnut that suggests "'tis a poor piece of cloth which can use no embroidery," and he embroidered in a mesmerizing manner.

In many senses he was a kindred spirit to the skilled storytellers featured in the pages that follow or, at least to my mind, that's the case. At any rate, the half-dozen examples of fiction linked to the deer hunter's world immediately bring him to my mind. Along with being a key factor in shaping my life and career as a writer, he also stirred my soul with storytelling. That's precisely what these tales do.

Archibald Rutledge arguably resides in a class by himself when it comes to a skillfully spun whitetail tale, and if you aren't stirred by the doings on Curlew Island, there's a genetic void in your imaginative DNA. Duncan Dobie's pair of offerings leaves little doubt that he one of the modern masters of writing on deer, while Arthur Macdougall reminds us of why he has long enjoyed prominent places in the literature of the outdoors.

THE KINGS OF CURLEW ISLAND

By Archibald Rutledge

Initially published in the January, 1923 edition of Outer's Book-Recreation, *this wonderfully gripping tale subsequently was included in three of Rutledge's books*—Heart of the South *(1924),* Those Were the Days *(1955) and* The World Around Hampton *(1960).*

It was Richard who showed me the huge antler—a dropped horn from a whitetail buck. Massive to a degree rarely seen, not less than five inches it measured around the handsome beading. Moreover, there were nine clear points, none mere craggy excrescences; they were genuine tines. Architecturally the beam was perfect. Of course, it was gray from weathering, and it had lost some of its impressive weight; nevertheless, I had never seen a trophy which interested me more. Wild woodland beauty and romance, caught and made permanent, were in such an object for me.

"Well," I asked, "and where did you find it, Richard?"

"Cap'n," said the smiling negro woodsman, "you done already know."

"On Curlew Island?"

He nodded.

"This year?" I asked.

"I picked up this horn a month ago," he replied—and here his tone took on a seriousness which actually thrilled me—"and this same buck I done see no later than Wednesday, this same week Wednesday."

"And you mean to tell me, Richard, that he was wearing a top hat like this?" I questioned, eyeing the tremendous antler and then the dusky trapper.

"He done ordered a larger size this season," the negro assured me, a smile creasing his face as a crack in front of a knife creases an overripe watermelon.

When it comes to sporting matters of this kind, I am inclined to be abrupt. "When do we start?" I asked shortly.

The suddenness of my question did not surprise Richard. He knew me too well. Almost from the cradle we had hunted deer together in the wilds of the Carolina coast country. And he was very well aware that while the years may change the color of a hunter's hair, and perhaps the sprightliness of his step, they cannot touch the fiber of his heart.

"Today would be a good day to go, Cap'n," Richard suggested.

Toward the westward-sloping November sun I glanced appraisingly. Then I looked toward the lonely barrier island, five miles away across the lonely sea marshes beyond many a solitary bay and creek and sound. To reach Curlew Island, we would have to row through winding creeks, which from the stormy inlet north of the island spread octopuslike arms far through the vast retiring marsh.

"Your boat—you have it here, Richard?"

The negro pointed toward the landing before my house. "I didn't even tie her up," he answered, "'caze I knowed you would go."

Yes, he knew me well.

Four hours later, Richard and I were actually on Curlew Island. Darkness had fallen, but it was a scented mild and starry darkness. To me, it seemed that we had come to a world of sea-winds, sea-stars and strange, lonely beauty. To us came the perfume of dew-drenched myrtle and oleander, the mournful organ music of the mighty pines, the fluting of a passing flock of yellow-legs. I heard the wings of wild ducks winnowing the warm air. The roar of the surf from the front beach sounded incessantly.

We had come to a strange, wild place, Richard and I, and we had come for a romantic purpose. And despite the fact that his name may spoil the romance of it all, I must mention that Scramble, Richard's dog-of-all-work, was with us. You will look in vain among the ancestors of the First Families for Scramble's forebears; nevertheless, he was all dog.

When I questioned Richard concerning his favorite's lineage, he told me that Scramble's mother was a fice and his father a woolly dog.

Having hauled our boat into the myrtle thicket, we made our way down the dim trail, glimmering now in the starlight that led to the old cabin, which the negro on his occasional trapping trips to the island was accustomed to occupy. On either side of us were black thickets, full of perfumes, rustlings and the hush of listeners. Three times I distinctly heard deer bound away from our approach. You can't mistake the running of a deer; that light, incisive thudding of his precise and trimly handled hoofs. And once I saw a tall flagtail, vividly white for a moment, which suddenly vanished down a dark woodland aisle.

"I think, Cap'n, we might walk a little careful," Richard said casually.

"We are liable to fall over ourselves," I agreed, not understanding just what he meant.

"Not that," he corrected me; "but I mean you mustn't make no mistake and tramp on that big rattlesnake what done kill my other dog."

His calm warning nettled me.

"Richard, what are you bringing me into—here in the dark? Why in the world didn't you tell me about this business before we left home? We shouldn't have come down here in the night," I added bitterly. "If the stag has eighteen points on his head, the diamondback probably has as many on his tail."

Like most men on a dark and lonely road, my attitude toward a rattlesnake is wholly conciliatory. I would just as let him have the broad highway to himself."

"I done kill the mate," Richard told me.

"Large one?"

"My dogs ran into them by an old oak stump, Cap'n. I kill one snake, and the one snake done kill my dog Poacher. The other snake get 'way under the stump. I lost one snake and one dog," he ended.

"How long did Poacher live after he was struck?" I asked.

"He didn't live at all. Nothing don't live after getting what he got. The snake strike at Scramble, too, but Scramble make a sharp dodge."

"That's what I feel like doing now, Richard. Confound you! I suppose the island is full of these little friends of the hunter."

"Just these two," the negro assured me, and I knew him well enough to trust his word on matters of woodcraft.

"How long was your snake?" I persisted.

"Bad luck to measure a rattlesnake, Cap'n. But, if you had his rattles at a frolic, you wouldn't need no jazz-band. He was a swamp rattler—about eight feet long, I think. But he was the smaller and the tamer of the two."

"Real thoughtful of you, Richard, to save the big one for me, and me for the big one. But yonder's the old cabin in the clearing."

Dimly in the open space in the forest before us there appeared the squat and staggering building that I had dignified by the name of cabin. It stood in an arena-like place of sparse bushes and white sand. About it gathered huge oaks, seeming to meditate in the calm starlight. It was with real relief that I left the darksome, haunted woods and entered this old clearing. An object could at least be discerned on the pale sand—an object like an eight-foot diamondback, let us say.

But whatever resentment I had against Richard was soon dissipated. With a bright fire of dry driftwood, he soon had the cabin cheerful while he prepared an excellent supper. Then there were smokes. All seemed well. Life was worthwhile, despite reptiles and such.

When I retired, it was to dream of stags with tree-like antlers parading before me, begging to be favored with a soft-nosed bullet from my .250-3000.

Next morning, before the dew was thinking of drying, I began in earnest my stalk of the great buck of Curlew Island. I had not been out an hour before I knew that Richard had told me a true thing when he said that this particular deer made his home on this island. I first struck the master stag's track in the black mud on the marshy edges of a freshwater pond. Wonderful was that track. The mud's consistency was tough; the track was therefore not exaggerated in size.

"But this must be a calf," I said to Richard; "aren't there still some wild cattle on the island here?"

"Yes," the negro agreed, "but the track you see here is the track of the Curlew King."

"Sounds romantic," I said. "The Curlew King. Well, we're here to do a bit of dethroning."

We followed the track—Richard and I. It led from the pond side into a marshy basin; thence it traversed a wild reedland, wherein wound many animal paths. In this wilderness of reeds were hummocks of cedar, underbedded with soft golden broomsedge—ideal drowsing places for deer.

Thrice out of such shelters we jumped deer—two does and a sprightly buck bearing spikes. They rocked away in standard fashion. We were hardly interested in them. The track we were upon belonged to an entirely different kind of creature. But it led into the gross myrtle jungle between the reedy wasteland and the sea. We seemed to lose the trail on the margins of this desperate thicket.

While each of us was wondering just what to do, and while the light and warmth of the morning sun sifted genially down upon us through the piney boughs, both of us detected some object lying down. It was not 30 yards off, and it was nestled in the most deer-like fashion on the brink of a vivid green savanna.

Richard caught my arm and pointed with a steady black finger.

Slowly I lifted my rifle, but then I lowered it.

"Did you think it was the King?" I asked him in a whisper. Then, with more assurance in my tone, I said, "It's nothing but a cow. I can't see its head; but if I'm not mistaken, Richard, it's a dead cow."

Together we approached the prostrate creature. It was a heifer, newly dead. So clean and beautiful was her coat and so prime was her condition that I knew her death must have been a violent one. I thought she might have tripped in a hole and broken her neck. Such an accident sometimes occurs. But Richard discovered the truth concerning her fate.

"She did fall," he said, in answer to my guess as to the cause of her fate, "but she was like poacher; she was dead when she fell."

"A snake?"

"Not *a* snake, Cap'n, but *the* snake. There's just one snake can do a thing like this."

"I suppose so," I agreed, feeling creepy and beginning to eye the near landscape with that singular alertness that awakens in a man who senses he is in sudden and deadly peril.

"In the neck," Richard was saying, lifting the cow's lank head and pointing to a dread swelling at a place where the great artery comes from the heart.

"Come on, Richard," I said impatiently, "don't start that snake talk of yours. We are after a deer, not a diamondback."

"That's so, Cap'n," the negro agreed, "but if that cow couldn't smell him and so done tramped on him, I might do the same thing. I ain't ready to tramp my last tramp yet. The Lord knows I ain't quite ready to sail on the Jasper Sea."

Now, as you know, I had come to the island for pleasure and excitement, yet a sense of dread and distaste was coming over me. But I was determined to shake it off.

"We should have brought Scramble," I said, changing the subject.

"He is a good varmint dog," Richard said, "but he ain't so good on snakes—'cept in the dodging line."

"Snakes be hanged!" I exclaimed; "I'm thinking of deer."

Down an old wood road that was densely flanked by a semi-tropical jungle we trudged. Richard had put me a little out of humor, and no man in a bad humor can do any decent stalking.

"Cap'n," said Richard after awhile, "do you know what I done think?"

"Well?" I queried, hinting by my tone a certain disrespect for any thoughts that the negro might be having.

"I done think," he said "that Curlew Island ain't got just one King. There's the master buck and there's this same thing that keeps crossing our trail."

The negro admitted that I had the advantage of him.

"I'll tell you frankly. The trouble with us is that we are almost in a funk. Every time I hear a jaybird snap a twig I feel like breaking into a sprint. It takes real men to follow, stalk and bring down a stag like the one we're after. Do you believe we are men enough to do this? Suppose you let up on this infernal snake talk of yours. I for one have the creeps and the jumps, and I know if I see a lizard, I'll do a Brodie over these pine-tops."

"All right, Cap'n," the negro agreed, not in the least out of humor. "But please be careful."

"Hang it, Richard, suppose you go back to the cabin. I'll try to trail this deer alone for a while. You take Scramble out and see what you two can find in the way of varmints. Then you can get a good dinner ready. Look for me about dark."

"All right, Cap'n. If you don't come back," he added with kindly, unconscious gruesomeness, "I will come to look for you."

"Thanks," I said shortly, "but I will be able to get home myself."

Little did I then realize how much, ere that day was over, I should need the grim good man I was sending away.

With no further words, we parted in the lonely road. Richard returned to the cabin, and I struck off at left angles into a dim trail through the fragrant woodland. I was in the wrong mood to traverse such country, for I was too angry to be very quiet, as a stalker should be, or careful, which had been Richard's sound advice. Yet this mood did not remain long upon me.

I remembered the cause of my coming to his wild island. The vision of a stately crown of antlers once again rose before me. Yet, in such country, stalking is not easy. A hunter might pass within 20 feet of the couched king reposing in the brush, yet never see him.

Semi-tropical, languorous, baffling in its thickety beauty, the virgin dewy wildwood flanked my path. All around me were tawny jungles of palmetto, dense greenery of cassina and myrtle and beds of ferns of majestic height. Overhead there were moss-bannered oaks and old giant yellow pines murmuring musically.

On I walked through scented scenes that made me believe that in these woods the flowers never faded and the dew never dried. Yet they were silent woods. Few birds ever come to the island except shorebirds, that when migrating, descend upon it in countless thousands. Here and there I flushed a woodcock, which went away in his swift, enigmatic, thoughtful way, the thin sweet music of his wings sounding far.

Under almost every live oak, I could see where wild turkeys had torn up the trash; and under the big pines, they had raked the straw into long windrows. There's no food they prefer to the sweet mast of the long-leaf pine.

Twice I started does from the thicket-side. One of these glided gracefully through the myrtles, came to a halt in the dim road and stood for a moment, gazing in startled fashion in my direction. She was just the sort of graceful, mysterious creature to inhabit woods like these. Indeed, she seemed a fairy palpitation out of the heart of the lonely, beauteous forest.

It was now past noon, and November afternoons are short. From the forest trail, I turned eastward toward the front beach. The deer of Curlew Island have always had the greatest liking for the sand dunes. For all I know, they may, like human beings, love to watch the plunging surf and to listen to the rolling anthem of the beach. More likely, however, their fondness for open spaces is in proportion to the density of the forests, which by day they frequent.

A hundred yards from the beach, not so very far from where Richard and I had parted hours before, I came upon a long sandy slough. It was the kind of a place where shorebirds would delight to wade and feed, for it was marsh-margined, and it was about a half-inch under clear water. In the packed sand were scores of blurred trails, and one of these, seeming very large, I followed.

Just as it entered the forest to seaward of the savanna, I got one clear impression. There could be no doubt it was the track of the king. Nor was it an old track. A piece of damp sand, displaced by the heavy tread of the giant deer, still hung clingingly on the top edge of the impression. The thing looked hot, and I knew that if I had been a hound, I would have begun to trail.

I examined the ground further. I came to a wide bayou the consistency of chocolate. And what track did I see crossing it? Not the buck's, but a wide, deep track, almost straight, for the rattler does not wriggle when he crawls, and there were tiny cuts and creases in it which I knew had been made by a reptile's scales. Judging from the width and depth of the track, my friend had a body not less than a foot in circumference.

Apparently, I was on the trail of both kings. One I was eager to see; the other I loathed and dreaded. And why was it that this second sovereign kept crossing my path with sinister insistence? But I made up my mind not to be diverted from following the stag.

A curious stalk this was—trying to come up to one creature and at the same time trying to avoid another. I was, in a sense, both a follower and a fugitive.

Cautiously I stepped forward, stooping under dense tangles, insinuating myself through thickets while trying to be as noiseless as possible. Quite near me I heard a wild turkey run. A gray squirrel must have seen the turkey, for he barked coughingly. He knew that there was some cause for alarm. I was still on the track of the stag. I had managed to follow it, even in this jungle, because the earth there is soft and almost clear of grass. Slow was the work, for sometimes the very darkness of the shadows prevented my picking up the trail readily.

Northward turned the stag, and northward I followed. Two full hours I held the baffling, winding trail. Then I found the track making for the beach.

The sun was down when I came to thinning trees and felt the hale breath of the sea wind. Then I saw the mystic sand dunes, topped by their waving tufts of gray beach grass, and beyond them, in foamy tumult, the ocean.

In the lee of a bulky, storm-scarred red cedar, I came up quietly under its shelter. From this position, I looked carefully up and down the beach. It was the very time of afternoon for deer to visit the sands. But the rolling high dunes shortened the range of my vision. I therefore laid my rifle on the sands and pulled myself up into the first limbs of the cedar. From there, I could see as far as my eyes had vision for seeing. To the southward, the beach was bare—unless, nearly a mile away, the shadowy objects which I saw might be a troop of deer. Northward I turned my eyes.

At first I did not see the stag. He was between two huge dunes, and he must have been holding his head down. But now he walked boldly, majestically forward, mounting a bare sandhill.

Before my very eyes stood, all unconscious of his peril— the King of Curlew Island. More than a hundred yards away he was—larger than life in clear relief against the sunset line. He was within range, but my rifle lay on the sands under the tree. Though deer hunting has been my pastime since early boyhood, I was greatly excited.

"Richard didn't lie," I kept saying to myself as I eased my weight carefully down the tree. "That's the greatest buck on this island and in this country. His body isn't that of a giant—but his horns! I've seen antlers in my time, but not kingly crowns and chairs of state and all that. No, Richard didn't lie."

For a shot at the great stag, I had to do one of two things: either reclimb the tree—which was mightly awkward business with a loaded rifle—or reenter the woods, pass down parallel to the beach for 30 yards or more, so as to get clear of the shielding dunes, and then take a close shot from the forest edge. I decided on the latter course.

Sinking into the darksome cedar grove, I made my way as silently as possible through the borders of the dusky, fragrant wood. The twilight was fading. Momently I expected to be able to make my little maneuver toward the beach, but darkness was coming. And rather than lose precious minutes dodging in and out, I bided my time. At last, however, I turned beachward. And simultaneously with my turn, I heard the diamondback! My God, the thing seemed to be under my feet!

Insistent, shrill, querulously warning, the rattles whirred. The sound seemed everywhere. I was afraid to move. Always difficult to locate, this perilous note of menace was hopelessly so on the borders of this thicket. There was no light, save a dim jungle glow, eerie and misleading. Moreover, I knew this to be the snake I had been dreading. None other could sound his warning so formidably. I was so close that I thought I smelled the snake.

I could not locate him, could not see him, but very well I knew what his appearance was. I knew he was slothfully heaped in his rasping cold coils. Loathsome death was under my feet. Behind those grim jaws, articulated with the strength of steel, behind the faint chill pallor of his contemptuous lips, there lurked a dread secret.

All this I knew. And I knew that my business just now was not to kill a buck, but rather, to keep from getting killed. A single movement in the wrong direction might be my last one. I remembered that when my dear friend Bob King had been struck in the femoral artery by a diamondback, he had fallen to the ground unconscious, never to awaken in this life. Such a fate seemed now upon me.

Suddenly, I heard the patter of running feet. Then there came a dog's sharp yelp, and out of the darkness behind me, I heard a human voice call; it seemed to be coming out of another world.

"O, Cap'n!" shouted Richard cheerfully. The voice called me back from the realm of terror to the realm of reality. It brought me to myself. I forced myself to try to locate the snake. I heard the dog. He was baying the reptile. They were between me and the beach. I stepped backward into the thicket. A few moments later, I joined Richard in the dim woodland road.

"I thought you might need me," he said almost apologetically.

I thought of Kipling's,

"Though I've belted you and flayed you,
By the Living God who made you
You're a better man than I am, Gunga Din!"

"Is that Scramble back there in the thicket?" I asked.

"Yes, Cap'n. What he been baying near you? I don't hear him no mo'."

"He probably saved my life," I said. Then I told Richard of having seen the stag and of having heard the snake.

"Scramble is good at a sharp dodge," he said, "but I don't know how well he can dodge in the dark."

Here Richard gave a long whistle. To this there was no response.

"I was in danger, Richard," I said. "You came just in time."

"And we is such a long way from home," he responded, "to make 'rangments for a funeral."

"You've such a nice, tactful way of putting things," I said.

But the negro did not get my scorn. He was a dealer in elemental thoughts. To be struck by a big rattlesnake was almost surely to die; to die would undoubtedly necessitate certain arrangements, and in the nature of the case, these would devolve upon him. Thus he reasoned simply, naturally, and thus he spoke his thoughts.

And what of the buck? We left him for the night. It was now too dark to shoot, even on the glimmering dunes, and one of my strong aversions in deer hunting has been this business of wounding a fine deer and letting it get away. But in my mind, I could still see that magnificent creature gazing out over the somber twilight sea. Almost a phantom buck he was—a romantic shape of the rolling, ghostly dunes, a comrade of the wild sea waves, the mysterious marshes, the lonely forest.

"Is one thing good 'bout this cabin," said Richard as we made up to the structure bulking darkly in the faint starlight.

"No, rats. A rattlesnake," he explained, "especially a large one, likes to stay 'round an ole place like this and catch all the rats."

"Cheerful little thought," was my comment. "And Richard, if you have any more of these happy snake ideas, suppose you give all of them to me in one spoonful. I don't care for the broken doses."

As we entered the cabin, I felt uneasy all over, but Richard's blue-flame driftwood fire and his good dinner relaxed all my tension.

"Tomorrow," I said to the negro, "is the day. By the way, I hope Scramble gets back safely."

Richard laughed without feeling.

"Scramble, if you could see him now, would look like an accident that is done already happened."

"A daylight start," I said, "and tomorrow will be our last day on the island."

Dawn, with its aromatic sea winds, its blazing eastern star and the dewy spiceries shed by pines and myrtles, found us once more abroad in the island woods. Silent and faithful, Richard trudged beside me. He was grieving, I knew, over the loss of his second dog. Within half-an-hour, we were near the scene of our encounter of the evening before. Here, the island begins to narrow to its northward point. The end of it, jutting out into a tawny inlet, was not more than a half-mile from where we emerged from the woods upon the gray dunes. We mounted a high sandhill.

"It was off yonder, Richard, that I saw him," I said, pointing to a group of dunes down the beach.

It was not yet sunrise. Sea mist hung over ocean and beach and forest, yet beneath its filmy canopy, we could see far. The twilight of the morning shed its soft luster over the lonely ocean, the solitary sands, the silent, fragrant woods.

"Cap'n," said Richard, with more excitement than I had ever known him to show, "ain't that the king down yonder?"

My fascinated eyes followed his pointing finger. Far down the northern end of the beach I saw a shadowy form. There could be no doubt of its identity—we were looking at the stag of Curlew Island. What I had last night left on the sands was, after a long night's wandering, here again. He was taking a last look at the ocean before retiring into the forest for the day.

"Cap'n, I'm thinking that he can't get away from us today." Richard's voice was quiet and assured. "He is at the narrow end of the island, and to get back into the wide woods, he will have to pass us."

"We've cornered the king, Richard. But look, he's going up the beach now. He's going into the woods."

The splendid stag faded into the margins of the misty forest.

"Dat's all right," said Richard. "He's going to Eagle Pond to drink before he lies down. Come, Cap'n. I know the way."

No more perfect screen for a stalk could be imagined than was afforded us by the dense undergrowth through which we now, by winding animal paths, made our hurried and silent way. Richard led me ere long to a big palmetto whose broad fronds spread fanlike to the ground. Crouched behind this perfect screen, we looked out over the broad savanna before us. The place was about three acres in extent—a reedy clearing in the forest. Here and there were spaces of damp sand. Near the center of the savanna was Eagle Pond—dark and deep, and just now, fairly alive with mallards and teal.

"He will have to cross this place," Richard was telling me.

I am not familiar with the kind of buck that has to do as a hunter thinks he should, but I felt this deer would walk out into the savanna. It practically spanned the woods here. Moreover, it must have been a singularly attractive place for him.

Silence, stealing morning sunshine and the sweet music of wild ducks' wings attended our watch. A lordly eagle beat his way powerfully over the amphitheater. I heard a wild hen turkey give her plaintive call. The surf fell sleepily on the drowsy shore.

I was crouched low, my rifle thrust forward. I had everything in my favor for the shot of a lifetime—everything except the target itself.

Suddenly, silently, out of the mysterious forest he appeared. I felt very much like a friend of mine who, when his first buck walked out to him, exclaimed in a loud, amazed voice: "Lord, look at that!" and never thought of shooting.

But I tried to be cool and sensible. I measured the antlers with my eyes. Craggy, chestnut-colored they were, massive, symmetrical and with long tines. I knew he must be an 18- or 20-pointer. And the spread of the beams was phenomenal; it could not have been under 26 inches. What a head!

A hundred yards away the myrtles had parted, and now he came forth clear.

"Shoot, Cap'n!"

It was the voice of Richard, and over my hesitancy, he came as near groaning in spirit as he will ever come.

I lifted my rifle to take the bead. The buck lowered his great head. Now his head came partly up, and I could see the bulge in his neck. Even at this distance I thought I could detect a defiance, a challenge in his aspect.

Suddenly he whirled toward us, and for 20 paces he came head-on. Distinctly I heard him snort—the strange whistling snort of a buck's defiance. Then he charged down a stretch of open sand toward us.

I was amazed, for I saw no enemy. It could not be that he was charging us. A wild buck doesn't charge a man when he can do anything else. I had my rifle on him. But my finger did not touch the trigger. The buck's behavior compelled me to watch him. I stood up. On the white sand in front of the stag was the object. This was the king's antagonist.

Parting the palmetto fronds with a cautious hand, I saw the two fighters distinctly—the huge buck with his hair ruffled angrily forward, and the monstrous diamondback heaped in his ponderous coil. And Richard and I were witnesses to this combat of the kings.

The stag backed away, his grand head lowered and lolling with fury. He halted on the wet rim of the sand. I saw the reptile bulge himself, rising in his massive coils. I saw the spade-shaped head drawn back for the mighty drive. Then the buck charged.

When within ten feet of his enemy, he leaped into the air, drawing his four feet together into a close-bound sheaf of incisive spears. With deadly precision, he dropped on the chimera; and as quickly as had been his descent was the speed with which he cleared himself. With the grace that is born of wild strength, he rebounded from his wondrously accurate spring. In another moment he had whirled and had repeated his savage maneuver.

We watched, fascinated. We were there to kill the buck, but I could not shoot him.

He now desisted from his work. Standing with regal head held high, he was the picture of angry triumph. He had trampled the monstrous serpent to death. I saw dark blood running out on the white sand. The fight was over.

"Richard," I whispered, "you aren't saying 'shoot!' any more."

"He done make that snake pay up for killing Poacher and Scramble," he replied, frank admiration in his tone.

"Well," I said, "a hunter may on occasion be a killer, but he must first be a gentleman. Look what that stag did for us. We've no right to kill him."

"He is sholy the king," said the negro.

"Yes," I agreed, "and because of what he's done for us, we are going to let him reign."

"And to think, Cap'n," said Richard with a smile as we turned away from the strange close to our memorable stalk, "I don't even have to tell you no mo' to be careful how you walk."

STRANGE HAPPENINGS AT CHICKAMAUGA CREEK

By Duncan Dobie

One of the modern era's most talented tellers of whitetail tales, Dobie has, in a fashion harkening back to Charlie Russell's decorated Christmas cards or small runs of little books popular in the 1930s and 1940s as Yuletide mementos, made a practice of writing delightful deer stories and sharing them with friends and fellow sporting scribes at Christmas. This is a prime example of his noble enterprise. The story originally appeared in Whitetail Dawn *(2006).*

The hunter had been following a sparse blood trail for over two hours and it looked as though his greatest fear might be realized. The scant blood sign was beginning to peter out even more. John Forrest feared it might disappear altogether. Although he was sure he had made a lethal shot, serious doubt—the enemy of every competent bowhunter—was beginning to creep into his mind.

As always, John had been hunting with a recurve bow and, as always, he had been shooting instinctively, with no sights. Despite the difficulty of hunting this way, he seldom had to travel more than 100 yards to recover a deer he'd arrowed.

It was mid-September in northwest Georgia. Archery season had just opened the day before. John had taken more than a dozen deer with his 54-pound Hoyt recurve. Being a purist at heart, he had even taken two mountain gobblers with the old recurve, aided by a handmade wingbone turkey call.

Ever since first light on this second day of the brand-new archery season, however, the woods had become increasingly strange. All morning long John had heard an odd rumbling sound off in the distance, much like far-off thunder. Although the weather report had indicated patchy fog in the area just west of Chickamauga Creek where he was hunting, the skies were supposed to clear by late morning with little to no chance of rain.

To heck with the weather report, John had told himself shortly after first light. *That rumbling has to be a thunderstorm, and it sounds like it's headed my way.*

Now, as he painstakingly followed the blood trail across a series of rolling hardwood ridges, the curious thunder was getting louder. What's more, a peculiar mist began to roll in and fill the woods around him. It was like no other fog John had ever experienced, and it seemed to bring with it a strange odor, a powdery smell that permeated the woods.

Could there be a fire in the woods somewhere off in the distance? he wondered.

John rehashed the events of the morning over and over again in his mind. Having scouted these woods several weeks earlier, he had found a series of rubs and scrapes on a well-used trail that crossed a gap between two steep hardwood ridges. He had built a primitive brush blind on the downwind side of this natural saddle. He had hunted here the day before, opening day, with no luck.

The eerie noise had begun on this second day of archery season about an hour after daylight. It had continued all morning long, but the woods around John had remained quiet.

Around 10:30 a.m., three does came over the saddle. An hour later, the buck appeared. It was a nice eight-pointer with fairly long tines and a good spread, and it was walking rapidly down the trail. It kept looking back, as if something were following it. Being well hidden, John waited until the buck was within 20 yards. Then, quietly coming to full draw and aiming carefully behind the buck's shoulder, he released his arrow.

The shot appeared to be right on target. The arrow passed through the buck's mid-section just behind its shoulder. The buck turned inside-out and quickly bounded back over the saddle in the direction from which it had come. John recovered his blood-soaked arrow. Then, after waiting about 15 minutes, he began following a fairly good blood trail. Two hours later, the blood trail had all but disappeared.

Better find him soon, John thought. *That thunder's getting closer, and it's really starting to get hazy in these woods. If it rains, I'll lose the trail for sure.*

John decided to take a short break as he passed a large outcropping of rocks. He sat down on one of the high, flat rocks and carefully rested his bow across another.

It can't be a forest fire, he thought. *But it sure does have a strange smell to it.*

John pulled out a large chocolate brownie that his wife had made and started eating it. Just as he was finishing up, he heard another strange sound. This time it was very close. The noise appeared to be the distinct clanging of steel. Someone, or something, was coming through the woods toward him.

Must be some greenhorn squirrel hunter, he thought. *No one else would make that kind of racket walking through the woods.*

John was surprised to see three men with rifles emerge from the rolling mist 40 yards away. They were walking three abreast, and they were coming straight toward him. One of the men was limping slightly. As they drew closer, John's mouth fell open. Two of the heavy rifles the men carried were topped with long bayonets, and all three men were wearing the soiled, homespun uniforms of Confederate soldiers.

They must be reenacting a battle today over near the battlefield, John thought. *Maybe that's where all the noise is coming from. But they sure do look real . . .*

One of the men suddenly spotted John. Stopping dead in his tracks with a startled look on his face, he halted his two companions. All three men stared at the lone hunter sitting on the rock.

"Howdy," John yelled. "What brings you men out here in the middle of nowhere?"

"You from around here?" one of the men asked with a challenging tone.

"I don't live too far from here," John answered.

"What're you doin' out here," another asked.

"I've been following a wounded deer," John said, nodding toward his bow. "A buck. He's headed in the direction you boys just came from. You haven't seen anything, have you? I've been following him quite a while."

"Nope," one of the men said, staring at John's recurve bow. "A wounded buck's about the last thing we'd expect to see around these parts today."

"Are you huntin' with that bow and arrie?" one of the men asked.

"That's right," John said. "An old Hoyt recurve."

"It's a good thing you're deer-huntin'," the oldest of the three men

303

said. "We thought you might be a Yank."

"No, I'm not a Yankee," John said, smiling. "I'm a pure-blooded Georgia cracker through and through."

As the three Confederate soldier look-alikes stepped closer, they continued to size up the strange man with an even stranger weapon. John was wearing a dark green wool jacket that had belonged to his grandfather. It was ideal for bowhunting. He also had on an old pair of brown corduroy pants and old, western-style leather work boots. On his head he wore his favorite weathered felt hat with a copperhead skin hat band. To any stranger, he might easily have looked like a 19th-century homesteader, except for the modern bow.

The recurve bow with its attached quiver of arrows seemed to baffle the three strangers.

"Are you an Indian?" the oldest of the three men asked.

"No," John smiled. "But I take that as a compliment. The Cherokees and Creeks that used to live around these parts were great hunters."

John noticed that two of the men were extremely young, practically boys. *Probably still in their late teens*, he thought.

The third man had a heavy beard and was probably in his 30s. Their odd gray uniforms were all strikingly different in appearance. All three men looked as if they had just walked through a burning forest. Their uniforms and faces were smeared with dirt and grime. Only the oldest of the three wore a hat.

"It's been a long time since I've done any huntin'," one of the youngsters reflected. "I'm a sandlapper from Lower Carolina. We used to hunt the swamp country with buckshot and hounds when I was a boy. I've heard tell of people huntin' with a bow and arrie like that, but I've never seen it with my own eyes."

"Hell, you look like you still are a boy," John said in a friendly tone. "You don't look a day over eighteen."

"I'll be seventeen on December 20," the boy announced. "I been away from home a right long spell."

The second youngster spoke up. "You reckon you could spare a drink of water, Mister? We're plumb parched."

"I've got a little here," John answered. "You're welcome to it. I've also got a couple of apples if you're interested."

John held out his leather water bottle as the men stepped closer. Then, knowing that a good-size creek flowed into the much larger Chickamauga Creek somewhere just ahead, he added, "Didn't you boys just cross a big creek back there?"

"Oh, we crossed it, all right," the bearded man said. "That water ain't fit to drink, if you know what I mean." He made a strange face.

John had no idea what the man's comment was supposed to mean.

"You boys really look convincing," John said. "I didn't know anything like this was going on today. Where's the battle taking place?"

Just over the ridge, yonder," the bearded man answered with an incredulous look on his face. "Less'n a mile away. It was pretty rough out there today, but we give them bluecoats a run for their money. We got separated from our outfit early on, but we heard tell our boys sent 'em skedaddlin' all the way back up toward Chattanoogy. We done our part today, though. So we just been takin' it easy through these woods. We ain't in no hurry. I reckon we'll ketch up with our outfit 'fore the sun goes down."

"I haven't seen a soul in these woods all morning," John said. Then, as an afterthought, he added, "It's a good thing you're doing today. I had a lot of kinfolk who fought in the war."

"Which side?" the older man asked.

"The South, of course," John answered.

"They all dead?" one of the younger men asked.

"Why, yes," John answered. "They've been dead quite a while." Then, addressing the bearded man, John asked, "Where're you from?"

"I'm from east Tennessee," the man answered, putting the emphasis on the first syllable. "Ike, here, he's from Alabam."

The young man with the limp nodded. "We're with the 23rd Tennessee Volunteers," he added.

"Are those new Springfield rifles you boys are carrying?" John asked.

"Yep, we got 'em off a couple of Yanks," the man said. "They weren't needin' 'em any more."

"You men are bein' pretty hard on the Yankees, today, aren't you?" John asked kiddingly.

"Actually, they were pretty hard on us," the boy from Carolina answered, taking a swallow of water, "til we got the best of 'em, that is."

"We better be gettin' along," the Alabamian said nervously.

"Okay," the older man said. He looked at John. "Say, you mind partin' with one a' them-there apples?"

"Not at all," John said. "Here . . ."

John reached into his jacket and pulled out two red apples. The men took the apples.

"We hope you find your buck," one of the boys said.

"Me, too," John said. "I hope you find your outfit."

"We'll ketch up with 'em somewheres hereabouts," the Tennessean repeated. "You better be careful your own self, though. They's lots of stragglers roamin' these woods today." He smiled oddly.

The three men clambered off through the hazy woods and disappeared.

What a strange encounter, John thought. *They sure looked convincing. What a crazy day!*

Thirty minutes later John found his buck. It was stone dead, partially submerged in a shallow pool in the big creek. Oddly enough, the entire pool had turned a dark crimson color.

My buck couldn't have had that much blood left in him, John thought. Then he noticed that the red-stained water seemed to be coming from upstream.

John spent the next two hours dragging his buck out to the nearest dirt road. He then pulled his truck around and loaded the deer in the back. Just as he reached the paved highway on his way home, he noticed a historical marker near the intersection. Pausing at the stop sign, he read the inscription on the marker.

The Battle of Chickamauga

"Near this site on September 19 and 20, 1863, Confederate troops under General Braxton Bragg defeated the Federal Army in the bloodiest battle ever fought on Georgia soil. Over 30,000 men perished during the intense fighting. Much of the battle took place just east of this point along the banks of Chickamauga Creek, which, along with several smaller streams in the area, were said to have flowed red with blood for several days."

It suddenly dawned on John that he had heard somewhere the old Indian word *Chickamauga* meant *place of death*. In almost a panic, he quickly glanced down at his watch. Cold chills shot down his back. The date was September 19.

WHITE DEER ARE BAD LUCK

By Arthur R. MacDougall Jr.

The author's fictional Dud Dean stands out alongside similar characters such as Edmund Ware Smith's Jeff Coongate as timeless representatives of the outdoorsman in literature. This piece comes from Where Flows the Kennebec *(1947). It has previously appeared in various anthologies such as* Hunting Trails *(1961).*

The teeth of early winter bit at a man's ears. The November sky was wind-blown and implacable. I was waiting on the station platform for the northbound train. That train was late.

Joseph Danner was due. There was a telegram in my pocket that said so. Danner is a man of the world, a sophisticated metropolitanite. But he was born in a story-and-a-half house that squats in forlorn abandonment beside a narrow road that long since forgot the way out. The Danners are all gone, but the little house, grim and neglected in its afteryears, is evidence that their roots go far back in the Maine soil.

I sat on my full pack and wondered how much of an alien this last of the Danners had become.

Mat Markham was with me—that is, in a detached way. He sat on the off edge of the platform and smoked a corncob pipe. And his face was as blank of emotion and expectancy as a beaver bog in the midwinter moonlight.

Mat is the only successful guide I know who is the epitome of mirthlessness. But Mat is also a crafty, careful and skillful guide. As a cook among the old guides, he has but one equal, Dud Dean, who is his lifelong friend, although two men could not be less alike. Mat's cream of tartar biscuits are light, luscious masterpieces. And if there is time, and a suitable oven, Mat makes pies that are as good as those

Mother made. And as for his bean-hole beans, are they not famous from Bingham to the border?

But Mat had come with me not as a professional guide but as a friend and fellow hunter.

"I'd like to git me a deer," he had said, when I had suggested the project on a wage basis, "but I'm all done guidin' fer the year. Let folks wait on themselves."

When I had said that I was anxious that Danner have a pleasant week, and that he get his deer, Mat had said, "Thar's deer enough, but the woods is so dry that a deaf owl c'ud hear a deer mouse wiggle his ears. Can this Danner shoot?"

Danner had written me that he had not fired a rifle for ten years.

"Now, ain't that jist like them Babylonians? They hardly know which end of a gun is loaded, but they'll strike off fer the woods, expectin' all they need to do is pull a trigger, an' then all the wild things will fall out of the trees an' lay around with broken necks, er sunthin'."

So we sat there, Mat and I, waiting for the train to pull into Bingham. Down the track a whistle blew. Then we heard the engine's bell at the crossing.

There were only four passengers for Bingham, and Danner was one of them.

"Hey there, Mak," he called. "It's good to see you again. The last time was at the Lawyer's Club—a nice place for a parson! How are the prospects? Got one salted? I remember an uncle who always baited them that way. He claimed that such methods expedited business."

We shook hands. Mat reached out a paw, which Danner grasped when they were introduced.

"How do you do?" he said to Mat.

"I do jist as I dang please, part of the time," said Mat.

"What do you do the rest of the time?" asked Danner, with a tone of levity that Mat would detect and dislike, as he had the formal. "How do you do?"

"I guide," replied Mat.

In those days the train came in to the lower station in Bingham, waited, backed out and went on up to Kineo. By the time we had carried our duffel inside the coach, the train was leaving.

Danner and I talked. I don't think that Mat listened. At Moxie Station was a group of men and women, and manifest excitement. Mat

White Deer Are Bad Luck

got off to ask questions. He came back to us when the train started.

"It was jist as I guessed," he said. "Somebody got hurt—shot in the neck."

"Dangerously hurt?" asked Danner.

"We-el, the doctor they've sent for ain't got thar' yit. It was Joe Pratt. They lugged him out from in back of Bald Mountain. If I was goin' to pass jedgment, I'd say that Joe was back from his last trip."

"How did it happen?"

"Somebudy didn't wait—took him fer a deer. An' a man on his hind legs looks erbout as much like a deer as a deer looks like a stepladder."

"Did the poor devil who did the shooting come in with him?"

"Yup. He's thar. He's takin' on like a woman with her best hat lost in the wind, but that don't do Joe no good. They've got a feller from The Forks who can stop blood, but Joe's lost a lot of it. If they don't git a doctor purty quick, it'll stop all right."

"What do you mean by a fellow who can stop blood?"

"Why, I d'know. Never knew. Some does. It's a verse in the Scripture er sunthin'. Anyway, it's a secret amongst them that know it. A man can only pass it on to a woman. A woman can only tell a man. Them that knows it, an' has faith, can stop bleedin'. At least, so I've always hear'n tell. No, dang it! They *can!*"

Danner turned to me. "There's some more of it. I remember that, too. Folks believed it when I was a small boy. My uncle did."

To my surprise, Mat made a genuine effort to lighten our mood induced by the unhappy event at Moxie.

"So far as Joe's consarned," he said, "that's the way of all flesh: born slow, die quick. Joe had it comin' to him."

"Coming to him!" exclaimed Danner. "What do you mean?"

"I don't mean anything against Joe," Mat made haste to say. "But last week, he was foolish enough to shoot a white doe deer. That's the surest way to invite the blackest luck in the world: to shoot a white doe deer. Matter of fact, I never heard of a person who shot a white deer that didn't come to some v'ilent end, er at least to black trouble. It never fails."

"Oh," said Danner. "I remember now. The curse of the white deer. There was such a superstition when I was a boy. My uncle believed it. And there were many who shared it in those days. But as a matter of fact, superstition is common to all primitive and isolated societies."

"If ye'll excuse me," said Mat, "I want to go up front. See a feller who borrowed five dollars off me. He can't remember none too good."

Danner watched Mat, as the older man walked up the aisle. "My uncle," he said, "has been dead for thirty years. And I thought he was the last of men like that. Do many persons up here believe such nonsense?"

At Forsythe Siding, we left the train and shouldered our packs. A man with a packsack on his back is a symbol of other days and other ways than those of urbanity. Once out of the train and facing the wild lands, Mat became almost cheerful. This was his country, where he was at ease and at home.

"We ain't packin' enough grub to see us through the week," he said. "So we either shoot some meat, er we go ga'nt."

"That's businesslike," said Danner.

"Better keep it in mind," said Mat.

On the way to camp—the camp Mat had chosen for our headquarters—Danner talked as a man would want to if he had been away a long time but felt, even patronizingly, that he belonged. I answered when necessary. But Mat maintained an Abnaki silence, except for one utterance: "The deer are wilder'n hell's bells."

And they were. The ground was frozen. The leaves were dry.

We needed snow. And through the next day and the following, we hunted without sight of a deer. But the night of the third day, Mat reported that he had seen a white deer. The incident was startling, because white deer are rare.

"Was he a big one?" asked Danner.

Mat laid aside the hot buttered biscuit that he had been lifting to his mouth. That was the sort of question Mat would answer with ponderous consideration.

"Wa-al, maybe I've seen bigger bucks—white deer don't usually live to git real big—but I never did see a bigger *white* deer 'n this 'un."

"How many points, would you guess?"

"Don't need to guess. I had plenty of time to look him over, same as he did me. All white deer are foolish, I reckon. He's got twelve p'ints, an' he w'ud dress off a hundred an' eighty pounds, maybe."

"Man!" exclaimed Danner. "That was a good one. Did you miss him?"

The question was tactless. Men like Mat fit their guns. And when they shoot, they kill. Furthermore, Mat had already made plain how he felt about the shooting of white deer.

But Mat patiently restated his position. "Young feller, I don't ever plan to shoot any *white* deer."

"Surely you do not mean that you forfeited the chance to shoot at a head like that because the animal happened to be a sport! What is a white deer? Answer: it's a freak dropped by a normal doe. You would shoot at its dam or sire, why presume that this oddly marked offspring is attended by supernatural accruements?"

Mat's blue eyes squared away at Danner's. There was no anger in them, but a pity.

"Listen," he said ponderously. "I knew a feller by the name of George Sands. George was inclined to be sure of his own powers an' talked erbout them. So some of the young fellers bet George a dollar that he c'udn't lift himself in a bushel basket. An' the durn fathead tried it. He lifted until he was red in the face an' pooched. Then the ash handles let go, pulled out from the rim. 'Thar!' says George. 'Yer see I c'ud have done it, if these danged handles had held.'

"What I mean is that a man can't lift himself in a basket. We're mortals. A college eddication don't alter that by one-hundredth of an inch. If thar's anythin' that a college sh'ud learn a man, it's that he don't come out an inch taller. But you city squirts want to come up here an' tell us folks that has learned things the hard way that what we *know* is true hain't so. An' then, like damfools, ye're surprised if we don't swallow it. Crotch!"

Danner stared at Mat. "Oh, well, heck," he said, "let it go at that. You make the best biscuits I ever ate."

It was wise to change the subject. But the incident spoiled the evening. We could feel Mat's glumness.

During the next day, when I met Mat, he said. "Do yer really think this perfessor Danner w'ud shoot that white buck if he was to see him? If yer do, thar hain't no two ways erbout it. An' I'm goin' home. Don't want no truck with unasked trouble, myself."

"Danner is a lawyer, not a professor," I said. "I don't think that you need to worry about him shooting the white buck."

"Becuz, I'll be condemned if I didn't jump that critter ag'in this forenoon," explained Mat. "Yer really don't think this perfessor w'ud be sech a punkinhead, eh?"

"I am confident he wouldn't," I said. But I was wrong.

That day, when we were returning to camp, the white buck and a normal doe jumped from the cover of a patch of young fir.

Danner's .30-06 hit his shoulder, and he fired before Mat could bellow, "Don't do it!"

"Missed him!" said Danner, with obvious disappointment.

Mat was angry and agitated, and he did not try to hide his emotions.

"Yer better thank God, er your own foolishness, that yer did miss him," he said. "An' I am done—goin' home. Crotch, I w'udn't even consider shootin' that natural doe becuz of her comp'ny. An' you blaze away at the *white* buck!"

I knew that Mat had made a masterly effort not to overindulge in adjectives, and that he was profoundly moved and disturbed.

"Oh, come now," said Danner. "That was a handsome creature. Its legs and ears are standard. And there's a big brown patch on his ribs. At least, that's only half bad luck!"

"That buck," said Mat, "is as white as they usually come. I never see but one pure white deer, an' I hain't sure she warn't ancestral. [Mat meant spectral.] As fer *shootin'* this one, if ye'd hit him, it's likely that we'd all have run right plum inter bad luck. Even shootin' at him may be enough to bring it on."

Mat looked like an earnest if not brilliant prophet. Even Danner sensed the man's utter concern and alarm.

"Mat," he said, "I'm sorry. Let's talk it over when we have eaten and rested. We're on edge now."

Mat grunted. "Thar's nothin' to talk," he said. "All is, if yer propose to shoot at *white* deer, yer can count me out of your comp'ny, right now."

Danner looked at me. I could only shake my head. In the first place, I had been provoked at my own stupidity, which had led me to stare at the departing white buck when I should have shot at the doe for we needed meat at camp. Now, however, I was relieved that both the buck and his little doe had gone free.

The day had been cold and gray. There was the promise of snow in the sky and in the wind. The camp was pleasant with its smells of good warm food, the purring of the hardwood burning in the stove, and the lamplight, which is not so much a light as the presence of a color.

But to my disappointment, Danner provoked more talk about white deer. Taciturn Mat became evangelistically determined to convert the unimaginative and skeptical lawyer. It was the only time in all the years I have known Mat when his astringent vocabulary was overworked.

Once started on the project, he told incident after incident, all illustrating the curse of the white deer.

Danner threw in words such as bosh, taboo, totemism and the like.

I was uncomfortable, as a man always is in the presence of genuine conviction pitted against skepticism. I would cheerfully have given ten dollars for more light in that little cabin than the small oil lamp achieved. And all my efforts to change the subject were ignored by the zealot on each side of the debate.

At last, Mat grew weary of his own unaccustomed loquaciousness. "Mak," he said, "I wish this friend of your'n had more *sense*."

Danner laughed. "I'll sleep on that," he said.

Mat pulled a cap down over his ears and went outside to inspect the weather. We heard him knock the ashes out of his pipe. When he returned, he seemed to have rid himself of his perturbed mood.

"Fellers," he said, "whatever 'it' is, it's spittin'. I sh'udn't wonder if it snowed enough to make good trackin' tomorrow."

So we went to bed—nothing settled, nothing achieved. I resolved to talk to Danner in the morning. Mat felt too profoundly about the ill omen and its aftermaths to be ignored. And if I had to choose between the friendship of Mat or Danner, the latter could go to New York. There was no doubt in my mind about that!

The next sound I heard was Mat's voice, mournfully reminding me that it was almost noon. But morning was still in obeisance, bowing the knee to the night. And the bit of earth I saw from the doorway was cold, white and uninviting.

Breakfast waited while we washed, and Mat went after another pail of water.

"Joe," I said, "this may seem to be an unusual and even unreasonable request, but I must ask you not to shoot at that white deer again, should you see him today."

Danner gurgled in the pan of ice water, grabbed a towel and looked up at me. He was amused.

"Why should one listen to you? After all, it seems that you are a neutral, not belonging to either school of thought about freakish deer."

"Mat feels this business too earnestly," I said. "After all, there are deer enough."

"Did you mean that?" demanded Danner.

"I did. And I do."

"Well, for gosh sakes. I give you my word. Far be it from me to disturb the peace of the upper Kennebec!"

I liked Danner more than ever before for that speech.

We partook of Mat's good breakfast, closed the camp for the day, and followed Mat into the shivering world. A great horned owl flew like a shadow out of a gaunt, naked tree.

Mat halted. "That is a crotchly bad sign," he said.

Danner said, "To heck with the signs and the seasons. Today, I'm out to shoot anything that comes along on all fours, except a blue ox and that white deer of yours, Mat."

"He sartinly hain't *mine*," said Mat, with a sober haste.

I hated that cold, sticky morning—it laid clammy hands on a fellow, and I looked back at the warm camp we had left like the lady from Gomorrah, while I marveled at Mat and Danner, who had accepted the weather as if it were not.

Furthermore, I didn't know where we were after we had walked for a half-hour. And I suspected that Mat did not know because of the dull light and the rapidly falling snow.

At last, we came upon the edge of a little wild meadow, a dry bog. There in the open the large, squashy snowflakes fell in an endless, whispering confusion.

Mat turned to me and whispered, "B'crotch, I can't rec'lect this place—can you?"

So we stood there watching and pondering our situation. It was Danner that heard the deer. There was a curling line of alders near the center of the meadow. And a deer was feeding there, but was half concealed in the alders and somewhat blotted out by the snow. It stood broadside to us. There was no doubt that it was a deer, or that it was a normal, brown creature.

This was our last day of the hunt. We had come to it without so much as the chance to shoot a deer, unless one counted Danner's wild shot at the white buck, which Mat would not do, of course. Therefore, Mat was anxious.

"Make it quick," he said to Danner.

Danner raised his heavy rifle, aimed and fired. In spite of that dim light and the blurring snow, Danner's lead had been deadly. The deer slumped as if it had been knocked between the eyes.

"Good on your head!" said Mat. But it was only said when we saw a deer leap to its feet—no, not leap, for it seemed to rise, and to get off at top form and speed.

Danner appeared to be possessed by astonishment—unable to act. I slammed my own rifle to the shoulder, but Mat was seconds ahead of me. His .30-30 sounded like a dull thud in the snow-blanketed country. The running deer plunged forward, came up again, but went down when Mat fired a second shot.

"Thar!" said Mat, as excited as a grocer weighing out half-a-pound of prunes. "Thar, I reckon we got that 'un, if we did have to shoot up the whole landscape to do it."

Danner was ashamed. "I thought," he explained, "that he had gone down for keeps after I fired."

"So did I," said Mat, as we walked out into the little opening. And of course, Mat would go first to the spot where the deer had stood when Danner fired, for there the story began.

"Ju-das priest!" he exclaimed when he reached the spot, a few steps in front of Danner and me.

There lay a doe—dead where it fell, hit cleanly in the heart— dead beside that black ribbon of a small brook within the alders.

"Judas an' the priest," said Mat, turning from the dead doe to a spot where there was no snow on the gray-brown meadow grass. "Thar's where another one bedded down."

"Then I did get mine," said Danner.

"Yes," said Mat, "but what in the devil have I shot?"

And he left us to follow the second deer's tracks. When he came to an abrupt halt, Danner shouted, "Got him?"

Mat was slow to reply. At last, he said, "B'crotch, Mak, I've gone an' shot that *white* buck—killed him deader'n a stun heap."

Danner stared at me. Then he sat down, or collapsed, in the slush.

"Oh, mygosh! This is comedy; Greek comedy undefiled. Oh, mygosh!"

I went to Mat; I think that I ran. Sure enough, there lay the white buck. The last shot had smashed its heart. Mat had removed his cap. His stiff gray hair was awry, and on his face was the expression of an extrovert shipwrecked on the foam of perilous seas in fairy lands forlorn.

"Wa-al," he said, "what's done is done, an' who in God's world can undo it? If I had only waited a min-it, but no, I had to shoot b'fore thar was time to look it over. So I've gone an' killed that *white* buck."

With that speech finished, Mat got out a jackknife and began to dress the white buck of the Forsythe country. Once he looked up to Danner and me.

"I wish you fellers w'ud unload your guns," he said, "becuz if I've got to be shot, I w'ud rather it 'ud be done by strangers."

Knowing that Mat meant what he said, I unloaded my rifle. Danner unloaded his.

"While ye're erbout it," said Mat, "unload mine."

"How would you like to have that nice, fat doe of mine?" asked Danner. "I would like to trade deer with you."

Mat was impressed. He looked searchingly at Danner. But his mind added up two and two and then stuck to it that the result was four.

"Danner," he said, "that's a handsome offer, but it w'udn't come to no good fer either of us. This is a danged deceitful world, where a feller with the best of intentions is apt to be led astray. But a man has to take his own consequences. I shot this white buck."

I have made my report. Now you know how it happened. Mat Markham shot a white buck—a big white buck with 12 points. Mat sold that buck for 50 dollars. An out-of-state hunter who had more money than fortune at deer hunting went home with that beautiful creature. I saw Mat pocket the money as if in a daze.

"Not that it'll ever do me any good," he said.

That was 20 years ago. I am sure that the 50 dollars have not changed hands since then. Moreover, Mat has enjoyed robust health and enough good fortune to satisfy a citizen in this good land that the Lord God gave to us. But Ecclesiastes is still the sum of Mat's conclusions concerning the lot of mortal man in this vale of tears. And to this day, he insists that it is p'ison bad luck to shoot a white deer.

REVENGE OF THE BIG DEER

By Duncan Dobie

This story originally appeared in Texas Trophy Hunters *magazine and also forms Chapter 2 of Dobie's* White Tales and Other Hunting Stories *(1989).*

They called him Big Deer. The great beams of his wide-spreading antlers were so thick, and his huge tines were so long, that the only name anyone could think of to call him when they saw him was just—a damned big deer! Big Deer had been hanging on the paneled wall of Buck Breedlow's den for going on five years now. People had been admiring the head and making a fuss over the incredible antlers ever since Buck had brought the trophy whitetail home on a cold December afternoon.

Buck owned a 300-acre farm down in Black Swamp County. Next to trying to eke out a living growing a few crops, he loved to hunt whitetails more than anything else in the world. Every year when the season rolled around, you could bet that Buck and a handful of his close friends would be out combing the woods for big-antlered whitetails every chance they could get.

You could also just about lay money that Sam Greer, a distant cousin of Buck's who was so far down the line that even Buck couldn't say for sure where he stood in the family tree, would just happen to drop by for a visit, and by pure coincidence, would just happen to have remembered to bring his favorite deer rifle. He would plant himself at Buck's house for pretty darn near the entire season, or at least until he succeeded in killing himself a farm-fed buck.

Now, there was always someone visiting at Buck's farm—an old friend or a loved one who had long ago moved away, or some of his wife's people, perhaps — but Buck had closer relatives he had neither seen nor heard from in 20 years, and it was always strange to everyone how Sam Greer seemed to pop up right at the beginning of deer season every year, like a migrating buzzard headed south for the winter. To make matters worse, he came from somewhere up north, and few of Buck's friends could tolerate the man they all pegged as "that golderned, loud-mouthed Yankee!"

The bad reputation was well justified, too. It had always been a mystery to everyone who knew him why Buck would put up with Sam Greer's antics year after year. Buck was a law-abiding citizen, and he believed in going by the rules. So did all of his friends. He and his crowd hunted strictly in season, and never killed more than the legal limit of bucks or shot a doe unless one of them possessed an appropriate tag.

With Sam Greer, however, anything went. He would leave no stone unturned in coming up with devious ways to collect his venison. For starters, he would bait deer with corn and salt wherever he could get away with it. Spotlighting at night along the road was a favorite pastime. And, he thought nothing of shooting does or six-month-old fawns whenever the opportunity presented itself. In short, he was an outlaw!

It had long been rumored that Sam Greer had been the one responsible for setting fire to a broomsedge field in order to flush some deer out of an adjoining thicket. And being as how things had been extremely dry the year this ill-fated event took place, the fire had burned up an old abandoned homeplace and some 50 acres of a neighbor's woods before Buck and other volunteers had finally put it out.

All fingers had pointed to Sam Greer as the culprit. Furthermore, Sam had ended up shooting an illegal doe that day. But blood is thicker than water, and since Buck could never prove anything, he reluctantly put up with this thorn in his side year after year with an amazing degree of forbearance. However, it did seem at times that Buck's blood was running mighty thin.

Rumor further had it that on the day of the fire, Sam Greer had spotted Big Deer bedded out in the briers near the old homeplace that had been destroyed. Without telling anyone about what he had seen, Sam Greer had unsuccessfully tried just about every dirty trick that a person with such bloodthirsty malice could think of to end the life of the huge buck.

Some other hunters had seen Big Deer in the same general vicinity that day, as well as the enormous doe that had been keeping him company. It turned out that Sam Greer had later shot the unfortunate doe, calling the action "a grievous but honest mistake."

In truth, he had missed a shot at Big Deer, and when the large doe ran out in front of him moments later, he wasted little time in taking advantage of this "last-ditch opportunity."

Buck had been forced to call in the game warden, who was also a personal friend, and Sam Greer had been made to pay a healthy fine. The other local hunters thought he had gotten off light, though, saying that a buck as fine as Big Deer ought to have an equally impressive mate to carry on the tradition.

Buck's friends all said that it was a real crime that the doe had been taken before she could produce Big Deer's offspring.

It was shortly after that, toward the end of the season, after Sam Greer had paid his fine and gone home, that Buck Breedlow got lucky one afternoon and dropped Big Deer in his tracks as the lone whitetail stood out in the middle of a barren field. Buck's friends were all glad for him, but most of his hunting companions maintained that Big Deer never would have been taken by legal means if it hadn't been for the fact that he had lost his mate, and was still heartbroken and disconsolate over the matter.

In any event, the whole community made a big fuss over Buck's hard-won trophy. Several of his closest friends convinced him that he ought to have the head of the huge whitetail mounted. After that, just about everyone who stopped by Buck's house for a visit asked to have a look at the wide-antlered monarch. Occasionally, people Buck didn't even know stopped by to marvel at the amazing 12-point rack.

Three years to the very day after Big Deer had been shot, late in the ongoing season, Sam Greer unexpectedly drove up in front of Buck's house late one afternoon. Sam had been laid up with back trouble for the first part of the season. However, not wanting to miss out altogether, he had made it down to Black Swamp County for the last few days of hunting. Buck was hoping he wouldn't see his distant cousin that year, and the disappointment showed on his face when he opened the front door and saw him standing there, grinning from ear to ear.

It also happened that a favorite aunt of Buck's wife was visiting from Omaha. Since she was already occupying the guest room, Buck had no choice but to let Sam Greer sleep in the den, offering him the use of the seldom-slept-in hideaway sofa bed.

As Sam went to bed that night, full of excitement and nervous energy about the next day's hunt, he cursed the mounted animal gazing down at him from the wall over the sofa bed. After all, not only had the crafty buck eluded him, it had also caused him to pay a steep fine.

Sam Greer never knew what hit him that night. He died in his sleep without so much as a twitch, as quietly as a newborn baby asleep in its crib.

You see, the nail holding the heavy mounted form of the trophy buck mysteriously broke in half sometime during the night. Big Deer, top-heavy from his huge antlers, came crashing down right on top of the sleeping hunter. When Buck found Sam the next morning, two of Big Deer's long tines were buried deep in Sam's chest, one right through his heart.

An appropriate investigation followed, but a coroner's jury found neither Buck nor Big Deer guilty of any wrongdoing. Buck was completely exonerated. Big Deer was hung right back up in the same spot—only this time a stronger nail was used—and people still continued to drop by from near and far to admire the legendary whitetail.

However, not one single person slept in the hide-away sofa bed after the tragic incident, including Buck's aged mother-in-law, whom he later tried to entice to sleep there on a number of occasions.

The only damage done to the head was a slight wrinkle on one side of the deer's nose and mouth that had not been there previously. Now, when people look up at Big Deer, they swear he's smiling!

A RIFLE NAMED 'SLEIGH BELLS'

By Edmund Ware Smith

A selection from For Maine Only (1959), *this is vintage Smith in every sense—a Maine setting, colorful characters, humor, subtle irony and most of all, superb storytelling.*

Any rifle has a history—a story—and many rifles have strangely begotten names. This is the story of a rifle named "Sleigh Bells."

It begins on a warm, still morning in May when Al Foster boated me across Grand Lake in Penobscot County, Maine, to my cabin on the wilderness shore. I had no inkling that I was on my way to discovering a secret concerning a buck deer I had shot almost 30 years before. There was something weird and haunting about it, because the secret was Henry Dennison's. Pop Dennison was my father-in-law—and he had been dead for more than four years!

I have no convictions about communication after death, one way or the other, but I hope Pop knows I have found him out, and perhaps he does. To me, it's a heartwarming thought. He was such a vital and dynamic personality that I don't have to listen very hard to hear the echo of his *basso profundo* chuckle over my discovery. You could call it leftover laughter.

Pop Dennison, more than anyone, got me interested in deer hunting, the Maine woods and log cabins—including the one that loomed closer over the bow of Al Foster's boat that day in May, 1956. But when Al put me ashore, I wasn't thinking about Pop and the buck I'd shot so long ago down on Second Chain Lake, which had been totally out of mind for years.

Presently, I was to do some intense thinking about both, but for the moment, I was pre-occupied with the purpose of my trip to the cabin, which was to take inventory of its contents with the idea of selling out—lock, stock, the works.

My wife and I had built this cabin, and many of the things in it, mostly with our own hands. We had lived in this remote and beautiful spot for ten incomparable years, and it was high in our hearts. The decision to sell had been tough to make and hard to take. But it made sense. We had reached the age where a gale on the lake was a hazard, rather than a bright challenge; the toting and hauling a burden; and the 29 miles to a telephone too far for peace of mind. But as I waved goodbye to Al Foster and walked alone up the path to the plank porch, I thought of the rich experience of our life here, and it pulled hard.

The wake of Al's boat followed along shore, and you could hear the little waves breaking. In the distance, the boat was a speck, and its motor sounded like a bee under a derby hat. I looked straight across at the long, dark peaks of The Traveller Range rising 3,000 feet above the lake, saw the snow patch on Big Traveller and the bald eagle doing a slow, superb lazy eight in a thermal above Birch Point. Then I turned, opened the cabin door and stepped inside. And the ghosts came stalking, one by one, with their sad whispering. They were nudging me toward Pop Dennison and his secret about that buck deer, but of course, I didn't know it at the time.

Just inside the cabin door was a floorboard that had been loose for years. I went in and stepped on it to see if it would make its familiar squeak. It did. Then I walked into the kitchen and looked at the woodstove.

This spring, there would be no ritual of lighting the first fire in this wonderfully familiar stove. What manner of man would succeed to the ritual? Would he love it, as we had? Whoever he might be, I said to him: "Mister, you've inherited one hell of a good cook stove."

I had said it aloud, and the sound of my voice startled me. This was no good. If I didn't get going on the inventory, it would be but a matter of minutes before I'd be talking to myself—and *believing it!*

Al Foster had agreed to pick me up at noon for the trip back across the lake to my car. I had about two hours to finish my melancholy job. So I got out a pad and pencil, started by itemizing everything in the kitchen, and worked systematically through the cabin. I wound up in my den, where my deer rifle hung on the wall pegs.

This rifle is an old Model .32 Special Winchester, half magazine. It has a sling ring on the receiver, and when I took the rifle down, the ring tinkled in the lonely stillness of the cabin, and the sound gave my memory a terrific clout.

It's ridiculous what an insignificant stimulus, like the *plink* of metal on metal, can do to a man's thoughts. On second consideration, it isn't ridiculous at all, because memory is one of the great marvels of life.

For example, by a simple exercise of remembering, you can be in two places at the same instant. Actually, I was standing in my log cabin on Grand Lake. But the sound of the sling ring had given me such a yank that to all intents and purposes I was also a hundred-odd miles away, down in Hancock County. The time had changed, too. It was early in November, 1926—30 years ago. And, I was standing in Pop Dennison's deer hunting cabin that we had built the summer before . . .

We had built the cabin at the head of Third Chain Lake in what was then virgin deer-hunting country. It was 12 hard miles by canoe from Pop's permanent camp at the foot of Dobsis Lake. Pop's annual hunting trip at the Dobsis camp had already been an institution for years. The select personnel, known as "The Old Bunch," consisted of Harry Wheeler, Bill Howell and Pop. The guides were Harley Fitch, Harley Fenlayson and Roy Bailey.

The 1926 hunting trip was extra special, extra exclusive, because it was Third Chain Cabin's christening. The trip's planning, which began weeks in advance, had a pioneer zest that was contagious. I had dropped heavy hints for an invitation, but Pop didn't field any of them.

"I haven't seen the big woods in fall yet, Pop. What are they like?"

"Wonderful," said Pop, and described them at length.

"I hope I cut enough firewood last summer," I said.

"If you didn't, we'll cut some more."

Just because I was a mere kid of 26, with no deer hunting history to speak of, I was excluded from this all-important trip. And I had spent most of a treasured summer vacation helping Roy Bailey build the peeled spruce cabin where these old, over-privileged characters would be sheltered. I had patched and painted the canoes they would use, toted in their cookstove, tarpapered their roof. And they had cast me aside, depriving me of my rightful adventure.

The crowning misery was when Pop showed me his nonresident Maine hunting license with the deer tags. But no! The crowning misery was when, as though conferring an honor, he asked me if I'd like to drive "The Old Bunch" from Framingham, Massachusetts, where they lived, to the night train at the North Station in Boston where they would embark for Maine—and Third Chain Cabin.

If I wasn't green with envy and frustration, I felt that way.

I helped them aboard the train with their duffel bags and rifles, and wished them luck, while inwardly hoping the cabin roof would leak and the stove would smoke. When the train pulled out, I stood glumly at the gate, reading the scheduled stops on the bulletin board: Portland, Bangor, Lincoln, Mattawamkeag, Forest Station, Vanceboro, St. John, Halifax, and all those wonderful places I couldn't go to. Then I drove home through the frosty night, bruised with self pity.

Three or four days later, I received a cock-eyed telegram from Lincoln, Maine. As near as I can remember, it read like this:

GALLOP THE SHALLOP AT FIRST CHAIN WEDNESDAY
(signed) *POP*

Some telegram! But what else could you expect from that artful, bald-headed, stumpy-built bundle of wisdom? It is a known fact—a matter of written record—that Pop Dennison wrote some of his annual reports to his stockholders in blank verse. If you don't believe this, and I don't blame you, check the reports prior to 1950 of the Dennison Mfg. Co., Framingham, Mass.

The whole shenanigan of the 1926 hunting trip is characteristic of Pop Dennison and the way he did things—always with careful staging, and elements of suspense, mystery and surprise. He'd probably been planning his stunt for weeks. Rather than say outright: "Ed, you join us at Third Chain Cabin after The Old Bunch has had a few days together," he had sweated me dry, just because he knew my ultimate delight would be magnified by ten.

Incidentally, it was no cinch in those days to get from Third Chain Lake to the town of Lincoln to send a telegram. And, just as Pop had intended, the telegram itself took some decoding. After about an hour's mystification and torment, I figured it out for what it was: a command invitation to take the Tuesday night train from Boston to Lincoln, get a ride from Lincoln to the head of Dobsis Lake Wednesday, find someone to boat me down Dobsis to First Chain Lake Carry, where, if I hunted in the right place, I would find a "shallop," which meant canoe. "Gallop" meant hurry. By means of the canoe, and several hours paddling and poling through the three Chain Lakes and their connecting streams, I would eventually arrive at Third Chain Cabin . . .

Thirty years later, in the den of my Grand Lake cabin, I could feel myself smiling. I was smiling at the sound of Pop Dennison's voice. It was almost as if he were actually speaking, saying to The Old Bunch that fall at Third Chain: "Wait till Ed gets that telegram. His lid will fly off."

It had, too.

The telegram reached me Tuesday afternoon, a few hours before train time. And I didn't even own a rifle, let alone a Maine hunting license or a ticket on the night train. I asked and got permission from my boss for a few days off, including that Tuesday afternoon. I telephoned my wife, and found she had been in on the scheme all along. Then I went down to Federal Street in Boston to the late Bob Smith's Sporting Goods Store and bought a hunting license and a secondhand rifle. The rifle was an old Model .32 Special Winchester, half-magazine, with a sling ring on the receiver.

Because of my intense remembering of Pop, it seemed weird and spooky to be holding that same rifle now, in my own cabin. Pop had spent a night in this cabin. His hands had held this rifle. Would I list the rifle on my inventory, leaving it to the unknown future owner of this beloved place? How would I describe it?

"One .32 Special Winchester carbine, excellent condition."

No! The description was vastly over-simplified. It ought to tell how, after I found the "shallop," or canoe, on First Chain Lake, I laid the rifle along the gunwale, tossed my knapsack in the bow and paddled up the lake; how the shod canoe pole sounded on the rocky bottom of Second Chain Stream; how the shell-iced puddles cracked under my moccasins on Third Chain Carry, and how the middle thwart of the canoe bit into the back of my neck as I lugged across into Third Chain; and then the big moment when I hauled the canoe ashore under the leaning cedar at the cabin, and Pop Dennison opened the front door and waved both hands, and hollered: "Hello, boy! Hello! Hello! I see you made it."

I couldn't remember when I'd been so happy.

"Where's the bunch, Pop?" I asked.

"Hunting. They'll be back."

"Do they like the cabin?"

"They're bats about it. What you got there? A new rifle?"

"Sure—new secondhand."

I handed it to him. He checked to see if it was loaded, and I awaited his approval of my pride and joy. No approval of any kind was forthcoming—nothing but a stern look in Pop's steel-blue eyes.

"What's the matter with it, Pop?"

"The essential of still-hunting for deer is stillness."

"Okay, I'll be still."

"Not with this," he said, shaking the rifle so that the sling ring tinkled. "You might just as well go forth to the beech ridges with a bell dangling from your neck."

"What'll I do? Hunt with a slingshot?"

"No. I'll fix that confounded ring."

He got a piece of soft, white grocery string and wound the ring all around. When he had looped the end under the last two turns and cut it off, he shook the rifle again, and you couldn't hear a thing.

"There," said Pop, handing me the rifle, "from now on, it's up to you."

It was too late in the afternoon to hunt the long beech ridge back of the cabin, so we sat on the porch and watched the sun get low over Duck Lake Mountain, and as the shadows lengthened, the hunters drifted in and told their several tales.

Bill Howell, with Roy Bailey guiding, had shot a buck where Killman Pond Stream came into the lake. Harry Wheeler and Harley Fenlayson had fallen asleep in the sun and dry beech leaves. When they woke up and stirred the leaves, three deer broke cover within a few yards of them.

"Just another 'caught napping' episode," said Harry.

Harley Fitch, hunting alone, brought in a fat, dry doe, and we had fresh liver for supper. Pop told about the noise my rifle made, and the Old Bunch promptly named the rifle "Sleigh Bells."

"Ever had buck fever, Ed?" Bill Howell asked.

"No. 'Course not."

"Old hand, hey?" Roy Bailey asked me.

"Sure."

"How many deer all told have you actually accounted for?" Harry Wheeler asked.

"Four—so far."

No one believed me—which was fair enough, because I had multiplied the truth by four.

"Wait till tomorrow," I said. "I'll bring one in. You'll see."

Pop Dennison said: "The steam that blows the whistle never turns the wheel."

"How many people at home did you promise venison to?" Bill Howell asked me.

"Just three or four guys in my office," I said.

"Poor, starvin' guys," said Harley Fitch.

As the kid member of the party, I was the target for all the jokes; and I had talked big. I had better produce. But in two days of hard hunting, my sad score was only three porcupines, and Pop wrote in the cabin diary: *Ed Smith and his rifle, Sleigh Bells, are doing well in Quill Pig circles.*

The third afternoon I came in early, my moccasins soundless on the pine needles on the path to the kitchen door of the cabin. I heard voices in the cabin and stopped, not intending to eavesdrop, but getting trapped into it. Pop Dennison was talking to Roy Bailey, and this is what he said:

"I'd dearly love to have that boy get a deer. Will you take him with you tomorrow?"

Roy said he would. He said he knew where there was a big buck working in the old burn over toward Second Lake. Then Pop said: "Make it casual, Roy, so Ed won't suspect us."

I ducked back up the path and started whistling, and they came to the kitchen door to greet me, none the wiser.

That night I couldn't sleep. Pop Dennison wanted me to get a deer even more than I wanted it myself. I had to make good—for Pop. I was suddenly weighed with responsibility to this devious and exciting old man, who was my father-in-law. I was no longer hunting for myself. I was hunting for Pop—and for the vicarious triumph he would derive from my success—if any.

The next morning at daylight breakfast, Bill Howell said his feet hurt. "I think I'll take a day off," Bill said.

That left Roy Bailey free to guide me, and I knew that was the way Pop had rigged it. None of them had any idea I knew what was cooking, and so, just out of devilment, I said to Bill Howell: "I'll stay in camp with you, Bill. We can play cribbage."

When I saw Pop Dennison's face, I could have bitten out my tongue. He was hurt and shocked by my implication that I had quit cold, or—worse—didn't like deer hunting.

"It's your last day in camp!" he said.

"Did you forget?"

"For a second, I did. No cribbage for me—just the long, brown ridges."

"Good! Good for you. How'd you like to go with Roy?"

"Wonderful," I said. "I'll make us some sandwiches, and we can get going."

I made the sandwiches with thin slices of cold deer liver left over from breakfast. Pop followed us a little way up the trail back of the cabin. Then he slapped me on the shoulder and said: "Good luck to you," and turned back. Now, Roy and I were alone, cat-footing through the ghostly gray beeches.

I had already known Roy Bailey for several years. We had fished salmon together on spring trips and been on canoe trips in summer, and worked together building Third Chain Cabin. But Roy was a hunter at heart, and still is, and I caught the fever from watching him work—three or four slow, careful steps, then a pause, and his head turning slowly, eyes searching, peering, listening. His rifle was an old favorite—a .45-70 with cartridges almost as big as your forefinger. Sometimes, when the angle was just right, I could read the number of his guide's license carved in the stock of his rifle. It was "8820."

We were traveling east toward Killman Pond swamp. We crossed the swamp and turned north toward the old burn, where a fire of years before had reached Second Chain Lake. We had entered the burn at a distance of a hundred yards or so when Roy stopped, tense. He moved his hand in a beckoning motion, and I knew my chance had come, and I started shaking like a twig in a current.

Roy beckoned again, and as I moved up to him, I stepped on a dry stick—and a deer blew, blew again, and I heard the animal's hoofs thud as he took off.

Roy looked around at me, a small, wry grin on his lips. I was sick. Anyone that would step on a dry stick at a time like that wasn't fit to be in the woods. What would Pop think when he heard about it?

Roy pointed to a nearby spruce blowdown, and we went over quietly, and sat down on it.

"I'm some still-hunter," I whispered.

"Never mind," he whispered. "Take it easy. Let's eat our sandwiches."

Roy took a big bite from his sandwich, and it bulged his cheek. I nibbled at mine. The new growth after the burn was dense, and black stumps loomed here and there. A jay screeched and a red squirrel chattered—and behind us we heard a crash, and the thud of hoofs. Something caught the corner of my eye, to my left—beyond where Roy was sitting. It was the motion of a spruce branch, and I focused on it.

The growth was so thick that it was like sighting through a pipe.

The branch moved again, and I saw the magnificent head and neck of a buck.

"I can see him!" I whispered.

"Go ahead and shoot," Roy whispered.

I reached down, picked up my rifle and cocked it. The ivory bead front sight settled into the notch of the rear sight—and the shot broke open the silence, and Roy and I quickly stood up, our liver sandwiches lying on the green moss where we'd dropped them.

"Did you see the deer?" I asked.

"No. But it must have been the same one—circling to get us sized up. Did you hit him?"

"No. When I fired, he just disappeared."

"Where was he?"

I sat down on the log again, and sighted the spot with my rifle. Roy got the line and walked slowly to the spot through the tangle.

"Come on over here," he called back, and I did. The big buck lay on the green moss, dead from a clean neck shot, and Roy was shaking my hand and laughing. I thought of Pop Dennison and couldn't wait to tell him.

"Fire three shots," Roy said. "Pop'll hear them, an' come. I'll bet he ain't far."

Pop heard the shots and came. He was all out of breath, and his head gleamed with sweat.

"Boy!" he said. "You're white as a sheet. Go and sit down. What a wonderful head—the buck's, not yours."

Now that it was all over, I felt weak as a starved kitten. I sat on a stump, while Roy and Pop bled the deer and dressed it, then skewered the heart and liver on a forked alder.

"Hey, Pop," I said. "You sure got here awful quick. Were you following us?"

"Oh-o-o-o . . . well, not exactly. Thought I'd like to be around."

What could you ever do to repay a guy like Pop? What he loved best, outside of home and family, was hunting. He had just given up a morning's hunting because of me. He had given up another day of it so he would be at Third Chain Cabin to greet me when I arrived from Boston. And he had made the long hard trip out to Lincoln—

personally—to send me that crazy telegram.

I would never catch up with him, and I would be a long time understanding his works and ways. But sitting on that stump, looking down at my buck, I had what I then thought was a flash of pure inspiration. Much as I wanted that handsome trophy for myself, I would have it mounted by the best taxidermist I could find—and I would give it to Pop! It would surprise hell out of him. He'd think I was having the nine-point head mounted for myself, but all the while it would be just for him.

Now, after that inspired moment on Second Chain Burn, I know the secret of the deer head, and how Pop kept it locked for all the years in his eloquent skull. If it weren't for the tinkle of the sling ring on old "Sleigh Bells" that morning in my cabin, I'd never have found it out. The string that Pop had wound on the ring had been long since removed by a gunsmith who had re-glued the rifle, otherwise no tinkle.

I put the rifle back on the pegs on the wall of my den and listened. I could hear Al Foster's boat coming, but I couldn't see it yet. I was thinking of the literally open-mouthed astonishment in Pop Dennison's face when, in the winter of 1927, I had presented him with the deer head, beautifully mounted.

"No!" he said. "Oh, Ed—no! You can't give me that."

"I could give you anything."

"But—this is *yours*."

"No, Pop, it's yours—for keeps."

"Do you really mean it?"

"Sure. I want you to have it—and I really mean it."

My mother-in-law, Ma Dennison, was with us at the time of the presentation. She looked quizzically at the mounted head and said to Pop, "Where will we put it?"

"Over the fireplace in the dining room," said Pop, unhesitatingly—and, until Pop's death, the big buck of Second Chain Burn looked down for about 25 years on every meal that was served at the long, oak table in the house on Juniper Hill in Framingham; and sometimes, Pop would interrupt his carving, turn and look up at the head, and say: "That's Ed's buck—the one he shot on Second Chain Burn."

I looked from my den window out over Grand Lake and saw Al's boat rounding a distant point. My time was about up, and I thought of the last time I saw the deer head. Pop Dennison died in 1952, missing his 75th birthday by four days. He lived an unusual life and died on an unusual day—a day which occurs just once every four years—February 29th, Leap Year.

Some months afterwards, Pop's widow gave the deer head to me. I was quite touched. But at the time, I had no place to hang the head, and no place to store it, and I suspected that my wife didn't regard it too highly as a decoration for the cabin. So I gave the head to Pop's first cousin, Lew Bement. Lew gave it to a friend of his named Jack Wechter, who has a kind of club room, and at this writing, it hangs in Jack's place near Greenfield, Massachusetts.

As Al's boat drew closer, I tried to visualize the deer head hanging in Jack's club room, but I could just see it where it hung originally, for all those years, over Pop's dining room fireplace.

"Harry," Ma Dennison must have said, innumerable times, "I don't like that deer head. We ought to have an oil painting of a ship."

"What? Don't like that head? Why, it *belongs* there. And we've got a ship painting in the living room."

There was something wrong with that dialogue, even though it was imaginary. Pop's secret was right on top of me. Why would anyone want a trophy that he hadn't shot himself, unless he was furnishing a museum or a club room? Pop Dennison never cared much for trophies anyway—except the white buck he shot on his last hunt, just a few years before his death.

"Pop," I said to him, "now I know! You thought I'd be hurt if you didn't accept that deer head. So you made a twenty-five-year show of liking it and no one ever knew you didn't, least of all me."

Al's boat had landed, and I took old "Sleigh Bells" down to the shore with me, and Al saw me lugging it and said: "This isn't deer-hunting season."

"The hell it isn't!" I said. "I was just on a hunt down on Second Chain Lake."

Al looked up at the cabin, then back at me.

"Say," he said, in a puzzled way, "did I hear someone laughing? Just a moment ago?"

I did a double take. Of course, everyone will say that Al heard me laughing at my discovery, but it might have been Pop Dennison's leftover laughter that he heard, because I think I heard it myself.

PART SIX

TRICKS OF THE WHITETAIL TRADE

An appreciable portion of today's outdoor magazines seems to be obsessed with features of the "how to" and "where to" genre, never mind that much of the greatest deer material ever written falls into distinctly and distinctively different categories of coverage. Selection of material for inclusion in this anthology leans heavily away from what is currently popular. After all, if you go back to what I would term the golden age of outdoor writing in America, a period beginning shortly after the end of World War I and extending into the 1960s or 1970s, careful perusal of that era's magazines will reveal a pronounced inclination for storytelling—"Me and Joe" accounts or first-person pieces where some master of the craft takes readers along on a vicarious adventure.

Still, there always has been and always will be a place for instructional pieces, and those who handle them best educate even as they tell stories. The finest classroom teachers, those we remember long after our school days lie behind us, somehow managed to instill important information while making the process enjoyable. Similarly, masters of conveying the joys of being afield teach even as they titillate.

Here, we have a quartet of selections proving that point, with two of them coming from Larry Koller's admirable book, *Still-Hunting the Whitetail,* one from 20th century "great" Ted Trueblood, and an opening day delight from the dean of modern bowhunters, M. R. James.

WOODCRAFT AND WHITETAILS
By Lawrence Koller

This is Chapter 4 in Koller's magnum opus, Shots at Whitetails *(1948). There are various reprints of the book, the most recent in 2000 with a new introduction by the then editor of* Deer & Deer Hunting *magazine.*

Of the many tales written around the drama of hunting whitetails, each one tends to stress the importance of woodcraft to the hunt's success and enjoyment. Aside from deer taken each season by pure luck—and believe it, that number is substantial—a knowledge of woodcraft plays a critical part with every sportsman. The still-hunter draws heavily on his knowledge of the woods during every moment on the hunt, for on this knowledge hinges the entire outcome of his trip. Even deer hunters who gang up on drives, following the accepted practice of most club-hunting, must possess the fundamentals of deer tactics and behavior to qualify on the score sheet.

Perhaps the original interpretation of our word "woodcraft" goes back to pioneer days, when its literal translation—craft of the woods—stemmed from its place in the era's economic picture. During those times, familiarity with the woods and its wild people had a direct bearing on the survival of early civilization. Food in abundance, clothing and shelter were provided for the woodsman with enough knowledge and skill to avail himself and his family of Mother Nature's benevolent gifts. All were there for the taking.

Today's thoughts of woodcraft still swing back unconsciously to the early days, even though today's woodsman applies his knowledge only to increase his recreational pleasure and further appreciation of Nature's gifts, still here abundantly.

A New Generation of Whitetails

Much of the thrill and charm of deer hunting is influenced by our conscious knowledge of the whitetail's role in the romantic days of the Indian and buckskin-clad woodsman. Any glimpse of these splendid creatures along our wooded highways and parks will stop even the most blasé individual—sportsman or not—with a quickening of the pulse and a thrill of secret pleasure, as though he had been favored by an infinite glance into the pages of nature's book. Much of this same effect is captured by the deer hunter.

Of all our outdoor pursuits, none except deer hunting is so wreathed by the aura of romance, none so connotative of our hidden pride in our American ancestry during its uphill climb for world recognition.

The whitetail possesses every quality of a top-notch game animal—a position it undoubtedly commands—sufficiently to place it on the top shelf in every hunter's library of gamebirds and animals. No other game is so adapted to changing conditions and the increasing spread of mankind's so-called civic improvements. The automobile and good highways, accused of ravaging the country of its small game and fish, seem to have simply awakened the competitive spirit in the whitetail. He flourishes now in many regions where he was unknown before the days of the machine age.

Our point is that the whitetail is so skilled in self-concealment and self-reliance that it requires the best of woods skill to beat him at his own game. In addition, most hunters of long experience agree the deer of today is infinitely wiser than his ancestors of 50 or even 25 years ago. Just as the hunter has increased his knowledge of the hunt, successive generations have planted new, or newly sharpened, instincts in our current deer herd. Thus, we must indeed know our deer if we would eat venison.

The study of woodcraft in its general sense offers an enormously widespread field, of such scope that a lifetime of effort would scarcely scrape off the top surface of possibilities. Still, the richer we are in this knowledge, the richer we become. Each action and habit of wild creatures dovetails inescapably into the lives of its brethren, so that each new bit of information gleaned in trips afield adds immeasurably to what we have seen before. Unfortunately, most of us can devote but little time to days in the woods and fields, spent simply in studying wildlife, however desirable this may be.

Our actual hunting trips, then, must be the sole means of enriching our knowledge of woodcraft; and fittingly enough, it is this absorption of woods lore on our hunting trips that forms the major part of our deer-hunting pleasure.

Action in deer hunting, unlike other sports, occurs quickly, exists for only a few seconds—thrill-packed though they may be—then it's all over, ending in a successful bag or a heart-breaking missed opportunity. These few seconds of action may have been days or weeks in preparation, for bucks aren't seen every day in the woods by even the best hunters. These days, though, should have been made profitable by observation of deer signs, tracks, runways, antler rubs and bed-downs, giving the hunter further information for subsequent days in the woods.

In this chapter, we will confine our discussion to that branch of woodcraft dealing with deer and deer hunting. We shall attempt to interpret the signs and existing knowledge of whitetails to the hunter's advantage. We must qualify these observations by stating the whitetail is often a most paradoxical animal. The one statement of fact that can be definitely and unequivocally made is that no one knows exactly what any one deer will do under any given set of conditions, not even the deer itself. The best we can hope to do is anticipate probable reactions with knowledge gleaned from previous experiences.

Finding Deer in New Areas

In strange deer country, both novice and expert hunter are faced with the problem of finding the deer. The novice usually elects to find a high spot overlooking as broad an expanse of territory as possible in the hope a deer will walk out within his line of vision. If by lucky accident he happens on a spot near feeding grounds or a well-defined crossing, he might get his shot—if he waits long enough. But as a rule this hit-or-miss method of hunting produces little results other than cold feet and discouraged impatience.

The experienced deer hunter wastes no time watching barren ground. His first move in new territory is to locate feeding grounds, bed-downs, runways and crossings to the best of his ability. He understands that movements and behavior of whitetails under normal conditions are influenced by only three factors: food and water, suitable cover for daytime hideouts, and the process of moving from bedding grounds to food and back again.

The logical tactic is to locate these runways and feeding grounds and wait from some vantage point at times when deer are most likely to be feeding. All this, of course, is under normal conditions. But two factors that exist during hunting seasons might induce wide changes in deer behavior. These are the rut and heavy concentrations of hunters.

With hunters tramping through almost all available cover and feeding grounds all day, deer constantly move from one hideout to another, sufficiently breaking their normal routine so that no rules of conduct apply. Then, during the rut's height, all deer, bucks in particular, constantly move, spending little time feeding or resting.

Any hunter who has killed a buck just after the rut can appreciate the tremendous amount of energy a buck expends during this period, taking little food in the process. Almost without exception, bucks taken after this period are exceedingly thin, almost to the point of emaciation, young bucks being affected to a greater degree than older animals.

Whitetail hunters must bear those two facts in mind, for they control hunting conditions to a great extent. However, there are many times when neither influence is present, and a hunter must employ straight woodcraft to find deer.

First, the matter of feed. It's a recognized fact that deer feed little in heavily timbered areas, for the heavy top foliage discourages the production of undergrowth. Deer are browsers almost exclusively, feeding on the tender tips of second-growth timber and underbrush, although they're not averse to grazing off a farmer's young wheat or rye. Whitetails don't favor any one type of food to the exclusion of any other. Rather, they select a varied diet from among the existing hardwoods and evergreens. The small, pyramid-shaped nuts of the beech and acorns of all species of oaks are especially favored by deer during early fall, perhaps to the partial exclusion of other food available at this time.

The important point to bear in mind is that deer can only obtain good browsing on low second-growth vegetation, regardless of the species. It's useless to look for feeding grounds in heavy timber, unless large numbers of acorns or beechnuts are dropping in these areas.

When looking for feeding grounds, the deer hunter examines the tips of low-growing branches at about waist level, which is the preferred browsing height, looking for freshly nipped-off ends, evidence of recent feeding. He goes through heavy timber looking for beech trees bearing nuts or oaks laden with acorns. If there is evidence to indicate nuts and acorns are dropping yet none can be found on the ground, this also indicates deer feeding, though it's not conclusive. If these areas are well populated with squirrels, it might be squirrels and not deer reaping the harvest.

As a rule, though, hunters can detect squirrel workings quickly by the breaking of the acorn shells and the pulverized results of nibbling. Feeding deer make a thorough cleanup of acorns, shells and all.

These observations, plus fresh tracks on feeding grounds, are certain proof of recent deer activity, but the novice might have trouble determining the track's freshness. If leaves are falling, it's simple, for some of the older tracks will be covered. If the ground is mossy, none but very fresh tracks will show. In firm, moist ground, a fresh track appears glazed at the bottom and old tracks appear dull.

Almost the same holds true for deer droppings. These little, dark, elongated pills are dropped in bunches, and their freshness can be determined by their shiny surface coating. Old droppings are invariably dull on the surface and are firm and hard. It's good practice to pick up these little pills and squeeze them. If they're soft, you can bet they haven't laid long.

Locating bed-downs is a somewhat tougher problem, for in most cases, the terrain and weather influence the whitetail's choice of a resting place.

The deer inhabiting an area of good feed and cover usually leads a well-ordered life. He feeds in much the same areas every day; valley slopes, low ground between ridges, and along the edges of heavy timber. The best year-round deer feed is found in low places, with the exception of scrub oak and acorns. Most whitetails prefer high ground for bed-downs: ridges, hillsides and knolls where they can be sure of detecting danger well in advance of its arrival.

The procedure of traveling down to feeding grounds and back up to higher ground for bedding is the most common of whitetail characteristics. It usually results in some well-defined runways connecting in some measure the two areas, for deer are creatures of habit. Although they seldom use the same spot twice running for a bed, they frequently use the same general area, perhaps the same slope or ridge. These spots can only be found by the most thorough search of likely ground, and even then, only the freshest beds remain as evidence.

Fresh beds are well defined. Leaves will be pressed flat in an oval-shaped area about three feet long and two feet wide. Fresh droppings are almost always found near the beds, as are fresh tracks. But after a day or two, the leaves once again fluff up to their original shape, aided by wind and moisture, destroying all evidence. Of course, the easiest way to locate a bed is to jump a deer, but this requires some skill in still-hunting and approach, or else the deer sneak off without being seen.

With bedding grounds and feeding areas located, it's simple to find well-defined runways somewhere between the two. This might be a good time to explain the difference between "runways" and "crossings." Deer hunters constantly use these terms interchangeably, yet they are not the same. A runway is a well-defined path followed by deer, whereas a crossing is a more general area where deer are likely to pass through.

Whitetails, with customary caution, dislike traveling the same beaten path day after day unless it is most convenient for them. We find runways, then, through thick cover—scrub oak, laurel, rhododendron and other tough going where travel is almost impossible except on worn paths. Runways often follow brooks hemmed in by deep gullies, or go under rocky ledges and through swamps where deer have little choice except to follow a single path.

On the other hand, when more open timber or cover is reached, they wander off a few yards on both sides of the line of travel, still keeping within the limits of a crossing, but not following a definite line. These crossings are often found in ridge "saddles," below knolls, through narrow strips of timber between open fields or meadows, or between heavy swamps or dense thickets.

At few times will a whitetail reveal himself completely in open fields willingly, unless it's after dark, near sundown or sunrise, or when afflicted with rutting fever. When he approaches these clearings, he usually skirts the edges, taking as much protection as the cover affords.

As a rule, though, deer keep their runways clear of growing twigs and branches by browsing as they travel, and this browse line is a dead giveaway.

Crossings aren't quite so easy. Perhaps the best plan for their location is to study the territory for spots previously mentioned—"saddles" over or between ridges, and such. Then, minute examination of the ground should reveal clues: fresh tracks and old tracks in profusion, droppings, indications of feeding and, during the rutting season, antler rubs on saplings. These rubs are perhaps the most obvious hint of deer travel in any location, and usually they are numerous during the hunting season.

The general opinion on antler rubs is that bucks use this method to remove their velvet after the antler has hardened, thus polishing and staining the antlers in the process. I cannot subscribe to this theory. I believe rubbing occurs mainly when the rutting season is about to begin or has already started. The buck's antlers start to harden in late summer and early fall, and by mid-September are usually free of any signs of velvet. Yet rutting might not begin until late October or November, and if the observant hunter scouts the woods before the period begins, he will find few, if any, rubs on saplings and brush. Later, however, during the hunting season and after the rut, rubs will be noted in profusion through the same areas.

I believe rubbing is performed by bucks while leading up to the mating process, merely to show off their various good points to the courted doe. In much the same manner, hunters will often see shallow holes about two feet across dug through the leaves down into the soil, with leaves and dirt thrown to one side and scattered for several yards. This the buck performs with his front hoofs, pawing at the ground like an angry bull, again to give himself a good buildup with susceptible females.

Observations made at game farms throughout the country indicate that bucks remove velvet by digging it off with their hind hoofs. This velvet is attached to a thin skin, and once this is broken through with a sharp hind hoof, it peels readily.

In my years in the deer woods, I have examined thousands of rubbed saplings, and I have yet to find a trace of velvet or skin on the ground below, though plenty of rubbed-off bark is often present.

As an additional point, every experienced hunter has noted flat spots rubbed on the antlers just forward of the burrs, indicating still further that all, or nearly all, of the rubbing is done with the bases of the antlers at or near the burrs. If removal of the velvet were the primary objective, the antler would show no concentration of rubbing at one point.

Now, if many of these rubs are noted throughout deer country, it is almost conclusive evidence the rut is on or has already passed. This can only be determined by close observation of the peeled area and the condition of peeled bark on the ground. I usually peel some bark off the first rubbed sapling I see at the beginning of the season's hunt and leave it on the ground with bark already rubbed off. I come back in a day or two and compare its condition with the rub, and from this, I can form a fairly accurate idea about the rub's age.

All this might seem like unimportant detail in a small matter, but the success of a hunt often is made or broken by the rutting season. While the rut is on, deer constantly move. Bucks chase does over a wide area, and does that have already bred are running and hiding from the bucks.

Likewise, the white-tailed buck loses a great deal of his natural caution during this period, and will blunder along runways and through crossings in pursuit of the doe with much less than usual caution. A high percentage of the odd deer stories that come out of the woods each season can be attributed to the height of rutting fever.

With light snow on the ground, the problem of locating feeding grounds, runways and so on is at once simplified. It resolves itself into the single operation of finding tracks and following them, watching surrounding cover for evidence of feeding, and of course, runways and crossings are at once evident. However, when snow covers the ground, deer are much more on the alert. They realize they can be seen more easily, so they stay close to good cover during all daylight movements.

In all of our heavily hunted areas, which include most of our best deer-hunting territory, larger bucks stay off by themselves. They find a safe hiding place for their daylight bed, usually on a ridgetop covered with scrub oak or laurel, moving off the bed only after dark or at dusk. They travel down to low ground for nocturnal feeding, then return again to the ridge for rest.

These big fellows are lazy and unsociable throughout the year, with the single exception of the rutting season. At that time, they single out one or two older does and stay with them for the greater part of the season, protecting them from the attentions of the younger bucks until their job is done. Then they retire to their old stamping grounds until the next season. Most of their travels are made after dark, regardless of moonlight or pitch-blackness, and as the restless urge of early fall seeps in, they become more and more furtive until the mating season begins.

Throughout the year, they permit no intrusions by young bucks into their chosen bailiwick, and they demand no company of the opposite sex. All of these old bucks seem to realize the often-careless female brings bad luck, and they fight any of the association except for the few weeks of the actual mating season.

Needless to point out, these bucks carry the heaviest racks and often the fattest venison and are highly prized by hunters. But it requires the best of skill and utmost patience to take these trophies by fair means. A "lone wolf" buck knows all the answers to a hunter's bag of tricks, but with a little luck on his side, a good hunter can bring him to earth.

If a big buck is located in a given area, much missionary work must be done before the season in attempts to locate his haunts and feeding grounds. All runways and crossings must be examined for the imprint of heavy hoofs. If the buck is large, he will have a much longer stride than the average deer as well as leaving a deeper impression of hoofs. This can only be determined by comparison with other tracks, but it's a good rule.

When a definite runway is located near his bedding ground, a black silk thread can be tied across it at waist level. If it can be conveniently done, the thread should be examined every night and morning to determine whether he leaves his bed by that route or approaches by it, for often separate runways are used for coming and going. Of course, if the ground is soft enough, a preponderance of tracks in one direction will give this information.

From then on, killing one of these big bucks is a matter of watchful waiting, taking a stand at daylight or moving in late in the afternoon in the hope he will leave his bed before dark or delay his return until after dawn. It might require much patient waiting, but these big fellows aren't taken every season and the time is well spent.

The Whitetail's Eyes and Nose

Discussing woodcraft and deer hunting at once brings up the subject of the whitetail's powers of sight, scent and hearing. There is little doubt their hearing and sight are better than our own, and their powers of scent very keen.

The most careful observers agree, though, that the whitetail's sight power is overrated. Deer always seem to have trouble establishing the identity of visible foreign objects unless these objects make a slight move. In the case of a hunter on a stand, if a deer is within only a few yards, even the winking of an eye is enough to start him off in a hurry.

On the other hand, I have had deer approach within 25 yards and pass by with hardly more than a glance, even though I was in full view, when I was virtually motionless.

The whitetail places little faith in any one of his several senses, unless alarmed. If he hears a strange noise, he usually waits to see just what has caused it. If the wind brings him man-scent, he sometimes bides his time until sight or sound confirms his suspicion. This natural curiosity has contributed directly to the untimely demise of more than one big buck.

Perhaps in strictly wilderness areas or regions remote from human activities, the whitetail is much more conscious of man's intrusion and alarmed more easily. But in areas where deer are taken in cover near farmlands or in any populated section, human scent is so often in a deer's nostrils that he pays little attention unless the scent is accompanied by more tangible evidence of danger. In most cases, this is a matter of near proximity or of an individual deer's experiences.

Any whitetail that has had a few close brushes with unfriendly nimrods possesses a much higher IQ rating than his less-sophisticated relatives. Deer learn rapidly, with little teaching. Their senses become more acute, or they develop a keener recognition of facts established by the life processes of seeing, hearing and smelling.

In the early 1940s, I located a big buck through a little preseason scouting. I found him bedded atop a ridge in densely thatched scrub oak. In that refuge, he was safe from any still-hunter, for the most careful stalking couldn't bring an approach within a hundred years without alarming the deer. By a bit of luck, I found a well-defined runway approaching the bedding grounds through a tiny uphill ravine, and it was there I elected to head him off, if possible.

I picked a good stand at the base of an uprooted red oak, giving me a view down the little ravine of about 50 yards, and far enough away so that deer using the run would pass by with little possibility of spotting me.

With a definite project in mind, I eagerly awaited opening day, almost sure of a good shot. But my luck didn't hold out. Just the day before the season opened, our deer-hunting territory was blanketed in a nice snowfall of several inches, followed by a cold rain that quickly formed a most unsatisfactory crust. This made still-hunting in any form out of the picture and tramping through the woods a hardship.

Nevertheless, at dawn that first day, I crunched up the hill for a noisy half-mile to my site. The dead air hung heavily over the hillside, sharply cold and pleasantly tingling on my cheeks. Hoarfrost formed lacy fringes on tree trunks and branches soon to sparkle with the first rays of the sun. Off across the valley, a bluejay sounded an early alarm as he policed his beat, his coarse, excited shrieking cutting crisply through the heavy silence and echoing among the white-bearded hemlocks along the slope. A beautiful morning to park quietly on a stand to listen and watch, I reflected, but that would be all.

On my stand, or seat—for I had snuggled down well concealed against the huge oak roots. I amused myself by watching big clouds of vapor streaming out from my nostrils and lips. Trees were cracking and popping gently in the cold and a red squirrel chattered peevishly across my ravine. Soon the sun rose, spreading a deep pink over the white-blanketed forest floor, magically electrifying the frost-covered tree trunks and branches.

About a half-hour after sunup, I heard faint crunchings down in my ravine. As I listened, the sound increased in volume and came nearer. Just a steady mixed *crunch, crunch*, sounding like a herd of deer in the quiet air. Then quickly the sound materialized into deer; first a sleek doe, head bobbing, ears waving an out-of-step beat as she daintily lifted a slim hoof for each quick stride. At her tail was another doe, somewhat smaller, just as sleek, just as dainty, but with erect head and ears laid back.

Steadily the procession grew until five tawny-coated does drifted by, closely followed by a tiny spike buck. Directly in front of my tree the leading lady stopped, halting the line momentarily. She swept me with a quick glance, then lifted a slim hind leg and scratched her right ear. The red disc of the morning sun behind them made a striking tableau, for each one had suddenly stopped all movement.

As I held my breath momentarily, they all swung their heads over their shoulders and looked back down the ravine. *Ah!* I thought, *here follows the object of my main interest*.

Then, without another glance in my direction, they moved on up the ridge.

I waited with pounding pulse for my buck to make some sound to indicate his approach, but after 10 minutes had gone by, I gave up hope.

Then I again heard the confident crunching step as my buck came up the ravine, but when he was almost within sight, his hoofstep faltered, then stopped. I knew he couldn't wind me in that dead air, and I was sure he couldn't see me. I tucked my chin still farther into the collar of my coat to keep the telltale breath vapors from fanning out before me.

Hesitantly now, his crunching hoofs came on until I could just see a faint movement through the saplings, then he stopped. There he stood, stamping his hoofs, suspicious now but not quite sure just what to do.

My view offered no possibilities for a shot until he emerged from those saplings, so I resigned myself to rigid immobility, but it was of no use. He snorted twice, stamped his hoofs again, then turned and jumped down the runway.

I never saw that deer again, alive. But as a matter of record, one of my hunting pals killed him two days later from this same stand. That morning had brought a gentle, warm rain, and at about the same time, the buck came up the little ravine without hesitation to meet his doom. He was a nice specimen, carrying ten big points.

To this day, I am convinced he could see my breath through those saplings and so took alarm. He was an old-timer, wise in the ways of hunters and cautious in the extreme. This incident is unusual and proves nothing beyond the fact that big bucks don't get that way by being careless.

It is possible this buck was well aware of the noisy progress of his travels through that deep, well-crusted snow. Perhaps this alone made him doubly cautious; so cautious that his senses were more alert than ever to possible danger. He might have picked up a tiny wisp of man-scent drifting from my stand, or seen some slight movement through the saplings caused by breath vapors.

At any rate, he was sufficiently alarmed, giving me no opportunity to place a shot. But two days later, when a warm rain had softened the crust, melted the snow and beaten down any possibility of drifting man-scent, he walked unconcernedly past this same stand, giving my partner a perfect, deadly shot through the neck.

The matter of the whitetail's keen vision is more closely associated with hunting methods than with woodcraft, yet it is sufficiently important for discussion. It is hardly possible that their sight powers are more acute than the normal human's. It is more logical to attribute their ability to pick out a hunter quickly to their intense familiarity with their daily haunts. Any foreign object in their home woods must be as apparent to them as would be a frog on our living-room floor. Yet, if the hunter remains still, their attention will wander and they will forget about the strange object.

Many authorities on whitetails maintain deer are not color-conscious, and that it does no harm to wear red clothing in the woods. This theory I reject. It is incredible to me that the creative force that so lavishly spreads such vivid coloring throughout the land could at the same time create any creature without inherent ability to absorb it visually. I do subscribe to the opinion that the wearing of red in any form has little effect in alarming deer, but not for the same reason.

During fall, the home covers of white-tailed deer are blotched in many ways with brilliant reds—sumac, red oak and some maples—to name three. What is more natural than to assume that a deer glancing casually at a hunter on his stand should mistake his red cap and coat for a scrubby red oak or a low sumac?

Deer are much more sensitive to alarming sounds than to the sight of strange, unmoving objects. Many times, I have had does stand, quietly watching me from distances of only a few yards. But a single snap of my fingers would be enough to produce a quick, frightened reaction that would send them bounding and snorting to safety.

A decade or more ago, when old Abe Wykoff conducted the Buck Mountain Hunting Club in Sullivan County's Oakland Valley region, I was almost run to earth by two does.

One morning, Abe and I were hunting together, still-hunting the slopes on a long narrow hogback. Following our usual custom, I was covering the river side of the slope, Abe the back side that slanted down to the Hartwood Club. I had just discovered a well-defined runway coming down the slope in a long angle and was investigating it where it passed between two husky oak trees only about a yard apart.

At this precise moment, Abe's rifle cracked once, then again, and in a matter of seconds two deer came over the hill in full flight, pounding down the runway toward my somewhat untenable position between the big oaks. My first glance labeled both deer as does, both badly frightened and bounding in high gear. When the leading doe was three jumps away, I waved my arm enthusiastically, thinking this would shy her off. Quickly then, I jumped behind one of my oak trees, barely clearing the run for the two deer as they bounced by.

I suppose a good loud yell might have frightened them enough to swerve them off, but I didn't want to alarm any buck that might be following. Both these deer were blindly alarmed and might easily have knocked me down if I had stood in the run.

Minutes later, I found that Abe had neatly dispatched the six-point buck that had been escorting these does, so my pains to keep quiet were unnecessary. Normally, of course, both these deer would have spotted me at once, but I am convinced that only a loud shout or a shot from my rifle would have swerved them from the runway.

In like manner, many frightened deer, both bucks and does, have been known to run headlong into danger, even though such danger was visually apparent.

Inversely, though deer are highly sensitive to strange sounds, the usual woods noises bother them not at all. This, too, is fortunate for the still-hunter, or else he would rarely get close enough to see a deer. Any deer must be hard put indeed to distinguish the step of the hunter's foot from the myriad rustlings of squirrels, the dropping of nuts and acorns, and the clamorings of crows and blue jays.

Such sounds of the hunter's progress that he must make to move in the woods are not in themselves alarming unless the deer can confirm them by seeing or smelling the hunter. Snapping of heavy twigs underfoot, breaking branches and rolling rocks are, of course, all taboo. Such noises form little or no part of the usual woods complement, and deer quickly detect them as foreign.

Deciphering Buck Tracks

It is regrettable that of the hundreds of thousands of deer hunters spread throughout our white-tailed deer country, only a few spend sufficient time in the woods for absorbing some knowledge of deer habits. Most hunters of my acquaintance seem content with their knowledge after they think they can establish the identity of the bucks' tracks from that of the does. And strangely enough, each hunter of some experience has decidedly definite ideas on this subject.

For my part, although I have spent almost two decades in hunting deer in some of the best covers of the East, I am never positive of the buck's track, unless I have seen the deer making it.

Perhaps I have heard as much discussion of the subject from the hunter's viewpoint as any other individual in the East. Over the gun counter, in hunting clubs, at sportsmen's meetings, in the deer woods, and in mountain taverns my ears have been bent with numerous positive rules for such identification. But still I remain unconvinced, for no two sets of rules seem the same.

First, the size of the track is no criterion. Larger females will most certainly have hoofs of greater length and width than the hoofs of small bucks. Another factor is the type of terrain the animal uses. Deer living in soft, swampy ground or an area of heavy coniferous timber will develop a larger hoof. Deer that climb rocky ridges and rock-studded slopes will have smaller, sharper hoofs. I have killed several large bucks on the Shawangunk Mountain range in Lower Sullivan and Ulster counties, all of which had comparatively small hoofs. This mountain range is of heavy limestone with many jagged outcroppings and generally rock-covered. Deer living and feeding on this range keep their hoofs in a well-trimmed condition. In the swampy Wolf Pond area of Sullivan County, only a few miles north of the Shawangunk Range, the deer have somewhat larger hoofs.

During the latter part of December 1946, one of my hunting friends and I skinned out our two bucks at the same time. One of these deer was unusually large, carrying a dressed weight of 212 pounds. The other was a normal eight-pointer that dressed out at 131 pounds.

In the normal process of skinning and butchering, we had disjointed the legs and thrown them into a single pile. Later, when we came to sorting out the respective hoofs, we would have been forced to pick at random were it not for the slightly longer and heavier leg of the larger deer. Certainly, there was no apparent difference in the hoof sizes. In addition, I have had ample opportunity during the past two decades to examine the carcasses of thousands of white-tailed bucks. I am still unconvinced the larger bucks carry the largest hoofs.

Depth of hoofprint is the more obvious indication of a buck's weight, plus the length of stride, both of which must be compared with other tracks made in the same vicinity. This gives an initial foundation for the hunter's deductions.

The fat, heavy buck shows a marked tendency to walk with front hoofs wider apart than the doe or small buck. Also, these bucks usually show an inclination to toe-out with the front hoofs.

In following a group of tracks (in snow), there are some distinguishing characteristics that will help hunters pick out the buck's track—if there be one in the herd. The does have a tendency to wander aimlessly when the herd is moving; the buck is more purposeful and direct in his movements. The doe track will wander off the runway, then weave back.

Often she'll playfully jump over a small bush or log, seemingly just for the fun of it. Her whole attitude as evidenced by the dainty hoofprints is much less concerned with a direct objective than is the buck.

The whitetail buck seldom engages in the female frivolities. His walking stride is calm and purposeful. He seldom turns abruptly to feed on a shrub just off the run. Rather, he walks directly to the feeding spot. He engages in no playful antics such as the doe tracks indicate. There is little bush- or log-jumping to be found in the evidence of a buck's hoofprints.

Often an entire group of does will fan out through crossings, covering an area 15 or 20 yards wide, as they precede the buck. The buck's track will usually be found, firm and purposeful, following up through the center of this welter of trails. Then again, the more wary old-timers will follow the doe herd, but at a distinct distance apart. If the hunter discovers one of these lone trails showing a marked tendency to stray off a bit from the rest of the herd, he can bet his stack there is a buck ahead.

In snow less than four inches deep, the buck consistently gives away his sex by dragging his front hoofs. The doe lifts each hoof daintily, then places it down. A buck carrying heavy neck and shoulders will not trouble to lift his hoofs clear of the snow. His dragging forehoofs leave a distinctive line behind each print. Of course, in heavy snow any deer will drag its hoofs to some extent, so the hunter must use judgment in making a decision.

Much has been said about the spreading of a buck's toes as a distinguishing characteristic. To me, a spread-toe print means only a heavy deer, whether it be buck or doe. Any running or loping deer will leave a spread-toe print, particularly in firm soil.

The woodsman who has opportunity to observe all the points we have mentioned will add up all of them before drawing a conclusion. In fact, the whole thing is not too important, because we must find the buck himself. Many times, though, we are forced to decide whether to follow a set of fresh tracks, and we might be able to save a day's wasted hunt if we can make a logical and accurate interpretation. At any rate, the study of deer prints never loses its charm for a deer hunter. Rather, it adds to the fun of a day in the woods.

Misconceptions About the Snort

There exists still another item of sex differential in deer that has caused many a clubhouse argument: the "snort" of the whitetail. Almost every hunter who spends much time in deer country has heard a deer snort. The sound is simply a whistling blast from a deer's nostrils, usually made when a deer is alarmed. It's also caused by the deer's effort to rid its nostrils of the nose-bot. The deer bot is a worm-like parasite that afflicts whitetails in certain areas, but usually isn't fatal by itself.

Commonly, it is the deer's ability to rid itself of these bots by blasting them out through the nostrils that helps determine if the deer will survive the vitality ebb of a hard winter.

However, it is a prevalent belief among hunters that only the buck snorts. This idea is so widespread that any snorting deer faces immediate danger during the hunting season.

During one of my still-hunting trips in the lower Catskills, I was working a big beech ridge. I had been in the woods about an hour and had not yet heard or seen any other hunters, so I was unprepared for a sudden burst of rifle shots that crashed out directly ahead of me. Seconds later, two does crashed by just below me, unaware of my presence. Just beyond me they stopped, looked over their backs in the direction they had left, then shaking their tails, they quietly trotted down the slope to the valley below.

A light powdering of snow covered the ground, so soon I could see two red-capped hunters following the trail made by the does. They were so occupied that neither hunter saw me and would have passed by if I hadn't whistled. I dropped down the hill then to talk with them.

"How long have you been standing there?" they both asked. "Didn't you see those two bucks go by?"

"Well," I said, "I certainly saw two deer go by, but if there had been any bucks, you'd have heard some shootin'. Just what made you fellows think they were bucks?"

Both shifted their feet a bit and looked at each other before the older man spoke up.

"Well, we had just come up on this ridge, and these deer were bedded down in some brush. When they heard us, they both snorted and jumped on up the ridge. We could see their flags for quite a ways, so we started to pump it at 'em. We're glad we didn't connect. That's the first time either of us heard of a doe snorting."

And so it goes. I have heard numerous incidents parallel to this one, and from widely separated regions, so the idea is by no means peculiar to a few deer hunters.

In this same connection, "way back in the early '30s," I had joined an Oakland Valley deer-hunting outfit called The Beaverdam Club.

On my first day's hunt, just after daybreak, I had found a tiny scooped-out gravel bank up on the mountainside near the camp. The boys had been taking gravel out to repair the winding wood road over the mountain to Beaverdam Pond. The bank was just so deep that I could barely look over the rim from a spot within the scooped hole.

I had a good view from this spot. With only my head exposed above ground level, I could cover the little ravine running down the steep slope to my left. The whole white-birch slope to my right and the valley below was in easy view for just a shift of the eye. This, I decided, would be a good spot to spend an hour, while the deer still would be on the early morning feed.

Hardly had I settled down to wait when two deer came into view, gently picking their way down the ravine edge toward the valley below. They were not alarmed, and would wander a bit from the ravine to the low second growth to nip off a tender bud now and then as they progressed, ever coming closer to my stand in the gravel pit.

Finally, they were only a few yards from my head when the lead doe discovered me. At once her head was thrown erect, sensitive ears cocked in my direction. Then, she lowered her head slowly and, at this close range, I could see her nostrils quivering as they sucked in air, filtering it for a taint of danger.

But the wind was right and she could find nothing to fear. Still, she was mighty curious, so she raised a slim foreleg and stamped it to the ground with an audible thump. Finding that I could not yet be frightened into moving, she again stamped. Meanwhile, her companion doe had inched forward cautiously until they were nose to flank. Then, incredible though it might seem, they each stamped and thudded their dainty forehoofs into the hard ground, no doubt still expecting to frighten a move out of me.

At last, satisfied no buck was tagging along behind, I broke the tableau quickly by yanking off my cap and waving it. The response was electric. Both does jumped into the air with loud snorts, reversing their field as they headed back up the slope, bounding as though they were on springs—tails flying erect—and snorting at every jump. At the top of the ridge they stopped, shook their heads, snorted a final blast and walked off into the white birches, snapping their flags in evident disgust.

Becoming at Home in the Woods

In bringing out some of these more intimate details of deer behavior, I have a definite purpose. There is a growing tendency among the great bulk of the deer-hunting clan to pursue whitetails in a hit-or-miss manner. For any man to gain the fullest success and enjoyment from his hunting each year, the whitetail must be made a hobby—a hobby of study that is as gratifying as the killing of the deer itself.

True, many men are fortunate enough to kill a deer the first time they set foot in whitetail country. This is not exceptional. Purely by the law of averages alone, some small percentage of greenhorns will kill their buck, because with thousands of hunters in the woods each season, some are bound to run across a deer. But the man who can kill his buck year after year is one who has a keen knowledge of woodcraft and deer behavior. No detail of deer lore is too insignificant to be overlooked.

There is much more to killing a buck than finding good deer country and spending a few days hunting it. Any woodsman worthy of the name covers his hunting grounds with hawk eyes. He studies his topographical maps and from these alone—virtually without seeing the land itself—he can often locate the sections where deer cross from valley feeding grounds to hiding places in swamps and bedding grounds on ridges. These maps are invaluable to the deer hunter in familiarizing himself with areas to be hunted. Such maps may be had from the United States Geological Survey, covering in quadrangle sections almost any area in the country. The maps show elevations as contour lines, and all roads, trails and streams in any given area.

It is a far cry from covering alder thickets with a good English setter or crouching in a duck blind on the sound to the successful hunting of white-tailed deer. This writer does not wish to disparage small-game hunting, for no one else enjoys that sport to a greater degree. However, I have always felt that such hunting calls more for good shooting ability and good dogs than for an abundance of woods lore.

Successful deer hunting is the true test not only of a sportsman's shooting skill, but of his specific knowledge of woodcraft and of his intelligent application of this knowledge.

A knowledge of woodcraft includes much more than a thorough understanding of deer habits and movements. The hunter himself must be at home in the woods, be able to detect good cover and feeding grounds at a glance, know his territory well enough to account for the movements of his pals, and above all, be sure of his own position through every minute of the day. In small covers near farmlands and settled communities, this is no problem. In the "back-country" and semi-wilderness areas, it is not so easy. Individuals vary much in this quality of directional sense, but every hunter can acquire enough of it to give him perfect freedom of movement in any territory he might like to explore.

OPENING DAY BUCKS
By M. R. James

Opening day in any sport carries a special cachet. It is a moment of great anticipation, occasional triumphs and, almost invariably, special delights. Arguably, no contemporary whitetail scribe is better suited to convey the magic of the day than James, the founder of Bowhunter *magazine and the dean of modern bowhunters. In this selection from his* Of Blind Pigs and Big Bucks *(2002), he gives us a piece that captures the flavor of the moment even as it conveys worthwhile information on how to approach the deer hunter's day of days.*

D eer season was less than an hour old when the eight-point buck stepped out of a multiflora rose tangle. He paused only briefly, standing watchful at the edge of the weedy clearing. In front of him a well-tracked trail meandered through the sumac beside a brushy fenceline bordering the opening, finally vanishing into a stand of shadowy hardwoods. Within seconds, apparently satisfied that nothing was amiss on this quiet October morning, the buck began walking toward the treeline in that purposeful, no-nonsense gait of a whitetail with a specific destination in mind.

He never made it. I shot him through the chest at 12 yards as he passed broadside beneath my treestand in a fencerow oak. Scant seconds later, I saw him go down kicking after a brief dash for the safety of the woods. With no real need to wait before taking up the blood trail, I was soon kneeling beside my opening day trophy, admiring the heft of his rack, appreciating the sleek beauty of yet another whitetail whose daily early autumn routine had proved to be his undoing.

Unlocking the door to this kind of early season bowhunting success is no mystery. The key is found in proper preparation and a knowledge of daily deer activity within a given hunting area. And while the element of luck—both good and bad—certainly enters into the outcome of any hunt, I'm convinced that bowhunters who rely mainly on the fickle whims of Lady Luck to help them fill their deer tags are going to fail more often than not. All of the consistently successful deer hunters I know make their own luck through hard work—and as that familiar axiom suggests, the harder people work, the luckier they become!

I tagged that opening day buck after thoroughly checking out my hunting spot many weeks ahead of the season opener. Once my late-summer scouting trips pinpointed a well-used travel route between feeding and bedding areas, I had only to select an appropriate ambush site and keep tabs on travel patterns.

By late September, the sticky-fresh rubs sprouting overnight on fenceline saplings told me one or more bucks were in the vicinity. And I knew from past experience that a nearby low-limbed oak offered an ideal vantage point where I could hang my portable stand to take advantage of prevailing winds.

After trimming several shooting lanes, the rest of my pre-season preparation, by comparison, was easy. It consisted mainly of checking and rechecking equipment, making time for daily shooting sessions, honing broadheads and savoring the anticipation of another opening day.

True, three-plus decades of whitetail hunting experience has given me an advantage over some less experienced hunters; however, I firmly believe any deer hunter can increase his or her odds of early season success by understanding a few basic facts, and then applying a handful of practical tips. Following are half-a-dozen key points to keep in mind as you plan for your opening day bowhunt:

No matter where deer live, early season whitetails have basic daily routines built around keeping their stomachs full and their hides free of perforations created by broadheads and bullets. Identifying active feeding and bedding areas is the first step along the road to success. While a deer's food sources and places of concealment may change with the seasons, your prehunt scouting forays can help you keep tabs on movement patterns and plan the best ambush site.

Remember, most veterans agree that knowledge of the hunting area and well-placed treestands situated along daily travel routes are the most effective way to tag your buck. But be careful! Never unduly disturb any feeding or bedding areas. And once you've settled on exactly where you'll hunt, resist the temptation to check it out again and again. The scent you'll leave—and inevitable encounters with deer—will cause them to become increasingly wary.

Just before opening day, place your stand(s) where deer are most likely to pass during their routine daily travels. Then show up opening day primed for action.

Hunting undisturbed deer is another key to consistent success. Inevitably, early season whitetails are less cautious than they were at the tail end of last hunting season when the orange-clad hordes finally departed and silence returned to the hills and fields. Warm spring days and abundant summertime browse may lull deer into a state of semi-relaxation. But they wise up fast! At best, the people suddenly traipsing around the fall woods will only make them suspicious; at worst, the activity will cause them to abruptly change their daily routines and timetables. This is especially true of bigger bucks, which have survived several hunting seasons.

Perhaps the very best time to really get to know any hunting area is just after the deer season ends. The bare winter woods are open, rubs and scrapes easy to locate, and you don't have to worry about spooking game while checking out every woodland nook and cranny.

Early spring scouting trips spent looking for shed antlers are other worthwhile efforts. But as another deer season approaches, try to keep your scouting trips brief yet meaningful. Where terrain permits, scout from a distance with binoculars or a spotting scope.

Again, don't contaminate your hunting area with human scent any more than necessary.

While its possible to restrict scouting activity on private or leased lands, public hunting areas are another matter. Here, you must accept the fact you're not going to have the woods to yourself—and plan accordingly. I've taken my share of whitetails on public lands by setting up in places where hunting pressure is most likely to push deer seeking to get away from the opening day crowds. This generally involves getting off the beaten path and arriving early, well ahead of the other hunters.

Natural whitetail crossings—wooded ridgetop saddles, fingers of brush or timber connecting farmland woodlots and trails cutting through bottomland bogs, for example—hold promise for public land bowhunters willing to walk back in and wait for itchy-footed latecomers to push deer past them. I normally stay in my stand longer where hunting pressure is heavy than when hunting undisturbed whitetails on private land.

And don't pass up the opportunity to sign up for special whitetail hunts on military bases or to go on out-of-state hunts in unfamiliar territory. Just because you can't do much, if any, scouting ahead of time doesn't mean it's a lost cause. You can learn something each time you go afield.

Upon arrival, simply apply the same principles of locating fresh signs of deer activity and positioning a stand along well-used trails. Sit back, be patient and allow natural deer activity—or wandering hunters—to move animals past your stand.

Remember, too, even though early season whitetail bucks may be feeling the first faint stirrings of rut, they aren't going to show the same interest in does that comes as the season moves along. Rattling might lure curious bucks but typically isn't as effective as during the pre- and post-rut period. Ditto for rutting scents, which offer the odors of receptive does (although food and curiosity scents may be effective early in the season).

Calling can work, and I've taken several early season bucks with the help of subtle vocalizations. Moderation, I'm convinced, is a key in any of these ruses. Overdo it with the rattling antlers, the deer scents or the deer calls, and you're likely to alert far more deer than you might attract.

Whenever in deer country during the open season, always keep evidence of your presence to an absolute minimum. Watch the wind direction at all times (a thread tied to your bowstring works well) and keep breezes in your favor as much as possible. Finally, realize that every step you take—and everything you touch—helps spread your scent and warn whitetails that you're around. Never relieve yourself near where you'll be hunting.

Rubber boots—or at least footwear with rubber soles—can help minimize scent, but keep in mind that every leaf you brush against and every branch you push aside is a potential warning sign to keen-scented whitetail. Also, perspiration can be an early season problem, especially if much walking is involved in getting to a favored stand. A dusting of common baking soda will help, as will unscented deodorants; however, I know some serious bowhunters who routinely pack their hunting clothes in a plastic bag and change after reaching their hunting area.

Mosquitoes and ticks often are an early season hazard. Taping the cuffs and sleeves of hunting pants and shirts can be an effective tick deterrent. But a routine check at bath or shower time is always a good idea.

Lyme disease is a very real threat in parts of the country, and this is especially true among hunters who handle deer without realizing whitetails are frequently unwitting hosts of these pesky woodland bloodsuckers. Although any good insect repellent will discourage bites and stings, some hunters refuse to smear or spray themselves with any odiferous stuff for fear of alerting deer. Here's where lightweight, bug-proof headnets and jackets can come in handy.

Cool mornings and evenings in autumn, with temperatures climbing substantially during the day, are common early season conditions. This can pose certain meat care problems for the successful bowhunter. Always field-dress the deer as quickly as possible and hang the carcass in a well-shaded spot to speed cooling and draining of the blood. I always wash and wipe the body cavity before hanging, and then use pepper or a game bag to keep flies, bees and other winged pests away from the meat.

As a rule of thumb, if the temperature climbs above 45 degrees for any length of time, you should make time to promptly deliver the meat to a game-processing facility or butcher it yourself. Warm weather can cause the meat to sour and spoil a lot of mighty fine meals. Don't ever take chances with your venison during these warm spells.

Today's burgeoning whitetail populations and generous bag limits offer most modern-day bowhunters opportunities undreamed of a few short years ago. In many states, multiple deer tags and extended seasons are the rule. It's quite possible to arrow an early season whitetail, and with a supply of tasty venison secure in the freezer, continue hunting—for more meat or one of those big-racked bucks that haunt all hunters' dreams.

Bowhunting the late-season rut, when bucks are constantly on the move and their full attention is on romance, is indeed a special time for deer hunters. But opening day and the early season should never be overlooked as a prime time to score.

The deer are out there, waiting to test your planning, patience and hunting skills. For my money, there's no better reason to grab a favorite bow and head for the door.

HUNTING WHITETAIL DEER

By Ted Trueblood

This material comes from Chapter 16 of Trueblood's The Hunter's Handbook *(1954). In the course of a half-dozen pages, the author, one of the giants of mid-20th century outdoor writing, touches on a variety of tactics ranging from tracking in snow, careful observation of feeding habits, still-hunting and driving deer.*

Thanksgiving vacation came with a foot of snow. Clarence Brown and I decided to go deer hunting. We loaded our camping outfit into his old car and drove out into a cutover area of northern Idaho that was literally crawling with whitetail deer.

It was rolling country, streaked with streams, dotted with cedar swamps, and sprinkled with areas of big white pine stumps where the second growth was higher than the head of a man standing on the tallest of them. There were deer tracks everywhere.

We started hunting by following the first fresh tracks we found. They wandered around aimlessly for a mile or so, then went down into a swamp. We followed them until the brush became so dense that we couldn't squeeze through and then we lost them. We backed out and picked up another set. They, too, terminated in a cedar swamp.

After repeating this procedure a couple more times, we decided it was futile. The deer apparently were feeding at night and going into the swamps to spend the day, and even if we could follow them there, we would have to be within a few yards of our quarry in order to see it and get a shot.

That evening we waited as late as we dared along the edge of one of the swamps, hoping to see a deer as it came out. The next morning we took stands near a swamp before daylight with the intention of stopping any deer that might be returning to cover for the day. Both of these plans failed.

Our next attempt was for one of us to force his way through a swamp, making as much noise as possible, while the other slipped along quietly outside and circled around the end. We took turns driving and tried this scheme several times, but it didn't work.

The remainder of our time was spent wandering around more or less aimlessly, watching the spots where tracks were thickest and trying all other ideas that seemed to hold any promise of success. We returned to school without having seen a deer.

My respect for the sagacity of the whitetail was practically unlimited at the conclusion of this first hunt, and it has remained at a high level ever since. They have been more successful in coping with civilization than any other big-game animal. In fact, there probably are more whitetails in America now than there were when the Pilgrims landed. I have seen them practically within the limits of New York City and in some of the wildest, most remote parts of the Northwest, and they were equally at home.

White-tailed deer are hunted chiefly by three methods: driving, still-hunting, and with hounds. The last is most common in the South. Some northern hunters consider it unsportsmanlike to run deer with hounds and shoot them with buckshot, but that is only because they haven't hunted in southern covers. The dog-work there is as much a part of the game as it is in quail hunting, and without them it would be utterly impossible to get a shot.

Of the three methods, however, still-hunting is the one that I prefer. I feel that it places the hunter and his game on a more nearly equal basis. The man has the advantages of his rifle and better vision. The deer's lie in his better senses of smell and hearing and his ability to move more quietly and much more rapidly. In most cases, too, he knows the area in which he dwells far better than does the hunter. He knows where the safest thickets are and how to sneak out of one when it is invaded and reach another without being seen.

The first step in successful still hunting is to evaluate these factors. The deer can smell you at much greater distance than you can see or hear him, therefore you must hunt into or across the wind. He can hear you long before you are within rifle range, so you must move cautiously to avoid unnecessary noise. He can travel many times more rapidly, consequently you will gain nothing by attempting speed.

On the other hand, he can't see you when you are motionless (regardless of the color of clothes you wear), but you can see him standing still, even when he is partly screened by brush. And your rifle will enable you to kill him as far away as you are likely to see him in timber country.

Ordinarily, I am no enthusiast for tracking. When I begin a hunt, however, I do like to follow the tracks of an undisturbed deer to see what he is eating and what kind of cover he goes into to spend the day. On that same first day, I'll try to get a good idea of the general lay of the land; I'll watch for any unusual concentration of tracks that might indicate a crossing or route of travel between nighttime feeding areas and daytime hideouts, and if I see any beds, I'll try to determine how recently they were occupied.

Of course, I'll carry my rifle and if I happen to get a shot, fine. I won't feel bad if I don't, however. It really is pretty futile to start into a new territory without any idea of where the deer are, what they're eating, or how they're moving and expect to get one. Spending the first day acquiring as many facts as possible about the country and its inhabitants helps to put me on a more even footing with them.

I may discover, for example, that the deer have been eating apples in an abandoned orchard. Before I leave, I'll pick out the best possible approach to the best spot from which to watch it. The next morning, I'll likely be back well before daylight, and I'll have a fair chance to collect my buck as soon as it's light enough to shoot.

If I don't get a shot then, I'll leave that vicinity entirely and come back late in the afternoon. I'll make myself comfortable—downwind, of course—and sit motionless until it is too dark to see the sights. That is, unless I get my buck first, which I will be likely to do unless some other hunter alarms them or the wind shifts and betrays me.

Any place that deer feed is worth watching, but it is futile to expect to find them there during the middle of the day unless a storm is approaching. Sometimes just before a storm all kinds of game feed actively all day. Ordinarily, however, since we can't shoot at night, the only time we can expect to get a shot at a feeding deer is early in the morning or late in the evening.

I think that a still-hunter might kill just as many deer in the long run if he spent the hours from mid-morning until mid-afternoon in camp, but I don't like to do it. After all, I go hunting to hunt, not to sit in a tent or cabin and stare at the stove.

Occupying one's time to good advantage during the middle of the day is not always easy, however. Aimless walking is not the answer. Just what offers the best chance for a shot depends on circumstances.

If there are a lot of hunters stirring around, then deer will be moving to keep away from them. Watching a crossing or even an opening through which they have to pass in sneaking from one daytime cover to another is a good bet. Even if you can't find such a spot, sitting in any vantage point that gives you a good view in several directions provides a fair chance for a shot. The motionless hunter always has the advantages of being in a good position from which to shoot, of not being winded and, many times, of getting a shot at a motionless or slow-moving target.

Deer ordinarily don't do much wandering around during the day unless they are disturbed, so when you have your hunting territory to yourself, it is up to you to find them.

Your first day's exploration should have given you some idea of the kind of spots in which they are bedding down. Those occupied by the better bucks always will be difficult to approach. There will be cover nearby to screen his escape and yet he will be lying in a position that enables him to watch his back trail.

Jumping a deer from its bed and then shooting it probably is the most difficult thing a deer hunter can undertake, but it is possible. When you leave camp, walk briskly until you come to the area you want to hunt, then slow down. You want the wind in your face, even if it is very faint, and you can determine its direction by sifting a handful of powdery snow, crumbled leaves or the dust from a rotten log through your fingers.

Take a few steps, then stop and look in all directions, including the rear. Whitetail deer often let a hunter pass and then slip away in the other direction. After you have scrutinized everything in sight carefully, advance again. As I stated earlier, you can't outrun a deer anyway, so your best bet is to move slowly, carefully and quietly. It doesn't matter if you walk only half-a-mile in half-a-day: you'll have a better chance to see a buck than you would if you covered 10 miles at a breakneck pace.

Following tracks in fresh snow is fascinating, but it frequently is fruitless. If they were made late at night or early in the morning, however, only an hour or two before you struck them, you do have a chance to get a shot if you work it right. Observe what the deer was doing as you walk along. Was he feeding? Looking for a spot to spend the day or traveling rapidly?

Successful tracking doesn't mean moving at a rapid pace with your nose to the ground. Stop frequently and look ahead. Study the lay of the land and attempt to figure out where the deer would be apt to go. If the tracks appear to be headed for a likely spot for him to spend the day, stop and check the wind.

Get it right, even if this involves leaving the trail entirely, and approach the cover from downwind. In fact, if you think a buck might be in a certain thicket, it is a good idea to leave his tracks and come up to it from another direction. He'll be watching his back track.

Now, work up toward your objective as though you had all the time in the world. Don't snap a twig nor scrape a single branch. Try to find the best angle from which to see into the cover and move cautiously to right and left occasionally, since changing your viewpoint even a few yards opens up an entirely new vista.

It is not a bad idea to circle a thicket entirely, provided there is no breeze. If you see your buck's tracks coming out, you can resume following them without wasting time. If they don't come out, you know that you have to work your way on in and take a chance on seeing him there. Of course, if there is any air current whatever, you would not dare to get upwind from the spot where you expect your quarry to be. He'd slip out without your ever seeing him. Naturally, too, there would be no point in attempting to circle an entire swamp. Deer often bed down in a small stand of evergreens or other dense cover, however.

Driving deer, while it requires less knowledge of their habits and of woodcraft in general than still-hunting, still should not be attempted blindly. All game has certain escape routes that it follows when alarmed. Knowledge of these from previous experience in the territory to be driven is a tremendous advantage. Lacking it, you need good judgment in locating the stands.

In general, a whitetail will follow concealing cover as long as possible before making a break across a clearing. Consequently, ends of the stringers of cedar or alders that extend from a swamp—if that is the spot to be driven—should be watched. He will follow a depression rather than a ridge, and when he crosses from the drainage of one creek to another he will go through a saddle rather than over a knob. Stands should be selected with these things in mind as well as the peculiarities of each locality.

Generally, it is best to drive downwind whenever possible. The deer will move ahead of the drivers and approach the stands without smelling the hunters stationed there. Of course, this causes deer to slip out the sides or double back whenever they can. They ordinarily won't travel with the wind unless they are so badly frightened that they are running headlong.

The beaters should stay fairly well in line and make plenty of noise, not only to frighten the game but to keep informed of each other's whereabouts. Of course, the hunters who will occupy the stands should be on location and standing motionless well ahead of the time that the beaters approach.

The distance between the drivers naturally depends upon the number available and the width of the cover to be driven, but they should not be too far apart. I once watched from a vantage point on a mountainside as a buck and two does slipped between two hunters who were scarcely 50 yards apart. It is amazing how clever they become at cutting back and how well they can take advantage of any cover available.

Of course, it is the whitetail's cleverness that makes hunting him so fascinating. There would be no more sport to getting a buck than in shooting a farmer's sheep if the deer were equally stupid. And, even more important, there would be no deer to hunt.

STILL-HUNTING THE WHITETAIL

By Lawrence Koller

This selection, Chapter 5 of Koller's book of the same title (1948), combines the story of a notable still-hunt with general information on the technique.

Sunup was moments away as I stood on the roadbank near the little old schoolhouse. Earl and Eddy had just dropped me off and had gone up the winding dirt road to the next farmhouse. They would park the car there and hunt up on the big hardwood ridge that parallels the course of the majestic Delaware River. I was to hunt on up this ridge and meet them a mile or so beyond.

Tale of a Still-Hunt

How quiet and lifeless were the slopes and valley below me! The quiet gray beeches stood like guardians among the little white birch and sumac by the roadside, gleaming damply in the early daylight. Now and then a heavy water drop would fall with a thunk on the dead-leaf carpet below. It had rained the night before—a soft, warm fall rain, bringing off the last reluctant leaves and opening the door to the hunter.

It was opening day some 10-odd years ago. We had decided to hunt here, in the Cahoonzie area of southwestern Sullivan County, purely on my say-so that it was good deer country. Of course, all of us knew there were whitetails in this area, but we had not yet hunted here for deer. I had, however, been over the section we were to hunt a few weeks before with the setter. I had combined grouse-hunting with a little exploration, and had decided the country offered good possibilities.

At that time I had been more or less driven out of my old stamping grounds near Wolf Pond by the heavy infiltration of new and reckless deer hunters. I had decided this year I would seek new hunting fields, where still-hunting would once again be practical and enjoyable.

Perhaps no one can say just why he picks a definite spot for a new hunting ground. On my grouse-hunting trip, I had found many tracks, some well-defined runs, and evidence of deer feeding on acorns and beechnuts up on the big ridge, now above me. But I knew many other places where deer sign was just as abundant. Perhaps on the day I had been here before, the beauty of the country impressed me and now had lured me there again.

It had been a glorious, golden fall day. Riotous color had filled the woods—the warm reds of the young oaks, the pastel yellows of the beeches. Waxy-orange bittersweet berries clung to the tumbledown stone fences and clambered over dark green cat-briers like living drapes. Here, I had found grouse and the delicate heart-shaped prints of deer.

Topping the ridges were long lines of towering hemlocks, standing guard over their progeny in the struggle for sunlight among the heavy white birch. Ground-pine and creeping hemlock carpeted the white birch grounds, almost concealing great beds of wintergreen and partridge berries. And over all was the rich glow of October sunlight.

In the valley below, the Shinglekill gurgled and chattered on its journey to the Delaware. Both brook trout and the heavier browns were even now lying in the gravel-bottomed riffles, ready to spawn. To me, trout and whitetailed deer have always been closely associated. Perhaps because many of my deer have been killed near trout waters, or perhaps because in both there breathes the never-ending beauty of the wilds.

The first pink rays of sunrise bathing the top of the ridge above stirred me from my reverie. It was time now to get up on that ridge and look for my buck. Behind the little school ran a low ridge, gently sloping upward to meet the big ridge that I felt should be the resting place of at least a few deer. Slowly, reluctantly, fearful of making any sound that might break the spell of silence, I began the climb.

My shoe-pacs fell softly on the sodden leaves. I brushed through little hemlocks whose evergreen feathers dropped tiny showers at my intrusion. Every half-minute or so, I stopped to look down each slope of the ridge, watching for deer sign as I progressed. Soon I headed into the base of my big ridge. Now the timber changed abruptly from small white birch and poplar to the heavy-trunked red oaks and big beeches. The beech is ever a lovely tree. Its smooth gray bark gives an impression of quiet, firm dignity, a strong contrast to the rough, black trunks of oak and hard maple.

The woods were indeed quiet that morning. The air had but a touch of chill; no breeze moved the last remaining leaves of the aspens—nothing but a *put* as an overburdened raindrop dripped from a high twig.

I struck a fresh track and stopped to study it. The prints were deep in wet leaves, wide-spaced and toed-out; they were heading for the ridge. It was apparent this deer had spent the rainy night before down in the valley hemlocks, either feeding or in shelter from the rain, and was making for the ridge to bed down.

I took the trail to the top. It was easy to follow in the sodden leaves. But at the top of the ridge, the trail became fainter as it led through long stretches of moss and over rocky ledges. Finally, I gave it up altogether to concentrate on covering the long hogback before me.

For an hour I carefully walked the ridge-top, swinging first right, then left, that I might watch both sides of the slope. Much of the time I stood to listen and watch, but I heard nothing more than the scurry of a gray squirrel as he dashed for a den tree, or the distant *pow! pow!* of a rifle. Then I turned to step around a big stump, and a movement in a white birch stand to my left brought me to a halt. I could see moving bodies in the brush and now and then a slim foreleg, but no heads.

In a moment, two deer came out of the white birch and headed up the ridge. Both were does, or at any rate no antlers showed. I decided to wait for a bit and watch their back trail for any following buck. But for 15 minutes no other deer showed, so I took off again following the ridge and, in a sense, following the two does.

My route crossed many deer signs; fresh tracks coming up from the valley below and crossing over the ridge; many droppings sprinkled in the runs through laurel and rhododendron. Almost every visible track must necessarily be fresh, for the rain would have successfully obliterated all those before its coming. Here on a small poplar near a rocky ledge a buck had rubbed the bark—long shreds lay on the ground at the butt. No tracks were visible here; it must have been rubbed some days before. All these signs were heartening. Perhaps this ridge would develop into a deer hunter's Utopia.

At last I reached the crest of the hogback. Beyond, the ridge sloped gently down to the valley of the little farm near where my pals were to be hunting. Quietly and slowly I worked down the slope, aware now of a gentle breeze fanning my left cheek and murmuring in the topmost hemlock boughs. The sun was much higher now. The early rose glow had changed to a pale yellow, penetrating to the forest floor in the beech and white birch stands, but failing to dispel the moist and morose shadows of hemlock and buck-laurel. *Deer should be bedding now,* I thought. *Not much chance to find any yet on the move.*

In my musing way, I had passed a big windfall of white oaks, lying off the shoulder of the ridge, heavily leaved tops pointing down the slope. The uprooted trunks lay crisscrossed upon each other with the thick, brown dead leaves clinging to the branches in a high mound. I had stopped then for a moment, to wonder at the perversity of a flighty wind in singling out for destruction this particular clump of white oaks. And as I stood here, my eye dropped to fresh deer tracks, tracks that headed toward this windfall.

Obeying the normal urge, my feet turned toward the fallen trees. No more than two steps did I make when, with a bursting crash, a fine buck bounded out from behind the screen of leaves, hightailing it for the crest of the hogback. As he jumped, his antlers had flashed in the sunlight, and even as my rifle came up, both antlers and long white flag were bobbing over the low brush.

My first fright over, I settled down to stopping him short of the ridge- top. Swinging with him, my front sight touched his knees as I tightened the trigger. With the crash of the .250, his forelegs crumpled on that last bound, his nose slid to the leaves and his chunky body swept over in a high-arching somersault. He made one game effort to regain his hoofs, but the second bullet threw a tuft of hair from the far side of his neck and he thumped to the ground again, stretched out in death.

As he lay on the damp forest floor, I marveled, as I do over every deer I have killed, at the dead-whiteness of his white hair and the tawny gray of his body coat, so similar in color to the leaves on which he lay. His antlers shone dully, hinting of many rubbings on the soft-barked saplings on his ridge. The main beams swept forward and upward, topped with 10-inch-long tines. His was not a magnificent head of wide spreading beams and many points, but simply the grand, sturdy crown of an adult eight-point buck.

And now, I reflected, as I dropped down on a log to steady my quaking knees, my hunting was over and the hard work—yet a labor of love—must begin. I had to get him out.

The Right Territory and Conditions

An experience such as this is the deer hunter's dream. On the day that I have related, still-hunting conditions were ideal. Each circumstance had been in my favor: quiet, damp woods, a gentle breeze favoring my direction of hunting, and the common, natural tendency of the white-tailed buck to remain hidden even at the close approach of the hunter. It was mere chance that I discovered the fresh tracks, turning me toward the deer's hiding place; and at once he knew the jig was up—therefore his mad dash for safety.

It is in such a fortuitous hunt, when Lady Luck smiles, that the sportsman reaches the greatest heights of hunting thrills and pleasure. True still-hunting will ever be a solitary effort, one in which the successful hunter can take the greatest pride of accomplishment. He has outwitted our most cautious and instinctively clever species of wildlife at its own game. The satisfaction of taking a white-tailed buck by still-hunting methods alone can never be approached by killing a buck that has been driven to the stander.

Of course, still-hunting poses myriad problems. Much of our good deer-hunting territory is not well suited for still-hunting. For example, the heavy scrub-oak territory of many Pennsylvania counties makes a close approach to deer almost impossible. A large portion of New York's Sullivan County is heavily thatched with scrub oak, laurel and rhododendron, so the hunter can never approach deer without driving them ahead, far out of seeing or shooting range. Many sections of deer country abound in similar obstacles to the still-hunter.

The ideal type of cover for still-hunting is the rolling, many-ridged hardwood lands, where timber is heavy enough to discourage dense undergrowth. This is not to say that virgin-forest growth is good deer country, for generally it is not. Rather the best still-hunting country is a combination of big hardwood ridges and small valleys covered with good, low undergrowth for deer feeding grounds. An example of such country can be found in the Northville area of New York state.

Here, in the southern foothills of the Adirondacks, at the northern extremities of Sacandaga Reservoir, lies just this type of rolling hardwood country. The tiny valleys lying within these hills are well thatched with small white birch, cedar, poplar and alder, as well as many other types of good deer feed.

The Catskill area offers many good still-hunting sections: Slide Mountain near Phoenicia, the Red Hill section farther south near Claryville, the whole Upper Neversink River Valley—to name a few.

Heavy spruce areas such as we find in the western Adirondacks are difficult to hunt. Vision is limited to the extreme in such areas by the constant walls of evergreens. Under these conditions deer can gain a safe hiding place in a few bounds, in almost any direction, giving little opportunity for a shot.

But good still-hunting areas can be found in any state where the whitetail is numerous—Vermont, New Hampshire, Michigan, Wisconsin or Maine, or whatever state happens to be the hunter's choice.

Most of my deer country is discovered on fishing trips, for actually a deer hunter never stops hunting, even on his summer jaunts. Many of my best hunting experiences have been enjoyed in areas I scouted during summer. After arming myself with topographical maps of my chosen area, I would be ready to hunt when opening day came around.

Another and perhaps more important problem for the still-hunter is the abundance of other hunters in his area. Still-hunting is hardly practical when many hunters are tramping the woods in groups of two, three or even more. The deer become highly alarmed in any section where hunters are on the move all day, so much so that the slightest noise will tend to send them off at top speed. Deer under these conditions of heavy hunting have had their routine of natural habits broken. They feed little, if at all, during daylight and bed down in the heaviest thickets they can find.

There is a personal element, too, under such a setup. It is hardly advisable for any hunter to go pussyfooting through deer country if there are many hunters strewn throughout the area. There is ever the thousand-to-one chance that a slowly moving hunter can be mistaken for a deer by one of his brethren. It is highly important, then, to pick your still-hunting grounds with a view to hunting pressure as well as abundance of deer and favorable terrain.

However, we do have many sections of good deer country where still-hunting methods are the only practical means to kill your buck. We speak now of the great wilderness areas of Michigan's Upper Peninsula, the North Woods of Maine, a great portion of the Adirondacks, or any true wilderness area accessible to hunters only by trails or waterways. Here, the deer are continually in a wild state, unfamiliar with the sight or scent of man. Perhaps many deer are born, live a normal span of existence and die without having seen a man. Hunting these deer successfully requires the best of woods craftsmanship.

It is just this type of hunting the writer prefers, but unfortunately, few of us have the time to devote to such a trip. Wilderness hunting involves considerable preparation, complete camping gear, and a knowledge of woodlore in sufficient quantity to make an extended stay outdoors a pleasure rather than a hardship. Its great compensation rests in the hunter's opportunity to disassociate himself from the humdrum existence and the platitudes of normal living. Here, the hunter must be virtually self-sufficient. He must walk many miles over dim trails carrying his camping and hunting gear on his back. He must depend on his wits and ability to provide a good bed, good food and reasonable living comfort in camp. But most of all, he must lean heavily on his still-hunting knowledge and ability to bag his buck. Any buck killed under these conditions will ever be the most highly prized trophy in a sportsman's collection.

And in wilderness areas there is no other way to kill deer. No methods of deer hunting other than still-hunting are practical. The terrain is of great scope. There may be many deer, but the animals are scattered over thousands of acres of timbered woodland. The still-hunter must seek until he locates his deer.

Many times I have thought deer hunters are becoming soft. Most of us can find deer within a few hours' drive of our homes. We drive into deer country, park our cars and in five minutes are hunting in productive country. I must admit this is good. In many cases it means a man is able to hunt deer where otherwise he would never be able to enjoy this sport.

But in another sense, much of the true hunting spirit is lost if we hunt deer only under these conditions. The man who has the initiative to seek deer in wilderness areas is the hunter who gains the most from his hunting. Still-hunting is becoming a lost art in many sections, primarily because of unfavorable local conditions, but often because of general inertia on the part of the hunter. To those who say there are too many hunters coming into their favorite haunts, or that the deer are being killed off, we can advise turning to wilderness areas. There still are many thousands of acres of wonderfully scenic forests, abundant with deer, that have scarcely felt the tread of a hunter's feet. Let these men get maps of the areas they would like to hunt, study them well, prepare the necessary camping gear, and when the season is at hand, "go back in" for a week or two where there are still many wild deer for the taking if the hunter possesses the skill and intestinal fortitude to make the grade.

Defining the Term

"Still-hunting" is, as a term, slightly ambiguous. It is not to be confused with the common practice of sitting on a deer run all day—day after day—hoping a buck will come along sooner or later. This method can be highly successful, but it should never masquerade as still-hunting. Rather, it might be more aptly named "ambushing."

This difference in terminology was driven home to me quite a number of years ago, during my early days of deer hunting. I had driven up to Wolf Pond, right in the heart of Sullivan County's best deer hunting, one morning in the early part of the open season. When I reached the old hand-laid stone dam, there was a large party of hunters gathered atop the dam, waiting for good daylight before taking to the woods.

Sitting apart from this group was another hunter—advanced in years and no doubt, I thought, well learned in the art of deer hunting. I struck up a conversation by asking him if he was hunting with the gang.

"No," he said. "This bunch is going up in the scrub oaks and drive the hell out of 'em. They've been doin' it all week. Guess they killed one buck so far. But I'm going to take it easy and do a little still-huntin'."

I looked him over pretty carefully after that remark. He was bundled up in a heavy sheepskin coat, covering layers of wool shirts and sweaters. His feet were well covered with a pair of huge felt boots into the tops of which were stuffed at least two pairs of trousers. He carried a huge lunch basket in one hand with a giant-size "Thermos" bottle resting upright in one corner. In the other hand hung a double hammer-gun of ancient vintage. Quite an outfit, I decided, for a still-hunter. Then I made off up the trail to do a bit of hunting myself.

Later that day, I happened on this same character, sitting a few yards off the trail, but not more than a hundred yards from the Wolf Pond Dam. I stopped to ask him if he'd seen anything yet and he told me, "Only a couple of does."

"Thought you were going to do some still-hunting," I remarked.

"Well, by God," he replied, "don't you think for a minute that I ain't been. I been here all day—haven't moved a bit since sunup. This here's a mighty good run, and I know I'll get a shot if I sit here long enough." So much for that brand of still-hunting.

I do not intend to ridicule those who prefer to hunt deer by careful watching and waiting near runways and feeding grounds. Many times it is the only way to kill a wary old buck that has been outwitting still-hunters and deer drives season after season. The true still-hunter, as a matter of fact, does a great deal of watchful waiting as he moves over deer territory. Looking, stopping and watching with patience and care has many times filled a deer license, more often indeed than has barging through deer country without regard or respect for a deer's keenness of vision, hearing and olfactory senses.

The principal drawback in this ambush style of modified still-hunting is that the hunter sees but little deer country. More valuable in deer hunting than patient waiting is a true, firsthand knowledge of the movements of deer in the area. This can only be gained by moving quietly through the woods and swamps, studying tracks, runs, bedding grounds and all the many signs that the experienced woodsman can interpret in terms of deer lore. This is still-hunting's greatest boon.

Add to this that in cold weather only the most Spartan courage can keep a hunter on a stand hour after hour throughout even the shortest fall or winter day. Such hunting limits the scope of a sportsman's knowledge. I know a goodly number of men who hunt deer year after year, and of this group none have yet seen for themselves the telltale rub of a buck on a green sapling. These hunters lose most of the charm of still-hunting. Deer hunting for them becomes a battle with the elements, often antagonistic during the open season in any of the northern deer hunting zones.

Frankly, I lack the infinite patience and courage to face a bitterly cold day on a runway stand. Feet become painfully inanimate lumps of frozen flesh, fingers almost crackle with frost, and the entire human frame soon vibrates like a strummed harp. The entire picture is out of tune with the normal theme of deer hunting thrills and pleasure.

Overlooking Hidden Deer

The hunter who follows the still-hunting game alone adheres to a typical ritual. He works the lower feeding grounds during the early morning and late-afternoon hours. When the sun climbs above the treetops, he begins to look for bedded deer on ridgetops or along the edges of heavy swamps or thickets of evergreens. In any case, he covers ground slowly, traveling the route that will permit motion through the woods with a minimum of noise. Feet are placed carefully on moss or rock at every opportunity, keeping away from the noisy rustlings of dead leaves. He travels wood roads wherever possible to keep clothing from brushing noisily through the small branches.

Many times a hunter will give up still-hunting entirely when the woods are dry and noisy. This can be a serious mistake. Deer are not instantly alarmed at the noise of a hunter's footfalls in dry leaves. Logically, such a noise could be made by other deer, squirrels, partridge, wood mice or myriad other creatures. It is to be expected that deer will usually take off if they see the hunter after their attention is aroused by such noises.

On the credit side of the ledger, we can say a smart still-hunter will often spot his deer before its alarm sends it crashing away. Again, white-tailed deer have a habit of standing still at the hunter's approach if they think they are well-concealed, or that the hunter will pass them by.

I recall an incident that illustrates this tendency to remain quiet in attempts to go undetected. I was not hunting deer at the time, for the season was a few days away. Following one of my customs, I was hunting partridge in a favorite deer cover up on the Shawangunk Mountain range. It was a windy day with a decided fall bite in the air. The birds were wild, and my setter was ranging out a bit more than he would have been normally. Now and then he would pass out of sight and I would whistle him in. The air was filled with falling leaves, setting the whole mountain slope in motion. There were many deer signs, but so far I had not jumped a deer. Nor did I expect to, for I had taken no pains to conceal my movements or the dog's.

At last there was a time I failed to see Pep for several minutes. I found myself near a high ledge that dropped away below me for 15 or 20 feet. I was not yet near enough to the cliff's rim to see beyond, so whistling and calling as I went, I came to the edge for a look below it. I searched the long slope stretching down through the big timber below for several minutes, still whistling and calling for the dog. Suddenly he appeared by my side and at once, he stiffened and looked down over the cliff.

Following his lead, I too looked down, directly below the ledge.

Right at the base of the rock lay two deer, a forkhorn buck and a doe, both flattened out on the leaf-strewn ground as though they would like to sink still farther into concealment. For a space of several seconds they lay still, then in a single motion they leaped from their beds and disappeared along the ledge. The appearance of the dog was the factor that routed them out.

I had stood quite a bit just above them, shouting and whistling like a maniac, and I have no doubt they would have remained there in frozen immovability had not the dog appeared. I am also certain I would not have been aware of them if they had remained quietly huddled at the ledge base and had not the setter come at that moment. At no time was I more than 30 feet from these deer, but they managed to fight off any wave of nervous timidity with the knowledge they were well hidden.

Deer continually follow this practice of allowing the hunter to pass and then making off quietly in the opposite direction. It is fully as important for a lone still-hunter to watch his back trail occasionally as it is for him to be alert for deer ahead. Every time the hunter passes a heavy thicket or clump of evergreens or rhododendron he should stop and watch behind for a glimpse of brown sliding and shifting away through cover. And it's amazing to observe the ability of a sneaking deer to move with little noise, whether it be through scrub oak, tangled cat-briers or over crusted snow.

Weather has a bearing on a still-hunter's success. Ideal conditions are damp weather or the period immediately after rain or light snow. Dampness softens all woods noises and at the same time makes fresh deer sign more apparent. Connected also is the tendency of deer to hide during a storm and move about for feed directly after the storm clears.

A quietly damp day with little wind and with all dead leaves fallen clear of trees and brush makes an ideal day for still-hunting. I personally dislike still-hunting in windy weather. The thrashing of wind-whipped branches, the heavy sighing of evergreens, and the constant motion and rustling of dead leaves fills the ears to the exclusion of all other noises.

Yet I have several successful still-hunting friends who much prefer windy days. They maintain the noise of wind-swept forests effectively covers smaller noises made by their movements. Add to this the fact that with trees and brush constantly in motion, the hunter's movements are more or less concealed or made less apparent. I see the logic, but so far it has not worked out for me. I find that deer behavior on a windy day is skittish in the extreme, and that they often dash off at any slight alarm.

In my mind, the hunter who is most benefited by windy weather is one with defective hearing. Under normally quiet conditions, such a man is at a disadvantage. The deer can hear him long before he can detect their movements by sound alone. But on a windy day, every hunter must depend virtually on his eyes alone, and this factor places the sportsman with poor auditory senses on an equal footing with those of us who are more fortunately equipped.

Old George Drake, well-known to fishermen and hunters alike in the Lower Catskill region, had poor hearing during his last few years in the woods. But he continued to kill his buck with astonishing regularity. George was a woodsman of outstanding skill which he gained during his market-hunting days with an old muzzleloader. Several times he confided to me that the wind had helped him get close enough to a buck to be able to get his shot. Until the time of his death a few years ago, his vision in the woods was of the best, even though he could barely read the local newspaper at a close range. Nature might have helped balance the scales by enabling his old eyes to see well enough to overcome his other loss.

All other things being equal, the quiet day offers the best possible opportunities for the still-hunter. It is then he can match wits with whitetails on a more equal footing. I say "more equal" advisedly, for none of us can hope to be as familiar with any deer country as are the deer.

Using Maps to Pick Hunting Areas

An intimate knowledge of the terrain to be hunted is mandatory if the still-hunter would kill his buck by not merely trusting to luck. In wilderness areas of wide scope, no hunter will have the time to spend on preseason trips to learn the layout. It is here that topographical maps come into their own.

If the sportsman has a definite idea as to where he intends to hunt, it is advisable to acquire topographical maps of the region. I remember an incident that proved to me the infinite value of these maps.

A few years ago, a friend took me on a deer-hunting trip up into Warren County in the Adirondacks. We planned a week's stay back in the woods, so we prepared our camping gear and started off. After getting to the end of the road, we packed in and made camp. We had a grand hunt; each of us had his buck at the end of the fourth day. We packed them out after breaking camp and started for home after a week of glorious weather and ideal hunting in some of the best still-hunting territory I have ever visited.

The years passed, and my partner of this trip had moved out to the Midwest. Once again I wanted to make the trip back to this hunting spot, but I had no accurate idea how to reach it. The topographical map came to my rescue. I picked out two quadrangles covering the general area and, together with a state highway map, I was able to locate accurately not only the exact route by car, but even the trail we had taken to the camping spot. Many times since I have had occasion to seek new hunting and fishing grounds with these maps. Indeed, I am never without a complete set, covering most of my hunting and fishing grounds.

Of course, many maps are not up to date as to trails and highways, but the country is the same as it was the day it was mapped. By intelligent study of the individual quadrangles, an accurate mental picture of the terrain can be visualized. Streams, lakes and swamps are accurately detailed; contour lines show every elevation. Valleys and ridges, steep hillsides and cliffs are graphically detailed. In a word, no area can be strange to the hunter who studies a topographical map.

Any experienced still-hunter can pick out on these maps the areas to hunt. Crossings through ridge saddles can be determined, and swamp hiding places brought to light. Watering places and streams are, of course, at once evident, and if the still-hunter plans a camping trip, he is able to pick out the exact trail to carry him to good water.

The maps are roughly 16 by 20 inches, and if they are to be carried on a trip, as they should be, they can be pasted on cheesecloth or muslin, rolled up and carried in a mailing tube. Reposing on my den wall is a large map of the Catskills area, made up by joining quadrangles together, the whole mounted on muslin. I have it covered with various colors of map tacks pointing out deer areas, trout and bass waters, and any other facts of interest to my sportsmen visitors. I consider it one of the most interesting additions to my equipment.

Still-Hunting the Wind

It has often been advised by authoritative writers that the still-hunter should always hunt upwind. The purpose, of course, is to prevent man-scent from reaching the deer in advance of the hunter. No doubt, a deer can pick up scent for 200 yards if it's carried by a stiff breeze. Generally speaking, it is good advice to keep downwind of any game, particularly deer. I fear, however, that in some areas, the hunter will be hunting uphill and down dale all day long if he sticks to the letter of the rule. If the ridge we propose to hunt runs north and south and the wind blows east to west, we have little choice but to follow the ridge. Certainly, we will never hunt straight up the side of the slope and down over the other side merely to keep heading into the wind.

In every hunting problem, rules must be tempered with good judgment, and in this matter of hunting against the wind, there can be no hard-and-fast rule. A hunter's strategy is dictated, for the most part, by the lay of the land. And in rolling, hardwood white-tailed deer country, the contours of the land are broken up in many ways by cliffs, ravines, pinnacles and knobs. Wind direction over such terrain is fitful and flighty. One moment we will feel a touch on the right cheek, and as we move past a rock ledge, the breeze will come directly toward us. In mountainous areas, the bright sunlight, beaming down on a southern slope, will create a heavy updraft, nullifying wind direction on this slope. Many times in a single hunt I have found the breeze shifting in every conceivable direction.

If the wind is fairly stiff, these modifying factors will be overcome, but in any case the hunter will abide by the influence of the terrain. He must keep a general upwind direction if possible, but it is not vitally important that he face forever into the wind. A good crosswind, either to right or left, is every bit as effective in keeping away man-scent from deer, at least until the still-hunter is abreast of the quarry.

In hunting a ridge, I prefer a cross-breeze, keeping on the downwind shoulder of the ridge as I move slowly along. Deer often keep constant watch along the top of the ridge in both directions. They seem vaguely to expect a higher incidence of danger along the crest of a ridge. It is wise then to keep just far enough away from the top of the ridge to yet be able to see any movement upon it. In no instance, however, will a still-hunter move in a deliberate downwind direction—this simply advertises his presence to every whitetail in the area ahead.

The term "still-hunting" is in itself connotative of the hunter's actions while in the woods. Every effort must be made to move slowly and with a minimum of noise underfoot. The cracking of dead branches, the rattling of loose rocks and other carelessly made noises are definitely foreign to the progress through the woods of any wild animal, except possibly a black bear or a frightened deer. Primarily, the still-hunter is most concerned with seeing or hearing his deer before the deer sees him. His every movement must be directed to this end.

Strive to Move Slowly

The thought that much territory should be covered in a day's hunt must be abandoned. This single factor has contributed to many an unsuccessful day in a deer hunter's season. No one, even the best woodsman, can cover five or six miles of territory silently and with caution and see the movements of game within his travels. The watchword must ever be: Move slowly, watch carefully and listen closely. Each time the hunter comes to a strategic spot where deer might cross, let him stop, first picking a suitable background where his silhouette will not stand out in bold outline.

Deer are highly conscious of any new object in their home covers. If the hunter is foolish enough to permit his body to be seen against an open skyline or atop a rock-ledge or big boulder, he cannot, in all honesty, complain if he fails to get a fair shot at his buck. The best policy is to stand against a neutral background—a scrub-oak patch, a big tree trunk or a boulder, first being certain the background is large enough to cover his outline. Suitably placed, a passing deer might see him, but if he remains quiet and the wind favors him, there is every possibility the deer will not be alarmed.

There is still another important factor in watchful waiting. Often the most careful approach and intelligent observation will fail to give the hunter a look at his deer before it makes off. If the cover is good, and the buck has been making the area his regular hangout, the chance is great he will return shortly. Any prime, wise buck is reluctant to leave his home bailiwick unless he is badly frightened. The passage of an occasional hunter seldom routs a buck for long from his home coverts. The wise still-hunter who discovers fresh tracks leading away from an obviously good hideout will do well to spend a quiet hour waiting for the buck to come sneaking back home.

In any heavily hunted deer territory, the older bucks have a habit of selecting a good high ridge, a heavy scrub-oak thicket or some other spot where a hunter cannot approach without the deer's being aware of the danger. When one of these bucks locates such a safe spot for his hideout, it requires plenty of hunting to keep him away from it. He might be scared off by a still-hunter or driven out by a drive, but 10-to-1, he will make every effort to get back again, provided the source of danger has apparently left the area.

I have had the opportunity to kill several bucks this way after locating their hideaways. One of these deer bedded down on a narrow scrub-oak ridge. Through the middle of the scrub oaks and lying along the crest of the ridge ran an old abandoned woods road. Many years of disuse had filled the road with tangled blow-downs and small brush, making quiet progress impossible. By the process of elimination, I discovered this buck would take to this scrub-oak patch as soon as the first rifles began to crack after the opening-day sunrise.

Twice in as many days I jumped him out of the scrub, but never caught a glimpse of him. Then I decided it might be good strategy to drive him out to a stand, giving someone a shot. I gathered together six of my hunting pals and mapped out a still-drive, thinking he would run atop the ridge, follow it to the end and give a shot to the standers I had posted at the top of the ridge where it sloped down to the creek bed. But he was too wise for us. Twice we jumped him but he failed to run the ridge. He went down the slopes to the nearest swamp, and there was never a stander near his route. He eluded our efforts that year, but I decided to try for him again next season if he still used that scrub-oak ridge.

Before the whitetail season came around the next year, I looked carefully for his tracks. They were sprinkled all over the ridge. I found two fresh beds in the scrub oak, and nearby, a well-defined run where this buck had rubbed and gouged a small maple tree in pre-mating exuberance.

There were many signs he had been active on the ridge, but no tracks of other deer were evident. Apparently the ridge was not used by other deer, or else this buck had driven off outsiders.

I decided to wait for him on one of his runways after daylight on opening day. I waited and waited for two days but he never appeared. I believed then that he was leaving the ridge after dark each night, feeding in the lower valley areas, and returning before daylight each morning. His fresh tracks were much in evidence each morning so I could make no other deduction. Accordingly, at dark of the second day's hunt, I tied my black thread across the runways in two places. Next morning both threads were hanging limply.

By this time I was a bit desperate, so I decided to jump him out of his bed just to make him "git." I swung up over the ridge, fighting my way down the wood road. I went through to the end of the cover about a quarter-mile, then swung back through the scrub oak itself. I never heard the buck leave, but I found fresh tracks leading down toward the runway. The tracks indicated he was in a hurry.

Will He Return?

Satisfied that I had at least disturbed his siesta, I walked out to the edge of the scrub and dropped down on a mossy patch near his runway for a rest. Plowing scrub oak and brush for an hour had taken a little pep from my legs and shortened my breath to little pants. I soaked in a bit of November sunshine, listened to the red squirrels chattering and the little mountain brook gurgling below me. Suddenly, a gang of bluejays set up a raucous chorus over on the next little ridge, and then just as suddenly, flew off in silence. Disturbed by a hunter, I thought idly, wondering meanwhile if he had heard the buck come off the ridge.

I passed many minutes in this fashion, planning new stratagems to outwit this deer, for by this time he had become an obsession. In fact, I dreamed one night that I had killed him, but I had not dreamed in sufficient detail, so it wasn't of much help. I had not yet set eyes on this buck, but I could envision a great spread of antlers crowning a massive head and neck, an idea no doubt implanted by deep gouges in the trunk of the little maple he had rubbed.

Somewhat lost in this haze of thought, I gradually became aware of tiny noises, foreign to the normal sound pattern, filling my ears. I glanced across to the other ridge but saw nothing strange. Again I heard a mumbling footfall and rustling of twigs, but could not make out any movement in the low second-growth that separated me from the other hardwood ridge across the valley of the little brook.

Without warning, I saw sunlight flash on antlers as a buck moved slowly through the underbrush toward the brook, heading in the direction of the runway. He paused now and raised his head in my direction, lifting it until I could see the full wide spread of his long-tined antlers and the tips of his ears.

I waited until he began to move again, then I shifted my position slightly until I could bring the short-barreled Krag into line with his path. He was in no hurry. He stopped many times, probably to test the wind and listen for noises up on his scrub-oak ridge. Now he was quartering toward me, only 50 yards off, and still I could see no part of his body through the underbrush. Approaching the brook, he stopped dead-still in a little alder clump on the far bank.

For many minutes he stood there, his antler tips shifting right and left as he cautiously looked over the area ahead. Then, in a single leap, he cleared the brook and walked into a big white-birch clump. At the edge of the white birch lay his runway. My front sight rested on the runway where he should emerge, held at knee level. My breath again was short, but for a different reason. My heart click-clicked in my throat. I thought he never would show himself. The suspense was frightful.

Slowly he poked a black nose out of the birches, head low now, as he sniffed at the runway. His front hoofs came into the opening and my front sight lifted to his neck as he quartered toward me. I squeezed off the shot. The muzzle blast blotted him out of my vision for just a fraction of an instant and then he lay across the runway, all four hoofs in the air, kicking out his last moments. He never regained his hoofs nor moved from the spot where he first came to earth. The open-point bullet had blasted a two-inch section from his neck vertebrae.

Don't be Quick to Move

It was evident this buck never moved far from his hiding place in daylight. When alarmed, he simply moved off the ridge, crossed the brook and went up on another ridge, likely staying there until things quieted down, when he would again carefully pick his way back to safety. He was a fine animal with long wide beams and carried eight long points. His dressed weight was just over 180 pounds. A splendid buck added to my list of trophies, simply by watching and waiting in the luckily chosen proper spot.

A buck will often be aroused by a prowling hunter, and his natural caution will dictate moving. But until he has precisely located the hunter, he might remain hidden until he is certain in which direction the danger lies.

On two occasions, I have jumped bucks while still-hunting, bucks that jumped only at the noise of my approach and who then stood quietly waiting to spot the danger. One of these moved into a heavy spruce thicket and stood there many minutes. When I alarmed this deer, I had been fighting my way through some of this same spruce and any progress I made was far from silent. However, when I heard the deer jump just ahead, I stood still and watched carefully all about me on the ridgetop. I was aware that after the deer had jumped, I had heard only a few bounds, then silence. I suspected he might still be hiding in the heavy evergreens, so I waited for him to move out. The air was motionless, the day damp, giving any man-scent that might have carried from me a limited range.

As I stood there in the quiet of the spruces, I thought I could hear a faint sniffing noise. At first it puzzled me, but at last it dawned on me that my buck was a short way ahead, screened effectively and most likely wondering where I had gone.

Perhaps 15 minutes passed before he decided it was safe, and he walked out at right angles to his original flight. I could hear him moving through the spruce off to my right and then I caught a glimpse as he crossed a small opening in the green curtain. He moved slowly, stopping often to listen and watch, but at last he came out of the spruce thicket, giving me a standing shot at its edge. This was another buck I did not have to trail after the shot.

Normally, of course, a buck fully aroused will move quietly away and never be seen, but every so often we'll run across one who pulls just such a trick as this. It pays then to play hunches when still-hunting.

PART SEVEN

SHORT STORIES

For reasons that largely elude this editor, relatively little in the way of what might be termed short stories has been produced in the field of writings on whitetails. Such is the case if you compare the genre with other aspects of outdoor life such as bird hunting, fly fishing, gundogs and the like. Yet perhaps this is a situation where quality supplants quantity.

There can be no argument about the quality of the three pieces offered here, although nitpickers and naysayers might raise questions as to whether they all fall squarely in the short story genre.

Certainly, William Faulkner's "Race at Morning" qualifies. Few indeed are the magazines being published today that would give a selection of this length, no matter its merits, so much as a second glance. Similarly, Robert Ruark's "Mr. Howard Was a Real Gent," even in the slightly abbreviated form offered here, is two-fold or three-fold longer than what would be acceptable to today's publishers (it originally appeared as a column in *Field & Stream*).

Perhaps most surprising of all, and it is a testament to the manner in which *Sporting Classics* magazine has endeavored to be different throughout its almost four decades of existence, is Ryan Stalvey's "Blood Red Mackinaw." It reminds us that the sporting short story, while not exactly thriving in today's world, still survives and can hold a special place in readers' hearts.

So dig in; prepare to wrap up this excursion into the world of the whitetail in stellar fashion, and be prepared for some pure pleasure. After all, who could ask for much more than material from a Nobel

The Greatest Deer Hunting Book Ever

Prize winner, one of the finest of countless first-rate efforts from a blockbuster novelist, a selection from one of the earliest scribes to look at deer hunting in detail, and a modern incarnation of a venerable storytelling tradition?

MR. HOWARD WAS A REAL GENT
By Robert Ruark

Originally published as one of his immensely popular "The Old Man and the Boy" columns in Field & Stream, *this story appears as Chapter 6 in* The Old Man and the Boy *(1957). Although generally considered one of the finest of a consistently top-level series of columns, this is the only "Old Man" tale in which deer hunting forms the primary subject matter.*

The week before Thanksgiving that year, one of the Old Man's best buddies came down from Maryland to spend a piece with the family, and I liked him a whole lot right from the start. Probably it was because he looked like the Old Man—ragged mustache, smoked a pipe, built sort of solid, and he treated me like I was grown up, too. He was interested in 'most everything I was doing. He admired my shotgun and told me a whole lot about the dogs and horses he had up on his big farm outside of Baltimore.

He and the Old Man had been friends for a whole lot of years; they had been all over the world, and they were always sitting out on the front porch, smoking and laughing quietly together over some devilment they'd been up to before I was born. I noticed they always shut up pretty quick when Miss Lottie, who was my grandma, showed up on the scene. Sometimes, when they'd come back from walking down by the river, I could smell a little ripe aroma around them that smelled an awful lot like the stuff that the Old Man kept in his room to keep the chills off him. The Old Man's friend was named Mister Howard.

They were planning to pack up the dogs and guns and a tent and go off on a camping trip for a whole week, 'way into the woods behind Allen's Creek about 15 miles from town. They talked about it for days, fussing around with cooking gear, and going to the store to pick up this and that, and laying out clothes. They never said a word to me; they acted as if I wasn't there at all. I was very good all the time. I never spoke at the table unless I was spoken to, and I never asked for more than I ate, and I kept pretty clean and neat, for me. My tongue was hanging out like a thirsty hound dog's. One day, I couldn't stand it any longer.

"I want to go, too," I said. "You promised last summer you'd take me camping if I behaved myself and quit stealing your cigars and didn't get drowned and—"

"What do you think, Ned?" Mister Howard asked the Old Man. "Think we could use him around camp, to do the chores and go for water and such as that?"

"I dunno," the Old Man said. "He'd probably be an awful nuisance. Probably get lost and we'd have to go look for him, or shoot one of us thinking we were a deer, or get sick or bust a leg or something. He's always breaking something. Man can't read his paper around here for the sound of snapping bones."

"Oh, hell, Ned," Mister Howard said, "let's take him. Maybe we can teach him a couple of things. We can always get Tom or Pete to run him back in the flivver if he don't behave."

"Well," the Old Man said, grinning, "I'd sort of planned to fetch him along all along, but I was waiting to see how long it'd take him to ask."

We crowded a lot of stuff into that old tin Liz. Mister Howard and the Old Man and me and two bird dogs and two hound dogs and a sort of flee dog who was death on squirrels and a big springer spaniel who was death on ducks.

Then there were Tom and Pete, two kind of half-Indian backwoods boys who divided their year into four parts. They fished in the summer and hunted in the fall. They made corn liquor in the winter and drank it up in the spring. They were big, dark, lean men, very quiet and strong. Both of them always wore hip-boots, in the town and in the woods, on the water or in their own back yards. Both of them worked for the Old Man when the fishing season was on and the pogies were running in big, red, fat-backed schools. They knew just about everything about dogs and woods and water and game that I wanted to know.

The back seat was full of dogs and people and cooking stuff and guns. There were a couple of tents strapped on top of the Liz, a big one and a small one. That old tin can sounded like a boiler factory when we ran over the bumps in the corduroy clay road. I didn't say anything as we rode along. I was much too excited; and anyhow, I figured they might decide to send me back home.

It took us a couple of hours of bumping through the long, yellow savanna-land hills before we came up to a big pond, about 500 yards from a swamp, or branch, with a clear creek running through it. We drove the flivver up under a group of three big-water oaks and parked her.

The Old Man had camped there lots before, he said. There was a cleared-out space of clean ground about 50 yards square between the trees and the branch. And there was a small fireplace, or what had been a small fireplace, of big stones. They were scattered around now, all over the place. A flock of tin cans and some old bottles and such had been tossed off in the bush.

"Damned tourists," the Old Man muttered, unloading some tin pots and pans from the back of the car. "Come in here to a man's best place and leave it looking like a hog wallow. You, son, go pick up those cans and bury them some place out of my sight. Then come back here and help with the tents."

By the time I finished collecting the mess and burying it, the men had the tents laid out flat on the ground, the flaps fronting south, because there was a pretty stiff northerly wind working, and facing in the direction of the pond. Tom crawled under the canvas with one pole and a rope, and Pete lifted the front end with another pole and the other end of the rope. Mister Howard was behind with the end of Tom's rope and a peg and a maul. The Old Man was at the front with the end of Pete's rope and another stake and maul. The boys in the tent gave a heave, set the posts, and the two old men hauled taut on the ropes and took a couple of turns around the pegs.

The tent hung there like a blanket on a clothesline until Tom and Pete scuttled out and pegged her out stiff and taut from the sides. They pounded the pegs deep into the dirt, so that the lines around the notches were clean into the earth. It was a simple tent, just a canvas V with flaps fore and aft, but enough to keep the wet out. The other one went up the same way.

We didn't have any bedrolls in those days, or cots either. The Old Man gave me a hatchet and sent me off to chop the branches of the longleaf pine saplings that grew all around—big green needles a foot and a half long.

While I was gone, he cut eight pine stakes off an old stump, getting a two-foot stake every time he slivered off the stump, and then he cut four long oak saplings. He hammered the stakes into the ground inside the tent until he had a wide rectangle about six by eight feet. Then he split the tops of the stakes. He wedged two saplings into the stakes lengthwise, jamming them with the flat of the ax, and then he jammed two shorter saplings into the others, crosswise. He took four short lengths of heavy fishing cord and tied the saplings to the stakes, at each of the four corners, until he had a framework six inches off the ground.

"Gimme those pine boughs," he said to me," and go fetch more until I tell you to stop."

The Old Man took the fresh-cut pine branches, the resin still oozing stickily off the bright yellow slashes, and started shingling them, butt to the ground. He overlapped the needles like shingles on a house, always with the leaf end up and the branch end down to the ground. It took him about 15 minutes, but when he finished, he had a six-by-eight mattress of the spicy-smelling pine boughs. Then he took a length of canvas tarpaulin and arranged it neatly over the top. There were little grommet holes in each of the four corners, and he pegged the canvas tight over the tops of the saplings that confined the pine boughs. When he was through, you could hit it with your hand, and it was springy but firm.

"That's a better mattress than your grandma's got," the Old Man said, grinning over his shoulder as he hit the last lick with the ax. "All it needs is one blanket under you and one over you. You're off the ground, and dry as a bone, with pine needles to smell while you dream. It's just big enough for two men and a boy. The boy gets to sleep in the middle, and he better not thrash around and snore."

By the time he was through and I had spread the blankets, Tom and Pete had made themselves a bed in the other tent, just the same way. The whole operation didn't take half-an-hour from stopping the car until both tents and beds were ready.

While we were building the beds, Mister Howard had strung a line between a couple of trees and had tied a loop in the long leash of each dog, running the loop around the rope between the trees and jamming it with a square knot. The dogs had plenty of room to move in, but not enough to tangle up with each other, and not enough to start to fight when they got fed. Pretty soon they quit growling and lay down quietly.

We had two big canvas waterbags tied to the front of the flivver, and the Old Man gestured at them. "Boys have to handle the water detail in a man's camp," he said. "Go on down to the branch and fill 'em up at that little spillway. Don't roil up the water. Just stretch the necks and let the water run into the bags."

I walked down through the short yellow grass and the sparkleberry bushes to the branch, where you could hear the stream making little chuckling noises as it burbled over the rocks in its sandy bed. It was clear, brown water, and smelled a little like the crushed ferns and the wet brown leaves around it and in it.

When I got back, I could hear the sound of axes off in a scrub-oak thicket, where Tom and Pete had gone to gather wood. Mister Howard was sorting out the guns, and the Old Man was puttering around with the stones where the fire marks were. He didn't look up.

"Take the hatchet and go chop me some kindling off that lighter-knot stump," he said. "Cut 'em small, and try not to hit a knot and a chop off a foot. Won't need much, 'bout an armful."

When I got back with kindling, Tom and Pete were coming out of the scrub-oak thicket with huge, heaping armfuls of old dead branches and little logs as big as your leg. They stacked them neatly at a respectable distance from where the Old Man had just about finished his oven. It wasn't much of an oven—just three sides of stones, with one end open and a few stones at intervals in the middle. I dumped the kindling down by him, and he scruffed up an old newspaper and rigged the fat pine on top, in a little sharp-pointed tepee over the crumbled paper.

He put some small sticks of scrubby oak crisscross over the fat pine, and then laid four small logs, their ends pointing in to each other until they made a cross, over the stones and over the little wigwam of kindling he had erected. Then, he touched a match to the paper, and it went up in a poof. The blaze licked into the resiny lighterwood, which roared and crackled into flame, soaring in yellow spurts up to the other, stouter kindling and running eager tongues around the lips of the logs. In five minutes, it was roaring, reflecting bright red against the stones.

The Old Man got up and kicked his feet out to get the cramp out of his knees. It was just on late dusk. The sun had gone down, red over the hill, and the night chill was coming. You could see the fog rising in snaking wreaths out of the branch. The frogs were beginning to talk, and the night birds were stirring down at the edge of the swamp. A whippoorwill tuned up.

" 'Bout time we had a little snort, Howard," the Old Man said. "It's going to be chilly. Pete! Fetch the jug!"

Pete ducked into his tent and came out with a half-gallon jug of brown corn liquor. Tom produced four tin cups from the nest of cooking utensils at the foot of the tree on which they had hung the water bags, and each man poured a half-measure of the whisky into his cup. I reckoned there must have been at least half a pint in each cup. Tom got one of the water bags and tipped it into the whisky until each man said, "Whoa." They drank and sighed.

The Old Man cocked an eye at me and said, "This is for when you're bigger."

They had another drink before the fire had burned down to coals, with either Tom or Pete getting up to push the burning ends of the logs closer together. When they had a solid bed of coals glowing in the center of the stones, the Old Man heaved himself up and busied himself with a frying pan and some paper packages. He stuck a coffee pot off to one side, laid out five tin plates, dribbled coffee into the pot, hollered for me to fetch some water to pour into the pot, started carving up a loaf of bread, and slapped some big thick slices of ham into the frying pan.

When the ham was done, he put the slices, one by one, into the tin plates, which had warmed through from the fire, and laid slices of bread into the bubbling ham grease. Then he broke egg after egg onto the bread, stirred the whole mess into a thick, bread-egg-and-ham-grease omelet, chopped the omelet into sections, and plumped each section onto a slice of ham. He poured the steaming coffee into cups, jerked his thumb at a can of condensed milk and a paper bag of sugar, and announced that dinner was served.

He had to cook the same mess three more times and refill the coffee pot before we quit eating. It was black dark, with no moon, when we lay in front of the fire. The owls were talking over the whippoorwills, and the frogs were making an awful fuss.

The Old Man gestured at me. "Take the dirty dishes and the pans down to the branch and wash 'em," he said. "Do it now, before the grease sets. You won't need soap. Use sand. Better take a flashlight, and look out for snakes."

I was scared to go down there by myself, through that long stretch of grass and trees leading to the swamp, but I would have died before admitting it. The trees made all sorts of funny ghostly figures, and the noises were louder. When I got back, Mister Howard was feeding the dogs and the Old Man had pushed more logs on the fire.

"You better go to bed, son," the Old Man said. "Turn in in the middle. We'll be up early in the morning, and maybe get us a turkey."

I pulled off my shoes and crawled under the blanket. I heard the owl hoot again and the low mutter from the men, giant black shapes sitting before the fire. The pine-needle mattress smelled wonderful under me, and the blankets were warm. The fire pushed its heat into the tent, and I was as full of food as a tick. Just before I died, I figured that tomorrow had to be heaven.

It was awful cold when the Old Man hit me a lick in the ribs with his elbow and said, "Get up, boy, and fix that fire."

The stars were still up, frosty in the sky, and a wind was whistling round the corners of the tent. You could see the fire flicker just a mite against the black background of the swamp. Mister Howard was still snoring on his side of the pine-needle-canvas bed, and I remember that his mustache was riffling like marsh grass in the wind. Over in Tom and Pete's tent you could hear two breeds of snores.

One was squeaky, and the other sounded like a bull caught in a bob-wire fence. I crawled out from under the covers, shivering, and jumped into my hunting boots, which were stiff and very cold. Everything else I owned I'd slept in.

The fire was pretty feeble. It had simmered down into gray ash, which was swirling loosely in the morning breeze. There was just a little red eye blinking underneath the fine talcumy ashes. After kicking some of the ashes aside with my boot, I put a couple of lighterwood knots on top of the little chunk of glowing coals, and then I dragged some live-oak logs over the top of the lighterwood and waited for her to catch. She caught, and the tiny teeth of flame opened wide to eat the oak. In five minutes I had a blaze going, and I was practically in it. It was mean cold that morning.

When the Old Man saw the fire dancing, he woke up Mister Howard and reached for his pipe first and his boots next. Then he reached for the bottle and poured himself a dram in a tin cup. He shuddered some when the dram went down.

"I heartily disapprove of drinking in the morning," he said. "Except some mornings. It takes a man past sixty to know whether he can handle his liquor good enough to take a nip in the morning. Howard?"

"I'm past sixty, too," Mister Howard said. "Pass the jug."

Tom and Pete were coming out of the other tent, digging their knuckles into sleepy eyes. Pete went down to the branch and fetched a bucket of water, and everybody washed their faces out of the bucket. Then Pete went to the fire and slapped some ham into the pan and some eggs into the skillet, set some bread to toasting, and put the coffee pot on. Breakfast didn't take long. We had things to do that day.

After the second cup of coffee—I can still taste that coffee, with the condensed milk sweet curdled on the top and the coffee itself tasting of branch water and wood smoke—we got up and started sorting out the guns.

"This is a buckshot day," the Old Man said, squinting down the barrel of his pumpgun. "I think we better get us a deer today. Need meat in the camp, and maybe we can blood the boy. Tom, Pete, you all drive the branch. Howard, we'll put the boy on a stand where a buck is apt to amble by, and then you and I will kind of drift around according to where the noise seems headed. One, t'other of us ought to get a buck. This crick is populous with deer."

The Old Man paused to light his pipe, and then he turned around and pointed the stem at me.

"You, boy," he said. "By this time you know a lot about guns, but you don't know a lot about guns and deer together. Many a man loses his wits when he sees a big ol' buck bust out of the bushes with a rockin' chair on his head. Trained hunters shoot each other. They get overexcited and just bang away into the bushes.

"*Mind* what I say. A deer ain't a deer unless it has horns on its head, and you can see all of it at once. We don't shoot does and we don't shoot spike bucks and we don't shoot each other. There ain't no sense to shootin' a doe or a young'un. One buck can service hundreds of does, and one doe will breed you a mess of deer. If you shoot a young'un, you haven't got much meat, and no horns at all, and you've kept him from breedin' to make more deer for you to shoot. If you shoot a man, they'll likely hang you, and if the man is me, I will be awful gol-damned annoyed and come back to ha'nt you. You mind that gun, and don't pull a trigger until you can see what it is and *where* it is. *Mind*, I say."

Tom and Pete picked up their pumpguns and loaded them. They pushed the load lever down so there'd be no shell in the chamber, but only in the magazine.

The Old Man looked at my little gun and said, "Don't bother to load it until you get on the stand. You ain't likely to see anything to shoot for an hour or so."

Tom and Pete went over to where we had the dogs tethered on a line strung between two trees, and he unleashed the two hounds, Bell and Blue. Bell was black-and-tan and all hound. Blue was a kind of a sort of dog. He had some plain hound, some Walker hound, and some bulldog and a little beagle and a smidgen of pointer in him. He was ticked blue and brown and black and yellow and white. He looked as if somebody spilled eggs on a checkered tablecloth. But he was a mighty dandy deer dog, or so they said. Old Sam Watts, across the street, used to say there wasn't no use trying to tell Blue anything, because Blue had done forgot more than you knew and just got annoyed when you tried to tell him his business.

Tom snapped a short lead on Blue, and Pete snapped another one on Bell. They shouldered their guns and headed up the branch, against the wind. We let 'em walk, while the Old Man and Mister Howard puttered around, like old people and most women will. Drives a boy crazy. What I wanted to do was go and shoot myself a deer. *Now.*

After about ten minutes, the Old Man picked up his gun and said, "Let's go."

We walked about half-a-mile down the swamp's edge. The light had come now, lemon-colored, and the fox squirrels were beginning to chase each other through the gum trees. We spied one old possum in a tall persimmon tree, hunched into a ball and making out like nobody knew he was there. We heard a turkey gobble away over yonder somewheres, and we could hear the doves beginning to moan—*oooh— oohoo—oooooh.*

All the little birds started to squeak and chirp and twitter at each other. The dew was staunchly stiff on the grass and on the sparkleberry and gallberry bushes. It was still cold, but getting warmer, and breakfast had settled down real sturdy in my stomach. Rabbits jumped out from under our feet. We stepped smack onto a covey of quail just working its way out of the swamp, and they half scared me to death when they busted up under our feet. There was a lot going on in the swamp that morning.

We turned into the branch finally, and came up to a track that the Old Man said was a deer run. He looked around and spied a stump off to one side, hidden by a tangle of dead brush. From the stump you could see clear for about 50 yards in a sort of accidental arena.

"Go sit on that stump, boy," the Old Man said. "You'll hear the dogs after a while, and if a deer comes down this branch, he'll probably bust out there where that trail comes into the open, because there ain't any other way he can cross it without leaving the swamp.

Don't let the dogs fool you into not paying attention. When you hear 'em a mile away, the chances are that deer will be right in your lap. Sometimes they travel as much as two miles ahead of the dogs, just slipping along, not running; just slipping and sneaking on their little old quiet toes. And stay still. A deer'll run right over you if you stay still and the smell is away from him. But if you wink an eye, he can see it two hundred yards off, and will go the other way."

I sat down on the stump. The Old Man and Mister Howard went off, and I could hear them chatting quietly as they disappeared. I looked all around me. Nothing much was going on now, except a couple of he-squirrels were having a whale of a fight over my head, racing across branches and snarling squirrel cuss words at each other. A chickadee was standing on its head in a bush and making chickadee noises. A redheaded woodpecker was trying to cut a live-oak trunk in half with his bill. A rain crow—a kind of cuckoo, it is—was making dismal noises off behind me in the swamp, and a big old yellowhammer was swooping and dipping from tree to tree.

There were some robins hopping around on a patch of burnt ground, making conversation with each other. Crows were cawing, and two doves looped in to sit in a tree and chuckle at each other. A towhee was scratching and making more noise than a herd of turkeys, and some catbirds were meowing in the low bush while a big, sassy old mocker was imitating them kind of sarcastically.

Anybody who says woods are quiet is crazy. You learn how to listen. The Tower of Babel was a study period alongside of woods in the early morning.

It is wonderful to smell the morning. Anybody who's been around the woods knows that morning smells one way, high noon another, dusk still another, and night most different of all, if only because the skunks smell louder at night. Morning smells fresh and flowery, a little breezy and dewy and spanking new. Noon smells hot and a little dusty and sort of sleepy, when the breeze has died and the heads begin to droop and anything with any sense goes off into the shade to take a nap. Dusk smells scary. It is getting colder and everybody is going home tired for the day, and you can smell the turpentine scars on the trees and the burnt-off ground and the bruised ferns and the rising wind. You can hear the folding-up, I'm-finished-for-the-day sounds all around, including the colored boys whistling to prove they ain't scared when they drive the cows home. And in the night, you can smell the fire and the warm blankets and the coffee a-boil, and you can even smell the stars. I know that sounds silly, but on a cool, clear, frosty night the stars have a smell, or so it seems when you are young and acutely conscious of everything bigger than a chigger.

This was as nice a smelling morning as I can remember. It smelled like it was going to work into a real fine smelling day. The sun was up pretty high now and was beginning to warm the world. The dew was starting to dry, because the grass wasn't clear wet any more but just had little drops on top, like a kid with a runny nose.

I sat on the stump for about a half-hour, and then I heard the dogs start a mile or more down in the swamp. Bell picked up the trail first, and she sounded as if church had opened for business. Then Blue came in behind her, loud as an organ, their two voices blending—fading sometimes, getting stronger, changing direction always.

Maybe you never heard a hound in the woods on a frosty fall morning, with the breeze light, the sun heating up in the sky, and the "aweful" expectancy that something big was going to happen to you. There aren't many things like it. When the baying gets closer and closer and still closer to you, you feel as if maybe you're going to explode if something doesn't happen quick.

And when the direction changes and the dogs begin to fade, you feel so sick you want to throw up.

But Bell and Blue held the scent firmly now, and the belling was clear and steady. The deer was moving steady and straight, not trying to circle and fool the dogs, but honestly running. And the noise was coming straight down the branch, with me on the other end of it.

The dogs had come so close that you could hear them panting between their bays, and once or twice one of them quit sounding and broke into a yip-yap of barks. I thought I could hear a little tippety-tappety noise ahead of them, in between the belling and the barking, like mice running through paper or a rabbit hopping through dry leaves. I kept my eyes pinned onto where the deer path opened into the clearing. The dogs were so close that I could hear them crash.

All of a sudden, there was a flash of brown and two does, flop-eared, with two half-grown fawns skipped out of the brush, stopped dead in front of me, looked me smack in the face, and then gave a tremendous leap that carried them halfway across the clearing. They bounced again, white tails carried high, and disappeared into the branch behind me.

As I turned to watch them go, there was another crash ahead and a buck tore through the clearing like a race horse. He wasn't jumping. This boy was running like the wind, with his horns laid back against his spine and his ears pinned by the breeze he was making. The dogs were right behind him. He had held back to tease the dogs into letting his family get a start, and now that they were out of the way, he was pouring on the coal and heading for home.

I had a gun with me and the gun was loaded. I suppose it would have fired if the thought had occurred to me to pull the trigger. The thought never occurred. I just watched that big buck deer run, with my mouth open and my eyes popped out of my head.

The dogs tore out of the bush behind the buck, baying out their brains and covering the ground in leaps. Old Blue looked at me as he flashed past and curled his lip. He looked as if he were saying, "This is man's work, and what is a boy doing here, spoiling my labor?" Then he dived into the bush behind the buck.

I sat there on the stump and began to shake and tremble. About five minutes later, there was one shot, a quarter-mile down in the swamp. I sat on the stump. In about half-an-hour Tom and Pete came up to my clearing.

"What happened to the buck?" Pete said. "Didn't he come past here? I thought I was going to run him right over you."

"He came past, all right," I said, feeling sick-mean, "but I never shot. I never even thought about it until he was gone. I reckon you all ain't ever going to take me along any more." My lip was shaking and now I *was* about to cry.

Tom walked over and hit me on top of the head with the flat of his hand. "Happens to everybody," he said. "Grown men and boys, both, they all get buck fever. Got to do it once before you get over it. Forget it. I seen Pete here shoot five times at a buck big as a horse last year, and missed him with all five."

There were some footsteps in the branch where the deer had disappeared, and in a minute Mister Howard and the Old Man came out, with the dogs leashed and panting.

"Missed him clean," the Old Man said cheerfully. "Had one whack at him no farther'n thirty yards and missed him slick as a whistle. That's the way it is, but there's always tomorrow. Let's us go shoot some squirrels for the pot, and we'll rest the dogs and try again this evenin'. You *see* him, boy?"

"I *saw* him," I said. "And I ain't ever going to *forget* him."

We went back to camp and tied up the hounds. We unleashed the fice dog, Jackie, the little sort of yellow fox terrier kind of nothing dog with prick ears and a sharp fox's face and a thick tail that curved up over his back.

I was going with Pete to shoot some squirrels while the old gentlemen policed up the camp, rested, took a couple of drinks, and started to prepare lunch. It was pretty late in the morning for squirrel hunting, but this swamp wasn't hunted much. While I had been on the deer stand that morning, the swamp was alive with them—mostly big fox squirrels, huge old fellers with a lot of black on their gray-and-white hides.

"See you don't get squirrel fever," the Old Man hollered over his shoulder as Pete and I went down to the swamp. "Else we'll all starve to death. I'm about fresh out of ham and eggs."

"Don't pay no 'tention to him, son," Pete told me. "He's a great kidder."

"Hell with him," I said. "He missed the deer, didn't he? At least *I* didn't miss him."

"That's right," Pete agreed. "You got to shoot at 'em to miss 'em."

I looked quick and sharp at Pete. He didn't seem to be teasing me. A cigarette was hanging off the corner of his lip, and his lean, brown, Injun-looking face was completely straight. Then we heard Jackie, yip-yapping in a querulous bark, as if somebody had just insulted him by calling him a dog.

"Jackie done treed hisself a squirrel," Pete said. "Advantage of a dog like Jackie is that when the squirrels all come down to the ground to feed, ol' Jackie rousts 'em up and makes 'em head for the trees. Then he makes so much noise he keeps the squirrel interested while we go up and wallop away at him. Takes two men to hunt squirrels this way. Jackie barks. I go around to the other side of the tree. Squirrel sees me and moves. That's when you shoot him, when he slides around on your side. Gimme your gun."

"Why?" I asked. "What'll I use to shoot the—"

"*Mine*," Pete answered. "You ain't going to stand there and tell me you're gonna use a shotgun on a squirrel? Anybody can hit a poor little squirrel with a shotgun. Besides, shotgun shells cost a nickel apiece."

I noticed Pete's gun for the first time. He had left his pumpgun in camp and had a little bolt-action .22. He took my shotgun from me and handed me the .22 and a handful of cartridges.

" 'Nother thing you ought to know," Pete said as we walked up to the tree, a big blue gum under which Jackie seemed to be going mad, "is that when you're hunting for the pot, you don't want to make much more noise with guns than is necessary. You go booming off a shotgun, blim-blam, and you spook ever'thing in the neighborhood. A .22 don't make no more noise than a stick crackin', and agin the wind, you can't hear it more'n a hundred yards or thereabouts. Best meat gun in the world, a straight-shootin' .22, because it don't make no noise and don't spoil the meat. Look up yonder, on the fourth fork. There's your dinner. A big ol' fox squirrel, near-about black all over."

The squirrel was pasted to the side of the tree. Pete walked around, and the squirrel moved with him. When Pete was on the other side, making quite a lot of noise, the squirrel shifted back around to my side. He was peeping at Pete, but his shoulders and back and hind legs were on my side.

I raised the little .22 and plugged him between the shoulders. He came down like a sack of rocks. Jackie made a dash for him, grabbed him by the back, shook him once and broke his spine, and sort of spit him out on the ground. The squirrel was dang near as big as Jackie.

Pete and I hunted squirrels for an hour or so, and altogether we shot ten. Pete said that was enough for five people for a couple of meals, and there wasn't no sense to shootin' if the meat had to spoil.

"We'll have us some venison by tomorrow, anyways," he said. "One of us is bound to git one. You shot real nice with that little bitty gun," he said. "She'll go where you hold her, won't she?"

I felt pretty good when we went into camp and the Old Man, Mister Howard and Tom looked up inquiringly. Pete and I started dragging fox squirrels out of our hunting coats, and the ten of them made quite a sizable pile.

"Who shot the squirrels?" the Old Man asked genially. "The dog?"

"Sure," Pete grinned. "Dog's so good we've taught him to shoot, too. We jest set down on a log, give Jackie the gun, and sent him off into the branch on his lonesome. We're planning to teach him to skin 'em and cook 'em, right after lunch. This is the best dog I ever see. Got more sense than people."

"Got more sense than *some* people," the Old Man grunted." Come and git it, boy, and after lunch you and Jackie can skin the squirrels."

The lunch was a lunch I loved then and still love, which is why I'm never going to be called one of those epicures. This was a country hunting lunch, Carolina style. We had Vienna sausages and sardines, rat cheese, gingersnaps and dill pickles and oysterettes and canned salmon, all cold except the coffee that went with it, and that was hot enough to scald clean down to your shoes. It sounds horrible, but I don't know anything that tastes so good together as Vienna sausages and sardines and rat cheese and gingersnaps. Especially if you've been up since before dawn and walked 10 miles in the fresh air.

After lunch, we stretched out in the shade and took a little nap. Along about two, I woke up, and so did Pete and Tom, and the three of us started to skin the squirrels. It's not much trouble, if you know how. Pete and I skinned 'em and Tom cleaned and dressed 'em. I'd pick up a squirrel by the head, and Pete would take his hind feet. We'd stretch him tight, and Pete would slit him down the stomach and along the legs as far as the feet. Then he'd shuck him like an ear of corn, pulling the hide toward the head until it hung over his head like a cape and the squirrel was naked. Then he'd just chop off the head, skin and all, and toss the carcass to Tom.

Tom made a particular point about cutting the little castor glands. Squirrel with the musk glands out is as tasty as any meat I know, but unless you take out those glands, an old he-squirrel is as musky as a billy goat, and tastes like a billy goat smells. Tom cut up the carcasses and washed them clean, and I proceeded to bury the heads, hides and guts.

The whole job didn't take 45 minutes with the three of us working. We put the pieces of clean red meat in a covered pot, and then woke up the Old Man and Mister Howard. We were going deer hunting again.

The dogs had rested too; they had eaten half a can of salmon each and had about a three hours' snooze.

It was beginning to cool off when Tom and Pete put Blue and Bell on walking leashes, and we struck off for another part of the swamp, which made a Y from the main swamp and had a lot of water in it. It was a cool swamp, and Tom and Pete figured that the deer would be lying up there from the heat of the day and about ready to start stirring out to feed a little around dusk.

I was in the process of trying to think about just how long forever was when the hounds started to holler real close. They seemed to be coining straight down the crick off to my right, and the crick's banks were very open and clear, apart from some sparkleberry and gallberry bushes. The *whoo-whooing* got louder and louder. The dogs started to growl and bark, just letting off a *whoo-whoo* once in a while, and I could hear a steady swishing in the bushes.

Then I could see what made the swishing. It was a buck—a big one. He was running steadily and seriously through the low bush. He had horns—my Lord, but did he have horns! It looked to me like he had a dead tree lashed to his head. I slipped off the safety catch and didn't move. The buck came straight at me, the dogs going crazy behind him.

The buck came down the water's edge, and when he got to about 50 yards, I stood and threw the gun up to my face. He kept coming and I let him come. At about 25 yards, he suddenly saw me, snorted and leaped to his left as if somebody had unsnapped a spring in him. I forgot he was a deer. I shot at him as you'd lead a duck or a quail on a quartering shot—plenty of lead ahead of his shoulder.

I pulled the trigger—for some odd reason shooting the choke barrel—right in the middle of a spring that had him six feet off the ground and must have been wound up to send him 20 yards into the bush and out of my life.

The gun said *boom!* but I didn't hear it. The gun kicked but I didn't feel it. All I saw was that this monster came down out of the sky like I'd shot me an airplane. He came down flat, turning completely over and landing on his back, and he never wiggled.

The dogs came up ferociously and started to grab him, but they had sense and knew he didn't need any extra grabbing. I'd grabbed him real good, with about three ounces of No. 1 buckshot in a choke barrel. I had busted his shoulder and busted his neck and dead-centered his heart. I had let him get so close that you could practically pick the wads out of his shoulder.

This was *my* buck. Nobody else had shot at him. Nobody else had seen him but me. Nobody had advised or helped. This monster was mine.

And monster was right. He was huge, they told me later, for a Carolina whitetail. He had 14 points on his rack and must have weighed nearly 150 pounds undressed. He was beautiful gold on his top and dazzling white on his underneath, and his little black hoofs were clean. The circular tufts of hair on his legs, where the scent glands are, were bright russet and stiff and spiky. His horns were as clean as if they'd been scrubbed with a wire brush, gnarled and evenly forked and the color of planking on a good boat that's just been holystoned to where the decks sparkle.

I had him all to myself as he lay there in the aromatic, crushed ferns—all by myself, like a boy alone in a big cathedral of oaks and cypress in a vast swamp where the doves made sobbing sounds and the late birds walked and talked in the sparkleberry bush.

The dogs came up and lay down. Old Blue laid his muzzle on the big buck's back. Bell came over and licked my face and wagged her tail, like she was saying, "You did real good, boy." Then she lay down and put her face right on the deer's rump.

This was our deer, and no damn bear or anything else was going to take it away from us. We were a team, all right, me and Bell and Blue.

I couldn't know then that I was going to grow up and shoot elephants and lions and rhinos and things. All I knew then was that I was the richest boy in the world as I sat there in the crushed ferns and stroked the silky hide of my first buck deer, patting his horns and smelling how sweet he smelled and admiring how pretty he looked. I cried a little bit inside about how lovely he was and how I felt about him. I guess that was just reaction, like being sick 25 years later when I shot my first African buffalo.

I was still patting him and patting the dogs when Tom and Pete came up one way and the Old Man and Mister Howard came up from another way. What a wonderful thing it was, when you are a kid, to have four huge, grown men—everything is bigger when you are a boy—come roaring up out of the woods to see you sitting by your first big triumph. "Smug" is a word I learned a lot later. Smug was modest for what I felt then.

"Well," the Old Man said, trying not to grin.

"Well," Mister Howard said.

"Boy done shot hisself a horse with horns," Pete said, as proud for me as if I had just learned how to make bootleg liquor.

"Shot him pretty good, too," Tom said. "Deer musta been standing still, boy musta been asleep, woke up and shot him in self-defense."

"Was not, either," I started off to say, and then saw that all four men were laughing.

They had already checked the sharp scars where the buck had jumped, and they knew I had shot him on the fly. Then Pete turned the buck over and cut open his belly. He tore out the paunch and ripped it open. It was full of green stuff and awful smelly gunk.

All four men let out a whoop and grabbed me. Pete held the paunch and the other men stuck my head right into—blood, guts, green gunk and all. It smelled worse than anything I ever smelled. I was bloody and full of partly digested deer fodder from my head to my belt.

"That," the Old Man said as I swabbed the awful mess off me and dived away to stick my head in the crick, "makes you a grown man. You have been blooded, boy, and any time you miss a deer from now on, we cut off your shirt tail.

"It's a very good buck, son," he said softly, "one of which you can be very, very proud."

Tom and Pete cut a long sapling, made slits in the deer's legs behind the cartilage of his knees, stuck the sapling through the slits, and slung the deer up on their backs. They were sweating him through the swamp when suddenly the Old Man turned to Mister Howard and said, "Howard, if you feel up to it, we might just as well go get *our* deer and lug him into camp. He ain't but a quarter-mile over yonder, and I don't want the wildcats working on him in that tree."

"What deer?" I demanded. "You didn't shoot this afternoon, and you missed the one you—"

The Old Man grinned and made a show of lighting his pipe. "I didn't miss him, son," he said. "I just didn't want to give you an inferiority complex on your first deer. If you hadn't of shot this one—and he's a lot better'n mine—I was just going to leave him in the tree and say nothing about him at all. Shame to waste a deer, but it's a shame to waste a boy, too."

I reckon that's when I quit being a man. I just opened my mouth and bawled. Nobody laughed at me, either.

RACE AT MORNING
By William Faulkner

This famous piece is one of four stories that comprise the Nobel Prize winner's only outdoor book, Big Woods: The Hunting Stories of William Faulkner *(1955). It first appeared in the March 5, 1955 edition of the* Saturday Evening Post. *The tale was Faulkner's last published work on hunting and it carries undercurrents of the end of an era and the author's realization that a wilderness world he had known and loved would soon cease to exist. Faulkner was a passionate deer hunter who purportedly was quite reluctant to leave hunting camp to travel overseas to receive the Nobel Prize in Literature.*

I was in the boat when I seen him. It was jest dusk-dark; I had jest fed the horses and clumb back down the bank to the boat and shoved off to cross back to camp when I seen him, about half-a-quarter up the river, swimming jest his head above the water, and it no more than a dot in that light. But I could see that rocking chair he toted on it, and I knowed it was him, going right back to that canebrake in the fork of the bayou where he lived all year until the day before the season opened—like the game wardens had give him a calendar when he would clear out and disappear, nobody knowed where, until the day after the season closed. But here he was, coming back a day ahead of time, like maybe he had got mixed up and was using last year's calendar by mistake. Which was jest too bad tor him, because me and Mister Ernest would be setting on the horse right over him when the sun rose tomorrow morning.

So I told Mister Ernest and we et supper and fed the dogs, and then I holp Mister Ernest in the poker game, standing behind his chair until about ten o'clock, when Roth Edmonds said, "Why don't you go to bed, boy?"

"Or if you're going to set up," Willy Legate said, "why don't you take a spelling book to set up over? He knows every cuss word in the dictionary, every poker hand in the deck, and every whisky label in the distillery, but he can't even write his name."

"Can you?" he says to me.

"I don't need to write my name down," I said. "I can remember in my mind who I am."

"You're twelve years old," Walter Ewell said. "Man to man now, how many days in your life did you ever spend in school?"

"He ain't got time to go to school," Willy Legate said. "What's the use in going to school from September to middle of November, when he'll have to quit then to come in here and do Ernest's hearing for him? And what's the use in going back to school in January, when in jest eleven months it will be November fifteenth again, and he'll have to start all over telling Ernest which way the dogs went?"

"Well, stop looking into my hand, anyway," Roth Edmonds said.

"What's that? What's that?" Mister Ernest said. He wore his listening button in his ear all the time, but he never brought the battery to camp with him because the cord would get snagged ever time we run through a thicket.

"Willy says for me to go to bed!" I hollered.

"Don't you never call nobody 'mister'?" Willy said.

"I call Mister Ernest 'mister,'" I said.

"All right," Mister Ernest said, "Go to bed then, I don't need you."

"That ain't no lie," Willy said. "Deaf or no deaf, he can hear a fifty-dollar raise if you don't even move your lips."

So I went to bed, and after a while, Mister Ernest come in and I wanted to tell him again how big them horns looked even half-a-quarter away in the river. Only I woulda had to holler, and the only time Mister Ernest agreed he couldn't hear was when we would be setting on Dan, waiting for me to point which way the dogs was going. So we jest laid down, and it wasn't no time Simon was beating the bottom of the dishpan with the spoon, hollering, "Raise up and get your four-o'clock coffee!" and I crossed the river in the dark this time, with the lantern, and fed Dan and Roth Edmondziz horse.

It was going to be a fine day, cold and bright; even in the dark I could see the white frost on the leaves and bushes, jest exactly the kind of day that big old son-of-a-gun laying up there in that brake would like to run.

Then we et, and set the stand-holder across for Uncle Ike McCaslin to put them on the stands where he thought they ought to be, because he was the oldest one in camp. He had been hunting deer in these woods for about a hundred years, I reckon, and if anybody would know where a buck would pass, it would be him. Maybe with a big old buck like this one, that had been running the woods for what would amount to a hundred years in a deer's life, too, him and Uncle Ike would sholy manage to be at the same place at the same time this morning—provided, of course, he managed to git away from me and Mister Ernest on the jump. Because me and Mister Ernest was going to git him.

Then me and Mister Ernest and Ruth Edmonds sent the dogs over, with Simon holding Eagle and the other old dogs on leash because the young ones, the puppies, wasn't going nowhere until Eagle let them, nohow.

Then me and Mister Ernest and Roth saddled up, and Mister Ernest got up and I handed him up his pumpgun and let Dan's bridle go for him to git rid of the spell of bucking he had to git shut of ever morning until Mister Ernest hit him between the ears with the gun barrel. Then Mister Ernest loaded the gun and give me the stirrup, and I got up behind him, and we taken the fire road up toward the bayou, the four big dogs dragging Simon along in front with his single-barrel britchloader slung on a piece of plow line across his back, and the puppies moiling along in ever'body's way.

It was light now and it was going to be jest fine; the east already yellow for the sun and our breaths smoking in the cold, still bright air until the sun would come up and warm it, and a little skim of ice in the ruts, and every leaf and twig and switch and even the frozen clods frosted over, waiting to sparkle like a rainbow when the sun finally come up and hit them.

Until all my insides felt light and strong as a balloon, full of that light, cold strong air, so that it seemed to me like I couldn't even feel the horse's back I was straddle of—jest the hot strong muscles moving under the hot strong skin, setting up there without no weight atall, so that when old Eagle struck and jumped, me and Dan and Mister Ernest would go jest like a bird, not even touching the ground. It was jest fine. When that big old buck got killed today, I knowed that even if he had put it off another ten years, he couldn't 'a' picked a better one.

And sho enough, as soon as we come to the bayou, we seen his foot in the mud where he had come up out of the river last night, spread in the soft mud like a cow's foot, big as a cow's, big as a mule's, with Eagle and the other dogs laying into the leash rope now until Mister Ernest told me to jump down and help Simon hold them. Because me and Mister Ernest knew exactly where he would be—a little canebrake island in the middle of the bayou, where he could lay up until whatever doe or little deer the dogs had happened to jump could go up or down the bayou in either direction and take the dogs on away, so he could steal out and creep back down the bayou to the river and swim it, and leave the country like he always done the day the season opened.

Which is jest what we never aimed for him to do this time.

So we left Roth on his horse to cut him off and turn him over to Uncle Ike's standers if he tried to slip back down the bayou. Me and Simon, with the leashed dogs, walked on up the bayou until Mister Ernest on the horse said it was fur enough. Then, we turned up into the woods about half-a-quarter above the brake because the wind was going to be south this morning, and turned down toward the brake where Mister Ernest give the word to cast them, and we slipped the leash and Mister Ernest give me the stirrup again and I got up.

Old Eagle had done already took off because he knowed where that old son-of-a-gun would be laying as good as we did, not making no racket atall yet, jest boring on through the buck vines with the other dogs trailing along behind him. Even Dan seemed to know about that buck, too, beginning to souple up and jump a little through the vines, so that I taken my holt on Mister Ernest's belt already before the time had come for Mister Ernest to touch him. Because when we got strung out, going fast behind a deer, I wasn't on Dan's back much of the time nohow, but mostly jest strung out from my holt on Mister Ernest's belt, so that Willy Legate said that when we was going through the woods fast, it looked like Mister Ernest had a boy-size pair of empty overalls blowing out of his hind pocket.

So it wasn't even a strike, it was a jump. Eagle must'a' walked right up behind him or maybe even stepped on him while he was laying, there still thinking it was day after tomorrow. Eagle jest threw his head back and up and said, "There he goes," and we even heard the buck crashing through the first of the cane.

Then all the other dogs was hollering behind him, and Dan give a squat to jump, but it was against the curb this time, not jest the snaffle, and Mister Ernest let him down into the bayou and swung him around the brake and up the other bank.

Only he never had to say, "Which way?" because I was already pointing past his shoulder, freshening my holt on the belt jest as Mister Ernest touched Dan with that big old rusty spur on his nigh heel, because when Dan felt it, he would go off jest like a stick of dynamite, straight through whatever he could bust and over or under what he couldn't, over it like a bird or under it crawling on his knees like a mole or a big coon, with Mister Ernest still on him because he had the saddle to hold onto, and me still there because I had Mister Ernest to hold onto; me and Mister Ernest not riding him, but jest going along with him, provided we held on. Because when the jump come, Dan never cared who else was there neither; I believe to my soul he coulda cast and run them dogs by hisself, without me or Mister Ernest or Simon or *nobody*.

That's what he done. He had to; the dogs was already almost out of hearing. Eagle musta been looking right up that big son-of-a-gun's tail until he finally decided he better git on out of there. And now they musta been getting pretty close to Uncle Ike's standers, and Mister Ernest reined Dan back and held him, squatting and bouncing and trembling like a mule having his tail reached, while we listened for the shots. But never none come, and I hollered to Mister Ernest we better go on while I could still hear the dogs, and he let Dan off, but still there wasn't no shots, and now we knowed the race had done already passed the standers, like that old son-of-a-gun actually was a hant, like Simon and the other field hands said he was, and we busted out of a thicket, and sho enough, there was Uncle Ike and Willy standing beside his foot in a soft patch.

"He got through us all," Uncle Ike said. "I don't know how he done it. I just had a glimpse of him. He looked big as an elephant, with a rack on his head to you could cradle a yellin' calf in. He went right on down the ridge. You better get on, too; that Hog Bayou camp might not miss him."

So I freshened my holt and Mister Ernest touched Dan again. The ridge run due south; it was clear of vines and bushes so we could go fast into the wind. Now the sun was up, though I hadn't had time to notice it, bright and strong and level through the woods, shining and sparking like a rainbow on the frosted leaves.

We would hear the dogs again any time now as the wind got up. We could make time, but still holding Dan back to a canter, because it was either going to be quick when he got down to the standers from that Hog Bayou camp eight miles below, or a long time, in case he got by them, too. And sho enough, after a while we heard the dogs; we was walking Dan now to let him blow a while, and we heard them, the sound coming faint up the wind, not running now, but trailing because the big son-of-a-gun had decided a good piece back, probably, to put a end to this foolishness and picked hisself up and soupled out and put about a mile between hisself and the dogs—until he run up on them other standers from that camp below.

I could almost see him stopped behind a bush, peeping out and saying, "What's this? What's this? Is this whole durn country full of folks this morning?"

Then looking back over his shoulder at where old Eagle and the others was hollering along after him, he had to decide what to do next.

Except he almost shaved it too fine. We heard the shots; it sounded like a war. Old Eagle musta been looking right up his tail again and he had to bust on through the best way he could.

Pow, pow, pow, pow and then *pow, pow, pow, pow,* like it musta been three or four ganged right up on him before he had time even to swerve, and me hollering, "No! No! No! No!" because he was ourn. It was our beans and oats he et and our brake he laid in; we had been watching him every year, and it was like we had raised him, to be killed at last on our jump in front of our dogs, not by some strangers that would probably try to beat off the dogs and drag him away before we could even git a piece of the meat.

"Shut up and listen," Mister Ernest said. So I done it and we could hear the dogs; not just the others, but Eagle, too, not trailing no scent now and not baying no downed meat neither, but running hot on sight long after the shooting was over.

I jest had time to freshen my holt. Yes, sir, they was running' on sight. Like Willy Legate would say, if Eagle jest had a drink of whisky, he would ketch that deer; going on, done already gone when we broke out of the thicket and seen the fellers that had done the shooting, five or six of them, squatting and crawling around, looking at the ground and the bushes, like maybe if they looked hard enough, spots of blood would bloom out on the stalks and leaves like frogstools or hawberries, with old Eagle still in hearing and still telling them that what blood they found wasn't coming out of nothing in front of him.

"Have any luck, boys?" Mister Ernest said.

"I think I hit him," one of them said. "I know I did. We're hunting blood now."

"Well, when you find him, blow your horn, and I'll come back and tote him in to camp for you," Mister Ernest said.

So we went on, going fast now because the race was almost out of hearing again, going fast, too, like not jest the buck, but the dogs, too, had took a new lease on life from all the excitement and shooting.

We was in strange country now because we never had to run this fur before. We had always killed before now.

Now we had come to Hog Bayou that runs into the river a good 15 miles below our camp. It had water in it, not to mention a mess of downed trees and logs and such, and Mister Ernest checked Dan again, saying, "Which way?"

I could just barely hear them, off to the east a little, like the old son-of-a-gun had give up the idea of Vicksburg or New Orleans, like he first seemed to have, and had decided to have a look at Alabama, maybe, since he was already up and moving. So I pointed and we turned up the bayou hunting for a crossing, and maybe we coulda found one, except that I reckon Mister Ernest decided we never had time to wait.

We come to a place where the bayou had narrowed down to about 12 or 15 feet, and Mister Ernest said, "Look out, I'm going to touch him" and done it. I didn't even have time to freshen my holt when we was already in the air, and then I seen the vine—it was a loop of grapevine nigh as big as my wrist, looping down right across the middle of the bayou—and I thought he seen it, too, and was jest waiting to grab it and fling it up over our heads to go under it.

I know Dan seen it because he even ducked his head to jump under it. But Mister Ernest never seen it until it skun back along Dan's neck and hooked under the head of the saddle horn, us flying on through the air, the loop of the vine gettin' tighter and tighter until something somewhere was going to have to give.

It was the saddle girth. It broke, and Dan going on and scrabbling up the other bank bare nekkid except for the bridle, and Mister Ernest still setting in the saddle holding the gun, and me still holding onto Mister Ernest's belt, hanging in the air over the bayou in the tightened loop of that vine like in the drawed-back loop of a big rubber-band slingshot. Suddenly, it snapped back and shot us back across the bayou and flung us clear, me still holding onto Mister Ernest's belt, so that when we lit, I woulda had Mister Ernest and the saddle both on top of me if I hadn't clumb fast around the saddle and up Mister Ernest's side. When we landed, it was the saddle first, then Mister Ernest, and me on top, until I jumped up with Mister Ernest still laying there with jest the white rim of his eyes showing.

"Mister Ernest!" I hollered, and then clumb down to the bayou and scooped my cap full of water and clumb back and throwed it in his face. He opened his eyes and laid there on the saddle, cussing me.

"God dawg it," he said, "why didn't you stay behind where you started out?"

"You was the biggest!" I said. "You woulda mashed me flat!"

"What do you think you done to me?" Mister Ernest said. "Next time, if you can't stay where you start out, jump clear. Don't climb up on top of me no more. You hear?"

"Yes, sir," I said.

So he got up then, still cussing and holding his back, and clumb down to the water and dipped some in his hand onto his face and neck and dipped some more up and drunk it. I drunk some, too, and clumb back and got the saddle and the gun, and we crossed the bayou on the downed logs.

If we could jest ketch Dan; not that he would have went them 15 miles back to camp, because, if anything, he would have went on by hisself to try to help Eagle ketch that buck. But he was about 50 yards away, eating buck vines, so I brought him back, and we taken Mister Ernest's galluses and my belt and the leather loop off Mister Ernest's horn and tied the saddle back on Dan. It didn't look like much but maybe it would hold.

"Provided you don't let me jump him through no more grapevines without hollering first," Mister Ernest said.

"Yes, sir," I said. "I'll holler first next time—provided you'll holler a little quicker when you touch him next time, too."

But it was all right; we jest had to be a little easy getting up.

"Now which-a-way?" I said. Because we couldn't hear nothing now, after wasting all this time. And this was new country, sho enough. It had been cut over and growed up in thickets we couldn't 'a seen over even standing up on Dan.

But Mister Ernest never even answered. He jest turned Dan along the bank of the bayou where it was a little more open and we could move faster again soon as Dan and us got used to that homemade cinch strop and got a little confidence in it. Which jest happened to be east, or so I thought then, because I never paid no attention to east then because the sun—I don't know where the morning had went, but it was gone, the morning and the frost, too—was up high now, even if my insides had told me it was past dinnertime.

And then we heard him. No, that's wrong; what we heard was shots. And that was when we realized how fur we had come, because the only camp we knowed about in that direction was the Hollyknowe camp, and Hollyknowe was exactly 28 miles from Van Dorn, where me and Mister Ernest lived—jest the shots, no dogs nor nothing. If old Eagle was still behind him and the buck was still alive, he was too wore out now to even say, "Here he comes."

"Don't touch him!" I hollered. But Mister Ernest remembered that cinch strop, too, and he jest let Dan off the snaffle. And Dan heard them shots, too, picking his way through the thickets, hopping the vines and logs when he could and going under them when he couldn't. And sho enough, it was jest like before—two or three men squatting and creeping among the bushes, looking for blood that Eagle had done already told them wasn't there. But we never stopped this time, jest trotting on by with Dan hopping and dodging among the brush and vines dainty as a dancer. Then Mister Ernest swung Dan until we was going due north.

"Wait!" I hollered. "Not this way."

But Mister Ernest jest turned his face back over his shoulder. It looked tired, too, and there was a smear of mud on it where that ere grapevine had snatched him off the horse.

"Don't you know where he's heading?" he said. "He's done done his part, give everybody a fair open shot at him, and now he's going home, back to that brake in our bayou. He ought to make it exactly at dark."

And that's what he was doing. We went on. It didn't matter to hurry now. There wasn't no sound nowhere; it was that time in the early afternoon in November when don't nothing move or cry, not even birds, the peckerwoods and yellowhammers and jays, and it seemed like I could see all three of us—me and Mister Ernest and Dan—and Eagle, and the other dogs, and that big old buck, moving through the quiet woods in the same direction, headed for the same place, not running now but walking.

We'd all run the fine race the best we knowed how, all three of us now turned like on an agreement to walk back home, not together in a bunch because we didn't want to worry or tempt one another, because what we had all three spent this morning doing was no play-acting jest for fun, but was serious, and all three of us was still what we was—that old buck that had to run, not because he was skeered, but because running was what he done the best and was proudest at; and Eagle and the dogs that chased him, not because they hated or feared him, but because that was the thing they done the best and was proudest at; and me and Mister Ernest and Dan, that run him not because we wanted his meat, which would be too tough to eat anyhow, or his head to hang on the wall, but because now we could go back and work hard for 11 months making a crop, so we would have the right to come back here next November—all three of us going back home now, peaceful and separate, but still side-by-side, until next year, next time.

Then we seen him for the first time. We was out of the cut-over now; we could evena cantered, except that all three of us was long past that, and now you could tell where west was because the sun was already halfway down. So we was walking, too, when we come on the dogs—the puppies and one of the old ones—played out, laying in a little wet swag, panting, jest looking up at us when we passed but not moving when we went on.

Then we come to a long open glade; you could see about half-a-quarter, and we seen the three other old dogs and about hundred yards ahead of them Eagle, all walking, not making no sound. Then suddenly, at the fur end of the glade, the buck hisself gettin' up from where he had been resting for the dogs to come up, gettin' up without no hurry, big, big as a mule, tall as a mule, and turned without no hurry still, and the white underside of his tail showed for a second or two more before the thicket taken him.

It mighta been a signal, a good-bye, a farewell. Still walking, we passed the other three old dogs in the middle of the glade, laying down, too, now jest where they was when the buck vanished, and not trying to get up neither when we passed; and still that hundred yards ahead of them, Eagle, too, not laying down, because he was still on his feet, but his legs was spraddled and his head was down, maybe jest waiting until we was out of sight of his shame, his eyes saying plain as talk when we passed: "I'm sorry, boys, but this here is all."

Mister Ernest stopped Dan. "Jump down and look at his feet," he said.

"Nothin' wrong with his feet," I said. "It's his wind has done give out."

"Jump down and look at his feet," Mister Ernest said.

So I done it, and while I was stooping over Eagle I could hear the pumpgun go, *Snick'cluck. Snick'cluck. Snick'cluck* three times, except that I never thought nothing then.

Maybe he was jest running the shells through to be sho it would work when we seen him again or maybe to make sho they was all buckshot.

Then I got up again, and we went on, still walking, a little west of north now, because when we seen his white flag that second or two before the thicket hid it, it was on a beeline for that notch in the bayou.

It was evening now. The wind had done dropped, and there was an edge to the air and the sun jest touched the tops of the trees, except jest now and then when it found a hole to come almost level through onto the ground. And he was taking the easiest way, too, now, going straight as he could. When we seen his foot in the soft places, he was running for a while at first after his rest. But *soon* he was walking, too, like he knowed where Eagle and the dogs was.

And then we seen him again. It was the last time—a thicket, with the sun coming through a hole onto it like a searchlight.

He crashed jest once; then he was standing there broadside to us, not 20 yards away, big as a statue and red as gold in the sun, and the sun sparkling on the tips of his horns—they was 12 of them—so that he looked like he had 12 candles branched around his head, standing there looking at us while Mister Ernest raised the gun and aimed at his neck, and the gun went, *Click. Snick'cluck. Click. Snick'cluck. Click. Snick'cluck*" three times, and Mister Ernest still holding the gun, aimed while the buck turned and give one long bound, the white underside of his tail like a blaze of fire until the thicket and the shadows put it out.

Mister Ernest laid the gun slow and gentle back across the saddle in front of him, saying quiet and peaceful, and not much louder than jest breathing, "God dawg. God dawg."

Then he jogged me with his elbow, and we got down, easy and careful because of that ere cinch strop, and he reached into his vest and taken out one of the cigars. It was busted where I had fell on it, I reckon, when we hit the ground. He throwed it away and taken out the other one. It was busted, too, so he bit off a hunk of it to chew and throwed the rest away. And now the sun was gone even from the tops of the trees, and there wasn't nothing left but a big red glare in the west.

"Don't worry," I said. "I ain't going to tell them you forgot to load your gun. For that matter, they don't need to know we ever seed him."

"Much oblige," Mister Ernest said. There wasn't going to be no moon tonight neither, so he taken the compass off the whang leather loop in his buttonhole and handed me the gun and set the compass on a stump and stepped back and looked at it.

"Jest about the way we're headed now," he said, and taken the gun from me and opened it and put one shell in the britch and taken up the compass, and I taken Dan's reins and we started, with him in front with the compass in his hand.

And after a while it was full dark; Mister Ernest would have to strike a match ever now and then to read the compass, until the stars come out good and we could pick out one to follow, because I said, "How fur do you reckon it is?"

"A little more than one box of matches," he said.

So we used a star when we could, only we couldn't see it all the time because the woods was too dense and we would git a little off until he would have to spend another match. And now it was good and late, and he stopped and said, "Get on the horse."

"I ain't tired," I said.

"Get on the horse," he said. "We don't want to spoil him."

Because he had been a good feller ever since I had knowed him, which was even before the day two years ago when maw went off with the Vicksburg roadhouse feller and the next day pap didn't *come* home neither, and on the third one, Mister Ernest rid Dan up to the door of the cabin on the river he let us live in, so pap could work his piece of land and run his fish line, too, and said, "Put that gun down and come on here and climb up behind."

So I got in the saddle even if I couldn't reach the stirrups, and Mister Ernest taken the reins and I musta went to sleep, because the next thing I knowed a buttonhole of my lumberjack was tied to the saddlehorn with that ere whang cord off the compass, and it was good and late now and we wasn't fur, because Dan was already smelling water, the river. Or maybe it was the feedlot itself he smelled, because we struck the fire road not a quarter below it, and soon I could see the river with the white mist laying on it soft and still as cotton.

Then the lot, home, and up yonder in the dark, not no piece akchully, close enough to hear us unsaddling and shucking corn prob'ly, and sholy close enough to hear Mister Ernest blowing his horn at the dark camp for Simon to come in the boat and git us, that old buck in his brake in the bayou; home, too, resting, too, after the hard run, waking hisself now and then, dreaming of dogs behind him. Or maybe it was the racket we was making would wake him, but not neither of them for more than jest a little while before sleeping again.

Then Mister Ernest stood on the bank blowing until Simon's lantern went bobbing down into the mist; then we clumb down to the landing and Mister Ernest blowed again now and then to guide Simon, until we seen the lantern in the mist, and then Simon and the boat, only it looked like ever time I set down and got still, I went back to sleep, because Mister Ernest was shaking me again to git up and climb the bank into the dark camp, until I felt a bed against my knees and tumbled into it.

Then it was morning, tomorrow; it was all over now until next November, next year, and we could come back. Uncle Ike and Willy and Walter and Roth and the rest of them had come in yestiddy, soon as Eagle taken the buck out of hearing, and they knowed that the deer was gone, to pack up and be ready to leave this morning for Yoknapatawpha, where they lived, until it would be November again and they could come back again.

So, as soon as we et breakfast, Simon run them back up the river in the big boat to where they left their cars and pickups, and now it wasn't nobody but jest me and Mister Ernest setting on the bench against the kitchen wall in the sun; Mister Ernest smoking a cigar—a whole one this time that Dan hadn't had no chance to jump him through a grapevine and bust. He hadn't washed his face neither where that vine had throwed him into the mud. But that was all right; his face usually did have a smudge of mud or tractor grease or beard stubble in it, because he wasn't jest a planter; he was a farmer.

He worked as hard as any one of his hands and tenants—which is why I knowed from the very first that we would git along, that I wouldn't have no trouble with him and he wouldn't have no trouble with me, from that very first day when I woke up and maw had done gone off with that Vicksburg roadhouse feller without even waiting to cook breakfast, and the next morning pap was gone, too, and it was almost night the next day when I heard a horse coming up and I taken the gun that I had already throwed a shell into the britch when pap never come home last night, and stood in the door while Mister Ernest rid up and said, "Come on. Your paw ain't coming back neither."

"You mean he give me to you?" I said.

"Who cares?" he said. "Come on. I brought a lock for the door. We'll send the pickup back tomorrow for whatever you want."

So I come home with him and it was all right; it was jest fine—his wife had died about three years ago—without no women to worry us or take off in the middle of the night with a durn Vicksburg roadhouse jake without even waiting to cook breakfast. And we would go home this afternoon, too, but not jest yet; we always stayed one more day after the others left, because Uncle Ike always left what grub they hadn't et, and the rest of the homemade corn whiskey he drunk and that town whiskey of Roth Edmondziz he called Scotch that smelled like it come out of a old bucket of roof paint, setting in the sun for one more day before we went back home to git ready to put in next year's crop of cotton and oats and beans and hay.

Across the river yonder, behind the wall of trees where the big woods started, that old buck laying up today in the sun, too—resting today, without nobody to bother him until next November.

So at least one of us was glad it would be 11 months and two weeks before he would have to run that fur that fast again. So he was glad of the very same thing we was sorry of, and so all of a sudden I thought about how maybe planting and working and then harvesting oats and cotton and beans and hay wasn't jest something me and Mister Ernest done 351 days to fill in the time until we could come back hunting again, but it was something we had to do, and do honest and good during the 351 days, to have the right to come back into the big woods and hunt for the other 14; and the 14 days that old buck run in front of the dogs wasn't jest something to fill his time until the 351 when he didn't have to, but the running and the risking in front of guns and dogs was something he had to do for 14 days to have the right not to be bothered for the other 351.

And so the hunting and the farming wasn't two different things atall—they was jest the other side of each other.

"Yes," I said. "All we got to do now is put in that next year's crop. Then November won't be no time away atall."

"You ain't going to put in the crop next year," Mister Ernest said. "You're going to school."

So at first I didn't even believe I had heard him. "What?" I said. "Me? Go to school?"

"Yes," Mister Ernest said. "You must make something of yourself."

"I am," I said. "I'm doing it now. I'm going to be a hunter and a farmer like you."

"No," Mister Ernest said. "That ain't enough any more. Time was, when all a man had to do was just farm eleven and a half months, and hunt the other half. But not now. Now just to belong to the farming business and the hunting business ain't enough. You got to belong to the business of mankind."

"Mankind?" I said.

"Yes," Mister Ernest said. "So you're going to school. Because you got to know why. You can belong to the farming and hunting business, and you can learn the difference between what's right and what's wrong, and do right. And that used to be enough—just to do right. But not now. You got to know why it's right and why it's wrong, and then be able to tell the folks that never had no chance to learn it; teach them how to do what's right, not just because they know it's right, but because they know now why it's right because you just showed them, told them, taught them why. So you're going to school."

"It's because you been listening to that dam Will Legate and Walter Ewell!" I said.

"No," Mister Ernest said.

"Yes!" I said. "No wonder you missed that buck yestiddy, taking ideas from the very fellers that let him git away, after me and you had run Dan and the dogs durn right clean to death! Because you never even missed him! You never forgot to load that gun! You had done already unloaded it a-purpose! I heard you!"

"All right, all right," Mister Ernest said. "Which would you rather have? His bloody head and hide on the kitchen floor yonder and half his meat in a pickup truck on the way to Yoknapatawpha County, or him with his head and hide and meat still together over yonder in that brake, waiting for next November for us to run him again?"

"And git him, too," I said. "We won't even fool with no Willy Legate and Walter Ewell next time."

"Maybe," Mister Ernest said.

"Yes," I said.

"Maybe," Mister Ernest said. "The best word in our language; the best of all. That's what mankind keeps going on: Maybe. The best days of his life ain't the ones when he said 'Yes' beforehand. They're the ones when all he knew to say was 'Maybe.' He can't say 'Yes' until afterward because he not only don't know it until then, he don't want to know 'Yes' until then . . .

"Step in the kitchen and make me a toddy. Then we'll see about dinner."

"All right," I said. I got up. "You want some of Uncle Ike's corn or that town whisky of Roth Edmondziz?"

"Can't you say Mister Roth or Mister Edmonds?" Mister Ernest said.

"Yes, sir," I said. "Well, which do you want? Uncle Ike's corn or that ere stuff of Roth Edmondziz?"

BLOOD RED MACKINAW

By Ryan Stalvey

Ryan Stalvey, the editor-in-chief at Sporting Classics, *wrote this gripping piece of fiction for the January/February 2016 issue of the magazine.*

Inch by inch, the afternoon sun steadily dissolves, casting an orange and pink haze over the sparsely populated landscape of rural Pennsylvania. From the front window of a seedy boarding house, Curt Sloan peers through the unclean glass panes, then disappears back again into the lightless room. Inside, he paces the dusty hardwood floors, moving with the nervous stride of a high-strung animal sensing danger. His pacing interrupted by the occasional glance to the door, then out of the window again. At last, a little before nightfall, the door bell sounds. He rudely greets the delivery man, draws the shade, and places the mail-order package on the table beside a half-empty bottle of bourbon and an upturned glass. Completely exhausted, he sits down, lights a cigarette, leans his head back and closes his eyes, praying all the while that the liquor would finally be too much for him and he'd nod off.

Gradually the cigarette he is holding burns down to his thick fingers, rousing him from a few minutes of much-needed slumber. He thumps it out, tosses it into an ashtray and picks up the unopened parcel. The postmark reads Abercrombie & Fitch, Madison Avenue and Fifth Street, New York. He peels back the brown paper wrappings and opens the lid of the box. Eagerly he takes out a heavy, woolen garment, holding it in front of him. A wide smile grows across his face as he studies the red and black plaid coat.

"Perfect," he says aloud, thinking of the day to come—the opening day of deer season and the countless hoards of hunters that will pepper the Northern countryside in a spectacle of crimson red and blaze orange.

Yes, he affirms his thoughts, casting his gaze across the hardwood floor, past a pair of heavy-laced boots to the Winchester Model 94 leaning upright in the corner. *Just perfect—for MURDER.*

Curt lights another cigarette, freshens the glass, blows himself a smoke ring and watches it curl up and then disappear. *Alone, all alone in life,* he thinks and chuckles. Thoughtfully, he twists the glass in his hand, staring deeply into his drink, recalling his past and the person he despises most in the world, the one he holds responsible for his misfortune—his old pal, Sean Regan.

Curt is a hard man; he came up the hard way. He was born Curtis McKay Sloan, grandson to Irish immigrants. His ginger hair came from his father; ill temper from his mother. His father was a delinquent; his mother even worse. Abandoned at an early age, it was inevitable he would eventually succumb to his breeding. The only family he had ever truly known was the Regans.

He and classmate Sean Regan were as close as brothers and thick as thieves. Rarely was one seen without the other. They picked fights, stole cigarettes, drank beer, and chased skirts. Sean was the type who could fall down the sewer and come up with bottles of perfume in both hands. Curt was not, and regularly served as the scapegoat for their mischievous endeavors. Nevertheless, Sean's father was very fond of the rough-and-tumble Curt. Blood may be thicker than water, but there was no mistaking that Curt was Mr. Regan's favorite.

He often took the boys hunting up in the highlands. Curt was a natural—a dead-eye with a gun—and immediately took to the ways of the woods. Sean just tagged along. Still, he and Curt roamed through those hills like Indians. They knew every track and trail in the forest. On opening day of hunting season, the three always hunted from the same timbered hillside. Both boys had bagged their first bucks from this stand and it became a place of great sentimentality after the early death of Sean's father. Invariably, each ensuing deer opener Sean would insist the two of them pay homage to his father and hunt together from the spot which held so many tender memories. Sean usually kicked back, enjoying a reminiscent smoke while Curt would eventually wander off, hunting alone.

After graduation, they took over the Regan accounting firm under the title of Regan & Sloan.

Eventually, each began to go his own way. Sean settled down, got married, joined the church, and cleaned up his act. Curt did not. He knocked around aimlessly, rappelling even deeper into the devious. In addition to managing the firm's clientele, he began keeping books on the ponies and the boxing matches, and it wasn't long before he ran into trouble with the dice. Curt had thrown every cent he had to the wolves and when that was lost, he let it ride without a nickel's worth of credit. Sean had helped bail him out on numerous occasions, but this time he would have no part in it.

Curt was in deep. He was down on his luck and it was about to get worse. His debtors were leaning hard and with no gag to avoid payoff, he turned to the office kitty. The books were soon audited and an inquest made. Curt was the prime suspect, but without a witness for the prosecution it seemed he might get off. Then Sean testified against his old friend.

The sentence sent Curt away for 20 years on racketeering and embezzlement. In his warped imagination, Curt was bound by the unshakable conviction that he'd been double-crossed and played the patsy. He could tolerate the torture of prison, but his longtime friend's betrayal would indelibly weigh on his mind.

A six-by-eight cell can eat a man's soul; Curt's greatest conduit to the outside world was through his devouring hatred of Sean. With more than a mild discontent for his situation, he vowed he'd turn the tables and settle the score. Ultimately, countless hours of outlandish scheming gave way to a brilliant conception bordering on madness. *It would be all too easy*, he imagined, *aside from the sea, the forest is the best place to kill a man*, and he x-ed off the days on his calendar until his release. That time came sooner than expected when his sentence was reduced due to good behavior.

Presently he sits in the ratty room of a rundown boarding house, with the bourbon, the loneliness, and the anger that has been raking his insides for 15 years. It's getting late and he's tired, more tired than he can ever remember. He sets the alarm and turns in.

Only a few hours pass, his anxiety waking him long before the clanging alarm. A sense of numbness is over him as he grabs his mackinaw and rifle and steps out into the damp darkness toward the car.

The road is deserted as Curt leaves the boarding house carport and heads out into the silence of the night. He rides with the windows cracked; the crisp, clean air feels good on his face. The red and yellow neon sign of an all-nite diner flashes on-and-on, matching Curt's frenzied pulse. He's famished and considers stopping. *Ham and eggs with coffee would sure hit the spot*, he considers, but drives on. Ahead in the high beams, the vertical silhouettes of the trees click off one by one. It's as if he has driven all night when he finally arrives at the edge of the familiar haunt of his past. He steers the car off the asphalt and kills the motor.

Sean would be coming in later by way of the adjacent road, making his way to the traditional spot where he and his father and Curt had hunted so many deer openers before. Curt was sure of it—Dead Sure.

A thousand stars hang low in the blackness of a crystal-clear night, casting just enough light for Curt to find his way. The woods are the same as he remembered, but aren't. He ambles noiselessly through the bushes and around trees, then scales up the steep, brambly bank of a rocky crag, where he positions himself at the top of the ridge. Below him, a picturesque valley lies asleep in the moonlight. At daybreak the rising sun will be at his back, illuminating the opposite hillside—and Sean Regan.

He brushes the sticks and leaves from beneath him and settles into his post. The air is cool with the suggestion of winter. *Not long now*, he thinks. But it is. A lengthy hour passes. The tension within him grows more and more unbearable. Over and over again he strains his eyes into the darkness, peering frantically for the source of each and every little noise.

Once, in the delicate silence, he was certain he heard footsteps— nothing. It's cold and he had gotten there early, too early. The heat from his body has been sucked into his head by his fevored mind and he hunches his broad shoulders against the bitter wind cutting into him.

Easy pal, he thinks to himself, *some things can't be hurried*.

He fondles the cold blued-steel sideplates of the rifle. It has been quite a while since he last shot anything. Once a gun had felt comforting, like an extension of his own body, but now seems foreign. At any rate, the magazine holds eight rounds and he figures he can make good with one of them. Curt waits.

He spies the lit embers of a cigarette long before he hears the rustling of dry leaves. The glowing orange spec floats through the blackness before halting on the opposite slope. The scent of smoke left

behind on the pathway lingers on the breeze toward Curt.
It's you all right, he thinks, *I could follow you wearing a blindfold.*

As the dingy gray of dawn begins to creep through the forest, death is electric in the air and Curt Sloan sits on a powder keg of emotion. He struggles to control the raging fire within him as the dark silhouette of a man against the milky light of morning begins to develop the faint details of Sean Regan.

"I've got you now . . . fink," Curt whispers as he shoulders the Model 94. He gazes down the sights glad and kill-hungry, his face wrenched in twisted madness. He lowers his aim from Sean's head to his chest. With no hesitation his finger teases the hard edge of the trigger, when suddenly, his peripheral vision detects a blur of brown.

Curt pauses. BANG! A loud shot rings out, exploding the morning silence, and instantly a heavy-racked buck skids to a death thrash, kicking sideways in the valley floor below. But the shot hadn't come from Curt. In spite of himself, his obsession has made him careless; another hunter has taken a stand nearby. A kaleidoscope of thoughts and actions race through his mind and he hurriedly reshoulders the rifle. *Even better,* he reasons, *I'll be to Canada before they ever realize it wasn't an accident.*

But before he can redraw a bead on Sean, a youthful, exuberant voice cries out."Dad, I got him! I got him! He's a big one!"

From the opposite hillside Sean shouts back, "I see him son, you got him!"

Curt is paralyzed. He watches with a blank stare; his bloodshot eyes tell the story. His hands grow sweaty. The rifle feels as heavy as a barbell and he lowers the muzzle. A sickening pain rises up from his stomach, bursting in his brain like a shell. He feels as if he himself has been shot. He can hardly breath. The vulgarity of what he had almost done disgusts him. It's like looking through a dirty window into a filthy room.

In the valley below the lifeless body of a big buck lies peacefully waiting to be claimed by father and son. Curt inconspicuously withdraws, melting into the thick damp cover. He takes in a long, deep breath. His face is flushed, and glistening with perspiration; he takes out a handkerchief and blots the back of his neck. He is ashamed, but more than mere shame; he is left with a mindfulness of humanity.

And he laughs. He doesn't care that he laughs, and he laughs until he sobs. In the background he hears the jubilant chatter of Sean and his son. It takes some time for him to compose himself. There will be no thrilling race to the border. No sensational headline for him on tomorrow's front page. No daring man-hunt. No secluded hide-out. No sweet revenge.

He slips away to the winding path leading out to the car. *I'm hungry*, he thinks to himself, *I could sure go for some ham and eggs with coffee.*

PART EIGHT

BIBLIOGRAPHICAL NOTES
By Jim Casada

For those interested in additional reading on the wonderful world of the whitetail, options abound. One of the literary giants from the formative era of American literature, James Fenimore Cooper, gave us an enduring classic in *The Deerslayer* (1841). Two years later, Henry William Herbert, under the pseudonym Frank Forester, wrote *The Deer Stalkers* (1843), and over the ensuing years, a number of other books that included sections on deer hunting. Their efforts, and indeed virtually every book-length work of note on the whitetail to appear up through 1991, are covered in Robert Wegner's, *Wegner's Bibliography on Deer Hunting* (1992). For the serious student of the sport's literature or the bibliophile, it is a "must own" book.

That being duly recognized, more than a quarter of a century has passed since its appearance, and those 25 years have seen a far greater outpouring of whitetail literature than any comparable period in history. This situation is explained in considerable measure by the fact that the animal's resurgence, one of the great wildlife restoration sagas of the last century, has resulted in record populations and ample opportunity to answer the old question, "Have you got your deer this year?" in the affirmative. There are several magazines devoted exclusively or in large measure to whitetails, and a number of modern authors have built solid, successful careers writing about and photographing whitetails.

If you don't happen to possess a copy of *Wegner's Bibliography*, you still have a running start at forming a representative whitetail library in the "Notes on Contributors" section of the current work. The majority of our contributors have written extensively on the subject, and in many cases their careers feature multiple books devoted wholly or in large measure to deer hunting.

Archibald Rutledge, for example, was the author of more than 50 books during the course of his long and productive career. Virtually without exception his narrative works, almost all of which were collections of stories initially published in magazines, contain considerable deer-related material. In fact, whitetails, to a greater degree than any single subject, dominate his writing.

Although I find Rutledge's poetry less appealing, scores of his poems are on deer. For a reasonably complete list of his whitetail pieces and the place(s) where they appeared, see Jim Casada (editor), *Tales of Whitetails: Archibald Rutledge's Great Deer-Hunting Stories* (1992).

A number of other contributors, among them Jack O'Connor, Gene Hill, Charley Dickey, Robert Wegner, Edmund Ware Smith, Duncan Dobie, M. R. James and Theodore Roosevelt, have multiple whitetail hunting books or shorter deer pieces in collections to their credit. Then, of course, if you enjoy the selections from writers such Paulina Brandreth and Larry Koller, along with the blue-ribbon writers of yesteryear such as Philip Tome, Theodore S. Van Dyke and Meshach Browning, you will want to obtain their books and read them in their entirety.

It is impossible in the scope of a work such as this to provide anything approaching comprehensive coverage of books that have appeared since the 1991 cut-off date for *Wegner's Bibliography*. However, there have been so many works of major importance published since then, and so many major writers gracing the whitetail stage, that at least a selective listing seems advisable.

Current contributors to this book who have specialized to an appreciable degree on whitetails, and have published books in the last three decades include: Duncan Dobie, M. R. James, Ron Spomer and Robert Wegner—check the "Notes on Contributors" section. Also, two major anthologies of Jack O'Connor's writings, both edited by Jim Casada and published by Sporting Classics—*The Lost Classics of Jack O'Connor* (2004) and *Classic O'Connor* (2010)—appeared in this time frame.

Beyond these works, here's coverage of some important writers and their efforts in recent decades. A true gentleman of the whitetail world and a man whose study and photography of deer, along with writings on them, established him as a leading authority on the subject was the late Charles J. Alsheimer. His works include *Whitetail: The Ultimate Challenge* (1995), *Whitetail Behavior Through the Seasons* (1996), *Hunting Whitetails by the Moon* (1999), *Quality Deer Management: The Basics and Beyond* (2002), *Whitetail Rites of Autumn* (2003) and *Strategies for Whitetails* (2006).

Patrick Durkin, who served as editor of *Deer & Deer Hunting* magazine for a number of years, put together a selection from that magazine's pages in *The Deer Hunters* (1997). Treading in the literary footsteps of Paulina Brandreth, Kathy Etling has written *Hunting Superbucks* (2001) and *The Art of Whitetail Deception* (2003). Dave Henderson, the guru of using scatterguns for whitetails, has given us *Hunting Superbucks* (1995) and *Shotgunning for Deer* (2003). Greg Miller's efforts include *Aggressive Whitetail Hunting* (1994), *Greg Miller's Rub-Line Secrets* (1999), *Greg Miller's Greatest Whitetail Adventures* (2001) and *Bowhunting Forests & Deep Woods* (2004).

Biologists, notably John J. Ozoga, have contributed important works meaningful to a popular audience. Especially noteworthy is his "Seasons of the Whitetail" quartet, *Whitetail Autumn* (1994), *Whitetail Winter* (1995), *Whitetail Spring* (1996) and *Whitetail Summer* (1997). Another work written in a similar spirit is Valerius Geist's *Whitetail Tracks: The Deer's History & Impact in North America* (2001). Both of these writers worked closely over the years with Dan Schmidt, longtime editor of *Deer & Deer Hunting* magazine, and in addition to his stellar work with that publication, Schmidt has given us important books, notably as editor of *25 Years of Deer & Deer Hunting* (2002) and in *Whitetail Wisdom* (2005).

Another work of note that reflects the rapidly growing interest in management techniques designed to produce larger, healthier deer is *Quality Whitetails* (1995), edited by Karl V. Miller and R. Larry Marchinton. Recently, a key figure in the founding of the Quality Deer Management Association, Joe Hamilton, has brought together his longtime column for the organization's magazine in *Firepot Stories* (2017).

Finally, there are numerous books dealing with high-profile personalities or "stars" in the deer hunting world. These include, among others, efforts by a leading gun and hunting writer, Bryce Towsley, in *Benoit Bucks: Whitetail Tactics for a New Generation* (2003) and *Big Bucks the Benoit Way* (2008); Jim Crumley, *Jim*

Crumley's Secrets of Bowhunting Deer (1994); Mark and Terry Drury, *Giant Whitetails: A Lifetime of Lessons* (2003); Ken Dunwoody (editor), *Great Whitetail Hunts and the Lessons They Taught* (1995); Gregg Gutschow, *Life at Full Draw: The Chuck Adams Story* (2002); Dick Idol, *Legendary Whitetails* (1996); and Larry Weishuhn, *Mr. Whitetails' Trailing the Hunter's Moon* (2003).

In short, there's reading material to stock a bevy of shelves, provide hours without end of armchair adventure and challenge the most adventurous of bibliophiles. Such thoughts are heartening ones, because through books we are able to extend the joys of actually being afield many times over.

BIOGRAPHICAL NOTES
By Jim Casada

MICHAEL ALTIZER
Michael Altizer has written feature stories and his "Ramblings" column for *Sporting Classics* magazine for over a quarter-century. He is the author of *The Last Best Day: A Trout Fisher's Perspective* (2009) and *Nineteen Years to Sunrise* (2014). A native of southwestern Virginia and longtime resident of the eastern Tennessee mountains, Altizer's fly rods, rifles, shotguns, bows and cameras have accompanied him across much of the Americas and Europe, from the Atlantic Ocean to the Bering and Baltic seas, and from northern Alaska to southernmost Patagonia.

RICK BASS
Rick Bass is the author of more than 30 fiction and non-fiction books with his most recent being *The Traveling Feast: On the Road and at the Table with My Heroes* (2018). He lives in Montana and is a founding member of the Yaak Valley Forest Council.

PAULINA BRANDRETH (1885-1946)
Paulina Brandreth was possibly the first woman to write a deer hunting book. Under the pen name Paul Brandreth, she wrote *Trails of Enchantment* (1930), an enduring classic recounting her whitetail experiences in New York's Adirondack Mountains. Most of the work's 23 chapters are distinct (and distinctive) stories capable of standing alone, although the still-hunting technique is a constant through the book. Her storytelling is at a consistently high level. The book was reprinted by Stackpole Press in 2003 with a new introduction by Robert Wegner and an afterword by Mary Zeiss Stange.

MESHACH BROWNING (1794-1883)

A late 18th and early 19th century Maryland hunter, Browning reportedly accounted for close to 2,000 whitetails over the course of an adventurous life devoted to hunting deer and bear. Some of the most exciting of his exploits, which include catching deer in the snow and struggles with wounded bucks, are found in his *Forty-Four Years in the Life of a Hunter* (1859, with numerous reprints). One of his "hands to horns" struggles with a deer was depicted by noted artist Arthur Fitzwilliam Tait and subsequently used by Currier and Ives in a lithograph. Rob Wegner's Foreword to the reprint of Browning's book in the "Classics of American Sport" series provides excellent insight on the man and his milieu.

CHARLEY DICKEY (1921-1998)

Charley Dickey was for many years one of America's best known and loved sporting scribes. A generalist, he wrote on subjects ranging from deer hunting to trout fishing, outdoor photography to humor. Perhaps best remembered for his rare warmth and wit, he had an uncanny ability to go to the heart of things with a few well-chosen words. Charley wrote numerous books, with one of his earliest works being *Charley Dickey's Deer Hunting* (1977). Among the most important of his books are those anthologizing his magazine columns and stories. These include *Backtrack* (1977), *Opening Shots and Parting Lines* (1983) and *Movin' Along with Charley Dickey* (1985). He was a fixture in the pages of national magazines, *Georgia Sportsman* and *Southern Outdoors*; served as a columnist for the *Tallahassee Democrat*; and under the pen name Sam Cole wrote the back page column for *Petersen's Hunting*. Over the course of his career, Dickey garnered numerous honors including Southeastern Outdoor Press Association's Lifetime Achievement Award.

DUNCAN DOBIE

An outdoor writer for almost four decades, Dobie's stories and photographs have appeared in numerous books, magazines and newspapers. He was a regular contributor to *North American Whitetail* magazine for more than a quarter-century and served as the publication's editor from 2004 to 2009. His efforts include 11 books, most of which are about white-tailed deer. They include *Dawn of American Deer Hunting* (2015), *Whitetail Dawn* (2006), *Legendary Whitetails* (2012) and *Arthur Woody: The Legend of the Barefoot Ranger* (2017).

WILLIAM FAULKNER (1897-1962)

A giant of 20th century American literature, Faulkner is best remembered for his complex prose and tangled tales of his native Mississippi. His early writings were all poetry but after three semesters at the University of Mississippi, he turned to short stories and novels. He produced both in prolific fashion for the rest of his life. Awarded the Nobel Prize for Literature in 1949 for "his powerful and artistically unique contribution to the modern American novel," he also won Pulitzer Prizes for *A Fable* (1954) and *The Reivers* (1962). Deeply steeped in the traditions of the South and similarly influenced by the region's folkways, it is not surprising that his *oeuvre* included short stories on the outdoors. The four of them comprising *Big Woods* (1955) are part of a much larger body of work in the short story field.

FRANK FORESTER (1807-1858)

Frank Forester was the pen name of Henry William Herbert, one of America's first outdoor writers. English by birth, he established himself as a major U. S. literary presence while making enemies about as frequently as he published. He used his real name for his numerous novels and books on history, but all of his outdoor-related material appeared under the pseudonym Frank Forester. A frequent contributor to the early sporting magazine, *Spirit of the Times*, his works on the outdoors include *The Field Sports of the United States and British Provinces* (1849), *Frank Forester and His Friends* (1849), *The Deerstalkers* (1849), *The Fish and Fishing of the United States* (1850), *The Warwick Woodlands* (1851) and *The Young Sportsman's Complete Manual* (1852). These works have been reprinted many times, including several volumes by Eugene Connett's prestigious Derrydale Press. Intensely lonely, Forester committed suicide after a dinner party at which only one invitee appeared.

COREY FORD (1902-1969)

A prolific writer who produced screenplays, various works of non-sporting humor (frequently for *The New Yorker*), hundreds of outdoor-related stories and a number of sporting books, Ford is best remembered for his immensely popular column, "The Lower Forty" for *Field & Stream*. His outdoor books include *You Can Always Tell a Fisherman (But You Can't Tell Him Much)* (1958), *Minutes of the Lower Forty* (1962), *Uncle Perk's Jug* (1964) and five posthumously published anthologies, *The Best of Corey Ford* (edited by Jack Samson—1975), *The*

Corey Ford Sporting Treasury (edited by Chuck Petrie—1987), and a trio of books compiled by Laurie Morrow: *Trout Tales and Other Angling Stories* (1995), *The Trickiest Thing in Feathers* (1996) and *Cold Noses and Warm Hearts* (1996). A stalwart supporter of Dartmouth College, he left his extensive personal papers and literary remains to the institution.

MIKE GADDIS

A longtime contributor to *Sporting Classics*, Gaddis writes his popular "First Light" column and regularly contributes features. He is known for his carefully crafted, evocative pieces that often nourish nostalgia in an irresistible fashion. At times, he also indulges in a delightful turn of whimsy. A devoted "bird dog man," Gaddis is the author of *Jenny Willow* (2002), *Zip Zap: The True Story of a Dog and a Dream* (2006), *Legend's Legacy: The Hand at Our Shoulder* (2009) and *Turning for Home* (2014).

PARKER GILLMORE (1835-1900)

A peripatetic Scot who hunted big game around the world, explored for gold and was a soldier, Gillmore wrote under the pen name "Ubique." He was the author of numerous books, and several of those include accounts of deer hunting. Among his works were *A Hunter's Adventures in the Great West* (1871); *Prairie Farms and Prairie Folk* (two volumes—1872); *Prairie and Forest: A Description of the Game of North America with Personal Adventures in Their Pursuit* (1874); *The Great Thirst Land* (1878); *Adventures in Many Lands* (1879); *The Hunter's Arcadia* (1886); *Through Gasa Land* (1890); *Gun, Rod and Saddle* (1893); and *Leaves from a Sportsman's Diary* (1893).

GENE HILL (1928-1997)

Immensely popular as a columnist first for his back page "Parting Shots" in *Guns & Ammo* magazine, "Mostly Tailfeathers" in *Sports Afield* and "Hill Country" in *Field & Stream,* Hill was a master at writing short pieces capturing the treasured little things that mean so much to sportsmen. He had an uncanny knack for depicting simple pleasures in a deeply meaningful way. Gene Hill's tightly crafted vignettes appear in a number of books including *A Hunter's Fireside Book* (1972), *Mostly Tailfeathers* (1975), *A Gallery of Waterfowl and Upland Birds* (1978), *Hill Country* (1978), *Tears and Laughter* (1981), *Outdoor Yarns and Outright Lies* (1983—with Steve Smith),

A Listening Walk (1985), *Shotgunner's Notebook* (1995), *Sunlight and Shadows* (1996) and *Passing a Good Time with Guns, Dogs, Fly Rods, and Other Joys* (1997).

M. R. JAMES

The founder and longtime editor of *Bowhunter* magazine, noted hunter and member of the North American Archery Hall of Fame, M. R. James is in many senses today's Fred Bear. A past president of the Pope & Young Club, in 1999 he received the Outdoor Writers Association of America Lifetime Achievement award. His activities in archery span hunting for many species, but deer have always been a key focus of them. In addition to his many articles, his books include *Bowhunting for Whitetail and Mule Deer* (1976), *Successful Bowhunting* (1985), *My Place* (1992), *The Bowhunter's Handbook* (1997), *Of Blind Pigs and Big Bucks* (2002) and *Hunting the Dream: A Memoir* (2013). Additional information on James is available on his website, mrjamesbowhunter.com.

LAWRENCE KOLLER (1913-1967)

Lawrence R. "Larry" Koller was a well-known gun-writer whose works in that genre included *Golden Guide to Guns* (1961), *The Fireside Book of Guns* (1959) and *How to Shoot: A Complete Guide to the Use of Sporting Firearms* (1976), and well as scores of magazine articles. He also wrote a well-received work on *Taking Larger Trout* (1950), *Larry Koller's Hunting Annual* (1957) and the sections on whitetails and mule deer for *The Treasury of Hunting* (1965). His magnum opus was *Shots at Whitetails* (1948; republished in 1975). Koller also wrote about whitetails for *The Complete Book of Hunting* (1954).

ARTHUR R. MACDOUGALL, JR. (1896-1983)

A preacher who lived in Maine, Macdougall created a memorable character named Dud Dean. A professional guide, Dean shared his wisdom and tales in a delightful fashion in scores of pieces for *Field & Stream*. Many later appeared in books. Macdougall was personally present in the Dud Dean tales, and the underpinning for most of them had "Mak," as he was known to his friends, out fishing or hunting with Dean when the guide launched into one of his tales. Replete with Maine dialect and pithy philosophy, the stories not only bring Dean alive, but leave the reader feeling he had been present in person listening to the story. Macdougall's books include *Dud Dean Yarns* (1934), *The Sun Stood Still* (1939), *If It Returns with Scars* (1942), *Under a Willow Tree* (1946), *Dud Dean and His Country* (1946), *Doc Blakesley, Angler* (1949), *Dud Dean and the Enchanted* (1954), *The Trout Fisherman's Bedside Book* (1963), *Dud Dean: Maine Guide* (1974), *Adventure in a Model T and Other Due Dean Stories* (1980), and posthumously, *Remembering Dud Dean* (2002).

GORDON MACQUARRIE (1900-1956)

Gordon MacQuarrie stands in the front ranks of those who gave us the golden age of American sporting literature, but he doesn't exactly fit the framework of other writers of this era. He was America's first full-time outdoor newspaper writer and must also be reckoned as one of the first sporting humorists. For a quarter-of-a-century, up until his death from a heart attack, he entertained millions of readers and provided a literary legacy that shines as brightly today as newly burnished silver. He wrote more than 100 magazine pieces, most of which appeared in one of the "Big Three" (*Field & Stream, Outdoor Life* and *Sports Afield*) and from 1936 onward, he was the full-time outdoor man at the *Milwaukee Journal*. Much of his best work was posthumously anthologized in *Stories of the Old Duck Hunters and Other Drivel* (1967), *More Stories of the Old Duck Hunters* (1983), *The Last Stories of the Old Duck Hunters* (1985), *MacQuarrie Miscellany: Featuring the "Lost" Old Duck Hunter's Stories and Other Tales* (1987) and *Fly Fishing with MacQuarrie* (1995). Keith Crowley wrote a fine biography of the man: *Gordon MacQuarrie: The Story of an Old Duck Hunter* (2003).

JOHN MADSON (1923-1995)

John Madson was a highly accomplished freelance writer and conservationist who did considerable consulting and advisory work as assistant director of conservation for Winchester at the ammo-maker's Nilo Farms in Illinois. He contributed frequently to major magazines such as *Field & Stream, Outdoor Life, Sports Afield* and *Audubon*. His haunts, and much of his finest writing, focused on the upper Mississippi River and the vast prairies it drained. His books include *Out Home* (1979), *Where the Sky Began* (1982), *Up on the River* (1985), *Tallgrass Prairie* (1993) and posthumously, *The Elemental Prairie* (2005). He also wrote or co-authored a number of short wildlife natural history books aimed at a hunting audience.

JACK O'CONNOR (1902-1978)

Perhaps the best-known gun writer of the 20th century and a longtime fixture at *Outdoor Life,* O'Connor is most often remembered for his writings on firearms and North American, African and Asian big game. While mule deer, along with elk, moose and especially sheep were primary focal points of his American big game coverage, he did hunt whitetails and especially Coues deer. A prolific author, his major books include the novels *Conquest* (1930) and *Boomtown* (1938), along with numerous outdoor-related works—*Game in the Desert* (1939), *Hunting in the Rockies* (1947), *The Rifle Book* (1949), *The Big Game Rifle* (1952), *Complete Book of Rifles and Shotguns* (1961), *The Big Game Animals of North America* (1961), *Jack O'Connor's Big Game Hunts* (1963), *The Shotgun Book* (1965), *The Art of Hunting Big Game* (1967), *Horse and Buggy West: A Boyhood on the Last Frontier* (1969), *The Hunting Rifle* (1970), *Sheep and Sheep Hunting* (1974), *The Hunter's Shooting Guide* (1978) and the posthumously published *The Last Book: Confessions of a Gun Editor* (1984). There is a biography of him, Robert Anderson's *Jack O'Connor* (2002), and two anthologies of his forgotten magazine articles, Jim Casada (editor), *The Lost Classics of Jack O'Connor* (2004) and Jim Casada (editor), *Classic O'Connor* (2010).

THEODORE ROOSEVELT (1858-1919)

Most historians rank Theodore Roosevelt among the top echelon of American presidents alongside Washington, Jefferson and Lincoln, the three with whom he is depicted on Mount Rushmore. He was the father of our national park system, a conservationist for the ages (including being one of the founders of the Boone and Crockett Club), winner of a Nobel Peace Prize, a marvelous role model in leading what he termed "the strenuous life" and most significantly, a great sportsman.

We have had other sporting presidents who wrote books on the outdoors, but none come close to TR's verve, vivacity and productivity as a sporting scribe. For the TR fan, all of his outdoor works, from rare ones such as the highly collectible two-volume set he did with Edmund Heller, *Life-Histories of African Game Animals* 1914), to the often reprinted *Hunting Trips of a Ranchman* (1885), merit reading. His other books include *Good Hunting: In Pursuit of Big Game in the West* (1907), *African Game Trails* (1910), *A Book-Lover's Holidays in the Open* (1916), *The Deer Family* (with T. S. Van Dyke and others--1902), *Outdoor Pastimes of an American Hunter* (1905), *Ranch Life and the*

Hunting Trail (1888), *Through the Brazilian Wilderness* (1914), *The Wilderness Hunter* (1893) and the four-volume *The Winning of the West* (1889-96). The latter work is by no means exclusively devoted to hunting and natural history, but those subjects loom large in its contents.

There are numerous books dealing with Roosevelt as an outdoorsman. Among them are Hermann Hagedorn, *Roosevelt in the Bad Lands* (1921), Farida A. Wiley (editor), *Theodore Roosevelt's America: Selections from the Writings of the Oyster Bay Naturalist* (1955), Paul Russell Cutright, *Theodore Roosevelt, the Naturalist* (1956), R. L. Wilson, *Theodore Roosevelt, Outdoorsman* (1971), Paul Schullery (editor), *American Bears: Selections from the Writings of Theodore Roosevelt* (1983), Joseph R. Ornig, *My Last Chance to Be a Boy* (1998—on TR's Brazilian adventure), Jim Casada (editor), *Forgotten Tales and Vanished Trails* (2001), Lamar Underwood (editor), *Theodore Roosevelt on Hunting* (2003), R. L. Wilson, *Theodore Roosevelt: Hunter-Conservationist* (2009—issued by the Boone and Crockett Club) and Andrew Vietze, *Becoming Teddy Roosevelt* (2010). There are, as would be expected for a man of TR's stature, dozens of general biographies. The fullest, and as close to definitive as we are ever likely to have, is Edmund Morris' trilogy, *The Rise of Theodore Roosevelt* (1979), *Theodore Rex* (2001) and *Colonel Roosevelt* (2010). Serious students of the man will also want to own John Hall Wheelock, *A Bibliography of Theodore Roosevelt* (1920).

ROBERT RUARK (1915-1965)

Although often described as the greatest of all American outdoor writers, thanks to his columns in *Field & Stream*, most of which were subsequently published in book form in *The Old Man and the Boy* (1957) and *The Old Man's Boy Grows Older* (1961), Ruark was never a mainstream sporting scribe. Instead, he was a nationally syndicated and immensely popular newspaper columnist and a blockbuster novelist. During his lifetime, his writings on his boyhood hunting and fishing adventures with his grandfather, along with magazine stories and books on international big game hunting, were almost incidental to the main thrust of his literary efforts. However, in today's world he is best remembered for his writings on the outdoors, which included, in addition to the "Old Man" books, *Horn of the Hunter* (1953) and the posthumously published *Use Enough Gun* (1966). Collections of his magazine articles include Michael McIntosh (editor), *Robert Ruark's*

Africa (1991) and Jim Casada (editor), *The Lost Classics of Robert Ruark* (1996). There are three biographies: Alan Ritchie's *Ruark Remembered: The Man I Knew Best* (2006—edited by Jim Casada), Terry Wieland's *A View from a Tall Hill* (2000) and Hugh Foster's *Someone of Value* (1992). This is apparently the only whitetail story he ever wrote.

ARCHIBALD RUTLEDGE (1883-1973)

Almost certainly the most prolific American outdoor writer of the last century, Rutledge wrote thousands of magazine articles, thousands of poems (many with outdoor themes) and close to 60 books. While a number of his books were collections of poems or of an inspirational nature, the heart of his literary legacy are those full-length works comprised of hunting and nature stories. He never produced a book dealing solely with whitetails, but he wrote more about whitetails than anyone in the 20th century. The most important of his outdoor-related books include *Tom and I on the Old Plantation* (1918), *Old Plantation Days* (1921), *Heart of the South* (1924), *Days Off in Dixie* (1925), *A Plantation Boyhood* (1932), *An American Hunter* (1937), *Hunter's Choice* (1946), *Santee Paradise* (1956), *Those Were the Days* (1955), *From the Hills to the Sea* (1958), *The World Around Hampton* (1960) and *The Woods and Wild Things I Remember* (1970). Rutledge's youngest son, Irvine, edited and compiled a nice selection of his father's writings, *Fireworks in the Peafield Corner* (1986), and the University of South Carolina Press has published five anthologies, all edited by Jim Casada and all presently in print, of stories by "Old Flintlock," as the longtime Poet Laureate of South Carolina was known to family and friends. These are *Hunting and Home in the Southern Heartland: The Best of Archibald Rutledge* (1992), *Tales of Whitetails* (1992), *America's Greatest Game Bird* (1996), *Carolina Christmas* (2010) and *Bird Dog Days, Wingshooting Ways* (2016). *Archibald Rutledge: The Man and His Books* (2003), combines a short biographical appreciation of Rutledge with a detailed bibliographical look at his books by David Cupka.

EDMUND WARE SMITH (1900-1967)

For reasons that lie beyond this editor's ken, Smith is not nearly as well known as he should be. He represents for Maine, what contemporaries such as Archibald Rutledge, Nash Buckingham or Havilah Babcock did for the American South and what Corey Ford did for other parts of New England. In the person of the "One-eyed poacher of Privilege," Jeff Coongate, he created a truly memorable character. Altogether, he wrote hundreds of stories, and many of the best were collected in nine anthologies: *A Tomato Can Chronicle* (1937), *Tall Tales and Short* (1938), *The One-Eyed Poacher of Privilege* (1941), *From Fact to Fiction* (1946), *For Maine Only* (1959), *Upriver & Down* (1965), *The Further Adventures of the One-Eyed Poacher* (1947), *The One-Eyed Poacher and the Maine Woods* (1955) and *A Treasury of the Main Woods* (1958). He wrote one early novel, *Rider in the Sun* (1935), and Thomas Kinney edited a fine collection of some of his best material, *To Fish and Hunt in Maine* (1991).

BURTON SPILLER (1886-1973)

Perhaps most noted for his writings on grouse hunting and bird dogs, Spiller was actually quite varied in his sporting interests and in the subjects on which he published. Despite having only a grade school education and being close to 50 years of age before he did any significant writing, Spiller left an appreciable literary legacy. His work appeared regularly in national magazines such as *Field & Stream*, *Outdoor Life* and *Hunting & Fishing*. His books included *Grouse Feathers* (1934), *Thoroughbred* (1936), *Firelight* (1937), *More Grouse Feathers* (1938), *Drummer in the Woods* (1962) and the posthumously published, *Fishin' Around* (1974) and *Grouse Feathers, Again* (2000). He also wrote two fictional books for boys: *Northland Castaways* (1957) and *The Young Crusoes* (1959).

RON SPOMER

A prolific freelance writer and skilled photographer, Spomer has contributed to most of the major American sporting magazines and written columns for many of them. He writes the "Rifles" column for *Sporting Classics* and is a field editor for *American Hunter* and *Sports Afield*. A television show host and seminar speaker, Spomer also has a weekly blog which can be accessed through his website (ronspomeroutdoors.com). Among his numerous books are *Advanced Whitetail Hunting* (1996), *The Rut* (1996), *The Hunter's Book of the Whitetail* (2000), *Big Game Hunter's Guide to Idaho* (2000), *Predator Hunting* (2003), *Big Game Hunter's Guide to Montana* (2003) and *Big Game Hunter's Guide to Wyoming* (2008).

RYAN STALVEY

A gifted artist, talented writer and layout guru, *Sporting Classics'*

Editor-in-Chief Stalvey is a true renaissance man. Add to this repertoire his passion for sporting art and literature, and you see why he is the right man for the job. Follow him on Instagram @ryanstalveysportingclassics.

PHILIP TOME (1782-1855)

Philip Tome's fame rests on his autobiography, *Pioneer Life; or Thirty Years a Hunter* (1854—with a number of reprints), which recounts his decades of experience in Pennsylvania's Alleghenies. Much of his hunting for deer, which was commercial in nature, involved fire hunting, although he used other methods including stalking, hunting from stands at salt licks, man drives and using dogs. He eventually abandoned his market hunting, which had also involved killing wolves for a bounty and capturing live elk, to become a naturalist and preservationist. Robert Wegner provides a useful profile of Tome as an Introduction to the reprint of his book in the "Classics of American Sport" series.

TED TRUEBLOOD (1913-1982)

Born in Idaho, Trueblood was a dedicated conservationist and all-round sportsman who spent almost his entire career as a freelance writer. After early stints of newspaper work and a few years in New York with *Field & Stream* magazine, he returned to his native state and spent the remainder of his life there. He continued his close connection with *Field & Stream,* and a significant portion of his work was as a masthead presence, columnist and regular contributor to the magazine. A true "all rounder" in terms of subject matter, his books include *The Angler's Handbook* (1949), *The Fishing Handbook* (1951), *On Hunting* (1953), *The Hunter's Handbook* (1954), *How to Catch More Fish* (1955), *Camping Handbook* (1955) and *The Ted Trueblood Hunting Treasury* (1978). Much of the material in his books comes from previously published articles. Suffering from intensely painful bone cancer, he shot himself in 1982. His personal papers are housed in the Special Collections section at Boise State University Library.

THEODORE S. VAN DYKE (1842-1923)

Although a New Jersey blue blood who studied at Princeton, where he earned B.A. and M.A. degrees, Theodore S. Van Dyke was an avid hunter who moved to the Upper Midwest after completion of his studies to practice law but even more so to be close to good deer hunting. He later moved to the West Coast, again with hunting well to the forefront of his mind, and it was there he became the grand chronicler of still-hunting. The material for his most famous book, *The Still-Hunter* (1882), was first published serially in *The American Field*. Some indication of its enduring appeal is provided by the fact that it has gone through at least 17 editions and far more printings since its original publication. No less authority than Theodore Roosevelt called it a "noteworthy" work that approached for the first time "what may be called the standpoint of the scientific sportsman."

ROBERT WEGNER

The acknowledged dean of whitetail history and a trained historian who holds a Ph. D. degree, Wegner has devoted much of his life to study of the animal, its natural history, hunters and the literature of the sport. He was the editor and co-owner of *Deer & Deer Hunting* magazine and his seminal three-volume work carries the title of the magazine. The volumes in the *Deer & Deer Hunting* trilogy appeared in 1984, 1987 and 1990. His other works include the invaluable *Wegner's Bibliography on Deer and Deer Hunting* (1992), *Legendary Deerslayers* (2004) and *Classic Deer Camps* (2008).

CHARLES EDWARD WHITEHEAD (1829-1903)

Apparently Whitehead wrote only a single book, but the work was published in numerous editions and under two titles (the original one, from 1860, was *Wild Sports of the South*, but that changed to *Camp-Fires in the Everglades*, which was a new and expanded version, in 1891. There was a deluxe edition in 1897 and the book has been reprinted as recently as recently as 2018. The scope of its coverage, embracing not only various types of hunting and fishing but natural history, Native American lore and local folkways, suggests an author with a probing mind who was keenly aware of his surroundings and intensely curious about them.